"Strong, smart and capable, Riley will remind many of Anita Blake, Laurell K. Hamilton's kick-ass vampire hunter . . . Fans of Anita Blake and Charlaine Harris' Sookie Stackhouse vampire series will be rewarded."
—*Publishers Weekly*

"Unbridled lust and kick-ass action are the hallmarks of this first novel in a brand-new paranormal series . . . 'Sizzling' is the only word to describe this heated, action-filled, suspenseful romantic drama."
—Curled Up with a Good Book

"Desert island keeper . . . Grade: A . . . I wanted to read this book in one sitting, and was terribly offended that the real world intruded on my reading time! . . . Inevitable comparisons can be made to Anita Blake, Kim Harrison, and Kelley Armstrong's books, but I think Ms. Arthur has a clear voice of her own and her characters speak for themselves . . . I am hooked!"
—All About Romance

Praise for *Kissing Sin*

"The second book in this paranormal guardian series is just as phenomenal as the first . . . I am addicted!!"
—Fresh Fiction

"Arthur's world building skills are absolutely superb and I recommend this story to any reader who enjoys tales of the paranormal."
—Coffee Time Romance and More

"Fast paced and filled with deliciously sexy characters, readers will find *Kissing Sin* a fantastic urban fantasy with a hot serving of romance that continues to sizzle long after the last page is read."

—Darque Reviews

"Keri Arthur's unique characters and the imaginative world she's created will make this series one that readers won't want to miss."

—A Romance Review

Praise for *Tempting Evil*

"Riley Jenson is kick-ass . . . genuinely tough and strong, but still vulnerable enough to make her interesting . . . Arthur is not derivative of early [Laurell K.] Hamilton—far from it—but the intensity of her writing and the complexity of her heroine and her stories is reminiscent."

—All About Romance

"This paranormal romance series gets better and better with each new book . . . An exciting adventure that delivers all you need for a fabulous read—sexy shapeshifters, hot vampires, wild uncontrollable sex and the slightest hint of a love that's meant to be forever."

—Fresh Fiction

"Pure sexy action adventure . . . I found the world vividly realized and fascinating . . . So, if you like your erotic scenes hot, fast, and frequent, your heroine sassy, sexy, and tough, and your stories packed with hard-hitting action in a vividly realized fantasy world, then *Tempting Evil* and its companion novels could be just what you're looking for."

—SFRevu

"Keri Arthur's Riley Jenson series just keeps getting better and better and is sure to call to fans of other authors with kick-ass heroines such as Christine Feehan and Laurell K. Hamilton. I have become a steadfast fan of this marvelous series and I am greatly looking forward to finding out what is next in store for this fascinating and strong character."

—A Romance Review

Praise for *Dangerous Games*

"One of the best books I have ever read . . . The storyline is so exciting I did not realize I was literally sitting on the edge of my chair . . . Arthur has a real winner on her hands. Five cups."

—Coffee Time Romance and More

"The depths of emotion, the tense plot, and the conflict of powerful driving forces inside the heroine made for [an] absorbing read."

—SFRevu

"This series is phenomenal! *Dangerous Games* is an incredibly original and devastatingly sexy story. It keeps you spellbound and mesmerized on every page. Absolutely perfect!!"

—Fresh Fiction

Praise for *Embraced by Darkness*

"Arthur is positively one of the best urban fantasy authors in print today. The characters have been well-drawn from the start and the mysteries just keep getting better. A creative, sexy and adventure filled world that readers will just love escaping to."

—Darque Reviews

"Arthur's storytelling is getting better and better with each book. *Embraced by Darkness* has suspense, interesting concepts, terrific main and secondary characters, well developed story arcs, and the world-building is highly entertaining . . . I think this series is worth the time and emotional investment to read."

—Reuters.com

"Once again, Keri Arthur has created a perfect, exciting and thrilling read with intensity that kept me vigilantly turning each page, hoping it would never end."

—Fresh Fiction

"Reminiscent of Laurell K. Hamilton back when her books had mysteries to solve, Arthur's characters inhabit a dark sexy world of the paranormal."

—*The Parkersburg News and Sentinel*

"I love this series."

—All About Romance

Praise for *The Darkest Kiss*

"The paranormal Australia that Arthur concocts works perfectly, and the plot speeds along at a breakneck pace. Riley fans won't be disappointed."

—*Publishers Weekly*

Praise for *Bound to Shadows*

"The Riley Jenson Guardian series ROCKS! Riley is one bad-ass heroine with a heart of gold. Keri Arthur never disappoints and always leaves me eagerly anticipating the next book. A classic, fabulous read!"

—Fresh Fiction

Praise for *Moon Sworn*

"Huge kudos to Arthur for giving readers an impressive series they won't soon forget! 4½ stars, Top Pick!"
—*RT Book Reviews*

"The superb final Guardian urban fantasy saga ends with quite a bang that will please the fans of the series. Riley is terrific as she goes through a myriad of emotions with no time to mourn her losses . . . Readers will enjoy Riley's rousing last stand."
—Midwest Book Review

Praise for *Darkness Unbound*

"A thrilling ride."
—*Publishers Weekly*

Praise for *Darkness Rising*

"Arthur ratchets up the intrigue . . . in this powerful sequel."
—*Publishers Weekly*

By Keri Arthur

THE RIPPLE CREEK WEREWOLF SERIES
Beneath a Rising Moon
Beneath a Darkening Moon

THE DARK ANGELS SERIES
Darkness Unbound
Darkness Rising
Darkness Devours
Darkness Hunts

THE MYTH AND MAGIC SERIES
Destiny Kills
Mercy Burns

THE RILEY JENSON GUARDIAN SERIES
Full Moon Rising
Kissing Sin
Tempting Evil
Dangerous Games
Embraced by Darkness
The Darkest Kiss
Deadly Desire
Bound to Shadows
Moon Sworn

THE NIKKI AND MICHAEL SERIES
Dancing with the Devil
Hearts in Darkness
Chasing the Shadows
Kiss the Night Goodbye

DANCING WITH THE DEVIL

Keri Arthur

DELL
NEW YORK

2013 Dell Mass Market Edition

Copyright © 2001 by Keri Arthur
Excerpt from *Hearts in Darkness* by Keri Arthur copyright © 2001 by Keri Arthur

All rights reserved.

Published in the United States by Dell, an imprint of The Random House Publishing Group, a division of Random House, Inc., New York.

DELL and the HOUSE colophon are registered trademarks of Random House, Inc.

Originally published in different form in paperback in the United States by ImaJinn Books, Hickory Corners, MI, in 2001.

This book contains an excerpt from the forthcoming novel *Hearts in Darkness* by Keri Arthur. This excerpt has been set for this edition only and may not reflect the final content of the forthcoming edition.

ISBN: 978-0-440-24651-0
eBook ISBN: 978-0-345-53870-3

Cover design: Lynn Andreozzi
Cover illustration: Juliana Kolesova

Printed in the United States of America

www.bantamdell.com

9 8 7 6 5 4 3 2 1

Dell mass market edition: July 2013

For Pete,
who supported my dreams
when so few did.

DANCING
WITH THE DEVIL

One

SOMEONE FOLLOWED HER.

Someone she couldn't see or hear through any normal means, but whose presence vibrated across her psychic senses.

Someone whose mission was death.

The wind stirred, running chill fingers across the nape of her neck. Nikki shivered and eyed the surrounding shadows uneasily. She'd never been afraid of the dark before—had, in fact, found it something of an ally, especially in the wilder days of her youth. But tonight there was an edge to the silence, a hint of menace in the slowly swirling fog.

People disappeared on nights like this. At least, they did here in Lyndhurst.

She returned her gaze to the slender figure just ahead. This was the second night in a row Monica Trevgard had come to the park after midnight, and if the teenager had a reason for doing so, Nikki sure as hell hadn't found any evidence of it. Her actions to date made very little sense. The only child of one of Lyndhurst's—and possibly America's—richest men, Monica had spent most of her life rebelling against her family and their wealth. And yet, ironically, it was only thanks to her father's money that she was free to walk the streets tonight. Though nothing had ever been proven, it was generally acknowledged that John Trevgard had at least one judge and several police officers on his payroll.

Nikki smiled grimly. Trevgard would probably have been better off keeping his hand in his pocket and letting his only child spend some time in jail. Maybe a day or so locked behind uncompromising concrete walls would shock some sense into the girl.

It sure as hell had with *her*.

Shoving cold hands into the pockets of her old leather jacket, Nikki let her gaze roam across the fog-shrouded trees to her left.

He was still there, still following her, the man with darkness in his heart and murder on his mind. But not her murder, or even Monica's. Someone else's entirely.

She bit her lip. With two knives strapped to her wrists and her psychic abilities to fall back on, she was sufficiently protected. At least under normal circumstances. But the man out there in the darkness was far from normal, and something told her none of her weapons would be enough if he chose to attack.

Maybe *she* was as mad as Monica. Four women had already disappeared from this particular area. She should play it safe and go home, let Jake—her boss, and the man who'd become more of a father to her than her own damn father had ever been—take over the case. A teenager looking for trouble was going to find it, no matter how many people her father hired to follow and protect her.

Only, Jake had enough on his plate already, and his

night-sight had started deteriorating since he'd hit the big four-0 several years ago.

The sound of running water broke through the heavy silence. Though the fog half hid the old fountain from sight, Nikki knew it well enough to describe every chipped detail, from the wickedly grinning cherub at the top to the embracing lovers near the bottom. It was amazing what became interesting when you had nothing else to do but watch a teenager watch the water.

Only, this time, Monica didn't stop at the fountain. She didn't even look at it. Instead, she glanced quickly over her shoulder—a casual move that raised the hairs on the back of Nikki's neck.

Monica knew she was being followed. Tonight she was the bait to catch the watcher.

The bitter breeze stirred, seeming to blow right through Nikki's soul. She swore softly and ran a hand through her hair. It was nights like this, when she was caught between common sense and past promises, that she really hated being psychic. She would have run a mile away from here had it not been for her gift, which warned that death would claim Monica's soul if she wasn't protected.

And because she couldn't stand the weight of another death on her conscience, Nikki had no real choice but to follow.

They neared the far edge of the park. Streetlights glimmered—forlorn wisps of brightness barely visible through the trees and the fog—and Nikki's discomfort surged. Monica wasn't heading for the street or the lights, but rather toward the old mansion on the far side of the park. The place had a reputation for being haunted, and though she wasn't particularly afraid of ghosts, the one night she'd spent there as a kid had sent her fleeing in terror. Not from the ghosts, but from the sense of evil that seemed to ooze from the walls.

Of course, it might have been nothing more than a combination of knowing that a family had once been murdered there, and an overactive imagination. But still . . .

Monica squeezed through a small gap in the fence and cast another quick look over her shoulder. There was no doubt about it, the kid definitely wanted to be followed.

Nikki stopped and watched her walk up the steps to the back door. Her common sense told her not to follow, and her psychic sense told her danger lurked inside. She clenched her fists. She could do this. She *had* to do this. For Monica's sake.

Because if she didn't, the teenager was doomed.

She stepped forward, then froze. No sound had disturbed the dark silence. Even the breeze had faded, and the fog sat still and heavy on the ground. Yet something had moved behind her. Something not quite human.

Throat dry, Nikki turned. Out of the corner of her eye, she caught a hint of movement—a hand, emerging from darkness, reaching out to touch her . . .

Yelping in fright, she jumped back and lashed out with a blast of kinetic energy. Something heavy hit a nearby oak, accompanied by a grunt of pain. She stared at the tree. Despite the sound, there was nothing—or nobody—at its base.

Yet something had to be there. It didn't make any

sense—bodies didn't just disappear like that. She swallowed and ran trembling fingers through her hair. Disembodied hands couldn't emerge from the darkness, either.

Had it simply been her imagination, finally reacting to the overwhelming sensation of being followed? No, something *had* been there. Was *still* there, even if she couldn't see it.

Not that *that* made a whole lot of sense.

She turned and studied the dark house. Trouble waited inside. But so did Monica.

Ignoring her unknown watcher, Nikki climbed through the fence and ran across the shadowed yard. Edging up the steps, she slipped a small flashlight from her pocket and shone the light through the open doorway.

The entrance hall was small, laden with dust and cobwebs that shimmered like ice in the beam of light. Faded crimson and gold wallpaper hung in eerie strips from the walls, rustling lightly in the breeze that drifted past her legs. The house really hadn't changed much in the ten years since she'd been here last—except for one thing. The creeping sense of evil felt a hell of a lot stronger now than it had before. In fact, it almost seemed alive. Alive and waiting.

She swallowed heavily and directed the flashlight's beam toward the stairs. Motes of dust danced across the light, stirred to life in the wake of Monica's passing. She'd gone up. Up to where the sense of evil felt the strongest.

Gripping the flashlight tightly, Nikki walked through the dust, toward the stairs. The air smelled of decay and unwashed bodies. Obviously, it was still a haunt for those forced to scratch a living from the streets. It was odd, though, that there was no one here now—no one but Monica and whoever it was she'd come here to meet.

A floorboard creaked beneath Nikki's weight, the sound as loud as thunder in the silence. She winced and hesitated. After several heartbeats, someone moved on the floor above.

It wasn't Monica. The footfalls were too heavy.

Reaching into her pocket, Nikki turned on her phone. If things started to go bad, she'd call for help. Trevgard might not like the publicity a call to the cops would bring, but if it meant the difference between life or death—*her* life or death—then he could go to hell.

The staircase loomed out of the shadows. Nikki shone the light upward. Something growled, a low noise almost lost under the thundering of her heart. She hesitated, staring up into the darkness. It had sounded like some sort of animal. But what animal made such an odd, rasping noise?

One hand on the banister, the other clutching the flashlight so tightly that her knuckles began to ache, she continued on. The growl cut across the silence again.

It was definitely *not* an animal.

She reached the landing and stopped. The odd-sounding snarl was much closer this time. Sweat trickled down her face and the flashlight flickered slightly, its beam fading, allowing the night to close in around her. Nikki swore and gave it a quick shake. The last thing she needed right now was for the light to give out. It flickered again, then became brighter.

She moved on but kept close to the wall, just in case. At least she could use it as a guide, even if the peeling remains of the wallpaper felt like dead skin against her fingertips.

The hallway ended in a T. Moonlight washed through the shattered window at the end of the left-hand corridor. On the right, the darkness was so complete that the flashlight barely penetrated it. And while she knew it was little more than a result of shuttered windows at that end of the hall, it still seemed oddly unnatural.

It wasn't a place she wanted to go. Unfortunately, her psychic senses told her that Monica was down there somewhere. But that odd sound had come from the opposite side. Whatever it was, she had to check it out first. She wasn't about to risk being attacked from behind in a place like this. So she turned left.

Two doors waited ahead—one open, one closed.

Was it fear or instinct that warned against entering either of the rooms?

The wind whispered forlornly through the shattered window at the end of the hall, accompanied by a low moan that raised goose bumps across her skin.

It was definitely more human than animal. And it wasn't Monica. The teenager still waited in the darkness of the right-hand corridor. Nikki crept forward and peered around the door frame. The room was large, with a line of windows to the right, but the glass was so filthy it allowed little moonlight to filter through. She couldn't immediately see anything waiting in the shadows, but something *was* in there. The sense of malevolence was so overwhelming she could barely breathe.

So why don't you turn around and run?

The thought whispered into her brain, featherlight but hinting at anger. Nikki froze, fear squeezing her throat tight. Just for an instant, her mind linked with another. She tasted darkness and concern and the need to kill. This was the man she'd half seen near the fence, the man who'd followed her through the fog.

Turn around and leave. You cannot help the child now.

No. Why could she hear this man's thoughts? Telepathy had never been one of her talents, even though she'd been able to receive Tommy's thoughts well enough. *And who the hell are you to tell me what to do?*

I am merely trying to save your life. You will not like what you find here. Not in that room, and not with the teenager.

Yeah, right. Who was this person? A would-be prophet of doom? Hell, for all she knew, he might even be the source of the darkness she sensed waiting, even if her senses told her otherwise. *I have never run from anything in my life, and I don't intend to start now.*

The lie gave her courage. She took a deep breath and stepped into the room.

Michael Kelly hit the fence in frustration. The little fool had gone in, despite his warning. Or perhaps because of it.

She knew that danger waited. He could taste the fear in her thoughts, despite the distance between them. So why wouldn't she run? Why did she continue this fruitless pursuit? Given the strength of her psychic talents, she had to know the child was well beyond salvation.

He let his gaze roam to the far end of the house. Hidden by the darkness, evil waited for his next meal, ably served by his young companion. Unless *he* intervened, Nikki James would become the fifth woman to go missing.

Had it been anyone else, he wouldn't have cared particularly—not given the identity of the man who hunted her, a man he'd long hunted himself. But he'd been sent here tonight to save a life rather than trap and kill a murderer, and as much as he might want to do the latter, he could not. But Nikki's abilities added a dangerous dimension to his task. It was for those abilities, more than for her blood, that Jasper hunted her.

He turned and walked to the end of the fence. The sudden movement caused pain to shoot through his head, but he resisted the urge to rub the lump forming near his temple. He had deserved that—and more—for being so careless. But he hadn't expected the fool to use her kinetic abilities against him. Why, he couldn't say. He smiled grimly. Maybe senility was finally setting in.

He walked through the gate and headed for the garage. While he generally couldn't enter private homes uninvited, that restriction didn't apply to houses that had been long abandoned. He could go in unhindered, and do what he was sent here to do.

But Jasper was not in that house alone. Not only did he have the teenager at his command, but his living dead as well. Six against one were not the best of odds, even for someone like him. What Michael needed was a distraction. He slipped past the remains of the garage door and his gaze came to rest on an old gas can. He picked it up; liquid sloshed within.

Jasper hated fire. Feared it.

It might provide enough of a distraction to save Nikki James.

The room smelled awful—a putrid mix of stale urine, excrement and death. Nikki cupped a hand over her nose and mouth and tried not to gag as she swept the flashlight's beam across the room.

Something slid away from the light—a hunched, humanoid shape that smelled like death.

Nikki backed away. She didn't know what hid in the shadows and didn't really care to find out. She'd learned long ago that there were some things best left unexplored, and she very much suspected *this* was one of those moments. Perhaps if she retreated and closed the door, whatever lurked in the room would leave her alone. She knew from past experience that all the doors in this old house creaked; it was one of the things that had spooked her as a teenager. At the very least, it would give her warning if the creature decided to move.

She began to turn away, but stopped. A prickle of warning ran across the back of her neck. The shadows parted, revealing a tangled mass of long blond hair and pale, naked flesh.

It was female. And human. And yet . . . not.

What the hell . . . ?

The grotesque figure lunged at her. Fear slammed through Nikki's heart. Stumbling backward, she threw out her hand and thrust the creature away kinetically. It slammed into the back wall and grunted in either surprise or pain. But no sooner had it hit the floor than it was scrambling to its feet, its agility surprising.

Glimpsing movement to her left, Nikki whirled. A second creature ran out of the shadows, its face a mocking image of womanhood. Nikki reached again for her kinetic energy. The heavy steps of the first creature were already drawing close. Sweat—more from fear than exertion—trickled down the back of her neck. She thrust the second creature back through the doorway, flicked a wrist knife into her palm and spun around. The first creature charged, teeth bared and hands raised like talons. Talons that showed the remnants of red nail polish. Nikki backed away, wanting to defend herself and yet suddenly reluctant to use her knife against another woman—even if that woman appeared dead set on killing *her*.

Then the second creature came back through the doorway, and the choice was taken out of her hands. She threw the first woman back kinetically and side-stepped the leap of the second, slashing at it with the knife. The blade cut through the creature's skin as easily as butter and blood sprayed across them both. Nikki blanched and scrubbed at it with the sleeve of her jacket as she backed away.

The creature made no sound, gave no reaction, not even when its stomach began to peel open and its innards bulged out. It just spun around and charged again. Nausea tightened Nikki's throat. She swallowed and kept retreating, but her feet wouldn't move fast enough. The creature lashed out, and its blow flung her backward. She hit the wall, the flashlight went flying and for a moment she saw stars.

The creature made a second grab for her. Nikki scrambled away, but it caught her shoulder and pulled her to it. Talonlike fingers tore into her arm, and pain shot down to her fingertips. She gasped, fighting the sudden wash of nausea. The creature snarled, its breath fetid, full of death and decay. Nikki shuddered and slammed the heel of her hand into its face. For a split second, its hold weakened and she quickly reached for more kinetic energy. A sliver of pain ran through her mind—a warning that she was pushing her psychic strength too far. She ignored it and forced the heavy creature away from her. It flew across the room and smashed through the window, tumbling out of sight with a feminine cry of surprise.

Moonlight fanned across the darkness, lifting the shadows and touching the face of the second creature as it lumbered toward Nikki. For an instant, it resembled Jackie Sommers, one of the four women who'd recently gone missing. But if it was, what the hell had happened to her? How could someone go from being an average suburban mom to something that was barely even human, and in so short a time?

The creature snarled—and any resemblance to Sommers shattered. It took one ponderous step forward, then stopped. Nikki readied another kinetic lance. The shard of pain in her head became a torrent. She was going to have a hell of a headache tomorrow—if she survived that long.

Blood ran past her clenched fingers and dripped to

the floor near her feet. She had no choice but to ignore it. One move, no matter how small, and the creature would surely attack.

So why wasn't it attacking now? It simply stood in the doorway, shaking its head and snarling softly. It was almost as if it was fighting a leash of some kind.

And she had absolutely no desire to find out who—or what—held the end of it.

The creature snarled again—an angry, sullen sound—but turned and leaped out the nearest window.

The retreat sent a chill up Nikki's spine. She waited tensely for something else to happen. The breeze stirred the dust from the shadows, and the heavy silence returned.

After several heartbeats, she sank down against the wall and drew her knees close. For a minute she simply sat there staring at the shattered window, breathing deeply and letting the quiet settle over her.

Had the creatures survived? Given the first one's reaction—or lack thereof—to the knife wound, it was more than likely that, even if they *had* broken bones, it wouldn't stop them. And she wasn't about to walk over to the window to find out. She had no idea what they were capable of; for all she knew, they might be crouched on the ground below the window, ready to spring up and drag her outside the minute she showed her face.

But if both creatures had been desperate to destroy her, why did the last one retreat? The desire—maybe even the *need*—to shed blood had been all too evident in its eyes. Yet it had leapt out the window rather than attack.

Which could only mean it had been *ordered* to. Because, instinct whispered, whatever lurked in that darkness at the other end of the corridor wanted her for itself.

Moonlight played across the floorboards near her feet, highlighting the bright splashes of blood. She wasn't sure if it belonged to the creatures or to her, but she knew in the end it wouldn't matter. *He* would come for the blood. *He* would smell it and come for her.

She didn't know who *he* was, and she certainly didn't care. She had to get out of this crazy house. She had to escape, while she still could.

But what about Monica? Did she really want to leave the teenager alone to face her fate?

Yes.

No.

Nikki took a deep breath and released it slowly. It didn't do much to calm the fear swirling through her, let alone the indecision. At sixteen, Monica had barely begun to live. She still had so much to learn, so much more of the world to see. And yet it wasn't as if the teenager hadn't already had her chances. Time and again, her willful—and often violent—tendencies had gotten her into trouble, and time and again, her father's wealth and influence had gotten her out of it. But she never seemed to learn. She just plunged headfirst into the next catastrophe, seemingly hellbent on a path of destruction. Was it really worth risking her own life to save Monica's?

Nikki took another deep breath and pushed upright. Ten years ago she'd been faced with a similar decision and had left that teenager to his fate. He'd been a hell of a lot more capable of taking care of himself than Monica would ever be, and still he had died. This time around, she was not letting fate get the upper hand.

She eased off her jacket and studied the wound on her forearm. While the three gashes were bleeding profusely, the creature's talons obviously hadn't severed anything vital. She could still move her fingers, even if it did hurt like hell. She dug a handkerchief out of her pocket and wrapped it around the wound. Hopefully it would stem the flow of blood long enough for her to find Monica and get out of this house.

After putting her jacket back on, she walked over to retrieve her flashlight, only to discover it no longer worked. The reason was easy enough to discover—the battery cover must have popped when she'd dropped it and the batteries had fallen out. She had a quick look around, but couldn't find the damn things.

"That's just great," she muttered, thrusting the now useless flashlight in her back pocket. She'd have to cross the threshold into that utter darkness with only instinct to guide her.

Instinct that had proven somewhat unreliable in the past.

The hallway was quiet, but her gaze was drawn to the far end of the hall. Monica was down there somewhere. But so was the presence that tasted so evil.

She took a deep, calming breath, and walked to the intersection. Awareness tingled across her skin as she neared the stairs. She hesitated, studying the shadows that hid the staircase. The stranger had entered the house. *Michael Kelly*, Nikki thought. *His name is Michael Kelly*.

Nikki rubbed the back of her neck. Why could she read this stranger's mind? And why had he entered the house? Was he here to help her, or did he have something sinister in mind?

No answers came from the darkness, and the spark of awareness flickered and died. Nikki frowned but continued on. The rapid beat of her heart seemed abnormally loud in the silence. Her senses warned her of another door, even though she couldn't see it. She ran her fingers along the wall and touched a door frame, then the cold metal of a knob. Stopping, she listened to the silence.

Evil was near, maybe even in the room beyond this door. She clenched the doorknob so tightly, her fingers almost cramped and she wondered why in hell she was doing this.

Though she already knew. Monica reminded her of Tommy, the teenager she'd left to die so long ago. To appease his ghost—and to appease her guilt—she'd follow Monica through the flames of hell itself if that's what it took to save her, simply because she'd been unable to save Tommy.

Swallowing, she opened the door. Laughter greeted her—laughter that was young and sweet, yet somehow cold.

Monica.

The teenager stepped forward, her smile clearly visible despite the shadows that hid her face.

"Follow me," she said, her voice holding a sense of menace that went beyond her years, her eyes oddly flat, "for only a little bit longer, and you will have the answers you seek."

Then she turned and walked away. Instinct urged Nikki not to follow—told her to run as far and as fast as she could. Told her Monica wasn't worth dying for.

But it also told her that if she ran, saved herself, Monica would die in her place. And that was a burden she couldn't bear. Taking a deep breath, Nikki followed the teenager.

Straight into the arms of the devil himself.

Two

THE CREATURE CAME out of nowhere, bringing with it a rain of glass, deadly daggers that sprayed all around him. It hit the ground hard, tumbled to its feet, and charged straight at Michael, moving too fast to avoid. He slammed a fist into the creature's gut, but the blow failed to halt its momentum and the two of them went down in a fighting tangle.

Michael swore viciously. Every second he wasted with these creatures left Nikki James another second closer to death. The little fool had entered the room where Jasper waited. His enemy's hunger was palpable, a beast that filled the darkness.

Anger surged through him—a deep, dark fury he desperately tried to control. He needed a clear head, not a mind ruled by blood-rage. The creature wrapped its hands around his neck and squeezed. Michael laughed; the stupidity of these things was beyond belief. He reached up and wrenched its fingers loose, then gave a quick thrust with his knee, throwing the creature over his head. It smashed through the front door and disappeared inside.

He scrambled to his feet, and swung about, sensing the approach of a second creature. Instead of charging, this one slithered to a halt—and in that instant, Michael saw the silver blade it held.

Silver was as deadly to beings such as him as wooden stakes. He backed away. The creature followed him, the blade an argent flame promising death.

Foreboding ran through him. He had no time for this. The web of darkness was closing in around Nikki. He should have stopped her in the park, should have seized control of her mind and ordered her away from the child and this house.

But she was different from most of the mortals he dealt with. While he could read her surface thoughts easily enough, he hadn't been able to reach far enough into her mind to achieve any sort of real control. Not in the brief time he'd tried anyway. Her gifts were exceptionally strong. And if he couldn't immediately take control of her, it was doubtful that Jasper would be able to, either. But that would change if the bastard killed her. Jasper had the ability to call his victims from the grave, and if he *did,* her body and her mind were his to control. Unfortunately, death did not blunt the abilities of the undead. Not until the last bit of flesh fell from their bones and their brain rotted away, at any rate.

The creature lunged at him. Michael dodged the thrust of the knife, then grabbed the creature's wrist. Squeezing tight, he forced the blade from its grip and thrust an elbow into its face, shattering its nose. It howled—a high keening sound of distress. Michael cursed softly. The creature was an abomination, but who was the greater horror: the dead, or the man who not only kidnapped and killed them, but forced them from their graves?

Michael might not be able to kill Jasper right now, but he could give this creature some peace. Gripping its head, he snapped it hard sideways, breaking its neck. It fell to a lifeless heap at his feet. One down, five to go, if he included Jasper and the teenager.

He kicked the blade away with his foot, retrieved the can of gas and walked into the foyer. Undoing the lid, he sloshed the contents around the floor and up the walls. Anywhere and everywhere. It didn't really matter, so long as it burned.

Throwing the empty can into a corner, he dug a box of matches out of his pocket. The old house was tinder-dry. Along with the gas he'd splashed around, it would ignite like wildfire. Jasper's remaining creatures were all outside, so there was no one in the house except the four of them. Jasper wouldn't burn—he'd run the minute he smelled the flames. But that would still achieve Michael's goal—to get Jasper away from Nikki as soon as possible. Which left three behind. If Monica was too stupid to follow her lover, that was just too bad. Nikki was the one he had to get out. She'd be too dangerous a weapon in Jasper's hands.

Michael lit the match and flicked it in the direction of the can. Then he turned and ran for the stairs.

The door slammed shut behind her. Nikki spun but knew there was no escape. Childish laughter echoed through the silence, mocking her.

Monica, in league with the devil himself.

"You have done well with this one, my pet."

The soft voice was powerful. Hypnotic. It filled the room with its warmth, and yet her skin crawled in terror. Instinct warned her not to move, told her the slightest indication of fear would mean her death. But the beat of her heart filled the silence like a drum. He had to know—had to *feel*—her fear.

The air stirred. She stepped back quickly. The presence laughed—a low sound of amusement. Nikki clenched her fists. Energy tingled across her fingertips, but she didn't release it, instead retreating another step. Her back hit the wall, but she felt no better for its protection. If only she could get to the door . . .

"There is no escape for you now." The stranger's tone was oddly gentle, yet filled with the certainty of death.

Nikki edged sideways, one hand outstretched, searching desperately for the doorknob. It had to be close; she hadn't walked that far into the room.

"Look at me." The voice changed, became deeper, more alluring. "Look at me . . ."

Blue fire flared in the darkness. Nikki stared, mesmerized, as the flame grew brighter, transforming itself into a pair of sapphire eyes.

So beautiful.

So deadly.

Nikki swallowed and tore her gaze away. Her fingers touched the doorknob and clenched convulsively around it.

"No," he whispered. "Stay with me."

His words wrapped around her, seductive and compelling. Blue fire pinned her. She couldn't tear herself free of the commanding beauty of his gaze.

"Be mine."

Memories rose unbidden, and Nikki saw another time, another man, uttering the same words.

"No!" She flung out her arm, releasing the pent-up kinetic energy. The sapphire eyes vanished, then something heavy hit the far wall.

Anger hissed across the room. Nikki slammed the door open and ran for the hall.

Smoke swirled around her, a stench that caught in her throat and made her cough. *Christ, there's a fire.* But she couldn't stop. Not with evil so close. She reached the door to the hall and flung it open.

Only to find herself in hell. Wallpaper dripped fiery tears, and the stairs were lost to an inferno of red heat. The smoke was so thick it stung her eyes and made it difficult to breathe. She coughed and dashed the tears from her eyes. What was she going to do now?

Wood creaked behind her.

Run, she thought, and leaped into the hall, slamming the door shut behind her.

The heat was fierce, scorching her clothes and searing her skin. Heart pounding with fear, Nikki spun, not sure where to go. The smoke did a mad dance around her, making it difficult to get her bearings. If she couldn't use the stairs, she'd have to run down the hall . . . but which way was safest?

"This way," a voice said behind her.

Nikki jumped then turned. A figure emerged from the swirling darkness. Something deep within quivered in recognition. This was Michael Kelly, the man she'd sensed earlier.

"Trust me," he said, and held out his hand.

She hesitated. The dancing brightness of the flames revealed the finely chiseled planes of his cheeks, and a nose that hinted of foreign blood. It was a handsome face. A haunted face. One she could trust—at least for now.

She placed her hand in his and his fingers closed around hers, wrapping them in a heat that was fiercer than any flame. It was a reaction that had nothing to do with fear, and yet fear slipped through her anyway. It had been a long time since anyone's touch had affected her so strongly. That it was happening now, with a stranger who was undoubtedly as dangerous as the man she'd just fled, was terrifying.

He led her quickly through the fire and into another room. She kicked the door shut, and saw the only exit was the large window to her left. They'd have to jump.

Shit. Nikki thrust kinetically at the window. The glass burst outward, glittering like a thousand bright stars as it fell.

Wind rushed into the void. She blinked and looked at the ground far below. It was a long way down . . .

As if sensing her sudden reluctance, Michael grabbed her, swinging her into his arms.

"No!" she screamed, and shut her eyes as he ran toward the window.

He leaped into the night. The wind whipped around them, and, for an instant, it felt as if they were flying. The illusion shattered when they hit the ground. The impact wrenched her from Michael's grasp and pitched her roughly forward. She rolled down a slight incline and through several shrubs before coming to an abrupt halt against a fence.

For several seconds she just lay there, too stunned to move and just thankful to be alive. She'd bitten her tongue sometime during the fall and could taste the blood in her mouth, but other than that, everything seemed in working order.

And she was free from the house and the evil it contained. But the man with the hypnotic sapphire eyes was still near. She could feel his presence, though she wasn't entirely sure whether he was hunting her or simply running. It didn't matter. She was getting out of here—and fast.

She rolled away from the fence. Pain shot along her back, and she groaned softly. No doubt she'd have a colorful array of bruises tomorrow.

"Take my hand."

Every nerve in her aching body jumped. Heart in her mouth, Nikki glanced up. Michael's form flowed out of the night and found substance—just like a ghost, she thought with a shiver. Her gaze swept from the blackness of his clothing, which did little to hide the lithe, athletic nature of his body, to his face. It was an angelic face—beautiful, and yet in no way feminine. She thrust the thought away angrily. Looks, no matter how divine, were no indicator of soul. That was a lesson she'd learned the hard way long ago, and one she suspected she should heed now. Because while instinct might be telling her to trust this man, there was something in his manner, a darkness that seemed to hover around him, that made her wary.

"If you were going to throw me out a window," she muttered, "you could have at least arranged for a softer landing."

Though his eyebrows rose in surprise, a hint of a

smile that did strange things to her pulse rate touched his generous mouth. Nikki ignored both her reaction and his outstretched hand, and pushed herself into a sitting position. Her stomach churned and she took several deep breaths, battling the urge to be sick.

"We have no time," he said, concern touching his voice. "Please, take my hand and let's go."

She studied him for a moment, weighing her distrust against her desire to get the hell out of there, then looked back at the house. Bright flames were leaping from the ground-floor windows, reaching hungrily skyward. She had no idea where Monica was, but the evil was on the move. When it came down to a choice between the two men, her path was clear.

She took Michael's hand. He pulled her up easily, his strength at odds with his lean build. Surprisingly, he stood only three or four inches taller than her paltry five-foot-four. In the flame-filled confines of the hall, he'd appeared a lot bigger.

"He hunts us," Michael stated softly. He tugged her forward, following the fence line. "We must keep moving."

"What about Monica?"

Michael glanced at her. His eyes were endless pools of ebony. You could lose yourself forever in those depths, Nikki thought, and glanced away uneasily.

"The child accompanies her master. You were a fool to go in after her."

"She would have died if I didn't." Nikki took her hand from his and briskly rubbed a tender hip.

His expression was grim. "Death is the one thing that child no longer fears."

She frowned at him. "What do you mean?"

"Nothing." His shrug was oddly elegant. "Can you move any faster?"

She returned her gaze to the house, then nodded. He led the way, his pace quickening to a run. Yet unlike her, he moved silently, at one with the night. A ghost, she thought again, uneasily. She glanced at her fingers, remembering the gentle strength of his hand around hers. If he was a ghost, he was certainly a solid one.

"I am as real as you, Nikki," he said softly. His dark gaze touched hers briefly before returning to study the surrounding night.

She'd forgotten he could read her thoughts—just like Tommy had, so many years ago. Fear stirred, along with old guilt. Why did she trust Michael? She couldn't say, and that worried her.

"One of his creatures follows us."

Nikki looked over her shoulder. A dark shape lumbered after them. "Should we try to outrun her?"

"No. It can run faster than you ever could."

But not, she surmised from his tone, faster than he could. Why was he still here, offering his protection?

There was a flash of movement to her left. Before she could react, Michael thrust her sideways and spun to meet the creature's charge.

She hit the ground, tasting dirt. Spitting it out, she rolled back to her feet. The creature attacking Michael held a knife, the blade a blue-white flame against the night.

Michael seemed wary of it—something that struck her as odd. It wasn't a particularly large knife—at least, not when compared with the ones street kids used these days. Frowning, she grabbed a rock and threw it at the creature. It hit with enough force to make the creature stop and shake its head in confusion. It snarled and charged her. But somehow Michael was in front of it again, his movements so fast he appeared to blur. He spun, kicking the creature in the head. It screamed and staggered sideways, and Nikki suddenly saw its face.

It was another of the missing women. What in the hell had been *done* to them?

The creature lunged again and Nikki reached for kinetic energy. Despite the ache in her head, it surged in response. She focused it on the knife in the creature's hand. At the same time, she heard footsteps behind her.

She tore the blade from the creature's grasp and spun, hurling the knife at the approaching figure.

And saw that it was Monica.

Frantically, she flung another bolt of energy at the blade. The weapon flared brightly, as if in protest, then quivered and changed direction. It thudded hilt-deep into a tree trunk several feet to Monica's left.

The teenager took no notice. Nikki frowned. Despite the crackling of the flames that consumed the old house, the night was strangely quiet. The creature that had attacked them had to be dead, but what about the one that had been following them? Was it dead, or had it been ordered to retreat? Nikki didn't know, and she wasn't about to take her gaze from the teenager to find out.

Michael stood behind her, not touching and yet close enough that the warmth of his breath whispered past her cheek. Under normal circumstances, she would have stepped away. But the night had become something chaotic and strange, and she had a feeling she would need his protection before it was over.

Monica stopped several paces away. Nikki cleared her throat. "Your father wants to speak—"

"I don't care what that bastard wants. Tell him to leave me alone or he'll regret it. You, however, are more than welcome to keep following me. I think it could be profitable for us both."

The words themselves weren't overly threatening. It was the continuing absence of life in Monica's eyes, the menace in her voice, that was so disturbing. It was almost as if she'd become nothing more than a blank vessel for someone else's thoughts and words.

"Not as far from the truth as you might think," Michael said softly, obviously reading her thoughts again.

She crossed her arms, trying to ward off a sudden chill. The teenager turned and walked away, a slim shadow against the brightness of the flames beginning to leap from the upper-floor windows.

"We must go," Michael said quietly. "The fire department is on its way."

If the fire department was on the way, so were the police. Nikki glanced at the nearby houses. People were lined up at their fences, watching. She grimaced and returned her gaze to his. The wind tugged at his hair, blowing the night-colored strands across his face.

"What has happened to the women who attacked us?" she said, shoving her hands into her pockets. "What have they become?"

He hesitated, then shrugged. "They go by many names."

Word games were the last thing she felt like playing right now. Her head ached. Her arm ached. In fact, everything ached. She stunk of smoke and sweat and fear, and she wanted nothing more than to go home and soak in a nice hot bath.

But she couldn't, not until she'd talked to her boss. And to do that, she had to first make some sense of the night's madness. "So what in hell do *you* call them?"

He looked past her and she resisted the temptation to turn around, sensing that if she did, he'd be gone.

"I suppose it's best to call them zombies," he said after a moment, his eyes dark pools of anger when he met her gaze again. "They answer to the man who attacked you inside the house."

She laughed at the absurdity of it, but her amusement quickly faded under his watchful gaze. She remembered the wash of fetid breath across her face, the chill of flaccid flesh against her palm.

Remembered her impression that the women were dead, and yet not.

Zombies. *Hell's bells.* Monica was into something far weirder than any of them had realized.

A siren wailed into the silence and she glanced over her shoulder. A fire engine came around the corner. The driver must have taken the shortcut through the park to get here so fast. "So how do we explain the presence of zombies to the fire department?"

"We don't," Michael said, his gaze on the approaching engine. "And they will only find charred remains. The others have already left. As should we."

"If the fire's been reported, no doubt someone's mentioned seeing us out front. I'd better stay here and wait."

"I cannot." He looked past her again, then stepped back. "We will meet again."

"Wait!" she said, reaching out to stop him, not wanting to lose the comfort of his presence. "I . . . I don't even know your name."

"You lie, Nikki James."

He smiled and caught her hand, his fingers gliding across hers. Her skin tingled as he raised her hand to his lips, and while she would have liked to think the cause was the unusual warmth of his touch, she knew it was simply a response to the gentle kiss he pressed onto her fingertips.

She pulled her hand from his. He was a stranger, an unknown. She should be responding with wariness, not . . . fascination. She'd traveled that path once before, and it had ended badly.

His smile, when his gaze met hers again, had faded. "The fire department is almost here. You should be safe enough with them. The man you fear has left the immediate area anyway."

His words drew her attention back to the park. Yes, the sense of evil had departed. So had Monica. Yet she knew the danger was far from over. And she still had a client who wanted to see his daughter—whatever the cost.

"He may have left the area, but I doubt I've seen the last of him . . ." Then her voice faded, because Michael had disappeared completely.

Three

THE SCENT OF his enemy swirled around him, but it was faint, distant. Michael flexed his fingers and fought the urge to give chase. He'd come here to save Nikki James from the danger she faced tonight, and that had to be his priority. And it wasn't as if Jasper was about to go anywhere. Not now that the fiend knew *he* was in town. Michael crossed his arms and leaned back against the fence, studying Nikki. She wasn't, he thought, what he'd call beautiful, yet there was something about her, something that caught and held his attention. A life, a fire that made her glow from within *and* without.

Not that she was, in any way, ugly. She was on the slender side but had curves in all the right places. Her hair was long and dark; her eyes an unusual, smoky amber. It was a combination he'd been attracted to before—and look at the trouble *that* had gotten him into, he thought with amusement.

Like that other woman, *this* one was something of an enigma. There was something of the streets in her mannerisms, and yet it was tempered by an odd sort of innocence.

If the situation had been different—if *he'd* been

different—he might have tried to get to know her better. The rapport that had flared between them, if only briefly, was something he hadn't experienced in a very long time. He grimaced and thrust a hand through his hair: And maybe, after that, he'd fly to the moon. What the hell was he thinking?

He'd see her again, of that he had no doubt. Once Jasper's presence in Lyndhurst was reported, he'd be ordered to hunt down and kill the bastard. And while Nikki had escaped Jasper's trap tonight, he had tasted her abilities and would not let her go so easily next time. Which meant the surest way to find Jasper was to remain close to Nikki.

But *his* association with her could never amount to anything more than friendship. And certainly it would last no longer than the time it took him to stop Jasper. He could not change who he was or what he did, and both were extremely dangerous to someone like her. He and Jasper were similar in that regard.

So he waited, watching as she spoke to the fire brigade, was tended to by the EMTs and finally talked to the police; then he followed her home. By that stage, dawn was beginning to touch the sky with flags of red and gold. While Jasper could function for about an hour after dawn, it was unlikely he'd be doing anything more than finding a safe place to see out the daylight and plot his next move. For the moment, at least, Nikki was safe.

The wind gusted around Michael, thick with the promise of rain. He turned, and headed west. The sound of high heels on the pavement ahead made him slow down. The red haze of life flared before him—a prostitute, plying her trade.

The darkness stirred within him and hunger rose, eager to taste the sweet offering of life. The woman was alone and unprotected. It would be so easy to reach out and take what his body craved . . .

Michael shook his head. He could not help what he was, but he'd beaten that particular demon long ago. He *would* feed, but not now, not tonight.

And definitely not on anything human.

He strode past her. He'd left his car in a parking lot just ahead, across the road from an old hotel. It was the sort of place that looked, at least from the outside, to be the kind of establishment frequented mainly by prostitutes and junkies in need of a cheap place to crash. A place where no questions were asked, and where the proprietor did not care who rented the rooms as long as they paid up front. Certainly not an establishment he'd normally frequent, but it *was* the sort of place Jasper liked. And while Michael doubted he'd be lucky enough to have Jasper walk straight into his waiting arms, it was still worth a chance. Jasper liked easy prey, and an area like this provided an effortless hunting ground.

So why had he turned Monica, rather than simply killing her? It was decidedly out of character, and *that* was worrying. Michael collected his bag from his car, then headed across to the hotel and booked a room. Key in hand, he headed up the stairs. Once he reached the top floor, he stopped and scanned the area, more out of habit than any sense of danger. The red heat of life flared in several of the rooms down the hall from his own, but everything else was still.

He continued on. The threadbare carpet did little to muffle his steps, and the floorboards creaked under his weight. But at least that meant nothing human could sneak up on him—although it was the not-so-human he was worried about. He opened the door to his room and quickly looked around. Basic but survivable.

After dumping his bag on the bed and retrieving the bottle of red from within it, he found a corkscrew and glass, and moved back to the center of the room. Sitting cross-legged on the carpet, he relaxed.

Contact was instant.

You arrived safely.

The harsh whisper winged into his mind and made him wince. Would Seline ever realize how strong her telepathic voice was?

He opened the wine and poured himself a glass. *Yesterday.*

And did you manage to save Nikki James?

There was an odd note in her voice that had Michael's eyebrows rising. The old witch was up to something, and it wasn't *just* saving a life. *Yes. But there are complications.*

When are there not? Amusement laced her mental tones.

Jasper's here. And he's up to his old tricks again.

She sucked in a breath, the sound sharp over the mental line. Whatever she'd planned when sending Michael here, it hadn't included Jasper's appearance. *I was hoping that bastard was dead.* She paused. *Do you need help?*

Images of Jasper and his teenage lover ran through Michael's mind, as did the twisted images of the three remaining zombies. Five deadly beings against one. He grimaced. If he were a betting man, he knew who he'd place his money on. And if Jasper killed any more and called them back to life . . .

Even if I did, we can't risk anyone else. Jasper's killed two of our number already, and he now knows I'm in Lyndhurst.

Concern ran like wildfire through the link. *He has had a long time to prepare his revenge, Michael. You need to be extremely careful with this one.*

He's not the only one whose been preparing, Seline. It's a fight that's long overdue.

How will you find him before he finds you? Lyndhurst is a big town.

Michael smiled grimly. It was big, all right. But Jasper wouldn't run. Or hide. As he'd already said, the game was over. This time, the battle would be final. The prize would be life—or death—for one of them.

I have some bait.

Not Nikki, surely?

He had a sudden image of Nikki's eyes. They were such an unusual color—a warm, smoky amber that seemed to reflect the intensity of her emotions.

Yes. She's a strong psychic—very strong, in fact. Jasper craves her power. He will try to kill, then retrieve, her.

Seline sucked in another breath. *That is a dangerous game to play, Michael. Especially with her.*

Michael took of quick gulp of wine. *Why especially her? It's not like we haven't used the innocent before now as bait to catch our foe.*

This is different.

How? I was sent here to protect her, and I will. But we've been hunting Jasper for a very long time, and we cannot risk losing him again.

Seline was silent for so long, he was beginning to think she'd perhaps fallen asleep. But eventually she said, *What do you plan?*

Given Jasper seems to believe power is the only way he can defeat us, there's no doubt he'll go after Nikki again. I'm going to befriend her. Hopefully, Jasper will turn up quickly, and I can get rid of him before he kills anyone else.

Take care, Michael. You're playing for far more than you realize here.

He frowned. Seline obviously knew more about the situation—or at least about Nikki—than she was letting on. But he also was well aware there was no point in questioning the old witch. She'd tell him what she thought he needed to know, and nothing more. There was little else to add, so he bid her good night and broke the contact. Then he stretched his legs and yawned, trying to relax the tension cramping his muscles.

He picked up his glass and rose, walking across to the window. The blinds were open, and the pale light of the rising dawn streamed in through the glass. Michael leaned a shoulder against the window frame and sipped slowly at the wine.

The sun had killed many of his kind. Seeing it again was a pleasure he'd long thought lost to him. Thankfully, time had taught him otherwise. He lifted his glass to the dawn's light and watched it reflect through the ruby liquid. Wine was another pleasure he'd thought forever lost. He'd been told he could only survive by taking the life of others, that anything else would kill him. More lies. His altered metabolism might mean he couldn't consume food, but it didn't prevent him from taking in fluids. Wine would never sustain him, but it wouldn't kill him, either.

He took another sip and wondered what had happened to the woman who'd turned him. Dublin in the 17th century had been an unforgiving place, and he'd fallen under Elizabeth's spell so very easily. Or perhaps he'd just been desperate to escape the emptiness of his existence—even now he wasn't entirely sure. He had a sudden vision of Nikki, and smiled. In very many ways, she reminded him of Elizabeth.

The sun's light grew stronger. He swallowed the remaining wine in one swift gulp and closed the curtains. As much as he would have liked to watch the dawn color the sky, he had to sleep. There was much to do when night fell.

Nikki drove her ancient car into the first available parking space near the office. Climbing out was difficult; every muscle protested fiercely. Taking a deep breath, she leaned against the car for a moment, waiting for the various aches to subside. The painkillers the EMTs had given her were about as useful as a sun hat in a thunderstorm. Nor had the brief hot shower and clean clothes helped much. What she really needed was some sleep—nothing too long, just three or four days' worth. She grimaced and turned. Like that was going to happen.

A long, white limousine took up several parking spots in front of the single-story building that housed the agency. Monica's father. Nikki groaned. Just what she needed to finish a perfect twenty-four hours.

The cool breeze ran around her, rich with aromas from the bakery down the road. She took a deep breath, then sighed in pleasure. Fresh, hot donuts. Was there a better smell on this earth, other than chocolate?

Maybe a donut was just what she needed. And if nothing else, it would delay the confrontation with Trevgard for a good ten minutes.

Besides, she hadn't yet decided what she was going to tell the old fart. Shoving her hands in her pockets, she headed to the bakery and ordered a half dozen. No doubt Jake would need some form of sweetening, if he'd been entertaining Trevgard for long.

Energy boost ready, she walked back to the agency.

"Where the hell is my daughter?"

Trevgard's demand hit her the moment she opened the door. His fury hit a second later, as breathtaking as a punch in the gut. Yet behind the bluster, she sensed concern. Trevgard might look and act like an ogre, but right now he was a man very worried about his daughter.

She shrugged and slammed the door shut. "I don't know." Though it was an honest enough answer, it was not one Trevgard was likely to appreciate.

"Why not? I've been paying damn good money for this agency to keep tabs on who she's fraternizing with, and I certainly haven't been getting *that*, either. Moreover, I wanted her *here*, not out *there*, still roaming the streets!"

"Now, John, relax." Jake's voice was at its mildest—a sure sign he'd reached the end of his tether. "Just give Nikki a chance to explain what happened last night."

She laid the donut box on her desk and walked over to the coffee machine. "For a start," she said, pouring coffee into a mug that had seen better days, "I did manage to talk to her. She wants to be left alone."

"What? I told you yesterday that I'd had enough of this bullshit. *I* want to speak to her. Me, not you. Why didn't you—"

"John," Jake warned quietly.

She flashed her boss a smile of thanks. Trevgard on the warpath was not something she needed right now. Her headache was bad enough already.

"I couldn't bring her back with me because this time she *wasn't* alone, and her friends were a bit . . . protective."

To emphasize her point, she put down her coffee and took off her jacket. The white blob of the bandages stood out like a sore thumb. Trevgard's round face paled, his thin mouth twitching slightly, his anxiety obviously rising several notches. She wondered how he'd react if she told him four of those protectors were zombies. Yeah, right. After he'd stopped laughing, he'd probably arrange to have her locked away.

"Are you all right?" Jake asked, leaning forward. His blue eyes were concerned.

She nodded absently, her attention still on Trevgard. The sooner she could get rid of him, the better. There was a lot she had to tell Jake, and if she didn't get some rest soon, she'd collapse where she stood.

"I'll find her again tonight." Though what she

would do when she located Monica again was an entirely different matter.

"And how will you achieve this miracle?" Trevgard asked, tapping stubby fingers against the desktop. "It's taken you nearly a week to get this far."

She raised an eyebrow and glanced at Jake. He could field this one. She wasn't about to explain that their problem stemmed from the fact that Monica was as slippery as an eel when it came to finding *and* keeping track of her. A teenager getting the better of a seasoned professional investigator wasn't good for business. Trevgard was powerful enough that he could make or break their agency. All it took was a word or two with the right people.

"Lyndhurst is a big place, John." Jake's deep voice was calm, despite the flicker of annoyance she saw in his eyes. "Up until now, we've been using conventional methods to track Monica. Tonight we'll try something different."

"Like what?"

Trevgard's gaze shifted between the two of them, his distrust evident. But then, he'd made his multimillions the hard way—trusting few, working long hours, and saving every penny. It was a pity his daughter wasn't a little more like him.

The image of sapphire-blue eyes swam briefly through Nikki's mind and her hand shook, splashing coffee on the carpet. She sat down quickly and hoped Jake hadn't noticed. It would only lead to questions she didn't want to answer right now. Not with Trevgard in the room, anyway.

"We'll need something of Monica's. Something she wore a lot," Jake said quietly.

"Why?" The older man's question was gruff, full of suspicion.

"Have you ever heard of psychometry?"

"No." Trevgard's gaze narrowed. "What is it?"

Jake's smile was so bland, Nikki had to sip her coffee to hide her grin.

"Psychometry is the ability to hold an object and sense some of the history of its owner. If the link is strong enough, you can sometimes use it to trace the owner."

"Yes? So?"

"So Nikki has that ability. We think we can use it to track your daughter."

"If she has this ability, why hasn't she used it before? What are you two trying to pull?" Heat suffused his cheeks, making them look mottled. And making him look uglier, if that was even possible.

"It's what we consider a last-ditch option, because it wipes Nikki out." Jake shrugged. "But it works. If you don't believe us, why don't you talk to Anita Coll? Nikki found her daughter alive and well, two days after the cops had given up."

Trevgard suddenly looked thoughtful. Definitely no fool—despite outward appearances. He might not like the agency or their methods, but he would use them—and anyone else—in order to bring back his wayward daughter.

He nodded abruptly. "All right. There's a charm bracelet Monica wore up until a week ago. I'll bring it to you—but if you think I'm going to let it out of my sight—"

"Fine," Jake interrupted smoothly. "But don't touch the bracelet yourself. Use cloth to pick it up, and carry it in plastic. Too many people handling an object can interfere with Nikki's ability to get a reading."

Nikki opened her mouth to protest about Trevgard being present when she made the attempt, but snapped it shut when Jake glared at her. She sipped her coffee again instead and seethed in silence. Did Jake really expect her to find Monica with Trevgard breathing down her neck? Her talent wasn't always reliable, and distractions only made matters worse.

Trevgard rose. "I'll go get it now."

"Fine. But don't bring it back until . . ." Jake hesitated, and Nikki held up six fingers. "About six this evening. Nikki has to rest first."

The older man grunted and strode to the door.

"Phew," Nikki said, once he'd gone. "Talk about a powder keg. He'll end up in the hospital if he's not careful."

"He's worried, believe it or not. But you're right, he's definitely in line for a heart attack at this rate." Jake relaxed back into his chair. "And don't say the world would be better off. It's not polite."

"Neither am I." She yawned. "Sorry. It's been a long night."

"Once you tell me what happened, you can go home and rest."

"It's a long story, boss." And not one she was sure she could really explain.

"I have all day, kiddo."

She smiled wryly. He was as busy as she, and they both knew it. Though in his early forties, Jake didn't fit the typical image of a private investigator. Absent were the scruffy looks, clothes in serious need of an iron and scuffed shoes. His image was more the successful businessman. Not only did it put his clients more at ease, it also gave him an extra advantage on the job. His look at the office was very different from the one he used on the streets.

She dug out a couple of donuts, then tossed the box to him. He caught it deftly and ate in silence as she gave him an edited version of the night's events. She left out the zombies and the fact that they were, in fact, the four missing women, not sure if she could convince him of that until he saw them for himself.

He whistled softly when she'd finished. "Sounds like Monica's landed herself in something serious."

"It's more than serious. The man she's with . . . he's evil, Jake. Pure evil." She leaned back in her chair, shuddering at the seductive memory of those fiery blue eyes. "I don't think we have a chance of getting her away from him."

"We have to try."

She bit into her donut. Yeah, they had to try, but she didn't have much hope of succeeding. Evil had too strong a grip on Monica now.

Jake rose and poured himself a cup of coffee. "And the man who helped you, Michael Kelly? Where does he fit in?"

Nikki shrugged. "I don't know."

"There's too much here that we just don't understand. I don't like it, Nik."

She struggled against another yawn. "Neither do I. But there's not a lot we can do about it."

"I could take you off the case . . ."

"And who would take over? You?" She grinned at

him. "You're so busy now, you don't have time to scratch."

"True." He shrugged. "One of these days, I'm going to have to hire another investigator." He gave her a sympathetic look as the yawn she'd been fighting broke free. "Why don't you go home and get some sleep? You look dead on your feet."

His words revived memories of the fetid breath and cold flesh of the zombies. She shuddered again and rose. "That's an offer I can't refuse. I'll leave the rest of the donuts, in case you want them."

"An offer *I* can't refuse." Jake grinned and helped himself to another donut. "Just make damn sure you're back by six. I might be tempted to murder our client if I have to spend any more time alone with him."

"Then I'll make sure I'm late," she answered sweetly, and stepped out the door before he could throw something at her.

In the end, exhaustion and a broken alarm clock did make her late getting back to the office.

"What happened to six o'clock?" Trevgard said the minute she opened the door.

His voice was mild given the anger she could sense. She looked at the clock. It was nearing six-thirty, so he had every right to be annoyed.

"Yeah, what happened?" Jake asked, his irritation undisguised.

She grimaced. "Alarm clock."

Jake shook his head. It wasn't the first time she'd

been late, and he'd been telling her for weeks to replace the damn thing.

Nikki glanced at Trevgard. "I'm sorry to keep you waiting. Did you bring the bracelet?"

"Yes. Jake has it."

Jake passed her the bracelet, sealed in a plastic bag. She sat down, her stomach churning. She'd done this a hundred times. But never before had her life been at risk.

She frowned at the thought and opened the baggie, letting the delicate gold bracelet drop into her hand. Her skin tingled as she closed her fingers around the charms, pressing them into her palm. Shutting her eyes, she reached for the energy that would unlock their inner images.

Gradually, it came, and her psyche followed the invisible trail until she began to see images.

A factory. Three floors. Broken windows. Dark. Her mind seized the pictures, storing them for examination at a later point. She had to go with the flow or risk losing it. She didn't have the strength for a second try.

The smell of the sea . . . the creak of boats. Inside . . . evil. She recoiled. *Oh God, he's here!*

Panic took control and, for an instant, the images faltered. Now she understood her earlier intuition. Evil was here in the darkness—and it was hunting *her.* Her fingers twitched against the bracelet, but she fought the instinct to break contact. Time was running out for Monica. Nikki had to find her quickly, and this was the only way to do it.

Sweat beaded her brow, but she reached again for the images.

Stairs . . . a basement. Two rooms, three. In the fourth one, Monica. Naked. Two strange marks on her neck but no blood, either there or elsewhere. Unconscious, but alive.

Then something hit Nikki hard, drawing her into darkness, snaring the very essence of her soul as securely as a fly in a web.

And the spider laughed in demonic delight.

Four

ONLY THE HARSH notes of her breathing broke the silence.

There was nothing to see—nothing beyond a deep void of darkness. Yet something—or someone—was near. She wasn't here in this darkness, only her psyche was, but nevertheless she rubbed her palms down her thighs and it felt real. *God,* she thought, *what sort of game is this?*

Soft laughter stirred the night, filling the void with its corruption.

She closed her eyes. He was here, in the cage that had captured her spirit, and there was no escape. Energy pulsed above her head—a net of power that somehow held her prisoner. If she stayed here too long, she would die.

Was that his aim?

Sweat trickled down her back. Fists clenched, she watched as a golden shaft of light spread across the darkness. It revealed a makeshift bed. On it lay Monica.

There was no sense of death, yet Nikki could see no signs of life. It was almost as if the teenager hovered somewhere between. Shivering in apprehension, she wondered what other surprises her abductor had in store.

As if in answer to her question, more laughter slid around her. Heart working overtime, she turned.

He flowed into existence from a patch of midnight, a maneuver that reminded her oddly of Michael. But the man before her now—no, he was more a boy, albeit a boy with the physique of a body builder— appeared maybe fifteen, sixteen years old, yet strong. Powerful. Hauntingly beautiful . . . and totally evil.

"Monica is mine."

His whisper sliced through her, and she responded, "Why are you doing this to her? To me?" Her voice came out high, almost childlike. She swallowed, trying to ease the dryness in her throat.

"She has what she wanted." His blue eyes began to change. Began to burn with a sapphire flame.

She licked her lips. "And that is?"

He moved a step closer. Horror held her immobile.

"What do all the rich want?" he replied. "Power. Eternal life."

His answer made no sense. "And what do you get in exchange?"

His smile was charming. But cold, so cold. "What makes you think I would want or need anything from her?"

"Because you do not seem like a caring, sharing type to me."

He laughed. Her skin crawled. "Let's just say she has assets I desire."

"And me?" she asked, fearing the answer.

"You, my pretty, are the first to elude my call. And you *certainly* have assets I desire."

He reached out, brushing her cheek with a hand. Her skin stung and bile rose in her throat. She longed to run, but even the simple act of breathing had become difficult. His hand slid lightly down her neck and across her breast. She closed her eyes, digging her nails into her palms to stop herself from screaming. She'd be damned before she gave him *that* pleasure.

He laughed and her eyes flew open. Hunger stirred deep in the bright heart of his gaze.

"So brave," he whispered. "So very brave. Our association will be an interesting one, indeed."

She shuddered, her mind screaming a denial her lips refused to utter. His gaze became a sapphire fire.

So bright.

So blue.

She watched, enthralled, as death closed in.

Night had settled across cloudy skies by the time Michael made his way through the last of the stockyards. The cattle had stilled their restless stirring now that he no longer walked among them, and the distant rumble of the traffic made little impact on the hush surrounding him.

He reached the last fence and stopped, leaning his arms against the rough railings. The red flare of life burned in the buildings opposite, and his hunger, though sated, stirred sluggishly. Would the desire for the sweet strength of human blood ever completely leave him? While control was not a problem these days, the yearning still ran through his veins—an addiction that refused to die. It was frustrating, but he couldn't change what he was. Once you underwent the ceremony and turned from human to vampire, the only other option open to you was death. And he certainly wasn't ready for *that*.

He half shrugged, and his thoughts turned to Jasper—and Monica. She was not the first young woman turned by a dance with the devil, but she was the first *rich* young woman Jasper had targeted. Perhaps the fiend had realized having heiresses under his control would lead to an easier and more luxurious lifestyle. He wouldn't be the first vampire to come to that conclusion. Life, especially a life as long as a vampire's, was definitely more comfortable with money behind you.

Michael climbed through the railings, then broke into a run, moving quickly along the road that would take him back to Lyndhurst. A quick check earlier in the day had revealed the town had five detective agencies. After three calls, he'd found Nikki's. He glanced at his watch. It was nearly six-thirty—she should be there by now.

What he did depended very much on Nikki's reaction to him. Still, one way or another—willing or unwilling—she *would* become his bait.

The sounds and smell of humanity swirled around him as he approached the business district. The streets became more crowded, forcing him to slow down. He might be able to prevent most people from seeing him, but he couldn't prevent them from feeling the impact of his body if he ran into them. And the last thing he needed right now was to stir up hysteria. The recent disappearances of four women had caused enough trouble. Much more, and Jasper might feel it necessary to leave. Despite his assurance to Seline,

Michael knew that Jasper wasn't stupid enough to stick around if things became too difficult. There was always another city, another time. Their final battle might be long overdue, but Jasper had time to spare. He could wait until the situation was right, the odds were on his side.

Nikki's office came into sight. Lights shone brightly through the windows. Nikki was . . . He stopped abruptly, a cold sensation he once might have named fear running through him.

Energy shimmered across his skin—a powerful cord of evil that held Nikki's mind captive. He took the building's front steps two at a time and opened the door. Two men looked up as he entered. One stood near a desk, the other was kneeling beside Nikki, one hand reaching out—

"Don't touch her!"

"What do you mean, don't touch her?" The blond stranger glared at him. Though he hunched over Nikki protectively, he made no further attempt to touch her.

No fool, this one, Michael thought as he knelt on the opposite side of Nikki's prone body.

"You might kill her," he said tersely, running his right hand a hair above her body, searching for some chink in the powerful shield surrounding her.

He heard the man's sharp intake of breath, but paid him little heed. Nikki's breathing was shallow and erratic, her heart straining under increased pressure. A body could survive only so long without the will, the essence, of its being.

And if she died, she would be Jasper's.

Power pulsed against his skin like a thousand dancing fireflies. He narrowed his eyes, studying its rhythm. Urgency beat through him, but he ignored it. She could die if he hurried . . . and die if he didn't.

Then the tempo of the dance faltered, weakening slightly and allowing him access. He reached out to her mind and swiftly followed the psychic cord through the darkness.

Fear assailed him again when he realized that Jasper was also attempting a mind lock, and that he was close to succeeding.

Nikki, don't look at his eyes! He charged the mental shout with all the power he could. He had to break the magnetic hold his enemy had on her mind.

Why?

Her reply was weak, vague. She was so close to giving in—yet, in her own way, still fighting. It was a miracle she'd held out as long as she had.

His eyes are so very . . . beautiful.

No! Nikki, look away!

Confusion stirred through the link, and hope soared within him. The more she fought against the net holding her captive, the weaker it would get. But Jasper was more powerful than Michael had realized if he could hold this net in place and still have the strength to attempt the possession of a mind as strong as Nikki's.

Fight him!

The net trembled, weakening with every second. Yet so was she. Psychic energy burned through him, but he held his weapon in check, denying the impulse to assault the net and kill his enemy. He didn't understand how the net entwined her mind, and if he tried to destroy it, he might destroy her, too. So he wouldn't attempt it unless absolutely necessary. He'd just have to wait, and catch her when she came free. If she came free.

Don't give in, Nikki!

Michael?

Her response was stronger this time. Wisps of urgency shimmered across the net, testing its boundaries, its strength.

A desperate surge of obstructing energy ran through the lattice, yet Jasper was faltering. A small tear appeared in its fabric. More energy flared through the net, but it was no longer enough to hold her.

Reaching out, Michael pulled her clear. Her spirit entwined with his for an instant—a gentle yet intense mingling that shocked him. Then she was gone and he was back in his body, feeling strangely empty.

He opened his eyes and lowered his hand, gently stroking the sweaty strands of dark hair away from her closed eyes. The link they'd just made could get them both into trouble. Whether she knew it or not, she'd created a bond that would not be easily broken. It could make things awkward, given that he had no intention of doing anything more than work to keep her safe . . . and use her to capture Jasper.

She opened her eyes and stared at him blankly. And, just for an instant, he saw an echo of evil in those smoky amber depths. How far had Jasper succeeded in his mind lock? There was no way to tell. And no way to know until he made his next move.

"Michael?"

"You're safe," he replied softly.

"Need to rest," she murmured, closing her eyes again.

He wasn't surprised. After what she'd just endured, she should sleep for a week.

"How is she? Will she be okay?" the blond stranger asked anxiously.

Michael ignored him, focusing instead on the big man near the desk. Frustration, fear and worry writhed through him, and he was clearly ready to explode. Slipping into the old man's mind, he ordered him into silence. Nikki needed attention. He didn't have the time for a war of words.

"She's fine," he said, returning his gaze to the blond man. "She just needs to rest."

"We'll put her in the room behind you. By the way, I'm Jake Morgan."

"Michael Kelly." He shook the offered hand absently.

"I thought you might be. How long will she be out?"

Michael shrugged. "A couple of hours, minimum. Tell your client to come back at ten. I will stay and keep watch over her." After all, what better way to start gaining her trust than by being here, guarding her, when she woke?

Jake nodded, not asking the questions Michael could see in his mind. Instead, he rose and crossed to speak to the older man. Michael hastily removed his previous compulsion.

He slipped his arms under Nikki's body and carefully lifted her. She was light. Too light, really. How in hell did she manage to maintain the energy needed to feed her psychic gifts when there was so little of her?

He took her into the next room—what looked to be

a small storeroom—and laid her on an old couch that dominated one wall. She stirred and opened her eyes.

"Don't leave me," she murmured.

Her gaze was filled with shadows and fear. He smiled and sat beside her. She shifted slightly, using his leg as a pillow. Closing his eyes, Michael carefully reached into her mind, calming the surface turmoil, stilling her fears—at least enough to allow her to sleep for several hours. That he could do this without her knowledge spoke of her desperate need for rest.

He opened his eyes and gazed at her. She looked so young lying there, almost childlike. Yet he'd caught the occasional whisper in her that spoke of a harsh past. He caressed her forehead, her skin like satin against his fingertips. And though he knew he could not afford to get more involved than he was already, he found himself wishing he could take the time to learn more about her.

But he'd long ago forsaken that sort of freedom. His life as a hunter of evil made any sort of relationship— even a fleeting one—dangerous. Getting involved emotionally with someone meant they could be used against him—and that was not a position he wanted anyone he cared about to be placed in.

It was a decision he'd never regretted.

Until now.

Darkness drifted through her dreams. It filled her mind, washing corruption through her soul. She fought it, desperate to be free, yet she couldn't break the chains.

In the distance she heard a voice whisper her name.

She turned toward the sound, following it desperately through the darkness.

Awareness surfaced. A door slammed in the front office. Trevgard returning, Nikki thought—and knew by the sudden leap of tension that both his patience and his temper were growing thin. She also became aware of Michael—of the firmness of his thigh against her cheek, of the gentleness of his fingers caressing her forehead . . . of his scent, an odd mixture of spice and earthiness.

She sat up abruptly, looking anywhere but at him, pushing her hair behind her ears. How did you react to a man who had saved your life and yet was still so much of an enigma?

"A simple thank-you would be sufficient," he said quietly.

She glanced up sharply. "I've never met anyone who can read my thoughts as easily as you." Tommy had been able to read her mind, but not so easily, unless she'd been angry or tired.

Michael shrugged, his ebony eyes regarding her warily. "Telepathic ability runs strong in my family. And I've honed its use over the years."

She had an odd feeling he wasn't speaking of blood relatives when he said "family." She frowned, then turned at the sound of approaching footsteps. Jake opened the door.

"I thought I heard voices," he said, stopping just inside the doorway. "I hate to rush you, Nik, but . . ."

"Trevgard's getting anxious," she finished. "What time is it?"

"A little past ten. I made a fresh pot of coffee. Want a cup?"

"Yes." She tried to ignore the ache that ran through nearly every muscle and pushed to her feet. "Michael?"

"If it's strong and black, I'll drink it."

He stood quickly, touching her elbow as she swayed slightly. She smiled her thanks and moved into the office, aware of Michael close behind her. Ready to catch her if she fell, she thought wryly. Three hours of sleep evidently wasn't nearly enough.

Jake placed a cup of coffee in front of her. Michael accepted his cup with a nod and leaned against her desk.

Trevgard swung around to face her as Jake returned the coffeepot to the hot plate. "So, did you find Monica?"

Nikki sighed. "Yes, I found her." She didn't mention the fact that his daughter might be dead. She didn't have the strength to face the old man's fury right now.

"And?" he demanded.

"And I'll try to bring her back with me."

Not alone, you won't.

She looked over at Michael warily, wishing she knew more about him. Instinct might be telling her to trust him, but she couldn't get rid of the niggling sensation that all was not as it seemed. Still, she wouldn't refuse his help. Nothing on this earth could make her go into that building alone. Not with a teenage madman on the loose.

"Then you really did see Monica? Really do know where she is?" Trevgard's voice held an odd mixture of hope and anger.

She returned her attention to him. "I think so. I know what the building looks like, and I've got a general idea of the direction; it's just a matter of driving around until I find it."

"What went wrong before?" Jake asked, moving back to his desk.

"Ever heard of out-of-body experiences?"

Jake nodded. "I've never believed in them, though."

She smiled. He hadn't believed in psychic talents, either, until they'd saved his life. "It was something akin to that. Except my spirit—soul, metaphysical body, whatever you want to call it—was forcibly drawn away from my body and trapped."

"How?"

"I honestly don't know." But she wished she did, so she could prevent it from happening ever again.

"It took a lot of psychic power to create and hold that net," Michael commented quietly.

Nikki regarded him thoughtfully. "And a lot of strength to pull me in. Yet he still had enough left to hold the intensity of the web as long as he did."

Jake's eyebrows rose. "Web?"

She took a sip of her coffee, then nodded. "Yes. A net of some sort held me captive. I don't know what he was trying to achieve. I wasn't really there. He couldn't physically harm me."

Though he could have killed her, had he held the net long enough, she realized.

"Control." Michael's expression was grim when it met hers. "He was after control."

"So I wouldn't be able to fight him if we ever met again." Cold fear ran down her spine. She had come so close.

"The man's a fiend." Jake swore and rubbed the

back of his neck. "I don't suppose you can give a description of him to the police?"

"Yes. Whether they'll believe it is another matter entirely."

Her boss grimaced. "Yeah. Our reputation's not exactly solid where they're concerned."

Trevgard made no comment, but she knew from the look in his eyes that their reputation was not exactly solid where he was concerned, either.

Smiling grimly, she said, "And it's not a man we're after, Jake. It's a boy."

Only Michael showed no surprise. Nikki had a feeling he'd known the madman's age.

"A boy?" Jake asked incredulously.

She nodded. "Maybe sixteen. As solid as a brick wall and as mad as a March hare."

Jake sighed and scratched at the blond stubble lining his chin. "Just what we need. Another psychotic in Lyndhurst."

"Lyndhurst specializes in this sort of thing, does it?" Michael asked, the mild amusement in his voice at odds with the sudden interest in his face.

Jake gave him a sour look. "It seems to lately."

"Enough!" Trevgard's gravely voice cut in. "This is not helping to find my daughter."

Though Nikki hated admitting it, he was right. She finished her coffee and rose. Trevgard took several steps forward, his body radiating the anger she could feel in his thoughts. He was ready for a confrontation.

"I'm coming," he announced. "I'll not run the risk of losing her a second time."

His company was the last thing she needed. She'd

be too aware of his anger and disbelief to concentrate on the fragile images that would lead her to Monica.

"No," Jake said. "Leave this to the experts."

"And I suppose he's an expert?" Trevgard sneered, jutting his chin in Michael's direction.

"Near as I know," Jake replied with a wry grin.

Trevgard grunted and looked away, and Nikki glanced at Michael. He stood beside her desk, arms crossed as he regarded Trevgard thoughtfully. He looked casual yet menacing, like a fighter about to step into the ring. He met her gaze and raised an eyebrow, a slight smile tugging on one edge of his mouth.

She grabbed her keys and jacket and stalked toward the door.

"Remember, use your phone," Jake called. "Let me know what's happening."

She acknowledged this with a wave of her hand and stepped outside. A blast of wintry air assaulted her. She shivered and put on her jacket. Michael stopped beside her, his gaze searching the streets, as if looking for someone. And while the light cotton sweater he wore emphasized the width of his shoulders nicely, it couldn't provide much warmth. She frowned, and hurried down the steps to her car. Lots of people didn't feel the cold, so why was she bothered by the fact that he apparently didn't?

"Want me to drive?" Michael asked as she opened the passenger's door.

She hesitated. If he drove, she could concentrate on finding the right building, and Monica. Nodding, she handed him the keys, then took the passenger seat and fastened her seat belt.

"Where to?" he asked, starting the car.

She closed her eyes and tried to pin down the elusive images. "Head for the docks. I'll know more when we get there."

"That's not where I expected him to be." He swung the car around and headed east.

A prickle of unease ran down her spine. Michael knew her attacker? And knew him well enough to have an expectation of where he'd head? "Why?"

He shrugged. "No reason. I just didn't expect him to be there."

"It sounds as if you know him."

"We've met before."

His voice gave little away, and the shadows hid any reaction she might have seen in his face. "Why the hell didn't you say anything before? You might know something that could have helped Monica—"

"Nothing can help Monica. The child has chosen her own path."

"But before—"

"It was still too late."

"Will you let me finish a damn sentence?" she exclaimed.

Michael smiled slightly and remained silent.

She chewed her lip absently and studied the street ahead. "Why are you in Lyndhurst?" she asked after a moment.

"I was sent to Lyndhurst to save you from the events of last night." He met her gaze briefly. "I remain here because Jasper is here, and it has become my task to stop him."

By "stop," she had no doubt he meant "kill." She shuddered. Was this casualness about life—and death—the darkness she sensed in him?

"Trust me, Nikki," he said gently. "I'll explain when I am able."

Yeah, right, she thought. *Heard that one before.* Tommy had been similarly fond of keeping her in the dark. "So that's his name? Jasper?"

Michael nodded. And when he didn't seem likely to say any more, she added, "Then tell me about yourself. Give me a reason to trust you."

He hesitated. And, in that instant, she sensed he'd give her nothing but lies and half truths. He might have been sent here to save her—and she'd love to know just *who* was behind that particular order—but it was Jasper who mattered now. Not her, not anyone else.

"I am a bounty hunter, of sorts," he finally volunteered. "I've been on Jasper's trail for several years now."

"Why?"

"Because he's a killer, and must be stopped."

She frowned. The slight edge in his voice suggested the reason was something more personal, but it was also a warning not to pursue it.

She returned her gaze to the street and her stomach lurched. They were nearing the docks. Taking a deep breath, she closed her eyes, reaching for images of the old building she'd seen earlier. She instantly knew its position—and knew something else, too. *He* was there, waiting for her.

"Turn right at the next street," she murmured, letting her instincts take control. "Then left. We're nearly there."

The smooth road gave way to broken concrete, which in turn became the rough timbers of an old wharf. The shadows of the nearby buildings drew close, crowding the narrowing alley. Michael eased the car past a row of Dumpsters and stopped in the small parking area beside the squat, ugly building.

This was it.

He touched her hand, entwining his fingers briefly in hers. Heat flowed, chasing the ice from her veins and making her skin tingle. "I can go in alone," he said.

She shook her head. She'd never felt afraid of the darkness before she'd met Jasper. One way or another, she had to get that back.

Nikki grabbed her phone and the flashlight from the glove compartment and slowly got out of the car. The wind was bitter, tinged with the smell of fish and putrid rubbish. She zipped up her jacket and joined Michael at the front of the car. Her shoulder brushed his arm, and an odd feeling of strength flowed through her. What was it about this man's presence that made her feel so safe? Especially considering the darkness she sensed within him?

She frowned, but didn't step away like she probably should, studying the building in front of them. Tin rattled noisily along the roof, and the wind whistled through the shattered windows lining the first two levels. The distant sounds of traffic were muted. She and Michael might well have been the only two people alive in this part of the world.

"I'll go first, if you like," he said, his voice oddly harmonious with the strangeness of the night.

"No. Let me lead. I'll feel any danger before it approaches."

"I'm not without some abilities of my own."

"But mine—"

"Just follow me, Nikki," he said in a voice that brooked no argument. "For once in your life, let someone else take control."

Anger surged. She clenched her fists, somehow resisting the temptation to throw him in the nearby ocean. "You have no right to say something like that! You know nothing about me—not who I am, or what I've been through."

He studied her for a minute, then nodded. "Fair enough. I apologize. I still intend to lead, though."

Nikki bit back a retort. He'd already moved ahead of her anyway.

She followed him into the shadows. The old building loomed above them like some misbegotten troll, frozen in darkness. The forlorn moan of the wind chased goose bumps across her skin. Perhaps it cried for the soul of the teenager locked within. Perhaps it cried for them.

She shivered and rubbed her arms. There was no sense of life within the building. No sense of death, either. She turned on the flashlight. Shattered glass gleamed diamond-bright in the light. Nothing moved except the rubbish, which the wind sent tumbling along the decaying brick walls.

Yet something waited.

"Nothing waits except the darkness and Monica, Nikki."

Michael was wrong. Jasper had been in this building, even if he wasn't currently. "I think he's set a trap of some kind."

"Perhaps." His fingers clasped hers gently. "Why don't you go back to the car?"

His hand burned against hers, and desire stirred briefly. Damn it, this was neither the time *nor* the place for such a reaction—and yet, it wasn't like she could exactly control it . . . especially if he kept hold of her fingers. She gently pulled her hand free. "I'm no coward."

"I wasn't suggesting you were."

"I know. But I can't back away from this." She hesitated, then added softly, "I won't let him make me afraid."

There was understanding in Michael's eyes. He nodded toward the doorway. "Shall we continue?"

No.

He looked at her, one dark eyebrow raised in query. She took a deep breath, and smiled. "Lead on."

She followed close on his heels as they climbed the front steps. His earthy scent filled every breath and chased away the more odorous smells that surrounded them. The door opened without a sound, revealing the dark interior. The air that rushed out to greet them smelled musty, full of decay. Michael's steps were sure despite the darkness, but the flashlight did little good. The night might as well have been solid.

After several minutes, she saw a faint gleam of silver in the darkness. Stairs, leading down.

Michael hesitated on the top step. She stopped just behind him and sensed him searching the darkness below. Wisps of energy ran through her mind, powerful enough to burn if she tried to capture them.

It was the first time she'd felt any hint of his power, and it made her own seem insignificant in comparison. A man with that much psychic energy could do anything he wanted.

An odd sense of foreboding ran through her.

"Monica's downstairs," he said after a moment. "Do you still want to continue?"

"Yes." There wasn't a hope in Hades she'd stay *here* alone.

Their footsteps echoed on the metal stairs, the sound scraping uneasily across the night. The flashlight flared against the thick darkness, yet revealed no secrets.

"Last step," Michael warned softly.

Her foot hit the floor. The wood underneath seemed to give, and she tensed.

"Old flooring," he commented, squeezing her fingers lightly. "It's probably rotten. You'd better wait here while I check it out."

She bit back an instinctive denial and tried to ignore the odd sense of loss she felt when the warmth of his presence left her. She held on to the banister and listened to the soft sound of his footsteps moving away.

"I've found Monica," he called after a few moments.

She could tell by his tone that he wasn't happy. She swept the flashlight in the direction of his voice, but couldn't see anything. "And?"

"She's still warm."

Warm, but dead; she knew without asking. She closed her eyes and took a deep breath. If she hadn't been such a coward last night, Monica might still be alive.

"Neither of us had much choice, Nikki. Don't condemn yourself for matters that cannot be controlled."

His words failed to ease the guilty ache in her heart. She could have tried harder. *Should* have tried harder.

"How did she die?" she asked, edging toward the sound of his voice. God, how was he seeing *anything* in this ink, let alone Monica?

His reply was terse. "Blood loss."

The floorboards moved a second time. Apprehension crawled up her spine, but she thrust it away. Michael had walked through here only a few moments ago. If the floorboards had held his weight, surely they'd hold hers.

"Did he mutilate her?" she asked, praying it wasn't so.

"No."

She took another step. "Then how did she die?"

The floor buckled. Wood groaned, as if ready to collapse. Imagination, she told herself fiercely, and took another step.

The floor bowed again, this time accompanied by an odd cracking sound. Sweat broke out across her brow. She cleared her throat. "Michael, I think something's wrong here."

"What?" His voice was sharp, alert.

"The floor." She frowned and took another small step. The boards seemed to bow even more.

"It's an old building," he reminded her gently. "Who knows what condition the pylons are in?"

A plausible enough explanation, but not the answer. She had the horrible feeling the whole floor was about to disappear beneath her. "It's more than that."

"Don't move, I'm coming back."

She swung the flashlight round in a tight circle. There was nothing to see but years of dust, stirred to sluggish life in the wake of Michael's passing. If Jasper *had* set a trap, surely Michael should have sprung it when he'd walked across this section. She bit her lip and took one more step.

It was one step too many.

The floorboards gave way, and she dropped like a stone into darkness.

Five

SOMETHING SHARP SKIMMED her side, tearing her clothes and scraping her skin, but her scream became a grunt when she hit something solid. She frantically gripped the old crossbeam that had stopped her fall, and hoped like hell it would hold. Far below, she could hear the roar of the ocean—a sound that promised death.

She couldn't swim. She could barely even dog-paddle.

There was another crack, the crossbeam gave way, and she plummeted once again, closer to the pit of darkness yawning at her feet.

She let go of the flashlight, flailing for something—anything—to stop her slide into oblivion. Her hands scraped against wood and she grabbed at it wildly. It shifted under the force of her weight, slipping several feet forward. For one heart-stopping moment, she hung motionless above the black pit, barely daring to breathe.

Then the wood—which was little more than a sharpened stake—cracked. She swung forward, desperate to find a more secure hold, jagged splinters tearing at her hands.

"Michael!" she screamed as her hands slipped farther down the old piece of timber. It cracked again, dropping her several inches closer to the pit . . . and death.

"Nikki!"

She looked up. Michael was leaning over the pit, reaching for her. She hadn't fallen as far as she'd thought, but that didn't make her position any less precarious. She shifted her grip on the wood and lunged for his outstretched fingers. His hand caught hers as more flooring shifted and dropped away.

"Your other arm," he ordered, his voice hoarse.

She released the timber and swung toward him. He caught her other hand, his grip like iron as she rocked back and forth. The sound of the ocean grew stronger.

But inch by precious inch, Michael moved backward, pulling her with him. As her feet came over the edge of the hole, he stood and pulled her upright. The night whirled dizzily around her and she closed her eyes, willing the sensation away.

Placing a hand under her elbow, Michael guided her to safety. Dark laughter flickered through her mind and she shivered. Jasper's trap might have failed, but he wasn't finished with her yet.

"That trap was not meant for you."

Her gaze shot to Michael's, even though she couldn't really see his features. "What makes you say that?"

"The strategically placed stakes. You were lucky you fell where you did. One step in either direction, and you would now be dead."

She shivered. "Why the hell would he even contemplate something like that?"

"Because it's a particularly nasty way to die." Michael stopped, forcing her to do the same. "Are you all right?"

He raised her hand, gently running his fingers over hers. Though his touch was still warm, this time it didn't do a whole lot to chase away the chill of knowing how close she'd come to death.

She flinched when he grazed several splinters. "A bit worse for wear, but otherwise in one piece." Her voice shook slightly, and she took a deep breath, trying to calm the desperate pounding of her heart.

"What about the cut on your side?"

Surprise ran through her. "You can see that?" How? It was pitch black and she'd lost her flashlight down the hole—not that it had been of much use, anyway.

His hesitation was brief, but nevertheless there. "I noticed it when I pulled you upright."

Liar, she thought, and wondered what he was concealing—and why he'd even bother. But all she said was, "It's fine."

"If it's fine, why are you still bleeding?"

He lightly touched her side and she winced. But again that uneasiness stirred through her. How the hell had he known?

"You should go back to the car and tend to the wounds," he continued, "you need to stop the bleeding."

She touched a hand to her side. It stung, but the blood wasn't pouring from the wound, no matter what he seemed to think. A couple more minutes wasn't going to matter. "The splinters hurt worse than the cut. Given that you can obviously see in this murk a hell of a lot better than me, can you pull them out?"

"I could, but I think it might be wiser if you went back to the car."

Why was he suddenly so determined to get rid of her? "No. I want to see to Monica first."

"There's nothing you can do, Nikki. Go back to the car and tend to your wounds."

"No." Something warned her not to leave the girl's body with this man. She might not find it again if she did. But . . . what in hell would Michael want with a dead teenager?

"You're a stubborn woman, Nikki James."

She smiled at the hint of exasperation in his voice. He'd only known her twenty-four hours, and already he'd come to that realization? It usually took people far longer to see through her polite veneer.

"And this is one of my good days," she replied lightly. "Now, would you please remove the damn splinters?"

"As you wish."

His hand caught hers and drew her a little closer. She stared into the darkness and tried counting to one hundred as he began to pull out the splinters. It didn't help a whole lot. She could no more ignore the sting in her hands than the warm brush of his body against hers.

"There," he said after a moment. "All gone."

"Good. Now we can go to Monica."

He smiled—though she couldn't say how she knew this. Perhaps it was little more than a quick caress of laughter in her mind. Or wishful thinking.

He placed a hand under her elbow again and led

her forward. The smell of decay tainted the air—a smell that had nothing to do with the sea or the rotting rubbish she kept tripping over. It was the smell of death. If only she hadn't dropped her flashlight—even a near-useless one would have been better than nothing at all.

Ahead, moonlight flickered through a few broken walls. The darkness shifted slightly, becoming less intense. Shapes loomed—old crates and half-demolished internal walls. Michael stepped through a shattered doorway and stopped. Though barely visible in the gloom, Monica lay before them. Nikki had an odd sense of serenity. This death was something the teenager had wanted.

She edged forward carefully then knelt beside the teenager's body and gently touched her neck. Though she didn't doubt Michael's word, she couldn't help hoping that perhaps he was wrong.

He wasn't.

Guilt washed through her. This death was partly her fault. If she hadn't given in to her fear and run from Jasper at the mansion, Monica might still be alive.

"Monica chose her fate. Nothing you could have done would've prevented this," Michael said, kneeling on the opposite side of the body. Nikki raised an eyebrow at the anger in his voice, but sensed it was aimed at himself rather than at her. He moved his hand, drawing her gaze back to Monica. "We should check her body."

"Why? She's dead. And as you pointed out, there's nothing much we can do about it now. Let's call the police and let them deal with her."

"I don't think that would be the wisest move."

She sighed and rubbed her temples wearily. She had a horrible feeling the night's surprises weren't over yet. "Why not?"

"Once I examine the body, I'll explain."

The thought of examining the dead girl further made Nikki's skin crawl. "What are you looking for?"

"Odd marks. A recent knife wound."

She raised an eyebrow but made no comment. Michael brushed the teenager's long hair to one side and bent to study her neck. And frowned.

Nikki rubbed her arms against a sudden chill. She knew what he'd found—she'd seen the two marks just before Jasper had snared her psyche. "Why are the odd marks and a knife wound so important?"

"If I find them all, I'll explain." He hesitated, then glanced up. "It might be quicker if you helped."

Though his tone was even, his irritation seared her mind. But how the hell was she going to help when she could barely even see him in this soup? Suddenly, she remembered her phone. She dug it out of her pocket, turned it on and put the flashlight app to good use. Its light flowed across the night, lifting the nearby shadows and lending warmth to Monica's pale skin. Nikki placed the phone on the floor next to her knee and gingerly lifted Monica's right arm. The smooth flesh felt cool, like meat just out of the fridge. Her stomach turned. While this wasn't the first time she'd seen a dead body, it was the first time she'd actually touched one. It seemed wrong, somehow.

"If she's dead, she won't mind," Michael said.

"Keep out of my thoughts," she snapped, frowning. "What do you mean, *if* she's dead?"

"I will *try* not to read your mind," he said, then added, "And I meant just what I said. Now keep checking."

"Not big on sharing, are you?" she muttered.

"Not under the circumstances," he said. "I'm here to catch a killer, nothing more."

And she and Monica were merely the means to an end. The thought annoyed her more than it should, but she continued her examination.

No unusual marks marred the creamy perfection of the teenager's skin. Nikki sat back on her heels. While she would have loved to be anywhere else but kneeling here beside a dead teenager, she owed it to Trevgard to find out what had happened—and maybe help bring her killer to justice.

The image of sapphire eyes rose in her mind, and she shivered. How did you bring a creature like Jasper to justice?

"You'd better have a look at what I've found," Michael commented softly.

His face was emotionless, giving no indication of what to expect. Phone in hand, she rose and walked around to his side. "Look at what?"

"Her wrist, for starters."

He pointed to Monica's wrist. A two-inch cut marred her skin. But the pale color of the scar indicated the wound was at least a week old. Nikki couldn't see how it was related to Monica's death. "And?"

"Now look at her neck."

She knew what she'd see, but squatted by his side anyway. Two small puncture wounds penetrated the skin. What she hadn't seen in the visions was the dried blood that ran from the wounds in a dark trail, disappearing behind Monica's pale blond hair.

Oh, *God*.

Michael had commented earlier that Monica had died from blood loss, yet there was very little blood near the body and no other obvious signs of injury. There might have been internal injuries they couldn't see, of course, and yet her mind leapt to a different, altogether more supernatural reason.

"So you're saying Monica died because . . ." Her voice trailed off and she closed her eyes, unable to voice the fear in her mind.

"She was drained by a vampire," Michael finished for her.

She took a deep breath and tried to control the turmoil running through her in panicked circles. It couldn't be true. Vampires didn't exist, damn it! They were a product of imagination, of fiction, *not* reality.

"Just as psychic powers don't exist?" Michael said, his voice gentle.

She glanced at him sharply. There was an odd expression on his face, as if her reaction was important in some way.

"That isn't the same thing at all!" she exclaimed.

"Why? Many people believe in psychic powers just as little as they believe in vampires. But does their lack of belief make those powers any less real?"

"No, of course not. But . . . *vampires*?"

"Look at her neck, Nikki. Remember the man she was with. Remember his evil."

She didn't need to remember. All she had to do was close her eyes and his image was there. "Being evil doesn't necessarily make him a vampire . . ."

"No, but drinking blood to survive does."

She shuddered. Monica looked so young, so peaceful. So dead. But if what Michael said was true, she might soon be alive again, as a vampire. According to legend, all it took was one little bite.

"Being the victim of a vampire does not mean you become one," he commented softly.

"It does in the movies." She rocked back on her heels and rubbed her arms, wondering why the room had suddenly become even colder than before.

"In reality, you become a vampire by sharing another vampire's blood in a special ceremony." Michael shrugged. "And only by mutual consent."

"So are you saying Monica *wanted* to become a vampire?"

"To some, the lure of eternal life is a powerful one."

"Not powerful enough, thank you very much." Why would anyone want to drink blood for eternity? And why would anyone want to live in night and darkness, never see sunlight again, never feel the warmth of it against their skin? If hell existed, then that was probably it.

Yet she remembered Jasper's mocking assessment of the rich, and suspected eternal life might be a strong lure for someone who basically had everything else she could ever want. "Besides, we can't be sure Monica went through the ceremony."

"No, but that cut on her wrist looks ominous."

She studied the half-healed wound. How could you tell an attempted suicide from an incision made during a special ceremony?

"You can't." Michael's voice was grim. "And that's why we must make sure she is *actually* dead."

She understood the intent behind his words well enough, even if he didn't come straight out and say it. "Why?"

"If she shared blood, she merely rests, waiting while her body undergoes the transformation."

"And have the movies got the methods of killing a vampire wrong, as well?"

He hesitated fractionally, then shook his head. "No. A stake through the heart will do it, as will the midday sun. Decapitation is the best method, though."

She raised an eyebrow. "And this is what you intend for Monica?"

His gaze searched her face. She wondered why. If he could read her mind so easily, surely he could taste her anger.

"It is for the best," he said after a moment.

Once again, he wasn't telling her everything. "The best for whom? You or Monica?"

"I am a hunter of evil, Nikki. I track it and kill it, and in the process make the night a safer place for people like you to walk."

"Don't give me that sanctimonious crap! You don't have the right to touch Monica. Her father needs her body back, at the very least. And with her head still on!"

"If I don't take her head, she will rise to aid Jasper." Impatience colored his quiet words.

Her anger rose another notch. She wanted nothing to do with any of this. Why had she let him onto this case . . . and into her life?

She swore and pushed upright, moving instinctively

away from him and toward the wall. Wintry air rushed through the shattered window above her head, but it failed to cool the anger heating her cheeks or the turmoil churning her stomach. At rest, Monica looked untouched by evil. It was easy to understand why Trevgard had refused to see his daughter as anything other than an innocent, even if the exact opposite was true. What would she say to him? Or to Jake? How could she face them if she allowed Monica to be mutilated? How could she face herself, in the long years of nightmares to come?

"I can't let you," she stated quietly, finally meeting Michael's watchful gaze.

His anger seared her mind. "You can't stop me," he warned quietly.

The threat behind the words shook her. Though he hadn't moved a muscle, he suddenly seemed so much larger, more threatening. The shadows moved in around him, obscuring his form, making him one with the night and the sense of evil that haunted the old warehouse.

Nikki clenched her fingers and felt energy tingle across her skin. Michael wasn't evil—not in the same way Jasper was. Yet she couldn't escape the feeling he wasn't entirely on the side of the angels, either.

"Are you willing to kill me to get to Monica?" she said.

His eyes were like chips of ebony ice. "Are you willing to die for the sake of evil?"

No. But she also refused to stand by and let him mutilate Monica's body. "If that's what it takes, yes."

Anger danced around her. She fought to breathe normally, trying not to let her fear show. She had a feeling Michael had spent too many years on his own, answering to no one but himself. He was, she sensed, neither one thing nor another—both light and dark, good and bad. She just had to hope the shadows in his soul didn't win tonight.

"Nikki, if this child becomes a vampire, she will be more dangerous than the man who hunts you. Can you live with that? With the death of so many innocents at her hands?"

She stared at him. How could anyone be more dangerous than Jasper? "I've been hired to find Monica and take her back to her father—in one piece. I'm just trying to do my job."

"And if she does turn?"

"I'll deal with it at that point."

A wave of fury rocked her back on her heels. The darkness crackled with energy and a sense of impending doom, but she stood her ground.

"You have no real concept of what you're letting loose!" Michael said, dark eyes glacial. The shadows around him began to retreat, but not the immediate sense of danger. "All right. Perhaps it is time for you to learn."

For an instant, he became something more than human—something akin to the evil that had stalked her. Her heart began to pound rapidly, a cadence that filled the tense silence. Something glimmered in his eyes—an echo of the powerful depravity she'd seen in Jasper's vibrant gaze. Underneath it lay the same desire for control.

Michael *wasn't* evil. Yet she couldn't escape the notion that her hunter and Michael were, in some way, connected. Damn it, she really had to find out more about both of them!

"What do you mean?" she demanded. Energy flowed across her fingers, yet she held her best weapon in check. She was not about to fire the first shot and start a war she had no hope of winning.

There was a long pause, then he shrugged and looked away. "Nothing. We will wait, as you wish."

The shadows no longer wrapped themselves around his body as he rose, and the impending sense of doom had fled with them. Yet the night was still ripe with uneasy tension.

"Come," he continued. "Let's go back to your car and call the police."

Though there was no emotion in his voice, there was still an edge of violence in his movements. This man had saved her life twice, yet she knew nothing about him—nothing beyond the fact that he could be very, very dangerous.

He turned to look at her, his eyes coal-black wells that told her little. Yet a flicker of emotion from his mind suggested that her distrust annoyed him.

"You have my word that I will not, in any way, touch or move Monica tonight. Is that enough?"

His soft tone hinted at anger, yet she heard no lie in his words. She nodded. After tonight, Monica would be in police custody. There was little he could do to her then.

"I shall lead, if you wish," he said, and offered his hand.

Why the sudden formality? Was it anger, annoyance, or something else entirely? Either way, taking his hand was the last thing she wanted to do—and not just because of the heat that always went through her at his touch. This man was dangerous, in more ways than one. And she'd be damned if she showed any weakness in front of him—despite the fact that she felt oddly safe in his presence.

She just had to hope this wasn't one of those rare moments when her instincts made a complete and utter hash of everything.

And that he wasn't right about Monica.

Michael crossed his arms and watched the two men bag the body. Even from this distance, he could hear the slow but steady beat of her heart. It was a gentle rhythm few humans would ever pick up—just a single beat every few minutes. His was much the same, except in times of stress, feeding, or sex. At least it was enough to keep his skin warm—being cold as death would have been awkward to explain.

He had no doubt the teenager would rise soon. Though it usually took about forty-eight hours, Monica appeared to be undergoing the change faster than most. She'd probably wake when night fell once more.

He should have killed her. What on earth had possessed him to make such a rash promise? All too often, he had witnessed the bloody rampages of the newly turned. And when their depth of malice and hate were as great as that he sensed in Monica, it was sheer madness to let them live. But he'd given his word to Nikki, and he intended to keep it. Whatever the consequences.

He had a sudden image of Nikki, face white and

eyes wide with fear, and frowned. He'd come too close to attacking her defenses in an attempt to gain control and make her do as he wished. Had he been alone so long that a simple act of defiance could tip him over the edge?

He sighed and rubbed a hand across his eyes. Whatever the reason, it didn't alter the fact that he'd have to watch himself. He was usually better at mastering the darkness. The last thing he needed right now was to let that control slip—especially when he was hunting someone like Jasper. That fiend would exploit any weakness he could.

The two men placed the teenager's body on a gurney and wheeled her out of the warehouse. Michael followed them.

Several police officers were still outside, questioning Nikki. He moved to one side, out of her line of sight, but her awareness washed over him anyway. He leaned a shoulder against the building's wall. Why was she so aware of his presence when so few could even see him while he was shadowed? Was it just her extraordinary psychic abilities, or had that brief mingling of their spirits formed a connection far stronger than he'd thought possible?

The sea breeze swirled, running chill fingers through his hair. Michael frowned and studied the distant shadows. A faint hint of evil lingered, mingled with the smell of the sea.

So Jasper had returned. Michael fought the urge to go after him, and instead looked at Nikki. The police officers towered over her, but they'd be no protection from Jasper. Or the zombies. No matter what he'd said earlier, keeping her safe was still a priority. Seline had wanted her saved last night for a reason, and while she hadn't actually shared that reason with him, he intended to keep doing it for as long as Jasper was on the loose.

Michael glanced at his watch and raised an eyebrow in surprise. It was after three A.M. They'd been here for nearly three hours. How many times could the police hear the same version of a story? Couldn't they see how tired she was? He was very tempted to unravel the shadows he'd pulled around himself and ask what in hell was going on, and was only stopped by the fact that the police were bound to start questioning *him*. And that could pose problems. His years of hunting evil had made him a lot of enemies, and he wanted his whereabouts kept secret from all except those he trusted.

The number of which he could count on one hand.

After a few more minutes, the two officers moved back toward the warehouse. Michael waited until they disappeared, then pushed away from the shadows and walked across to Nikki.

"Have they finished?" He kept a careful eye on the old building. He didn't want the policemen to return and spot him.

Dark rings shadowed Nikki's eyes, and her nod was barely visible. A stray wisp of hair fell across her face, and he had to restrain a sudden urge to tuck it behind her ear.

"They asked me not to leave Lyndhurst. It looks like I'm a suspect."

"And a pretty grubby one, at that." He smiled at her startled look. "Do you wish to go home, or to the office?"

"Home. They let me call Jake earlier and tell him what's going on. And he's given me tomorrow off."

"Good. You deserve it." He hesitated. "Shall I drive again?"

She shook her head. "No, I'm fine."

She looked close to exhaustion, but he handed over the keys anyway. Her fingers brushed his lightly, her touch cold against his skin and yet oddly warming. Which was just another warning that he'd really have to watch himself around this woman.

She unlocked the passenger's door, then moved around to the other side. Michael climbed in, studying the shadowed parking lot carefully. Jasper was still there, still watching. Hopefully, he'd follow. It would save him having to find the fiend again later.

Nikki fired the engine and turned the car around. Beneath its rumble came the sound of another car starting.

He smiled grimly. Jasper's behavior was sometimes too predictable. Once Nikki was safely home, Michael could resume his hunt.

"Penny for them," she said softly.

He glanced at her. Moonlight gilded her dark chestnut hair and softened the planes of her angular features. She was truly beautiful. A jewel he could not afford to touch.

He cleared his throat and glanced briefly out the window. "How safe is your house?"

"It's actually Jake's house, which he divided into apartments." She looked at him, a half smile touching her lips. "And just in case you were wondering, he's married to a lovely woman, and they do not live anywhere near the apartments."

"I wasn't."

"You'd be surprised how many people do."

"Actually, I wouldn't. It's the nature of humanity to suspect the worse."

She raised an eyebrow. "Is that an edge of bitterness I hear?"

"Perhaps." He shrugged. "To repeat the original question, how safe is your apartment?"

"It has lots of locks, I can assure you."

Which Jasper could pass with ease if she uttered the right words. All it took was a simple invitation. "Locks won't be much good if Jasper's friends turn up."

She gave him a quick smile. "I can scream very loudly."

He controlled the impulse to return her smile and watched the amusement fade from her eyes.

"I have my abilities," she finished quietly. "I can protect myself."

The hint of uncertainty in her voice suggested she wasn't as confident as she sounded. "And neighbors?"

"An old couple above me, and a drunk below. Not exactly reliable help in this sort of situation."

Not exactly reliable help in *any* sort of situation.

"I'll be fine," she added. "I've been in worse predicaments, believe me."

Her bleak tone stirred his curiosity. "Such as?" What could be worse than a vampire and his undead cronies after your body and soul?

She glanced at him, amber eyes suddenly as unreadable as her thoughts. "When you tell me your secrets, I'll tell you mine. We're here."

She parked the car in the driveway of an old Victorian. Michael climbed out and studied the building. A good coat of paint and a gardener would do wonders for the place. But no amount of paint could stop the rot setting into the window and door frames—neither of which would hold the zombies back for more than a minute.

"Would you like to come in for coffee?" she asked. "I've got some of the best mocha you've ever . . ." Her voice faded, eyes widening slightly as she stared at him.

Like she'd suddenly realized her impulsive invitation had just given him unlimited access to her home.

He smiled and reached out, tucking the stray stand of hair behind her ear. She shivered slightly at the brief caress, but didn't retreat.

"Thanks, but I better not. You need to rest."

"True." She gave him a smile that was more nerves than warmth, but her gaze went beyond him, studying the night.

And he knew that she sensed Jasper's presence.

"Nikki." He touched her arm lightly and felt the tremor that ran down it. "I'll stop him, whatever it takes. He will not touch you. Ever."

Empty words, when Jasper's darkness had touched her already. And Michael knew he couldn't prevent it from happening again—nor, in many respects, did he want to. She was still his best hope for luring Jasper in.

Her gaze searched his face. "Who sent you here to save me?"

He hesitated. "I'm afraid I can't reveal that."

Disappointment flitted through her eyes, and he found himself wishing that he could, just this once, be completely honest with someone. But he couldn't; too many lives depended on the secrecy of their organization.

He ran his hand down her arm and gently clasped hers. Her pulse skipped a beat, then began to race. Fear had no part in her reaction, just as it had no part in his own. "I'll see you tomorrow evening."

He raised her fingers to his lips and kissed them gently. She smelled of honey and cinnamon. Of life. Of everything he longed for, but had long ago lost. He released her hand and stepped away, moving back into the darkness of the ill-lit street. Her gaze followed him for a while, then she turned and went into the house.

He stopped and cast his senses into the night. Jasper was half a block away. Michael smiled grimly and cast a final glance at Nikki's apartment. He doubted Jasper would risk an attack with the three remaining zombies, not with dawn so close. And while there was still the possibility that Jasper had succeeded in getting enough of a hold on Nikki's mind to exert some form of control over her, the fiend couldn't force her to utter the words that would give him access to her home—there would be no point unless he was close enough to hear them being said. The invitation *had* to be spoken out loud, not thought. For the moment, she was safe enough.

Time to hunt the hunter.

Six

THE SHADOWS IN her room were filled with demons—
insubstantial wisps that mocked and threatened from
the safety of the gathering darkness, and creatures
that oozed an evil identical to Jasper's. Nikki swallowed and reached under her pillow. Her fingers
touched the blade of the old silver knife she'd hidden
there, and cold fire leaped across her skin. The demons fled, and the room became her own again.

Shifting slightly, she turned on the bedside lamp.
Pale light filled the room, but did little to ease the fear
sitting like a rock in the pit of her stomach. Had those
wisps been nothing more than a product of an over-
wrought imagination? Or was it Jasper, haunting her
dreams and using the demons to mock her? If he
could do that, could he do more? Could he somehow
control her?

She pulled the knife out from under the pillow
and examined it more closely. Light reflected off
its tarnished surface. It was part of an old setting
she'd found in a secondhand shop some time ago. She
had no idea how much silver the knife actually contained, or if it would be of any use against Jasper, yet
it had felt oddly comforting to have it under her pil-

low last night. And there wasn't a doubt in her mind that touching it had somehow made the demons disappear—whether or not they were from her imagination or a product of Jasper's sick mind.

Shivering, she rose and padded barefoot across the dusty floorboards to open the curtains. Though it was nearly six, the fast-fading light held just enough warmth to chase away the shadows and any lingering remnants of her dreams.

But if the gathering clouds were anything to go by, the night was going to be a bitch. The wind stirred the nearby oak, scraping branches against the windowpane and chasing shadows across the footpath below. People wearing heavy coats hustled by, intent on getting home before the rain hit.

She crossed her arms and leaned against the windowsill. If Jasper was a vampire, as Michael insisted, how was he able to send her images during the day? Weren't vampires little more than corpses during the sunlit hours? But, of course, it *was* almost dark . . .

Maybe a quick trip to the library was in order. Her knowledge of vampires amounted to little more than what she'd seen on television or a movie screen, and while Michael had told her some stuff, it couldn't hurt to do a little research.

Goose bumps chased themselves up her arms, due more to the chill in the air than the fear sitting like a lump in her stomach. She turned and grabbed her robe. What she needed right now was some coffee to warm her up.

She headed for the kitchen, turning the lights on as she went. To hell with the power bill tonight. She made coffee, then leaned against the counter, watching night sweep in and idly wondering what Michael had been up to all day. And whether he had a girlfriend somewhere.

Not that she should care, she reminded herself somewhat fiercely, because it wasn't like anything was going to happen between them.

The hairs on the back of her neck prickled a warning. Smiling, she reached for the phone. "Evening, Jake."

"I wish you wouldn't do that. It's very annoying."

The background noise told her he was calling from his car.

"Hey, it's one of the reasons you employ me, isn't it?"

"Yes. And it's still annoying."

If the tone of his voice was any indication, it had not been one of his better days. "What's the matter? Mary threaten to divorce your workaholic butt again?"

"Worse. Monica Trevgard just walked out of the morgue."

Nikki closed her eyes and tried to control a sudden burst of panic. So Michael had been right. She hadn't wanted to believe it, but . . . Now that the impossible had happened, what in hell was she going to do?

"Did you hear me, Nikki? I said—"

"I heard." She rubbed a hand across her eyes. They had to stop Monica, obviously. But where would a newly turned vampire go?

Home.

Michael's thought cut through her mind, knife-edged with anger. He had every right to be furious. Monica was loose because Nikki had refused to believe him. Yet even knowing the truth, could she have stood by and let him sever the teenager's head? She shivered and thrust the image from her mind.

Why home? Her thoughts were tinged with panic. She might have said she'd handle the situation if Monica turned, but now that she *had,* the thought of confronting the teenager scared the hell out of her.

Because she must. And because she will need to kill soon.

A chill ran through her soul. It was no secret that Monica hated her father. Trevgard was in danger.

"Still with me, Nik?"

Jake's voice made her start. She clenched her fingers around the phone. "Yes. And we have big problems."

"Nothing compared to the coroner's, I'd say."

"On the contrary. It's pretty much the exact same problem." She rubbed her eyes again, hoping the niggling ache behind her left eye didn't mean yesterday's headache was returning. "Where are you at the moment?"

"The corner of Jackson and Pacific."

"You'd better swing around to my place and pick me up. We have to get to Trevgard's as quickly as possible. I'll explain why when you get here."

Nikki, no!

She ignored Michael and hung up the phone. She finished her coffee in several gulps, which burned her throat, and walked back into the bedroom to get dressed.

Damn it, woman, wait for me. You have no idea—

It's my responsibility, she reminded him, quickly strapping her spare set of knives onto her wrists.

Don't go alone! Wait for me.

I'm not alone—Jake will be with me. She paused. *How long will it take you to get here?*

I'm over near the stockyards. It'll take me maybe twenty minutes—

The stockyards? Why the hell was he over there? Then she remembered what Jasper was. Maybe the fiend topped up on animal blood when he couldn't get enough human. *What about Jasper?*

Confusion ran down the link. *What about him?*

Well, isn't he the reason you're at the stockyards?

His hesitation was brief, but there. *Yes.*

It might be better if you chase him and leave Monica to us.

Not in this situation. A freshly risen vampire is one of the most dangerous beings you will ever encounter.

If she's that dangerous, we can't afford to wait even twenty minutes.

Nik—

No, she said, and cut him out of her thoughts.

She collected her coat off the chair, checked that her keys were in the pocket and grabbed the spare flashlight. At the front door, she hesitated, then turned and moved back into the bedroom. Rummaging quickly through her jewelry box, she found the small silver chain and cross Tommy had given her so long ago. Bitter memories rose; she shoved them away and fastened the chain around her neck. She had no idea if a cross would offer any protection against a vampire, but, like the knife under her pillow last night, she felt safer with it near.

Jake's sleek silver Mercedes pulled up as she stepped outside.

"What in hell is going on?" he growled once she'd settled into the front seat. "Why is it so important for us to get to Trevgard's?"

She grimaced. How did you approach the subject of vampires? "I left out a few details about Monica when we talked last night."

"Like what?" The look he cast her simmered with annoyance.

She hesitated and shrugged. Perhaps a direct approach was best. "Did the police happen to mention the manner of Monica's death when they broke the news to Trevgard?"

"No."

"It was blood loss."

He gave her a quick, surprised look. "The creep cut her up?"

"No. Her body was hardly marked at all. In fact . . ."

"Nikki . . ."

There was no avoiding the subject. "She only had two marks on her body. A small cut on her wrist that was days old and almost healed . . ."

"And?" he prompted, when she again hesitated.

"Two small puncture marks on her neck." She glanced across and met his brief, puzzled look. She must have given Michael the same sort of look when he'd pointed them out.

"And am I supposed to read something significant into that statement?"

"Think, Jake. Blood loss. Puncture marks . . ."

The car swerved violently as he jerked in surprise. Swearing under his breath, he straightened the vehicle and pulled over to the side of the road.

"For fuck's sake," he said, applying the hand brake

before turning in his seat, "are you trying to tell me Monica was killed by a vampire?"

"Yes."

"A *vampire*?" He stared at her. "You really believe Monica was killed by a vampire?"

"Yes. I saw the body, Jake. Apart from the puncture marks, the only other wound was days old and almost healed. And there was no blood around her. Or in her."

He snorted. "Your psychic senses are now telling you how much blood someone has in their body? Give me a break, Nik."

She smiled grimly. "If you don't believe me, why not call your friend at the morgue?"

He pulled out his cell phone. She stared out the window, watching the traffic roll past. They had to move fast if they wanted to save Trevgard.

"They never had a chance to perform an autopsy," Jake said as he hung up the phone.

"I'm afraid that's not the end of it."

"There's more?"

She nodded. "The walking dead."

"As in zombies?"

Though his voice was flat, she could see the disbelief in his eyes. "As in. I think there are at least three running around."

"Have you been smoking funny weed?"

"You know I haven't smoked in years, Jake. Nor have I gone insane."

He shook his head. "Psychic abilities I can believe in. Maybe even ghosts and extraterrestrials. But vampires? Zombies? No way, Nik."

How could she possibly convince him? He had to

be ready for what they might face at Trevgard's to-night. And yet, if she hadn't seen Monica's lifeless body last night, she'd probably have a hard time believing it herself.

"You've trusted my intuition before, Jake. Please just trust me one more time."

He rubbed the back of his neck uneasily. "But Dracula's only a piece of fiction. And zombies . . . well, I know some Polynesian Islanders will swear to their existence, but this is Lyndhurst!"

"So how do you explain the lack of blood in Monica's body?"

"There's no evidence to back up your story, Nik. And how in hell would I know, anyway? But it wasn't a vampire. It just wasn't."

"Then how did she just walk out of the morgue? Her body wasn't stolen, Jake. It *walked*." And presumably everyone at the morgue was in such shock that they didn't think to stop her. Either that or she'd somehow managed to give them all the slip. "There's no other reasonable explanation, Jake."

"A vampire is not exactly a reasonable explanation. Hell, for all we know, we've got some nutjob who enjoys draining the blood from his victims on our hands."

It was an apt enough description of Monica's lover. "So how *do* you explain Monica walking out of the morgue tonight?"

"I can't." His expression was determined as it met hers. "But it wasn't caused by vampirism."

Nothing she could say would convince him otherwise. He had to see it for himself. "Okay, but we still have to get to Trevgard's."

"Why?"

"She hates her father, Jake. Trevgard is probably the only person in town who doesn't know it. And I've got a real bad feeling she'll go after him tonight."

"Trevgard's got guards all over the place," Jake muttered, but threw the car into gear anyway and sped off.

She sighed in relief. He might not believe her, but at least he still trusted her instincts. She just had to hope they didn't arrive too late.

A part of her wished that she had waited for Michael—even if she couldn't have. Not and still make it on time.

"I don't suppose you brought your gun?" Jake asked, after a moment.

She shook her head. "You know I won't use it. It's locked up at home. Besides, bullets don't kill vampires."

"They might if you blow their freakin' heads off," he said, voice grim. "So, where's the boyfriend tonight?"

"Michael's not my boyfriend." And never likely to be. He held far too many secrets, and was too much of a loner. And was far too much like Tommy.

"If chemistry's anything to go by, he will be. Where is he?"

"You're imagining things, and I don't know."

He wasn't far away, though. She sensed that much. Somewhere, somehow, he was tracking her, furious that she'd refused to wait.

"Odd that he only turns up at night." Jake gave her a sardonic look. "He's not a vampire, too, by any chance?"

"Not likely." Yet as she recalled the darkness in his soul, she couldn't help shivering.

It took them ten minutes to get to Trevgard's. Jake turned into the driveway, then braked. Nikki bit her lip and studied the dark gates before them.

"No lights," Jake commented, peering through the windshield.

She stared at the gatehouse. Like everything else that Trevgard owned, it was ostentatious, more like a small house than the boxlike building she'd expected. Right now, however, it was as dark as the night itself. "No guard. I've got a bad feeling about this."

She wished Jake would just turn around and drive away, before it was too late. But it was her fault that Monica was loose. If she had allowed Michael to behead the teenager . . . The thought stalled. No, she'd had no option last night, just as she had none now. Jake couldn't go in alone, and the police had no idea what they were up against. And even if she told them, they'd never believe her. If Jake didn't, no one would.

"I guess we'd better check it out," she said softly.

He nodded. "Glove up. We don't need the police finding our prints if things have gone bad in there."

She dug her spare pair out of the glove compartment. Slipping them on, she slowly climbed out of the car. The gentle purr of the engine had little impact on the silence of the night. Jake removed his gun from its holster and held it by his side. She followed him, kinetic energy crackling around her fingertips.

Jake tapped lightly on the glass front of the guard's box. "Anybody home?"

No one answered. The wind whistled lightly through the darkness, rattling the branches in the nearby trees. Where the heck was the guard? Had he answered a distress call from Trevgard? And if he had, why weren't the lights on ahead?

Jake nudged her, then pointed to the left. She nodded and edged carefully around the small building, every sense alert. But there was no sign of life, no sign of activity. She reached the gate. It was locked.

After a few seconds, Jake joined her.

"The gate's locked," she told him.

"So's the door to the guard box," he replied.

"Should we break in?"

"It's either that or the gates." He shrugged and met her gaze. "I'm beginning to agree with your bad feeling. I don't think we can wait for the cops."

She nodded and sent a bolt of kinetic energy at the door. It crashed back on its hinges.

"Handy little trick," Jake said. "But it would be nice if you could learn to make a little less noise."

"Sorry. Nerves." She shrugged and waved him through. After all, he had the gun.

He stepped past almost tentatively. "I can't see anyone. Let's find some light."

She grabbed his arm. "Don't. Monica might ignore headlights if they go no farther than the drive, but this is a different matter."

Yet if Monica really was a vampire, wouldn't she sense their presence anyway? Just how close to reality did the movies come? She released his arm. "I have a flashlight."

Though it was little more than palm-sized, it provided enough light to see why no one made a fuss about them breaking in. The guard was here, all right. But dead.

Nikki handed Jake the light and shoved her hands in her pockets to hide their sudden shaking.

"If this is Monica's handiwork, she's one angry teenager," Jake said, kneeling next to the body. He pointed the light toward the guard's neck—or what remained of it. Nikki swallowed and turned away.

"There's not enough blood," he muttered. "With a wound this bad, there should be more blood."

Sweat broke out across her brow. "Monica's a vampire, remember."

"Or completely over the edge." He rose, face ashen. "We'd better call the cops."

"Yes." After discovering the guard, they had no real choice. "But we can't risk waiting for them. Not if we want to stop her. She can't be too far ahead of us."

Nikki retreated and studied the darkness as Jake made the call. With that done, he pressed one of the buttons in front of the guard's chair. The huge gates eased silently open, making them welcome.

But welcome to what?

They climbed back into the Mercedes and drove on, without the headlights. The night closed in around them, oppressive and still.

Through the trees, yellow light winked, starlike, from a window on the upper floor. The rest of the mansion was dark.

"Where are the servants' quarters?" she asked, studying the end of the house where the lone light shone. "Should we check that first?"

"Who is more important? Trevgard or the butler? I'd vote Trevgard—if only because he owes us money."

The butler hadn't exactly done anything to deserve

death at the hands of a vampire. But then, the only thing Trevgard was guilty of was giving his daughter everything she'd ever wanted.

The house soon loomed above them, oppressive and oddly threatening. Or maybe that was nothing more than knowing what might lie inside, waiting for them.

Jake stopped the car and gave her a grim look. "I really *don't* like the feel of this."

"Neither do I." She grabbed her flashlight and climbed out of the car. Nothing moved. The night was still, and the air was heavy with the promise of rain. Her psychic senses could find no trace of life. If Trevgard or any servants were here, they were no longer among the living.

"He's not here," a soft voice behind her said. "And two servants lie dead inside the house."

Nikki jumped violently and swung around. Michael stood two feet away, arms crossed as he stared at her. "Have you been inside?"

He hesitated. "No, but that does not alter the fact that Trevgard isn't here. Why didn't you wait, as I asked?" His voice was flat, devoid of the anger she could feel in his thoughts, and all the more frightening because of it.

"Because this is my fault, and my problem to deal with." She watched him uneasily. The darkness shifted in his eyes, becoming stronger. Just how different was he from the man he chased? "And how did you get here so quickly? I thought you were twenty minutes away."

"From your house," he said enigmatically, as Jake approached.

Nikki was suddenly glad her boss was there. Though she doubted he'd be much use should Michael attack.

"Michael," Jake said, surprise edging his voice. "Glad you could join us."

He stopped next to Nikki, close enough for their shoulders to touch. Nikki wondered if Jake could sense her sudden uncertainty about Michael.

"I got here as soon as I could. But not soon enough, I fear."

Jake barely glanced at the house. "Is Monica still inside?"

Michael's face was expressionless. "No. If she were, I would sense her."

Jake raised an eyebrow. "How?"

"Nikki's not the only one with psychic abilities."

"Really? And do those abilities allow you to move faster than a car? Because you certainly didn't arrive in one."

"No, I didn't." Michael's voice held an edge of annoyance. "But we're wasting time here. Monica's killing spree has only just begun. We have to stop her. Quickly."

Nikki pushed the hair out of her eyes. "To stop her, we have to find her. So unless you have some means of tracking her, I have to go inside and take something of hers to use."

"I can only sense her when she's close." Michael hesitated, frowning. "And if you enter the house, she'll know it. It's home ground, the place she's lived most of her life. She's connected to it."

"Another one who believes in vampires," Jake muttered.

Nikki ignored him. "Does that mean she'll come after us?"

He hesitated. "Maybe. It would depend on Jasper's plans."

Meaning Monica wouldn't make a move without his approval? Nikki rubbed her arms. "Is it true a vampire can't cross a threshold uninvited?"

Michael nodded. "Yes, but the rule doesn't work when it's your own threshold."

"Oh."

She glanced uneasily at the mansion. Monica had to be stopped before she could kill again. And if she didn't come to them, they had to go to her.

"Before we start worrying about Monica," Jake said, the tone of his voice suggesting he wasn't about to accept any argument, "I think we owe it to Trevgard to check his people. They may be still alive, no matter what you believe."

"It is a waste—" Michael began, but Nikki cut him off.

"It's still something we should do. Just in case." She handed Jake the flashlight, then shoved her hands into her jacket pockets. "Let's get this over with."

They walked to the far end of the house. Jake climbed the steps and approached the side door cautiously. Something flickered through Nikki's mind—a specter of darkness, of death. She studied the brightly lit windows above them.

The servants haven't been dead long.

Surprised, she looked at Michael. *How can you tell something like that?*

I can smell the blood.

His eyes were icy pools that somehow intensified,

washing darkness through her mind. Dizzy, she reached out, catching his arm, his muscles like steel under her fingertips. Then a shock of electricity hit her fingers, and a haze filled her vision. Suddenly, their minds merged, and she could see the bodies in the room above, feel the cooling heat of their flesh, could almost taste the sweet dark pools of blood . . . Her stomach rose and she blanched, shuddering.

Michael shook off her grip, shattering the contact between them. She staggered away from him, one hand held to her throat. Dear God, what sort of talent *was* that?

"Don't ever do that again, Nikki." His voice was harsh, but there was both surprise and anger in his expression. "It's far too dangerous."

He didn't explain how it had happened or why it was dangerous, and she didn't dare ask. Something told her she might not like the answers.

Jake twisted the doorknob, then said, "It's locked."

She turned away from Michael and gave a mental push. The door opened—gently this time—and Jake raised a surprised eyebrow.

She shrugged in reply and climbed the steps. Warm air rushed past her legs as she stopped in front of the open door. Light filtered down the stairs at the far end of the hall, but the rest of the house was full of uneasy shadows.

Jake swung the flashlight beam left to right, searching the darkness.

"Nothing." His voice was hushed, as if he too sensed death waiting. "I guess we'd better check upstairs."

Nikki grimaced. "After you." Then she turned to

Michael, who was lingering at the base of the steps. "Are you coming?"

"I can't go inside," Michael said quietly.

"But weren't you inside before?"

He hesitated. "Yes. But the police have been called, and while you two can give a plausible enough excuse for being here, I can't. I'll wait here and watch for Monica."

Jake motioned for Nikki to hurry. She hesitated, glancing back at Michael. "And if you can't stop her?"

"I'll warn you," he replied. "Do this fast. Remember, she'll be quicker than a rattlesnake, and twice as deadly."

"Thanks. Like I really needed to know that."

He smiled, but his eyes were as frightening as the house. "Go. Just take care."

After another second of hesitation, she stepped through the doorway and followed Jake. They climbed the stairs. At the top, death waited.

"Shit," Jake said, stopping in the doorway of the first room.

Though warned by the images she'd shared with Michael, her stomach still turned. The bodies were a twisted mass of flesh that no longer resembled anything human. Blood was everywhere. If it hadn't been for the bits of humanity scattered about, it would have been easy to think some kid had gone wild with a can of red paint.

"Monica obviously had more than one score to settle." Jake took several steps into the room. "And for a vampire, she's pretty damn messy."

Nikki gave him a sharp glance. His ironic half

smile told her he was only trying to make a tough situation somewhat easier, and that he still refused to believe Monica was actually a vampire. He picked his way through the smashed furniture and knelt next to the remains. Why, she had no idea. Certainly there was no hope of life in what was left of him.

Grab a piece of broken wood—preferably one that resembles a stake.

She frowned. *Why in the hell would I do that?*

It's wood, Nikki. Michael's mental tone was brusque. *Deadly to vampires when used to stab them.*

She picked up the smashed leg of a chair. A little too thick perhaps, but nicely jagged at one end . . . She blanched and almost dropped it. Where the hell had that thought come from?

Keep it. You have no other way to protect yourself should Monica attack.

I can run . . . But Monica was a vampire, and if all the legends were true, running wouldn't help much.

It was a thought Michael confirmed seconds later. *She is faster . . . by far.*

Nikki clutched the leg tightly. Jake rose from examination of the old man's body, his face pale.

"Well, if she used a knife to create this mess, there's certainly no immediate evidence of it." He ran a hand through his hair. "The police are going to love this."

"We have to stop her, Jake. Us, not the cops." She motioned toward the bodies. "They won't understand what they're dealing with."

"Nikki, *we're* not even sure what we're dealing with."

Speak for yourself, she wanted to say. But if the

sight of these bodies didn't convince him, nothing would.

"I still have to find something to help me track Monica."

"Well, do it quickly," Jake muttered sourly. " 'Cause we'd better be out of this house before the cops and Trevgard get here, or there'll be hell to pay."

"Especially when he discovers his precious daughter has become a vicious killer."

"There's no direct evidence it's Monica, Nik. Remember that." He motioned her out the door. "I've only been here once, but I think the bedrooms are at the other end of the house."

"Can we get to them from here?"

"I'm sure there's a shortcut, but I'm not familiar with it. We'll just have to take the long way around."

She followed him back down the stairs, glad to be free of the nauseous smell of death.

Monica's on the prowl, Michael warned. *She's heading back toward the house.*

Can you stop her?

Only if you want to sacrifice Trevgard. He's on his way, too, coming up the driveway now.

Hell. Nikki massaged her temples. This was all they needed. *Jake and I will be down in a minute . . .*

No, grab what you need first. Monica—and therefore Jasper—will sense me when she gets closer, and he won't waste his new toy by throwing her up against me. He turned her for a reason; otherwise, she would be as dead as his other victims. Which means we need to be able to find her again. Hurry, Nikki. You don't have much time.

Jake touched her arm, and she started.

"You all right?"

She licked her lips and nodded. "Monica's heading our way. And Trevgard just got home."

He didn't question her certainty, which was just as well. How could she possibly explain her connection to Michael when, in all the time Jake had known her, she'd never been able to do more than read a fleeting word or emotion?

"If the kid comes anywhere near us, I'll blow her head off," Jake warned, drawing his gun.

"The police will just love that." And there was every possibility that Jake would never even see Monica. Not if what Michael said about her speed was true.

"To hell with the police. The girl's a nut."

"I thought you said there was no direct evidence that she's the culprit."

"No, I said there's no direct evidence she's a vampire." He quirked an eyebrow at her. "That doesn't mean I believe she's innocent."

From what she knew about Monica, the teenager hadn't been innocent for a very long time. Boys, drugs and theft had all featured fairly regularly in her life from the moment she'd hit puberty. Not that she'd been an angel *before* then.

The flashlight beam was faint, barely penetrating the shadows now. She turned on the lights as they went through each room, knowing the time to worry about discovery had passed. Trevgard would know instantly that something was wrong, thanks to the open gates and the dead guard. And Monica would sense them regardless. At least the light banished the shadows and made the house appear less threatening.

They made their way quickly down the hallway and up another flight of stairs. Nikki entered the first bedroom. It had to be Monica's; she couldn't imagine Trevgard surrounded by flowery wallpaper.

Monica's coming fast. Whatever you want to do, do it now.

Trevgard? She held out her hand, palm down, and walked past the dressing table, trying to find a response from the jewelry scattered there.

Alive, but I knocked him out. She's in the house, Nikki. Move!

She couldn't. Not until she found something to track Monica with . . . but would she even need it, now that Monica was in the house and tracking *her?*

Yes, the sliver of darkness inside her whispered. *Because she won't die tonight. I have plans—for her, and for you.*

Fear swirled, but she ignored the dark whisper and continued searching for something that held Monica's vibes. Her palm tingled when she walked past the bed. Kneeling, she looked underneath. Something glinted in the darkness. Reaching out, she grabbed the locket from its bed of dust. Then she rose and looked at Jake.

"I've got what we need, but Monica's in the house."

"Okay, let's go." He raised his gun and led the way back into the hall.

She's near the stairs—coming up. Nikki, get out! Get out now.

How? She practically screamed the question. The stairs were the only way out.

The windows. Smash a goddamn window. Just— Watch out! She's . . .

She cut Michael from her mind and spun. A slender figure materialized behind her. Monica. Their gazes met, and Nikki stepped back. Monica's face was bloody, her mouth a thin line of rage. But her eyes were the most frightening. The bright blue depths had lost all hint of humanity.

Jake cursed and fired his gun. Faster than the wind, faster than any bullet, Monica winked out of existence.

Only to reappear behind Jake.

"Look out!" Nikki screamed, and blasted him with kinetic energy, thrusting him out of Monica's way.

The gun fired as he fell, the bullet smashing a mirror at the far end of the hallway.

The teenager shrieked and lashed out at Nikki. The blow smashed her sideways. She hit the wall hard, her breath whooshing from her lungs, briefly seeing stars. Blinking back tears, she shook her head and struggled into a sitting position.

Monica leaped at her. Cursing loudly, Nikki scrambled upright then lashed out with the chair leg. The teenager twisted away from the blow and threw up her arms to protect her face. The jagged edges tore into her arm, and the skin peeled away, blackening where the wood touched. Screaming in fury, Monica leaped again. Her weight hit Nikki like a ton of bricks, knocking the stake from her grip as she was forced to the floor again. Razor-sharp teeth gleamed brightly in the darkness; Monica's breath was fetid, full of death. Gagging, Nikki grabbed the teenager's arms, desperately holding the twisting, snarling girl away from her neck. Energy burned from her body.

The bolt hit Monica and flung her away. Agile as a cat, she landed on her feet and surged forward again.

Nikki scrambled out of her way and reached for another kinetic lance. But the girl stopped, eyes suddenly distant, like she was listening to someone.

Jasper, Nikki thought with horror. Monica snarled, took a step forward, and stopped again. Fighting her master's leash, Nikki thought, as a look of petulance crossed the teenager's face. It was an odd reminder that this was still a sixteen-year-old girl, whatever else she might have become.

But she was a teenager who *had* to die. Nikki quickly looked around for her stake, but even as she spotted it, Monica snarled, and winked out of existence.

No way, Nikki thought, and leaped for the stake. She hit the carpet and rolled, gathering the stake and throwing it hard in one fluid movement. The wood arrowed down the length of the long hallway . . . and stopped abruptly, suspended in midair.

Monica materialized. The wood had speared through her abdomen. Her face was twisted in agony, but she pulled the stake from her middle and again melted from sight. The bloody stake fell to the floor. Nikki grabbed it, turned and ran to Jake.

"I'm all right," he muttered. "Just a few bruises and a cut on my arm. Next time you decide to kinetically toss me, be a bit gentler."

"I'll try to remember." Nikki grabbed his good arm and helped him up. Though the air around them burned with fury, Monica had obeyed her master and had left the area.

Leaving Nikki wondering not only why Jasper had

let her attack them in the first place, but why he was now letting them go. What the hell he intended to do with them all.

Whatever it was, she thought with a shiver, it would *not* be good.

And it would involve death. Hers, Michael's, maybe even Jake's.

Foreboding ran through her. She ignored it and followed Jake out of the house—away from the death, the bloodshed and the ominous intuition it raised.

Seven

NIKKI LEANED AGAINST the front of Jake's car, lightly massaging her temples. Her headache was back with a vengeance, thanks to the long hours of questioning. And still the police didn't believe her. It was evident from the look in their eyes, the tone of their voices. They just couldn't accept a sixteen-year-old girl would be capable of such destruction.

And Nikki hadn't even hit them with the vampire theory.

She eased her weight from one leg to the other and studied the brightly lit mansion. Though Monica hadn't come back, her pain and fury continued to linger in the air. Maybe it was just an echo of the hate that radiated off her. Or maybe it was little more than the memory of the destruction the teenager had caused, combined with an overactive imagination. It wouldn't be the first time.

Voices rose briefly inside the house, and she couldn't help wishing Trevgard was as absent as his daughter. He currently strode from room to room like a general marshaling his troops, taking his anger out on anyone who got in his way. Both she and Jake had withstood a good ten minutes of his tirade before the police had decided to rescue them with more official questions. Her headache had started around then.

A wiry figure appeared in the doorway, looking around for several seconds before moving briskly in her direction. Nikki groaned. Just what she needed—another round of questioning with Detective Col MacEwan. They'd known each other for a long time. He'd arrested her several times during her early years on the streets, and was the closest thing she had to a friend on the force.

Which didn't mean they actually liked each other.

"I called the hospital." He came to an abrupt halt several feet away from her, his calm tone belying the anger she could see in his brown eyes. "Jake's cut needed a few stitches, but other than bruising, he's okay. They've let him go home."

She nodded her thanks and crossed her arms. MacEwan hadn't ventured outside just to say that. There would be more.

"I don't believe a word of the crap you and Jake spouted in there," he continued, "but I've no evidence to dispute it, either. So for the moment, you're free to go."

"Gee, thanks."

"I know you too well, Nikki, and I can taste a lie. When I find out what the two of you are hiding . . ."

He let the threat go and glared at her a moment longer. She returned his gaze evenly. She had nothing to hide—nothing but a truth he would never believe. After a moment, he grunted and turned around, walking back into the house.

At least she could finally go home. Pushing away from the car, she moved around to the driver's side.

She tugged on the door, then realized it was locked. And that Jake had the keys.

Damn. She'd have to walk. She kicked a tire in frustration, and turned to study the shadows. The gentle breeze held no trace of Monica, but with the teenager's speed, that didn't matter much. She could be out of the scope of Nikki's psychic senses and still be within killing range. Maybe Nikki should ask one of the police officers for a lift.

She glanced at the house and saw Trevgard gesturing angrily at some poor officer. *No way,* she thought, shoving her hands into her pockets to keep them warm. There wasn't a power on this earth that could force her back in the house with Trevgard. She'd had enough of his lectures to last a lifetime.

She headed down the driveway. The noise and lights gradually faded away, and the crunch of gravel underneath her boots grew louder. She turned left out of the gates and crossed the road to the softly lit sidewalk. The stately mansions lining either side of the street lay wrapped in shadows, and the silence hung as heavily as the clouds in the moonless sky. Yet this time, it wasn't threatening.

Ahead, a figure rested casually against a lamppost. His dark shirt emphasized the lean strength of his chest and arms, and his jeans clung just right to his legs. Michael. He looked . . . nice. More than nice, really.

His sudden smile sent warmth shivering through her.

"I thought you might like to get something to eat before you go home," he said, falling into step beside her and offering his arm.

She tucked hers through it. "It's close to midnight—there aren't many places open at this hour around here."

"I'll find us something. What kind of food do you prefer?"

Her stomach rumbled noisily. He quirked an eyebrow at the sound, and she grinned. "Actually, I could go for a really big burger."

His look was suddenly severe, though amusement danced in his eyes. "All that cholesterol?"

"That's just what I need—a health nut." She grinned lightly and met his gaze. "What would you suggest?"

"Only the best, of course."

The look in his eyes made her pulse skip a beat. She cleared her throat and glanced away. Perhaps linking arms with him wasn't such a great idea. The warmth of his body so close, the caress of her fingers against his arm—it was a reminder of how long it had been since anyone had held her. How long it had been since she had *wanted* to be held. And it was a dangerous desire when it was sparked by a man she knew next to nothing about.

"Lyndhurst doesn't have much in the way of decent restaurants at this end of town. It's pretty much all residential," she said.

"If I remember right, there's one not too far ahead."

He meant Roslyn's, but dressed as they were, they'd never get in—even if it hadn't been so late. "A hamburger suits me fine. Besides, they'll be getting ready to go home."

"We'll just have to persuade them to remain open," he said with a smile. "What did the police say?"

She blinked at the sudden shift in conversation. "The usual shit. That Jake and I aren't to leave town, blah, blah, blah."

"Did they believe Monica was responsible?"

"Nope. But then again, Jake wouldn't believe it either until she attacked him."

"How is his arm?"

"All patched up. The hospital's let him go." She hesitated, and met his gaze. "You said earlier that Monica had to come back home. Why?"

"A newly turned vampire must return to the place of its birth. I think it's part of the centering process. To understand what you have truly become, first you have to understand what you have lost." He shrugged. "The fledglings also have to find something of the past to carry with them through eternity."

"What the hell for?"

"Perhaps as a reminder that they, too, were once human?"

"Weird," she muttered, frowning. "You seem to know an awful lot about vampires . . ."

"I've studied them for many years."

"Why?"

He hesitated. "Because my brother was killed by one."

By Jasper, Nikki thought. That would certainly explain Michael's fierce determination to catch the man. Or vampire, as the case may be.

"Why didn't the wood kill her? I thought you said wood was deadly to vampires."

"It is . . . but like any weapon, you have to hit something vital. You punctured her gut. A wound like that will be painful and can take a long time to heal, but it's definitely not deadly."

Next time she'd make sure she actually aimed for the heart. "Why aren't we chasing her now? I have the locket—"

"And how will you explain the fact that you've stabbed Monica through the heart to the police?" he asked.

"I thought vampire bodies turned to dust when staked."

"Only in the movies. Admittedly, the sun will burn a vampire's flesh to dust. But otherwise, it's just a body, like any human body."

"Why can't we find her, stake her, then release her body back to Trevgard?"

"Because what I said earlier still applies. Jasper obviously has plans for Monica, and he will not allow it."

"So? If we find her, we find him—"

"No. Jasper isn't that foolish. He knows I'm hunting him. And he also knows me well enough to be aware that I'll hunt her first."

She frowned. "But he's more dangerous than she—"

"Ultimately, yes, but she hasn't been turned long enough to have her bloodlust under full control. And while Jasper *can* control her, it would amuse him to let her run loose."

Nikki lightly bit her lip, and said, "Can vampires rise after they've been killed? I thought it was part of the legend that vampires can heal any wound."

"Most wounds—which is why it is best to decapitate them *after* you've staked them. Once the head is separate, there's no chance of rejuvenation."

They came to the restaurant. Michael opened the door, and as he ushered her inside, she caught sight of a ring on his left hand. Was he married? It was a thought that disturbed her, yet there was also a part of her hoping he was. Resisting her attraction to him would be a whole lot easier.

A waiter approached, an apologetic look on his face. "I'm sorry, sir, but we've just closed."

"Surely you could reopen for half an hour?" Michael said, an odd edge behind the lightness of his words.

"I'm sorr—"

The waiter's words faltered as a sliver of power caressed the air. His eyes widened, became lifeless. A chill ran through Nikki. It was like Tommy, all over again.

She dragged her arm from Michael's and punched him in the shoulder. "Stop—"

He turned, and she took an abrupt step backward. Just for an instant, his eyes held a darkness that burned her soul.

The next moment, he blinked, and his gaze became guarded, wary. "Stop what?"

She took a deep breath. "Release the waiter. I . . . I don't like the food here anyway."

He hesitated before finally nodding. Power whispered around her, then the waiter cleared his throat and gave them another smile.

"I'm afraid the chef has already gone home for the night. I'm sorry, but we can't help you."

"Thanks," Nikki said, and spun, making a quick exit. The cold night air touched her fevered skin but wasn't responsible for the tremors running down her spine. Michael had controlled the waiter's mind too easily—as if it was something he did every day.

She stopped several houses down from the restaurant and took a deep breath. What kind of man so casually possessed the mind of others, forcing them to do as he asked? A man like Tommy, she thought. A man who just didn't care.

The back of her neck tingled with sudden awareness. Michael had stopped just behind her.

"I'm sorry," he said softly.

His breath brushed the back of her neck. She tensed, but made no move to turn around. "Why did you do it?"

"It's easier than arguing."

An honest enough answer—and so very similar to the excuses Tommy had used. "Could you control me as easily?"

He moved past her, his arm brushing against hers. Heat trembled across her skin. She rubbed the spot where their flesh had touched and watched him warily. His face was still, expressionless, but she sensed the turmoil beneath the calm exterior.

"Not without a lot of effort and time, I suspect," he said.

The clock on the Town Hall tower bonged into the silence. Midnight, the hour when all things dark and dangerous came out of hiding.

Things like Michael, maybe. She met his gaze again, the uneven pounding of her heart abnormally loud in the growing silence.

"If you ever try—"

"You would never know," he said quietly. "Just like the waiter never knew."

She clenched her fists in impotent fury. The ease with which he'd taken over the waiter's mind made it clear his abilities were very strong. She could so easily become a puppet to his will.

He swore softly and grabbed her shoulder, shaking her lightly. "I would never do such a thing to you."

Yet he wasn't averse to reading her mind. She wrenched free of his grip. "Unless you had no other choice."

She could see the truth of her statement reflected in his eyes.

"I have made a promise to keep you safe," he said softly. "Though I am a man of my word, I will not stay where I am not wanted. Do you still wish me to accompany you home?"

She opened her mouth to refuse, then hesitated. Intuition told her not to let this man go. She needed the protection he offered, even if she hated the darkness that seemed to be so much a part of him.

Because evil far worse waited for her, somewhere in the night.

She shifted her stance and crossed her arms. "If you are a man of your word, as you say, will you make me a promise?"

"What do you wish?" His reply was as guarded as his expression.

"Will you swear never to try to take control of my mind or make me do anything against my will?"

Something in his stillness spoke of anger. "If you trust me so little, yes, I swear."

There was a sudden distance between them, though neither of them had moved. It was for the best, she told herself firmly. They were still essentially strangers. Until she knew more about him, more about the subtle yet terrifying shifts in his nature, she had to keep that distance between them.

Because it was possible her hero was no true hero at all.

Michael walked quietly beside Nikki, aware of the tension and confusion churning her thoughts. He felt the same way.

Perhaps something within her recognized the darkness in him. Maybe that was why she now wore the small silver cross at her neck. Why she refused to trust him.

But why was her trust so important to him? He was here to keep her safe and to find Jasper, nothing more. She was his best, and quickest, means of doing the latter. Trust played no part in that.

The shadows moved on the other side of the street and Michael glanced across. It was only a young couple, strolling hand in hand. He looked away, studying the street ahead, unsettled by a surge of envy. Just for an instant, he had shared such intimacy . . . and it had felt good after so many years of loneliness.

Maybe Seline was right about the dangers of using Nikki as bait. But the threat wasn't just physical, as he'd presumed. It was emotional. Two days with Nikki, and unwanted wisps of emotion were raising their heads.

He frowned, remembering a whisper he'd caught from her thoughts. *Just like Tommy.* Had someone in the past tried controlling her?

It was something he wouldn't like to attempt, and

he'd had years to define and strengthen his gifts. Even Jasper would never gain full control over her—not while she was alive, at any rate. Her psychic abilities were far too strong to be leashed for long.

Yet from what he could gather from her thoughts, she was more terrified of Jasper's attempts to control her than of Jasper himself.

Which only made Jasper's task that much easier. He would use this fear against her—use it to beat her into submission, to bend her to his will. Then he would kill her, and she would be his.

Damn it, there had to be some way to get her to face the demon in her past, so the demon in her present could not get the upper hand.

And just who in hell had appointed him the keeper of her soul?

He sighed and glanced skyward. He didn't want to get involved with Nikki—not on any level. He just wanted to catch a killer, and he still had every intention of doing that. Only he didn't want to see her hurt in the process.

And when the time came to tell her he was a vampire? Michael glanced at her. When the time came, he'd walk away. He couldn't change what he was, and he doubted she could live with the darkness. Something told him there'd been far too much of it in her life already.

"Do you still want something to eat?" he asked, after a while. "I believe there's a pizza place not far from here."

"There is, but I'm no longer hungry." She didn't look at him as she spoke, and part of him wanted to make her.

They continued to walk in silence, and her pace increased as they drew close to her apartment building. He felt her anxiety to get inside, to be alone.

He stopped outside, as before, scanning the dark windows. He didn't sense Jasper or any of his minions within the immediate area. Maybe she'd be safe for the rest of the night. But just to be certain, Michael would stand watch across the road. He'd learned to expect the unexpected when it came to creatures like Jasper.

She turned, her gaze meeting his. "Thank you for walking me home."

Anger and confusion were still evident in her gaze. He nodded and resisted the urge to reach out and touch her. Hold her.

Something flickered in her eyes and she quickly stepped away. Michael frowned. Just how strong was the link she'd created? If she could merge with his mind, however briefly, it was more than possible she could read his thoughts. Maybe he didn't have to tell her he was a vampire. Maybe she already knew.

He watched her retreat, then turned and made his way across the road.

Dawn's light was spreading fiery fingers across the night sky when he finally stepped away from the shelter of the bus stop. The muted sense of life in Nikki's flat told him that she slept. It was time to begin his hunt.

It didn't take him long to return to Trevgard's mansion. He walked through the rapidly disappearing shadows, carefully avoiding the many police officers still present.

Monica wasn't near but her pain and desperate hunger lingered, providing a trail he could follow. He wondered if she'd found the item she would carry through eternity—given she'd been there long enough to murder her father's servants, she probably had. Which meant she more than likely would not be back anytime soon—unless, of course, Trevgard's murder was part of Jasper's plan.

Which it undoubtedly was. His victims were rarely as rich as Monica would be if her father died, and with the teenager now under his command, the money would be his in all but name. Jasper was certainly arrogant enough to believe he deserved the best. The only surprising thing was the fact it had taken him this long to do it.

Ironically, the need to find a better life had been one of the reasons behind *Michael's* turning. That, he thought with amusement, and his love for a woman who'd been a whole lot more than she'd seemed.

He glanced at the ring on his left hand. It was the item he'd chosen to carry though eternity, and had been made for his father by his grandfather, carved from the soft rock that abounded on their farm in Ireland. It was a constant reminder of the life he'd willingly forsaken; a reminder of the death he'd unwittingly caused.

It had been his father who'd discovered his body, and the shock had brought on a heart attack, leaving his mother to somehow scratch a living on land so poor even grass refused to grow on it. He'd returned once the blood-rage had left him, hoping to help in some way. But by that point, years had passed, and the struggle to survive had all but killed her. His oldest brother, Patrick, had given up on the farm and left in search of work elsewhere, and his four sisters had found themselves husbands and homes of their own. He'd nursed his mother through her final days, then buried her next to his father. And had vowed, at the foot of her grave, never to take another innocent human life.

A vow he had kept.

He continued past the mansion's porch and followed the scent out of the grounds. The sun was rising, and given resistance only came after about half a century or so of unlife, Monica would undoubtedly be tucked away in complete darkness somewhere.

He followed her scent through the half-light of morning. As he'd said to Nikki, it was doubtful that Jasper would be anywhere near his fledgling, but it was still worth tracking her down, on the off chance that he was. Hiding in the middle of a city as big as Lyndhurst held special problems for the likes of Monica and Jasper. Street people already occupied many of the abandoned factories and houses. And the one thing more important to a vampire than a place to wait out the sun was security.

Day sleep was a kind of death—one in which the mind was active but the body not—for younger vampires. You had to be sure you were safe in the hours when you were totally helpless. While Jasper *had* some sun immunity, neither he nor Monica had the choice of sleeping in motels, as Michael did. Because of his years and lifestyle, he could wake and protect himself if threatened. Monica could not. Jasper should have been similarly disposed, but given how strong the fiend had become of late, it was more than possible that he was capable of at least *some* movement.

Perhaps Jasper's constant quest for power had more benefits than Michael had realized.

The skies began to brighten. He quickened his pace, even though the sun would not provide any real threat to him for at least another couple of hours. The scent led him to an old warehouse and Michael stopped abruptly.

Fate had done the unexpected. Jasper *was* here.

Michael clenched his fingers, ignoring the desperate urge to rush into the basement where Jasper hid and crush the life from his old enemy. Jasper *wasn't* alone. Not only was Monica by his side, but so were the zombies—and now there were four of them again. Jasper had not been idle while Monica had kept Michael and Nikki—and Jake—busy. The four zombies would not be much of a problem in and of themselves, but he had no doubt Jasper had also rigged the warehouse to explode should he be attacked. He'd done it before, and killed over a hundred people in the process.

And, as it was, people were already working on the floors above, unaware that a monster lurked below. Michael could control minds easily enough, but not that many, and certainly not when Jasper was so close *and* awake.

He turned and walked away. He'd come back later, a few hours before dark, when Jasper and Monica were still asleep, and defuse the bomb, then burn this retreat to the ground. The building had an alarm—it would alert the people on the floors above, giving them time to get out, but it wouldn't save the evil that slept in its basement. Not if he timed it right.

Whistling tunelessly, he shoved his hands into his pockets and headed to the stockyards on the outskirts of town.

Eight

NIKKI ABSENTLY RAN the silver cross up and down its chain and watched people hurry past the foggy office windows. Everyone was bundled up against the bitter wind that raced the clouds across the morning sky. She felt no warmer, despite the heat in the office.

How did you stop a vampire?

Their encounter with Monica two nights ago had proven how difficult that might be. From the little Michael had said, she knew Jasper had been dead long enough to develop and refine his vampire gifts.

And if Monica was that fast as a fledgling, they'd never see Jasper, let alone get near enough to kill him. She crossed her arms and tried to ignore the ice creeping through her veins. Michael was right about one thing: Jasper and Monica *were* evil. They would kill, and keep on killing, until they were stopped. She just wished she wasn't the one who had to stop them.

She leaned forward and grabbed her coffee off the desk, wrapping her hands around the mug to keep them warm. Her thoughts turned to Michael. If the eyes were the window to the soul, what did his gaze tell her? That he was a man well versed in controlling his surroundings. That his secrets and knowledge were old. Perhaps centuries old.

She frowned and sipped her coffee. That was impossible, of course. And there were more than secrets in his eyes. There was also warmth, and a hint of passion that called to something deep inside her. She shivered lightly, and as much as she wished the cause was fear, she knew it stemmed more from desire. She'd been on her own for a long time now, and while she was happy, every now and again loneliness stirred. It would be nice to have someone in her life to hold her, be there for her . . . The thought died. Michael was not that person. Could never be that person. For some still undefined reason, he was here to protect her, and to hunt down Jasper. She was part of his mission. Nothing more, nothing less.

The office door opened. Jake stepped in, accompanied by a blast of wind that sent the loose papers on her desk scattering.

"It's cold out there," he muttered sourly. He threw his coat in the general direction of his desk and stalked across the room to the coffeepot. His bandaged forearm gleamed whitely as it peeked out from the sleeve of his dark blue sweater, but the wound didn't seem to be restricting his use of the arm in any way.

"Tell me something new," she said, returning her gaze to the street. Michael was out there somewhere. While it was obvious he could take care of himself, worry gnawed at her. Last night, her dreams had sent her a warning. Jasper was weaving a trap around them all, with Michael's death the grand finale.

"I've sent Mary on a trip to visit her mother," Jake said into the silence.

Nikki almost choked on a mouthful of coffee. In the ten years she'd known him, Jake had never been worried enough by an ongoing investigation to send his wife away.

His face was bleak. "If Monica is still alive after having that stake shoved in her gut . . . She'll come after us, Nikki."

Hunter and hunted, both. Great, she thought, and took another sip of coffee.

"At least I'm lucky," she said after a moment. "I have no one to worry about but me."

"You must have aunts and uncles out there, somewhere. Grandparents, even. All you have to do is find them, kiddo."

Yeah, she thought sourly. She had them. But they didn't want to know her. She took another sip of coffee and met Jake's curious gaze. "Mom told me her family refused to understand the nature of her gifts. They thought she was possessed by the devil. That's why she left when she was sixteen. And Dad couldn't cope with having a wife *and* a kid who were both strong psychics, and walked out on us both."

Jake shrugged. "Times change. You can't be sure how your kin would react to you now."

"Yes I can." She smiled bitterly, and bent to gather the papers from the floor, only to have them scatter farther as the door opened a second time. Michael stepped inside.

"Morning," he said, his dark gaze enigmatic when it met hers.

Intuition delivered two warnings, and her pulse

skipped a beat. The wall he'd raised last night would stay in place, and he had something to say she wasn't going to like. She gathered the papers, and sat back down.

Jake offered Michael a cup of coffee before moving back to his desk. "So," he said. "What can we do for you?"

Michael stopped near Nikki's desk. She had the sudden sensation of being caught in a small pen with two charging bulls and wondered why. Had Jake picked up on her uncertainty about Michael, or was something else going on? She leaned back in her chair and eyed them both warily.

"I came to help," Michael said evenly.

"Really," Jake drawled. "I find it interesting that Nikki didn't appear to need any help until you arrived in town."

Her breath caught in her throat. What made Jake think that? She glanced at Michael and caught a wisp of anger—the same dark anger that had threatened her in the warehouse. Then he looked at her briefly, and the anger died. Still, it was obvious Michael wasn't used to having his actions challenged.

"It might also be said that she would be dead had I not," he replied.

Jake leaned back in his chair and regarded him thoughtfully. "Why *did* you come to Lyndhurst?"

"I was sent here to save her life. I remain here to do that *and* catch a killer—the man who now chases Nikki."

Michael sat on the edge of Nikki's desk. He appeared very relaxed, very calm. He was not. Jake's doubt infuriated him, and she wondered why.

"Why?" Jake asked bluntly. "You're not a cop or FBI or anything else official, so who the hell do you work for? Is this a job, or a personal vendetta?"

"Both." Michael hesitated, and sipped at his coffee.

Deciding how much he should tell them, she thought, and wondered if there was anyone in his world he trusted enough to be completely honest with.

"Jasper killed my brother. A few years later, he killed a close friend of mine."

The truth, as far as it went, but nowhere near the full story, she thought. "I get the feeling there's more history than that between you," she said.

Michael glanced at her. His face was guarded, wary. "Ours is a battle that has been going on for many years. I have killed his brother, and I will kill him—not in retaliation, but simply because the bloodshed will not stop until he is dead."

"Which suggests there is very little difference between you and the man you hunt."

Michael's smile was bitter. "There's one big difference. I do not hunt innocents, nor do I drain the blood of my victims."

She shuddered, remembering the bloody mess Monica had made the night before. "You said you don't kill in retribution, and yet you killed his brother. Why?"

"Because they were twins who hunted and worked as one. Together, they'd killed over one hundred people before I stopped his brother, and Jasper has killed as many since."

Again, the truth as far as it went, but she sensed it still wasn't the whole story. "Why is he so determined to hunt me? We both know there's easier prey on the streets."

Michael drank more coffee, studying her for several seconds before answering. "Jasper hungers for things he can never have. Power, more than anything else. You have that power, Nikki."

"Yeah, but he's not getting it." She paused. "Or me."

If Jasper succeeds in killing you, he will call you from your grave and draw your power into himself even as the flesh rots from your body.

He'll make me a zombie, she thought, as bile rose in her throat. She swallowed heavily and took a quick drink. It didn't take the bitter taste of fear from her mouth.

I will not let that happen. I would kill you myself, if it came to that.

It was a chilling thought, and not one she found particularly comforting.

Their gazes met and the telepathic link between them became something a whole lot more. His mind embraced hers—a gentle yet intimate touch that caressed her body in a way no physical touch ever could. For several seconds she could do little more than stare at him as her heart raced and heat suffused her body. And suddenly all she wanted was to feel his lips on hers, his fingers on her skin, caressing and exploring . . . Damn it, not even Tommy had affected her this quickly, or this deeply, and that terrified her.

Jake cleared his throat and she jumped, tearing her gaze away from Michael's. What the hell was happening between them? And why did she feel like running as far and as fast as she could?

"So what do you plan to do?" Jake asked into the silence.

"I plan to kill Jasper before he can kill again."

"That's not exactly legal ... and I take it from your lack of answer about your employer that you aren't anything official."

"No. And with a creature like Jasper, I have no other choice," Michael said quietly. "You had a taste of what he is capable of in his fledgling, Monica."

"Then she *is* a vampire."

There was no disbelief in Jake's quiet statement now. Only an edge of fear Nikki could easily understand.

"Yes," Michael answered. "As Jasper is. But Monica is newly turned. Jasper has had over seventy-five years to refine his powers."

"Shit," Jake muttered, and stared morosely into his coffee. "So how do we kill a vampire? Chase it with a stake and cover it in crosses and garlic?"

Michael smiled, though no humor touched his eyes. "The cross works as a deterrent only because, historically speaking, they have usually been made of the purest silver. But any sort of silver can burn vampires that touch it, particularly the newly turned. As for garlic, I suspect it is only a deterrent for those with weak stomachs."

"So what's the proper method of killing a vampire?" Jake asked. "And how do you know so much about it?"

"As I've already told Nikki, a stake through the heart and decapitation are the best methods. Exposure to the noonday sun works, too. Either way, you must first find their daytime resting place."

"Why the noonday sun?" Nikki asked in surprise. "I thought exposure to any amount of sun would kill."

"In most cases, yes." He paused, and shrugged. His quick look told her that he wished this subject had never been raised. "Age has a lot to do with it. The more years of unlife you have behind you, the more tolerant you become to silver and the sun."

"So how old is this Jasper?" Jake asked.

"As I said, we think he was turned about seventy-five years ago. It would normally give him about an hour of immunity."

Which explained how he could affect her dreams right before night fell, she thought, feeling ill. "What about the zombies?"

"If you kill their master, they will die," he said, voice grim. "It's his life-force that's keeping them alive."

"Does putting salt in their mouths work?" Both in movies and in novels, salt was often mentioned as a deterrent for evil, and it had even been used as a means of stopping zombies.

A shimmer of amusement spun around her. "Well, if you shoved enough down their throats, they might choke to death . . ."

She scowled at him. "I'm being serious here."

"So am I." His amusement fled. "I don't honestly know if the salt would work. Break their necks, and they will die. Otherwise, as far as I know, they cannot. Not until their master does."

"How the hell is that possible?" she said. "How can he raise the dead and make them his slaves?"

Michael shrugged. "The ability to call the newly

dead back to life is an art that often runs in families. From what we know of Jasper, both his father and grandfather were animators, as well."

Meaning it predated his vampirism. Great, she thought, and wondered what other unknowns walked through the darkness, hiding from the sunlight and humanity's sight.

Be careful what you ask, Nikki, or you might just discover the answer.

A chill ran across her flesh—a premonition that perhaps the warning came too late.

"So what do you suggest we do next?" Jake said into the silence.

"We must hunt Monica first. The newly turned tend to be unbalanced and dangerous, especially those who, when alive, had no real love for their fellow humans." Michael smiled grimly, and added, "As you've already discovered."

"Which is where Nikki comes in."

Michael nodded. "Once she finds Monica's hideout, we'll go deal with her."

Kill her, he meant. Nikki shuddered then frowned, studying him. She suddenly had the odd notion that she was not included in his "we'll."

"Meaning we introduce her to the delights of sunshine." Jake frowned. "I don't know if I—"

"I'm not asking for help here. I can handle her alone." Michael paused. "And you are wounded—"

"Monica is my client's daughter," Jake cut in, his voice flat. "And thus my responsibility. As for the wound, I only got a few stitches; it's *not* a problem. If you go without me, I'll call the cops."

If the threat fazed Michael in any way, it certainly

didn't show. "Okay, come." His gaze met Nikki's. *Here it comes,* she thought. A statement she wasn't going to like.

"We should be relatively safe from attack during the day," he continued, his voice as neutral as his face. "But all the same, I think, for safety's sake, Nikki at least should go home, and stay there."

Jake stood quickly, forestalling her anger with raised hands. "Vampires I can handle, a battle between the two of you, however, is beyond me. I'm grabbing some breakfast." He threw on his jacket and headed for the door. He reached for the door handle, then paused and looked at Michael. "I wish you luck. After a statement like that, you'll need it."

Michael restrained the urge to stop Jake's retreat. As much as he'd counted on having the other man's support, any sign of psychic intrusion would only inflame Nikki further. As the door slammed shut, he took a sip of coffee and braced himself to face the storm brewing on the other side of the desk.

"Who in hell do you think you are, telling me what to do?" She glared at him, cheeks flushed.

"You're a liability," he said flatly. Granted, a liability he had no choice but to use, given his discovery yesterday afternoon that Jasper and his creatures had fled the warehouse via some damn service tunnels. The bastard obviously had better sunlight mobility than Michael had presumed and *that* was galling. If he'd known, he would have risked going out earlier into the sunlight to take them all out.

But risking his own safety was far different than

risking hers. He refused to do that any more than necessary. "Monica is not Jasper. In many respects, she's more dangerous because her behavior cannot be predicted."

"I managed to survive the other night. I can do it again. Jake's more of a liability than I am. At least I have psychic gifts to protect myself with."

"Yes, but Jasper's not after Jake. He's after *you*."

"Meaning I'm supposed to cower at home while you take care of the problem? I don't think so."

He couldn't imagine her cowering anywhere, but that wasn't what he was asking. "We could be walking into a trap, Nikki."

"And you'd rather risk Jasper getting his hands on Jake than me." She snorted softly and sat back in her chair, amber eyes narrowed. "You're a cold bastard, you know that?"

It was certainly a term he'd heard before. Many times. "Are you so eager to die, Nikki?"

"No." Something flashed in her eyes, and he suddenly realized she was no stranger to death. "But I'm even less eager for Jake to die in my place."

"I have no intention of letting that happen. I plan to use him as a guard, nothing more." If only because he didn't trust Jake's sense of honor—an honor that lay with the client, not with him. He wouldn't put it past the man to step in and stop the killing stroke in some vague attempt to reconcile the girl with her father.

"Then why not take me? My abilities make me more useful as a guard. At least I'll be able to sense the zombies before they approach."

Michael rubbed the back of his neck. She was making perfectly good sense, and they both knew it. "Nikki, I had a premonition. If you come with us today, you could fall into Jasper's hands."

"At last, some honesty." She hesitated, her face grim. "How safe am I at home, though? Jasper may not be able to cross a threshold uninvited, but the zombies can, can't they? What if he's using Monica as bait to separate us so he can snatch me?"

He had to acknowledge it was a possibility, however unlikely. "I doubt he'd make such an attempt in daylight. If things went wrong, there would be little he could do to help."

And yet Jasper *did* possess more mobility in sunlight than he'd guessed, so maybe he *could* step in. Could snatch Nikki.

"Monica is my responsibility. It's my fault she's out there, and I won't be left out, Michael."

He stared at her for a long minute, then slowly, almost unwillingly, reached out, lightly cupping her cheek. She closed her eyes briefly, as if savoring his touch, and turned her head, brushing a kiss across his palm. His skin burned where her lips touched, and an ache flared deep in his heart.

"Why, Nikki?" he said, softly. "What is it about Monica that makes you feel so guilty?"

She snapped away from his touch and rose angrily to her feet. "Keep out of my goddamn mind!"

"It doesn't take telepathy to realize that Monica reminds you of someone. Who?"

She crossed her arms and glared at him.

He met her gaze. "Who's Tommy?"

She swore and spun toward the windows, arms still

crossed, shoulders tense. "Tommy died a long time ago. He has nothing to do with any of this."

The rising tide of her guilt suggested otherwise. "Monica reminds you of him, doesn't she?"

Though Nikki still had her back to him, her bitter smile was an ache in his heart. "Actually, Monica reminds me more of me."

He couldn't see why. They were nothing alike. "Tell me about Tommy, Nikki."

She made a sharp dismissive motion with her hand. "There's nothing much to tell. He was the head of the street gang I ran with. He died when I was nearly eighteen. End of story."

Not if her pain was any indication. "Why were you on the streets? Did you run away?"

She snorted softly. "No. My mom died, my dad couldn't be found, and I didn't like the home the authorities tried to shove me into."

Which did nothing to explain why she empathized with Monica. The teenager might have run wild, but she'd still had a dad who cared and a home to go back to.

"How long were you in this gang?"

"Only four years." She hesitated. "But it seemed like an eternity."

"Why didn't you stay with relatives?"

"Because no one wanted me. They thought I was a witch, like my mother. They want nothing to do with me even now."

He scrubbed a hand across his chin. None of this made sense. He'd met a lot of street kids over the years, and they all had one thing in common—a fierce, do-anything-to-survive determination. Most had been little more than feral animals, their humanity almost lost in their quest for survival. And, as she'd said, four years was a long time on the streets. It was an experience that should have scarred her for life. Yet there was very little evidence of that, in her words or her actions.

"How were you involved with this Tommy?"

"That is none of your damn business."

Her voice was curt, her thoughts suddenly chaotic. In many respects, that told him all he needed to know. Her relationship with Tommy had been sexual. And, for some odd reason, she felt responsible for his death.

"Why does Monica remind you of him?"

"I told you, she doesn't."

"And yet you chase her because of what happened to Tommy."

She didn't deny it, just stood at the window, staring out.

"Why, Nikki?"

For a moment, he didn't think she'd actually answer, but she surprised him.

"Because I let him die." Her voice was so soft it was a more a whisper through his thoughts than anything he could actually hear. "And I've vowed to never let it happen again."

"There was nothing you could do to save Monica. She chose her fate long before you came onto the scene."

Nikki glanced at him. "You're wrong, Michael. I could have stopped this."

The certainty in her voice made him frown. "Monica performed the ceremony over a week ago. From that point on, her fate was ordained. It was just a matter of when."

"And it was the *when* I could have changed." She hesitated, then turned to face him. "Everyone has some good in them. Sometimes all it takes is one person's belief to change the tide."

He had an odd feeling she was talking more about herself than Monica. He wondered who had turned her tide. Jake?

She lifted her chin slightly. "None of this alters the fact that I won't be left behind today."

He scowled. Her tenacity annoyed the hell out of him, yet he couldn't help admiring her for it, either. "You're a stubborn wench."

"I never claimed not to be. And nothing you can do or say will stop me from going with you."

"I can tie you down and lock you up," he muttered.

"And I can use telekinesis to escape, then come after you."

He ran a hand through his hair. "I'm only trying to keep you safe, Nikki." Taking a sip of coffee, he watched her over the rim of his cup. If he couldn't stop her, he'd just have to find a way to keep her out of harm's way. And that wasn't going to be any easier than trying to talk her out of accompanying them.

She shrugged and gave him a rueful smile. "I know. But I've been looking after myself for a long time now. And I have to finish what I start."

In that, they were very much alike. He glanced at the door, aware of Jake's approach. The door opened and Jake peered around it.

"It seems safe to enter," he commented, doing so.

"But it's hard to judge who won. Those black looks are almost identical."

"Quit clowning around," Nikki growled. "I'm going."

"Ah." Jake glanced at Michael sympathetically. "She can be really difficult when it comes to doing something she doesn't want to do."

Michael smiled grimly. "I noticed."

"So, we stick to the mid-morning raid?" Jake moved over to his chair and picked up his car keys.

Michael took another sip of coffee and nodded. "It's the best time to win against *any* vampire."

And yet he had a notion it was not his time to win—in any way.

Nikki crossed her arms and leaned wearily against a metal signpost. Jake and Michael were standing several yards in front of her, barely visible through the mist of rain.

She wondered why Monica had chosen a train tunnel to hide in. There had to be more secure places about. And surely a child raised in opulent surroundings could never be comfortable with the dirt and constant noise inside the tunnel.

Not to mention the probability of being seen, or even caught. The area was a well-known haunt for street kids. Nikki's gang had often dared one another to race through the tunnels just as a train was due. She had no doubt kids still did that today. Some things never went out of fashion. And unless it had changed in the last ten years, there weren't many hidey-holes inside. So why come here?

There was no sense of Jasper here, though, so maybe Michael was right. Maybe it *wasn't* a trap. And yet she couldn't help that itchy feeling that said all wasn't as it seemed. She wrapped her fingers around the locket. The metal pulsed lightly—a single beat every few minutes. Monica's heartbeat, she now knew.

As Jake snapped the timetable closed, she walked across to the two of them. "What's the verdict?"

"Near as we can figure, a train isn't due for another twenty minutes." He shoved the timetable into his jacket pocket, then took the stake Michael offered him.

"I hope you're right. There's very little room to move in there when a train goes through."

Jake grimaced and studied the sky. "With all this damn cloud and rain, there's not much sunlight. That going to make a difference to Monica remaining asleep?"

"It shouldn't," Michael said, looking at the tunnel. "Are you certain Monica's inside, Nikki? No one else?"

"You can't tell?"

"I can't sense anything, but she might be hiding beyond the range of my senses."

"Oh." She glanced down at the locket in her hand. It pulsed steadily, and heat washed over her skin. Heat and hunger.

"Then yes," she added softly. "I'm certain."

Jake switched on his flashlight and walked toward the tunnel, becoming one with the gloom. An odd prickle ran across the back of her neck.

"It's not too late to turn back, Nikki."

Yes, it is. She gripped the barrel of her flashlight tighter and walked forward. Michael kept close, and she felt safer for it. Yet instinct said it wasn't going to be enough to save her.

She ignored the quick thrust of foreboding and watched the beam from Jake's flashlight dance across the darkness. Her own paled by comparison, barely piercing the gloom to either side. Maybe she should have stopped and bought some new batteries.

Their footsteps echoed through the silence. Could Monica hear them, even though her body was inert? Could she pass that information on to her dark master?

The tunnel swung to the right, and the darkness fully encased them. Past escapades returned to haunt Nikki, and she swung her light to the left. There had been a break in the wall near here, somewhere. She'd fled into it once in the face of an oncoming train.

Jake stopped so abruptly, she almost ran into him.

"Hole in the wall," he said, shifting his grip on the stake he held. "Wait here. I'll check it out."

Shifting her weight from one foot to the other, she watched him disappear. Though she couldn't sense anyone in the hole, a physical check was far safer than simply relying on her psychic senses.

Michael stood behind her, as silent and still as the darkness around them. Yet he reminded her of a coiled spring. He must sense danger ahead, like she did.

Jake returned. "Nothing," he said, sounding relieved. "Only garbage."

"Monica's still ahead." Nikki swept the light across the darkness surrounding them. She'd heard no sound, nothing to indicate there was anything or anyone else in this tunnel besides them and Monica, yet she had a sudden sense of movement.

"How far ahead?" Jake's question jostled harshly against the silence.

"I'm not sure. Not far."

He frowned and turned, leading the way once more. The yellow beam of his flashlight swung in the darkness, barely penetrating the thick gloom. It would be so easy to walk into a trap.

The locket in Nikki's hand pulsed again. She clenched her fingers around it and let her senses flare to life. Monica was on the move, running swiftly through the tunnel. But how, when it was mid-morning and she shouldn't even be awake? Nikki bit her lip. Something was happening, something she didn't understand.

Michael's tension washed heat across her back. Maybe he could sense the presence she merely guessed at.

"Jasper's not here," he said softly. "But the zombies are. They're moving Monica, meaning that Jasper's sensed our presence. I think you and Jake should go back. I'll continue the hunt for Monica alone."

"As I've said on numerous occasions, Monica is my client's daughter," Jake said over his shoulder. "You're going nowhere without me."

"You can never match the undead—not on strength or speed. You'll only get in my way."

Jake turned. His flashlight pierced the darkness, almost sun-bright. "And are you suggesting that *you* can?"

"Yes, I am." Michael hesitated. "I don't like the feel

of this. Take Nikki and head back to the entrance. You'll be safe there."

He was certainly determined to keep her away from Monica, Nikki thought. What was he afraid of—that she'd try to stop him killing her? Beheading her? "You need to accept the fact that Jake and I are here to stay, Michael."

"Damn it, Nikki, you've encountered the zombies once already. Do you really think you and Jake can survive four of them?"

Though annoyance barely touched his voice, it seared through his thoughts, almost burning her. She stared at him for several seconds. Perhaps he was right. She'd barely escaped an attack from two zombies. Add another two, and the odds weren't good— even with Michael on their side. Perhaps it was time to leave Monica to her fate.

Besides, she didn't like the feel of whatever was happening up ahead.

"Okay, I'm out. Jake?"

He shook his head. "I think we owe it to Trevgard to see this thing through."

Michael raised an eyebrow. "And didn't you promise your wife to take no foolish chances? Is Trevgard really more important than she is?"

Nikki glanced at him sharply. He'd obviously been reading Jake's thoughts, to know something as intimate as that. Maybe it was only her presence that stopped him from entering Jake's mind and forcing him to obey.

Jake glared at him. "Just how in hell did you know that?"

"As I said, Nikki's not the only one with psychic

abilities. But that's not important—what is is that Mary should be your main concern here, not Monica."

Jake glanced at her, his expression troubled. "All right, I'll go. But you can't behead Monica. At the very least, bring her out into the sunshine. If she's a vampire, that will kill her just as surely as anything else."

"Yes." Michael studied Jake for a moment, his expression giving little away. "What of your duty to Trevgard? When she burns, what story are you going to give him?"

"*If* she burns, I won't have to give him a story, because she'll simply have disappeared. Happens a lot in this town, believe it or not."

Michael nodded, then stepped into the shadows and disappeared.

"Damn," Jake muttered. "How did he do that?"

"He moves fast," Nikki muttered, although he hadn't. He'd only taken a dozen or so steps and before hesitating, out there in the darkness. She wondered what he had sensed. Wondered why she was still aware of his presence. "And the tunnel turns to the right a few yards away. That's why you can't see him."

Jake touched her arm lightly. "Let's go. The darkness doesn't feel quite as safe without your sinister friend around."

He was right. It didn't. Her sense of danger had increased twofold in the few minutes Michael had been gone. The quicker they got out of this tunnel, the better. Nikki turned and kept close to Jake as they began their retreat.

"What's that noise?" Jake said, after a few minutes.

Energy surged in response. Nikki clenched her fists and listened. The wind sighed past them, gathering speed. The next moment, the ground began to tremble.

"Christ," Jake continued. "A train. *Run!*"

Nikki's adrenaline surged, giving her feet wings. "The hole's only twenty feet or so away. Head for that!"

They ran through the tunnel, the duel beams of their flashlights creating a crazy pattern along the walls. And, just for an instant, they reflected brightly in a dead blue eye. Oh, Christ, the zombies . . .

"Jake, watch out!"

Around her, the night found form. Something grabbed her waist and swung her away, into the darkness. She screamed, but icy fingers covered her mouth, cutting the sound off. She tasted dirt and death, and bile rose in her throat. Struggling violently, she kicked and punched the creature that held her so tightly. Kinetic energy surged, but before she could release her weapon, something hit her head, and pain exploded.

Evil danced around her. *When my creature brings you to me, I will make you mine.* Jasper's thoughts were soft, as if spoken from a great distance.

No! She lashed out blindly with kinetic energy, fighting the zombie holding her. But when she wrenched it away, another quickly replaced it. Dimly, she felt a warm trickle of blood on her cheek, heard a distant scream of anger not her own.

Then nothing but mocking laughter.

Nine

A SLIGHT HISS was all the warning he got. Michael dodged, but not fast enough. The dart hit his forearm and spread fire through his veins. *Silver . . . the dart was made of silver.* Swearing softly, he pulled it from his arm. Three of the zombies were close, moving down a tunnel that ran parallel to his. The fourth was with Monica ahead, moving her to safety.

It made no sense. Why hide her in a place like this in the first place? Between the trains, the maintenance crews, and—if what he'd read in Nikki's mind was anything to go by—the kids who played down here, it wasn't exactly a secure spot.

The wind sighed past him, velocity increasing with every second. A train approaching. Either they'd misread the timetable or the train was early. Whatever the reason, they were running out of time. He turned and headed back to Nikki and Jake.

He'd barely taken a dozen steps when dizziness hit him. He staggered for several seconds then stopped, pressing his palm against the tunnel wall. It was real and solid, and most importantly, not moving. Frowning, he squinted into the darkness. Ahead, Nikki and

Jake were blurred shapes, a muted wash of red he could barely see.

He blinked and swallowed. There was a bitter taste in his mouth, and it had nothing to do with fear. *The dart had been drugged!*

The zombies came out of the other tunnel. Nikki screamed and her energy seared the air.

Something hit the side of his head. Michael dropped to his knees, battling to stay conscious as the night danced around him. Moisture ran down the side of his face. He licked it, tasting his own blood. The darkness within him rose—a demon that battled the lethargy overtaking his mind. He struggled upright, knowing time was running out. The train was almost upon them. He had to find Nikki and get out of this tunnel.

Her life-force burned fiercely through the darkness. Michael lunged toward her, but his legs felt encased in glue. He couldn't move with any sort of speed. Jasper's distant laughter mocked him. The darkness claimed the fire of Nikki's life-force, removing her from his sight.

And removing the warmth of her thoughts from his mind.

He swore and swung around to meet the charge of a zombie.

Punching the creature in the face, he knocked it back several feet. It landed on its rear, shaking its head and growling in confusion. Michael turned and ran on.

Jake was gamely battling against a second zombie. Michael leaped, kicking it away, sending it staggering across the tracks. Grabbing Jake, he thrust him into the safety of the hole and dived in after him. Two seconds later, the train screeched past, whirling dust and rubbish through the darkness.

Coughing, Michael pushed upright and leaned against the grimy wall. The wind was cool, but it failed to provide any sort of comfort. He closed his eyes and sent his senses winging back across the darkness. There had to be some trace of Nikki . . .

Nothing. Nor could he sense the zombies. *I hope the train severed their heads* . . . but given the way his luck had been running these last few days, they'd undoubtedly escaped. He took a deep breath.

As he'd foreseen, Nikki had been captured. He had no doubt Jasper would kill her. Then Michael would be forced to rekill her, just to give her the peace of death.

He'd known it was a possibility, but it still wasn't one he was ready to face. Not now, not ever.

He clenched his fists in the dirt, then slowly relaxed them. Really, what was the life of one more human if that was the price that had to be paid for Jasper's death? Even if that life was the woman he'd been sent here to save?

Yet the thought chilled him, and for the first time in years he wondered at the cost of his quest—both to himself and to those close to him. People like Nikki—who was by no means close, and yet could have been, had either of them wished it.

He closed his eyes and rubbed them wearily. She wasn't dead yet. At least he had the comfort—or maybe that should be *dis*comfort—of that knowledge. The connection she'd formed between them wasn't severed, just temporarily empty.

He wondered what Jasper was waiting for. He wanted Nikki's power; of that Michael had no doubt. And the only way he could claim it was by killing her.

Then again, Jasper was something of an egomaniac; maybe he wanted to break her first, just to prove he could, before he fully claimed her.

"Where's Nikki?" Jake's question rasped across the silence.

Michael opened his eyes and studied him. The heated haze of Jake's blood was a muted glow in the night. Purple patches marred his face and torso, bruises in the making, but otherwise he appeared unhurt.

"Gone. Jasper has her," Michael replied flatly. He blinked and switched from infrared vision to normal. The return of darkness was, in some ways, a blessing.

"*Fuck!*" Jake said. "What are we going to do now?"

"Nothing." Michael used the wall as a brace and rose to his feet. The drug in his system would probably take hours to dissipate and, with the sun strengthening toward noon, there was little he could do now but wait. "Except head back to the office."

"And make no attempt to find her?" Jake's voice was incredulous.

"I have no other choice," Michael bit back.

"Why the hell not? You said you were psychic, so why not use—"

"Because," Michael cut in, voice harsh, "I've been fucking drugged. I can barely think, let alone use my abilities to try to track down Nikki."

So much for control, he thought bitterly, and stepped out of the hole. A glint of silver caught his eye. He walked across the track and bent to pick it up. It was Nikki's silver cross. The small amount of silver within the charm tingled against his palm, but he ignored it. At least he had something of Nikki's to hold on to. Something to remember her by in the years ahead if things did go badly.

He glanced across at Jake, then strode through the darkness. There was nothing more they could do in the tunnel, and Jasper just might try to contact them at the office—if only to taunt them.

Tonight he would search.

And if Michael found him, Jasper would pay.

The darkness stirred, coming to life. It shifted . . . and disappeared.

Nikki blinked, wondering if her eyes were playing tricks. The night appeared silent, empty. Yet the more she stared into the darkness, the more certain she became that someone was there, watching her.

She shivered, but resisted the urge to rise from the cold concrete floor. Until she had an idea of where she was, there was no point in moving. Who knew what traps might wait in the darkness?

The minutes crept by. Sweat broke out across her brow, and fear crawled through her heart. Though there was no sign of Jasper in the heavy darkness, he was there, somewhere. The foul scent of his evil filled the air.

She clenched her fists and tried to still the sudden rush of panic. She had to stay calm if she wanted to survive. Taking a deep breath, she tried to contact Michael through their link.

Only he wasn't there.

Nothing was.

Her psychic abilities no longer answered her call. Bile rose in her throat and she swallowed heavily. What had Jasper done to her?

Laughter rolled across the night, a rich sound that made her skin crawl with terror.

"Your lover will not hear you."

Jasper's voice spun through the darkness, entwining her in corruption. She still couldn't see him . . . nor did she have any sense of him. What was wrong with her?

"He's not my lover." Her voice was little more than a harsh whisper that burned against her throat's sudden dryness. She licked her lips and tried again. "Why won't he hear me?"

The night stirred, and Jasper appeared. There was an almost terrible beauty in watching his perfect body find shape.

Suddenly she realized he was naked.

Her heart skipped several beats. Closing her eyes, she tried to control the terror squeezing her throat. Despite the soreness of her limbs, she sensed Jasper hadn't touched her yet. But he would. She didn't need her abilities to feel his hunger.

He laughed.

She resisted the urge to roll into a tight ball of fear and sat up instead. The concrete scraped harshly across her buttocks. Only then did she realize that she was as naked as he.

"When the form is so beautiful, why cover it?"

To emphasize his point, he struck a pose, showing the muscular splendor of his body. *Mad . . . He has to be mad.* She wrapped her arms around her knees, drawing them close to her chest. "What do you want with me?"

"Many things." The amusement fled his features. "Mostly, I want you to help me kill the man who murdered my brother."

"Never."

He laughed softly. "Oh, you *will* help me, pretty one."

She didn't bother refuting the statement again. Jasper smiled and walked to the far corner of the room, his movements grace itself. Nikki blinked, suddenly realizing she could see. Light seeped through the boarded-up window to her right, but it wasn't sunlight. It didn't hold the warmth or the strength. The fact that it was artificial, combined with the occasional roar of a car speeding past, suggested there was a street nearby. Freedom was so close . . . and yet so far. She had no doubt he would kill her if she so much as blinked the wrong way right now.

He turned, holding a syringe in one hand. Relief surged. That was why her head felt so fuzzy. He'd been drugging her.

"This won't put you out." His smile made her edge back slightly. "Only stop you from moving and cloud your gifts. I have no wish for you to call your lover so soon."

Fear held her immobile. Jasper knelt, slid the needle into her thigh and administered the drug. His hand caressed her skin, his touch hot, possessive. She closed her eyes and held her breath.

Jasper laughed and rose. Her eyes jerked open, and she watched him move to the bed. He was playing with her, she realized grimly. Tasting her fear, fueling its flames. Savoring it.

She knew then that he wouldn't physically touch her. Not for a while anyway. This man enjoyed violation of another kind—of the heart, the soul and the mind. Like a cat playing with its prey, he would toy with her until she broke.

Then he would use her to trap and kill Michael.

She had to escape this madman's grasp.

Footsteps whispered through the silence. Laughter surrounded her, provocative yet chilling. Not Jasper's. Monica's. Nikki closed her eyes, refusing to acknowledge the teenager's presence. Bedsprings squeaked as Monica joined her lover on the bed. After several more minutes came soft moans and the rustle of sheets.

All she could do was ignore the noise of their lovemaking and try to rest. Like Jasper's games, she knew this was meant to be some perverted form of torture. But if they hoped to shock her, hoped to encourage the first tiny cracks in her sanity, they were in for a surprise. She'd seen and heard a lot worse during her years on the streets.

Yet she couldn't help the tiny hope that daylight would arrive and drive them into oblivion. Or better yet, to hell.

Pain woke her. Her heart pounded, racing uncomfortably in her chest. She opened her eyes. Jasper knelt beside her, warm breath kissing her skin, his gaze burning with desire as he watched her . . . and sucked blood from her wrist.

Nikki screamed and tried to jerk her arm free. He

held her still, his grip bruising as he drained her life away. There was nothing she could do to stop him.

As the realization of death hit her, he finished drinking.

The hot ache where his razor-sharp teeth had penetrated her flesh eased. Smiling, still watching her every movement, he licked the remaining droplets. His tongue danced sensually across her wrist, and the two small holes healed over—they were visible, but no longer bleeding.

Horror filled every corner of her mind. It felt as if his depravity had somehow invaded her soul and left it stained. Jasper laughed, white teeth gleaming, canines still tarnished with her blood. She closed her eyes, desperate to control the rising tide of hysteria inside her. That's what he intended, what he wanted. Her hysteria. It was just part of his attempt to break her will.

She couldn't let him succeed. Not when Michael's life was at stake.

Jasper moved back to the bed, his bright gaze fixed on her. There was no life, no emotion, in his eyes. It was almost as if becoming a vampire had robbed him of all humanity. And yet, she had an odd feeling that even when he'd been alive, the look in his eyes would have been much the same.

She shifted uncomfortably on the cold floor, but her muscles were stiff and unresponsive. She still clasped her knees close to her chest, though the muscles along her thighs had long ago gone numb. While the protection it offered was only illusory, she didn't want her body exposed to this man.

"You have been missing for more than twenty-four hours. Do you think your lover is frantic yet?"

"He's not—" She stopped. What was the use? Jasper would never believe she and Michael were barely friends, let alone lovers. Madness had control of his brain, and he refused to hear anything beyond the boundaries of what he believed to be true.

He rested his forearms against his knees, face somehow more intense as he leaned forward. "He will suffer, as I suffered. He will feel you die, as I felt my brother die."

His voice was flat, chilling in its lack of emotion. Yet she couldn't help a soft snort of derision. They both knew that *wasn't* the real reason he'd snatched her. "Let's be honest here—making Michael suffer might be a bonus, but what you really want is my abilities in your control. Why not just kill me, and get it over with?"

Perhaps it wasn't the wisest move, asking a madman a question like that, but it was one she needed answered—if only to understand how long she had to get free of him.

"If I kill you now, and bring you back, your lover will merely return you to death. There would be nothing to savor in such a situation."

"And yet by keeping me alive, you risk losing not only me, but your own life."

He smiled. It was *not* a pleasant thing to see. "Perhaps the risk is part of the pleasure."

And perhaps, she thought, still eyeing him warily, he thought himself the more powerful of the two now. But to underestimate Michael's capabilities would be a very bad mistake, no matter how much stronger Jasper believed he was.

"Why haven't you tried to get me in a mind lock again, then?" she asked after a moment. He'd come so close the first time.

"At the time, you were unaware and ripe for attack. Were it not for your lover, I would have had you. Right now you are not so easy a target, even with your mind so clouded. I have no wish to deplete my own reserves when fear and drugs can more easily break your spirit."

And the pain involved would give him more pleasure, she thought. He smiled, and she wished—somewhat futilely—that the bastard would keep out of her thoughts. Fear curled through her stomach as she realized his canines had lengthened again. She had to keep him talking—keep him from thinking about her blood. It was her only hope. Every second she could delay whatever plans he had for her was another second Michael had to find her.

"Was your brother a vampire, too?"

His gaze narrowed slightly. He surely knew what she was up to, yet she sensed he was prepared to play along. At least for a while.

"He was my twin. My other half. I've been waiting a long time to confront his killer."

And probably a long time planning Michael's death. She moved her right leg slightly, trying to ease the numbness, but stopped when a hungry look flickered across his face. Holding still, she cleared her throat, trying to draw his attention away from her naked body. "Michael didn't even come to Lyndhurst for you."

"He may not have come here for me, but he re-mains here for me, and we both know it. And he will curse me long and loudly before he dies." He rose and picked up another syringe. "I must go out. Your blood, intoxicating as it was, will not fulfill my needs."

He slid the needle into her thigh and she bit back a yelp of pain. White fire flashed through her veins, and her pulse began to skip. Sweat broke out across her skin, though she felt chilled to the bone. The darkness began to move, began to moan and whis-per . . . and dancing images of every nightmare she'd ever suffered came to life around her.

She closed her eyes, battling for sanity. It wasn't real. It was only the drug. Jasper's hand caressed her arm, his touch hot with desire. She shuddered, but didn't move. Didn't dare.

"Have fun, beautiful one."

"My name is Jasper Harding."

His voice broke the numbness. She flinched, hold-ing her knees tighter, but otherwise not moving. Sweat ran in rivulets down her body despite the chill of the room. Every heartbeat was a shudder of fear.

The darkness writhed and danced with horrors un-imaginable. They prevented her from slipping into the oblivion of sleep, filled her with their madness, twisted her soul with their evil. She'd long ago given up telling herself it was only the drug. It was more than that now. He was back.

"Repeat it. Say my name."

She bit her tongue and ignored the urge to do as he

asked. The darkness ran across her skin as lightly as a spider, scalding her.

"Repeat it, and the fear will go. Everything will go."

"*No!*" She dropped her head to her knees and tried to deny the growing need to do as he asked. She'd rather face insanity.

Pain flared in her thigh. More drugs. She moaned. She wouldn't give in. She wouldn't . . .

Her mother's death replayed itself, over and over in the darkness. The look on her face as she'd waved good-bye to Nikki. The scream of metal as a runaway truck crushed her. Images of the twisted remains of the car entwined with blood and mangled body parts, none really distinguishable from the other.

Again and again she felt the caress of her mother's soul, her kiss of love, as she passed on.

Nikki screamed and cried and denied the night's insistence that her mother died because of her. Begged and pleaded for forgiveness, only to be mocked with vicious laughter.

And still the nightmare danced on.

Over and over she watched Tommy being beaten, her gaze hazy with the blood from a wound on her forehead. Unable to help him, her gifts useless with the pain pounding through her brain, she could only watch the three kids kick him.

Words mocked her. Her words, spoken the night before his death—praying for his soul to be sent to hell. She cried a denial to the darkness. The words had been spoken in anger and fear, and never meant.

But the night would not listen, and the madness danced on.

She heard the distant wail of the approaching police siren that frightened the thugs away. Suffered again the agonizing crawl toward Tommy. Felt the moment of his death as she held his bloody body in her arms, the touch of his soul as it passed on its journey toward eternal darkness.

Her curse, her fault. Over and over and over . . .

"Say my name."

The chant sang through her brain. She shook her head, the movement feeble. Everything ached—her head, her muscles, her heart. The night went on forever, and time became a frozen wasteland of madness.

Resist, resist. The weak litany overran his chant, helping her ignore it. Fire touched her leg, burned through her bloodstream.

The drug. Her heart shook with fear as the craziness danced in fevered delight.

"Jasper Harding."

The words were torn from her. She couldn't stop herself repeating his name, though her heart wept in bitter defeat.

The darkness stilled its dance. Sweet silence filled the void.

"Repeat it," Jasper urged, elation running through his voice.

"Jasper Harding," she croaked in reply. How long had she sat here? How long had she resisted the drug? It felt like forever, but it was probably little more than a day or so.

Fatigue trembled through her, but that in itself told her little. Her head swam, though she wasn't sure if the cause was lack of food or the drug. Her throat was parched, and it hurt to swallow, let alone speak. Jasper would kill her if he wasn't careful.

She studied the darkness wearily. She may have lost the battle, but not the war. Jasper couldn't guard her, or control her, twenty-four hours of every day. She'd beat him yet. If there was one thing she'd learned during her years with Tommy, it was that no matter how bad things seemed, you could never give up. Hope might be only a heartbeat away.

Jasper appeared out of the darkness, a presence she felt rather than saw. She closed her eyes, refusing to acknowledge him.

"Resistance is pointless," he mocked quietly. "You are mine now."

She made no comment. The chill air caressed her sweaty flesh, making her feel colder than she'd ever thought possible.

"Open your eyes." His voice had taken a commanding tone. "Look at me."

She fought the order as hard as she could. Yet her head rose, her eyes met his. Tears tracked silently down her cheeks.

Monica stood behind him, her blue eyes full of

hate. Behind them both, dawn's warm light danced through the shadows.

"Get the syringe."

Nikki's pulse leaped at his command. Jasper laughed as Monica turned to do his bidding.

"This time we'll merely put you to sleep. You fought a long but useless battle, pretty one. And we all need our rest."

Relief surged. At least the mad dance of nightmares was over. He stepped away as Monica knelt beside her. Motes of sunlight played across his flesh, raising red welts that disappeared as quickly as they appeared. She remembered Michael mentioning Jasper's lack of immunity to the sun, and wondered what time it was. Something told her it could be important.

"When we are all rested," Jasper continued softly, "you will become mine fully."

She'd kill herself before she ever let him take her. But meeting his mocking gaze, she knew how futile the thought was. She had no means to fight him, for a start. The drugs they'd been pouring into her body still blocked her psychic gifts, and who knew how long they'd take to dissipate. And physically, she doubted she'd pose a serious threat to even an ant right now.

"I shall enjoy taking your body, as I have enjoyed taking your mind."

Monica jerked, and liquid sprayed across Nikki's leg. She tensed, wondering if the teenager realized what she'd done. Monica met her gaze, her blue eyes dark with anger and hate. She glanced briefly at the needle, then back at Nikki. She knew it was almost empty. In her own strange way, Monica was offering a chance to escape . . . but only because she feared sharing the monster she called lover.

The teenager rose and threw the empty syringe on the shelf before joining Jasper on the bed. The arm she placed around his waist was possessive. Nikki wondered how much time Monica had left. Not much, if body language was anything to go by. Nikki's gaze met Jasper's. Malice gleamed back at her.

"Has Michael told you his secret yet?" he asked.

Nikki closed her eyes. She didn't want to hear anything else from Jasper, but not because she feared his lies. No, this time she feared the truth.

"Michael is one of us," Jasper said softly. "A creature of the night. A taker of blood."

"No." The denial was torn from her. Yet in her heart she knew he spoke the truth. It explained the darkness she'd sensed.

But Michael was not Jasper.

He laughed coldly. "Believe what you will, pretty one."

She ignored him, ignored the fear whispering through her thoughts. Michael might be a vampire, but that didn't make him evil. It made him dangerous, there was no doubt about that, but *not* evil. What it did provide, however, was another reason *why* she shouldn't get involved with him. She closed her eyes, allowing sleepiness to overtake her. She had to rest if she wanted the strength to escape, and discover the truth.

*   *   *

Michael leaned wearily against the wall, impatiently watching the sun. It was mid-afternoon, and every second until he could start hunting again felt like an eternity. For the last three days they'd followed every possible lead, yet had found no trace of Nikki or her captor. Everyone, even Monica and the zombies, seemed to have vanished off the face of the earth.

He touched the cross around his neck. The silver tingled against his skin and would, in time, burn him. He didn't care. It was Nikki's—all that he might ever be able to have of her.

He closed his eyes and reached again for the link. Darkness greeted him, a wall he could not traverse. At least she was still alive. He wouldn't have felt such a wall if she wasn't.

But until she was free of the chains holding her mind captive, there was little he could do to help her. Jasper had chosen his hiding place too well. It could take weeks to ferret him out. Indeed, the last time he had run for cover, it had taken Michael almost a year to track him down. Nikki probably didn't have that much time left.

All he could do was wait a few more hours and return to the hunt, however futile. He crossed his arms and continued to watch the afternoon crowds rush past. A thick curtain of lace protected him from the main thrust of the sun's heat, but he didn't dare go any closer to the window. He wasn't suicidal.

In the office behind him, Jake paced and swore into his phone. It was a futile exercise. They both knew there was little the cops could do that the two of them hadn't already tried.

Hunger washed through him. He ignored it. There

was no time to eat. The detour might mean the difference between finding some clue and not. He couldn't take the risk.

He sighed and cast his gaze back to the skies. The day had been appropriate to his mood—wet and miserable. Only recently had the sun begun to break the heavy blanket of clouds. He hoped it was a sign of better things to come.

Behind him, Jake slammed the phone down. "Damn those bastards."

"They're doing their best," Michael said softly.

"Well, it's not good enough!"

Nothing was good enough, Michael thought in bleak agreement. Not the cops' efforts nor theirs. Nikki was still held captive by evil, and God knows what he was doing to her . . .

He took a deep breath and shoved the thought away, but he couldn't escape the guilt so easily. This was his fault. He should never have let her go with them. Should never have left her in that tunnel. Had they been together, things might have turned out differently.

And while she might still be alive, he knew there could only be one reason for that. Jasper wanted payback for his brother's death, and he obviously believed Michael and Nikki were more involved than they actually were. He would make her suffer, knowing that Michael would also suffer. From imagination, and from the knowledge of the depravities Jasper was capable of.

"Damn it all, *we* should be out there ourselves." Jake swung around and snatched his coat off the back of his chair. "I can't sit here any longer. I'm going to look for her."

"I cannot."

Jake turned to face him. "Why the hell not? I thought the two of you—"

"*You thought wrong.*" Michael took a sharp breath and clamped down on his temper. "But what I do or do not feel has no bearing on the matter. I simply cannot go outside."

"Why? Afraid of the sun or something?"

"Or something," Michael muttered, and turned. It was not what he'd call an ideal time to be honest— but then, what time was? It would be so easy to just reach out and touch Jake's mind, make him trust . . . But he couldn't. Nikki would know. She'd sense the intrusion.

"Jasper and I have one thing in common. We're both vampires. I'll die if I walk outside right now."

"Which would certainly explain why you've been avoiding daylight." Jake paused, and added more slowly, "You're not kidding . . . are you?"

"No. While I do not drink human blood, I *am* a vampire."

"But . . . you're standing in sunshine now."

"Diffused sunlight. Watch." He reached forward, brushing aside the curtain to let the full force of the sun fall upon his arm. Instantly his skin began to turn red. He dropped the curtain back into place before the burn became too bad. "Because I have been on this earth a long time, I can stand some sunlight. Even so, if I went out there now, I'd only last ten minutes or so."

Jake leaned against his desk and ran a hand through

his pale blond hair. Michael could hear the struggle in his thoughts. Lord, it would be so easy to reach out . . . He ignored the urge and waited.

"Does Nikki know?" Jake asked.

It wasn't a question he'd expected. And though he could see fear in Jake's eyes, it wasn't the full-blown panic he'd half anticipated, either. "No. But I have no doubt Jasper will have told her by now."

"Hell of a way to find out." Jake swallowed slightly. "You don't drink human blood, you say?"

"No."

"Of course, I only have your word for that."

Michael returned his gaze evenly. "If I wanted to taste your blood, you wouldn't even have time to scream."

"Well, that's just great." Jake shuddered, then ran a hand across the sandy stubble on his chin. "In recent days I've seen zombies, and a supposedly dead teenager suddenly gaining inhuman strength and speed. I suppose it's not too much of a stretch to believe you're a vampire. Though I have to say, you don't act very vampirelike."

Michael raised an eyebrow. "And how many vampires have you met to make such a judgment?"

"Well, just Monica, but I've seen countless Dracula movies."

"The Dracula legend was based on a man. It has very little to do with reality."

"Tell that to Monica and this Jasper of yours. They're pretty much matching the legend."

"Becoming a vampire did not make Jasper what he is today. His thirst for blood was evident well before his turning."

"But turning has made him more unkillable." Jake hesitated, eyes narrowing slightly. "Why did he really snatch Nikki? To get back at you?"

"I believe so. He thinks I care for her—"

"Which, despite denials, you do."

"—and he wants to make me suffer before he kills us both."

"So you and Jasper have this personal vendetta, and Nikki, Monica and I were unlucky enough to get in the way."

Boiled down to basics, that about summed it up. Michael rubbed his forehead, wondering again if all the years—and all the lives lost—were worth the effort of chasing Jasper.

Then he remembered his brother, Patrick, and his friend, Jenna. And people like Monica, who was by no means innocent but still deserved more than the path of death and destruction that Jasper had initiated her into.

"As I said before, it's more than a personal vendetta. Jasper has to be stopped. And it's my job to do it."

"Why?" Jake's gaze was shrewd. "You're not in this alone, are you?"

Both were questions he wasn't prepared to answer right now. Risking his life was one thing; risking the lives of his fellow hunters by revealing too much about their organization was another. Jasper was still loose, and Jake might be next on the hit list. The less Jake knew, the better for them both.

"Sometimes it takes a vampire to hunt a vampire."

"In other words, mind my own business." Jake flashed a toothy smile that held very little warmth. "I guess we wait. I hope you don't mind if I keep my distance. Being around a vampire might take a little getting used to."

Michael smiled. Jake was all right. No wonder Nikki depended on the man.

"I just feel so damn useless sitting here," Jake continued with a sigh.

"We'll find her. Don't worry." Meaningless words, when all *he* was doing was worrying.

"Yeah, right."

The disbelief in Jake's voice annoyed him. Hope was the one thing they couldn't afford to lose. But the rebuke died on his tongue. It was fear that made Jake speak like that—a fear Michael could well understand.

An hour crawled by, and another. And then, finally, the sun was low enough for him to survive its touch. Michael pushed away from the wall. Now he could *do* something, instead of merely waiting.

Life suddenly sparked in the darkness of the link. He stiffened, reaching out swiftly. Turmoil, fear and confusion greeted him. Nikki didn't hear him, didn't acknowledge his presence. But it didn't matter. He knew where she was.

And Jasper was a dead man.

Puddles of yellow light splashed across the floor but did little to take the chill from the room or her body. She'd watched the gentle progress of the sun for the last few hours, lethargy holding her immobile.

But time and daylight would not wait for her. She had to move, had to get out of here before the day disappeared. The sunlight's waning strength said it was already late afternoon. There was so little time left.

Gritting her teeth, she straightened her right leg. Stiff muscles protested the movement, and her stomach churned. Head swimming, she slowly straightened her other leg.

Her arms were almost as difficult to move, stiff and leaden with cold. Her whole body felt numb with it, her skin icy to touch. But for the first time in ages, she felt stirrings of life in the void that had been her psychic gift. Massaging her legs, she glanced warily at the bed. Monica and Jasper lay still and silent, naked limbs entwined around each other. If they breathed, she couldn't see it. She had the perfect chance to kill them both, only she didn't have a weapon.

And, if she was being honest with herself, didn't have the courage. She had one chance—one small opportunity to escape—and that's precisely what she intended to do.

Her gaze slipped from them, and she noticed the door next to the bed. Until now, she hadn't even realized it existed. She bit her lip, then rolled over onto her hands and knees.

The effort sent the room spinning. She took several deep breaths, her gaze never leaving the figures on the bed. But they didn't stir.

Slowly she turned and put her hands against the wall, using it for support as she stood.

Still no movement from the bed.

Sweat trickled down the side of her face. She turned around until her back was braced against the wall. Sick tension churned her stomach, but she ignored it, focusing instead on the padlock chaining the door closed. She lacked the time and energy for finesse; she hit the lock with all the psychic energy she could muster. It literally exploded, the noise reverberating around the room. She held her breath, her gaze locked on the figures on the bed.

Still no sign of movement. Maybe they were playing with her, toying with her hopes like a cat with a mouse. She had a sudden vision of reaching the door only to have Jasper reach out and grab her, destroying her last hope of freedom.

It would be the ultimate trick. Still, there was nothing she could do but take the risk.

Her legs were like rubber. Every step she took felt like a mile. She kept her gaze on Jasper and prayed he didn't move.

She reached the door and pushed it open. Beyond lay a steep flight of stairs. She had been held in a cellar of some kind.

Gripping the handrail, she dragged herself upward. The ache in her legs was agonizing, and it seemed to take her forever to reach the top. When she got to the final step, she collapsed, bruising her knees and battling to catch her breath.

After a few precious seconds, she rose and staggered on, finding herself in a kitchen. Dust covered the mess of broken cupboards, smashed windows and falling plasterboard time and vandals had caused. If the thickness of the dirt was any indication, the house had been abandoned for years.

Her hopes of quick rescue plummeted. But then it had been a very stupid hope. Why on earth would Jasper pick a hideout in the cellar of someone's home?

The chance of discovery would have been too great. She walked on, skirting shattered glass and smashed floorboards, seeking an exit. She had to hurry. Exhaustion was a huge wall threatening to topple her over.

In the next room she discovered her clothes and shoes, thrown haphazardly in a corner. Her cross wasn't among them—not that it was important right now. She stopped long enough to throw on her jacket and jeans, and slip on her shoes. The rest she left. Time was moving, and so must she.

Panic crept past her guard and filled her limbs with energy. She ran down the long hallway, no longer caring about the noise she made. The front door loomed before her—locked. She pushed with her kinetic energy. The door exploded outward with enough noise to wake the dead.

She felt the urge to laugh insanely, but suppressed it with an effort. Madness was no escape—and of no use to her now.

Her eyes watered against the sudden glare of bright sunlight. She threw up a hand to protect them and staggered on. It didn't really matter where she ran, as long as it was away from the house and its occupants.

Stones shifted under her feet. The harsh sound of traffic assaulted her ears. Blinking rapidly, she recognized shops, a mall packed with people. Safety. Jasper wouldn't find her in such a crowd. Wouldn't dare kidnap her with so many witnesses.

Wouldn't have to, when all he had to do was call her name . . .

Heart pounding unevenly, she ran, desperate to get

lost in the evening crowds and the safe oblivion they offered.

Dusk began to streak the sky. She reeled like a drunkard and smacked into an old man. His curse followed her as she staggered on. She had to keep going, had to escape, before Jasper came after her.

"Nikki!"

Her heart stopped. *Oh Lord, he'd found her!* Without looking back, she ran on. Somehow Jasper had found her. Terror lent her feet wings.

Nikki!

The shout reverberated through her. She bit back a cry of terror. He was after her. She had to keep running.

Stop! Nikki, watch it . . .

A screech of tires filled her ears. Too late she became aware of the road, the traffic and the red car.

She tried to dodge, but the car hit her. And oblivion swept in as agony exploded.

Ten

THE HEAVY RUMBLING of traffic woke her some time later. Nikki shifted slightly, and cotton rustled against her skin, bunching near her thigh. A faint scent clung to the material—warm, musty and recognizable. She smiled, wondering how she'd come to be wearing Michael's shirt.

She opened her eyes and studied the room. A lamp that had seen better days sat on the table to her right, its pale light washing across the smoke-stained blue walls. Paint peeled from the ceiling above her, and across the room sat a small brown dresser that looked as if it would be more at home in a Dumpster than a bedroom. It wasn't her room, or her dresser. Her heart skipped several beats. Where was she?

A hand rested lightly on hers, enclosing her fingers in warmth. Michael. She closed her eyes briefly and wished he'd take her in his arms, tell her it had all been a nightmare, that everything would be all right.

But he didn't move, and maybe that was just as well.

"What time is it?" she asked softly.

"About ten at night. You were unconscious for a while."

The weariness in his voice tore at her heart. She turned her head to meet his gaze, and even such a small movement caused pain. She bit her lip, fighting the sudden sting of tears.

"Gently, Nikki. Your hip and left leg were badly grazed by the car."

He sat in a chair next to the bed, bare feet propped up on the mattress. His midnight-colored hair was unkempt and in need of a wash, his face etched by deep lines of exhaustion. Though he looked relaxed, there was nothing remotely casual in the way he studied her. In the dark depths of his eyes, she could see all her secrets, all her fears. All that had happened.

She swallowed uneasily and looked away. "I guess I'm lucky I'm only grazed. How did you find me?"

"I followed your thoughts."

If her thoughts were so open to him, why didn't he tell her if Jasper's mind-bending techniques had succeeded or not? "How long was I gone?"

"Two nights."

It had seemed far longer. She shivered and rubbed her wrist. Though the two puncture wounds in her skin had healed, her flesh still burned. "Where are we?"

"My hotel room. Your injuries didn't warrant a hospital, and this place is safer anyway."

"No it isn't. Jasper's forged a connection to my thoughts, Michael. He can find me anywhere, anytime." And there wasn't a damn thing she could do to stop him.

"I know." Michael's voice was calm as he shifted his feet and rose, but something in the way he moved spoke of violence. "He cannot get into this room. I've taken precautions."

She raised an eyebrow. "What sort?"

He hesitated. "Let's just say I'm friends with an old witch who has forgotten more about vampires than anyone else actually knows."

Given his closed expression, he wasn't about to tell her anything else about said witch. A thought he all but confirmed by adding, "How are you feeling?"

"Surprisingly enough, like I've been hit by a car." She watched him pour water into a glass. His clothes were disheveled and creased, as if he hadn't slept in days.

She wanted to reach out and caress the tautness from his shoulders, kiss the tension from his lips. Instead, she clenched her fists against the blanket. Was she insane? She wanted to touch a vampire in ways she'd never wanted to touch a man before . . .

"Michael, why didn't you tell me?" she whispered, ignoring the glass of water he held out to her.

The muscles along his arms went taut, momentarily straining against the restriction of his rolled-up sleeves. He slowly lowered the glass to the bedside table.

"I'm sorry, Nikki . . ." He hesitated and shrugged, avoiding her gaze. "I never meant for you to find out this way."

"Did you ever plan for me to find out at all?"

Again he hesitated, then, quietly, "I don't know."

At least he was being honest. And if she was being honest with herself, she had never, at any stage, truly feared him. Just the darkness within him, the darkness she now could name.

A darkness he would never be free of.

He held out the glass again and her hand shook as she accepted it from him, brought it to her lips. The cool water did little to ease the fire in her throat.

"I would never hurt you, Nikki."

She met his dark gaze and tried to ignore the trembling deep in her soul. She could understand him not telling her immediately, but surely he should have once they'd gotten deeper into the case. By not doing so, he'd only emphasized the fact that he didn't trust her. And that hurt more than anything Jasper could ever do to her.

Michael sat back in his chair, fingers entwined lightly in his lap. "There are things about me that you'll never know, Nikki. It's safer that way—for you, and for me. Trust me."

"Trust you?" She couldn't help a slightly bitter laugh. "Dear God, Michael, I've trusted you more from the very beginning than I've trusted anyone in my entire life!"

"And yet, deep down, you still fear me." His gaze met hers, reached deep into her soul. "I have never lied to you, Nikki."

"No." Her voice was terse. "You haven't. You just ask me to do what you cannot, or feed me half truths when it suits you."

He slapped his hands hard against the arms of the chair and thrust himself upright. "And would it have made any difference if I told you the complete truth? Would it have stopped you from entering that tunnel after Monica?"

"No." She watched him walk across to a small alcove that held an ancient-looking coffee percolator and a take-out container. "But there's still more you're not telling me. Who sent you here? Are you the only hunter working for them?"

He glanced around, one eyebrow raised. "No, I'm not. But my fellow hunters aren't important, not at the moment."

They might not be important, but the mere fact he didn't trust her with the information was. Did he fear Jasper's influence, or was there something more? "Yeah. Like you being a vampire wasn't important?"

"No, not like that." He took a mug from the bed-side table. "Are you hungry?"

Her stomach rolled at the thought of food. Considering how little she'd eaten during the last few days, she should be famished. She wasn't. "As long as it's something easy."

"I ordered in some soup."

Which was obviously what was in the take-out container. She nodded and closed her eyes, suddenly confused. How much did her need to fight with Michael come from Jasper? Would she end up betraying Michael, no matter how hard she tried not to?

"The mere fact you ask yourself those questions suggests his plan hasn't entirely worked."

Michael walked back to the bed and placed the steaming mug of soup on the bedside table. She sat up but ignored it. "But what happens if I *do* betray you?"

"We'll deal with that if and when it happens." He sat beside her on the bed and placed an arm around her shoulders. She leaned into him, savoring the warmth of his body.

"Unfortunately, we can't undo what's been done. You fight it, Nikki."

"And if I can't?" She rested her cheek lightly against his shoulder and tried to ignore the gentle strength with which he held her. Lord, it felt so right . . .

"Then we're all in trouble."

The grimness in his voice made her shiver. What would he do if she ever *did* betray him? Would he kill her, the same as he intended to kill Monica?

"Monica has to die because she's an out-of-control fledgling. You betraying me is hardly the same thing." His voice held a slightly bitter edge that pierced her heart. "When will you realize I would never hurt you?"

"I'm sorry." She bit her lip, regretting her thoughts the minute his arm left her shoulders. His touch had temporarily eased the tight knot of fear in the pit of her stomach.

He rose and retrieved the mug, handing it to her handle first. "Finish it. You need to get some nourishment back into your system. Give me a call if you want anything else."

"A call? Why? Where are you going?" She hated the slight edge in her voice, yet the thought of being alone filled her with fear.

"Nowhere. But it's been a long three days, I'm afraid."

Had he . . . eaten?

"I haven't." His answer was grim. "Do you think it was easy for me, knowing who had you? Imagining what he was doing?"

"I'm sorry." She hesitated, not sure what else to say, not sure how to take the touch of pain in his eyes. "How did you find me? Why were you even awake? I thought vampires had no choice but to sleep during the day."

"It was dusk, not daylight, when we found you. But everyone must sleep, Nikki, even those of us not quite human. Vampires do so during the day because, for the most part, the sun is deadly to us, not because our bodies literally shut down."

She remembered the sun touching Jasper's back, and the red welts it left there. "And feeding?" she asked softly, not really sure if she wanted to know the answer.

"I do not dine on human blood. Nor do I need to feed every day, as younger vampires like Jasper and Monica must." He hesitated, then added in a voice heavy with bitterness. "After three hundred years of existence, you learn to do without many things."

She blinked. Had she heard him right? He was *three hundred* years old?

"Yes." He sighed, and ran a hand through his unkempt hair. "Now eat, and rest. I'll be near if you need me."

He retreated to the chair near the window, and was quickly lost in the shadows of the room. Even though he was little more than ten feet away, it felt like a mile. Frowning, she ate the soup he'd given her, without really tasting it. When she'd finished, she placed the mug back on the bedside table and—though she wasn't tired—closed her eyes, determined to get some more rest. She had a bad feeling she wouldn't be able to later.

Her sleep was scrappy, though, and her dreams were filled with fear and madness, haunted by an evil that teased and mocked her. She woke to darkness a few hours later, her shirt twisted about her body and damp with sweat. Blinking the sleep from her eyes, she stared at the darkened room.

Something about the stillness told her she was alone, and her heart skipped several beats. But being alone wasn't what she feared. No, there was something else . . .

Like a siren's song, the call whispered through her mind, urging her to action.

Frightened, yet unable to resist, she threw aside the blankets and rose. Walking unsteadily to the windows across the room, she pushed the curtains open and stared out.

Darkness held the city in its grip. Somewhere down the street a clock tower chimed four times, and the street below was silent, empty.

Then the shadows moved.

Jasper. Smiling confidently at her, sure of her response.

Come to me.

Something deep within responded, wanting to do as he asked. She closed her eyes—fighting it, fighting him.

It's too late to fight. You are mine.

Never. I'll kill myself first.

His laughter sang through her soul, filling her with its corruption. Trembling, her heart beating so rapidly it felt as if it was going to tear out of her chest, she crossed her arms and turned from the window. It didn't stop the treacherous feeling of wanting to do whatever he asked. She took a deep breath, trying to gather her scattered wits. *Michael, where are you? I need you.*

What if he couldn't hear her silent plea for help? Well, she wasn't helpless, no matter what the demons in her mind might say.

Do not ignore me, pretty one.

She shivered, and battled for calm and the strength to resist as she returned to the window. *Where's Monica?*

Hunting us up something to eat.

Images filled Nikki's mind—visions hot with lust and violence. Her pulse quickened, as if stirred, and she blanched, feeling sick. Lord, why was this happening? What had he done to her?

You will beg me, pretty one. As Monica begged me.

He wanted her to hunt the night with him, become a slave to darkness and death and uncontrollable bloodlust. Revulsion turned her stomach. *I will never walk with you.*

Yet she could hear the uncertainty in her own assertion. Jasper was Tommy, only a hundred times stronger. If he gained control of her mind, she would never be able to distinguish her wish from his.

Never is a long time in my world. And I grow tired of Monica.

Why did you turn her?

As I have said previously, she has something I desire. Once her father is dead, she will inherit it all.

She shuddered. *Michael will stop you.*

As he protected you? Jasper's laughter echoed through her mind. *Really, my pretty, you should know better now.*

She clenched her fists, battling the urge to run as far as she could from the madman below. She was safe in this room. Michael had assured her of that.

Jasper was only toying with her, testing her nerve. And it took all the strength she had to remain still, to ignore his taunting whispers, to stare at him in silence.

Michael took the stairs two at a time, making no effort to keep quiet. Jasper had made little effort to conceal himself, and he would know that Nikki had called out to Michael. Just as Michael knew the zombies stationed around the hotel—five in total now, meaning Jasper had killed again last night—would move in on Nikki if he went after Jasper. Why they hadn't while Michael was absent from her, he couldn't say, although he suspected Jasper was merely playing games. Toying with his prey before he made his final, deadly assault.

He reached the third floor and ran down the corridor, only slowing when he approached his room. Even from this distance, he could feel her distress. Yet she resisted Jasper's call, which was more than Michael had truly expected.

He unlocked the door and stepped inside. Psychic energy danced around him, though he doubted if she was aware of his presence yet. She was using everything she had to resist Jasper. He clenched his fingers and took a deep, calming breath. Now was not the time to run downstairs and commit murder—however much he might want to. Not when the zombies were nearby and waiting. Nikki needed him.

She stood near the window, still wearing his old black shirt. It hung to her thighs and did little to hide her slender but shapely figure. He had never seen her look more alluring. Or more frightened.

"Nikki?" he said softly, not wanting to scare her by suddenly appearing by her side.

She jumped anyway and turned. "He's here." Her voice was steady despite the panic he could see in her eyes. "Across the road."

Michael stopped beside her and slid his hand down her arm, entwining his fingers with hers. The rhythm of her heart was loud and erratic, and her hands were like ice. He looked out.

Jasper waved at them.

Anger spurted through him. He clamped down on it, hard. "He's an arrogant bastard."

She swallowed. "He's calling me, Michael. He wants me to go to him."

"I know." He was really going to enjoy killing this bastard. "He's only testing you, Nikki. And, thankfully, now he knows his leash is not as strong as he had hoped."

But Jasper had yet to unleash his full power. Michael knew it, and she did, too. He could taste the fear in her thoughts.

"Why don't you go down there after him?" she asked.

Because he wants you dead, and the zombies are ready to complete the task should I leave your side. But he kept *that* thought to himself. "I wanted to make sure you were all right first."

"But why not go down now?"

"Because he won't be there anymore. He's just trying to unnerve you, Nikki."

"It's working." She untangled her fingers from his

and wrapped her arms around her body. Though he wished he could hold her, give her the comfort she seemed to want, he didn't dare move. Jasper still watched them. "He can't hurt you unless you let him. You have your abilities, Nikki. Use them to protect yourself."

She had to get past her fear. He couldn't be with her twenty-four hours a day. Besides, the best way to protect her was to kill Jasper. To do that, he would have to leave her alone.

She gave him a quick glance, and he wondered if this time she'd heard the thought. With the link between them growing stronger by the day, it was becoming increasingly hard to keep his thoughts to himself.

"He's leaving," she stated quietly.

Michael looked out the window and watched Jasper fade into the darkness, saw the blur of his body heat move quickly up the street. With dawn only a few hours away, he'd be off to hunt before retreating for the day into a dark space. No doubt there would be more murders for the *Lyndhurst Mail* to report to its troubled readers. Of course, they'd be even more troubled if they actually knew the dead were being raised and were roaming around Lyndhurst's streets.

He turned and drew her into his arms. She felt so soft and warm against him. He brushed a kiss against the top of her head and held her quietly until her tremors stopped.

"Thank you," she whispered, pulling away slightly.

Her eyes were bright, but not with fear. He could hear the unsteady pounding of her heart and knew its rhythm matched his own.

He raised a hand, gently brushing a dark strand of hair away from her cheek. Her skin was like silk under his fingers. He traced the outline of her jaw, then lightly brushed her lips. He wished he could taste their fullness, but that wouldn't be fair. Not when she was so frightened and Jasper remained free, trying to control her.

"You should rest," he said, seeing the sparkle in her amber eyes, watching the heat rise in her cheeks. God, she was beautiful.

"I've been asleep, Michael," she said softly. "What I want is for you to make love to me."

He studied her, noting the hint of desperation in her eyes, the fear in her thoughts. While he couldn't deny the attraction flaring between them, he also knew it had nothing to do with her sudden desire to make love. In any other situation, any other time, he might have taken what she offered, enjoyed her company until the job was done, and left, as he had with other women in the past. But he didn't want that with Nikki, and certainly not for the reason he could see in her thoughts. Somehow, it just didn't seem right to make love to her just so she could erase Jasper's taunts from her mind.

But damn, she felt so good in his arms . . .

He lowered his head and kissed her. He'd meant it to be brief, but her lips were soft and sweet under his, and he found himself wanting more. Her hand brushed his cheek as she moved it around to his neck, and he closed his eyes, pulling her closer, teasing her lips with his tongue. She made a sound that was almost a sigh, and opened her mouth, allowing him deeper access. He moved his hands down her back and cupped her buttocks, holding her softness against him.

He didn't want the moment to end, but knew it had to. No involvement, he reminded himself sharply. Lifting his lips from hers, he kissed her forehead lightly, and then rested his own against it.

"I can't do this, Nikki." Because Seline was right. He was playing for far more than usual with this case, and it wasn't just Nikki's life that was at stake. He had a suspicion that if he got involved with her sexually, it would start a fire he'd never want to put out. "It's not the right time."

A slight smile touched her warm lips. "It felt pretty right to me."

It had felt pretty right to him, too, and that was the problem. "I'm a vampire, Nikki. It's a fact that can never be changed. I live in a world of darkness, and tread paths no human can ever take." He hesitated, seeing her amber eyes darken. "I have made love to many women in my time, but they were little more than fleeting moments of pleasure. There can never be anything more for me. Vampires cannot love."

The lie tasted bitter on his tongue. But it was better she think him incapable of love. It would make things easier when he walked away.

"I'm not asking for anything more than one night, Michael." Her gaze searched his for a moment. "I don't want anything more."

Maybe she didn't, he thought, studying the dark auburn highlights in her hair. But could he hold her in his arms, make love to her, then simply walk away?

"Making love will strengthen the link between us,

Nikki," he said softly. "Can you risk that when you fear it almost as much as you fear the vampire?"

She glanced up sharply. "I don't fear you."

He smiled grimly. "No. You fear the darkness in me—the vampire. But I am not two beings, Nikki, so you cannot fear one side of me without fearing the other."

She closed her eyes and took a deep breath. "I don't care about the technicalities, Michael. I just want—"

Footsteps echoed in the corridor beyond the room. Someone was approaching the room. He placed a finger against her lips, quickly silencing her, and watched the heat of life get closer. After a moment, he relaxed. It was only Jake.

And just in the nick of time, too.

Smiling wryly, he glanced at Nikki. "Jake's here. And he's angry about something."

"How can you tell?" She rubbed her hands up and down her arms, a gesture that spoke of the fear he could see in her thoughts.

"His heart is racing, and fury runs through his thoughts."

"Something's happened."

He entwined his fingers with hers and squeezed them lightly. She smiled, then motioned him toward the door when Jake knocked.

Jake's gaze swept her. "Good to see you up and about."

"Thanks, but you didn't come all this way to check me out."

"No." His smile was anything but warm. "Have you heard the news?"

"No." It wasn't too hard to guess what had happened, though. Michael stepped aside, allowing Jake to enter. "Why?"

"Our vampires are active again. There's been a triple murder in Highgate Park."

Given Jasper had been here until a few moments ago, the murders had to be Monica's doing. Which at least meant Jasper couldn't raise the victims. "When did this happen?"

"About an hour ago." Jake grimaced and walked over to the small percolator. "The cops are still crawling all over the scene."

"You've been there?" Nikki said, surprise in her voice.

"No. I asked Mark to let me know if anything like this happened." He glanced across at Michael and added, "Mark's the crime reporter at the *Mail*."

"The bodies are still there?" Nikki asked.

Jake's eyebrows rose. "Why would you . . . oh. Zombies."

"It's not like we need more of them."

But more of them was what they'd get, Michael thought. With the cops crawling all over the crime scene, Jasper would be forced to feed elsewhere. But he'd call them back from the grave later, strengthening the numbers of his undead army.

"We have to stop Monica," Nikki stated. "And not just because she's a murdering bitch. Jasper wants Trevgard's fortune."

Jake frowned. "Why would a vampire want all that money?"

"Money is power," Michael said. "And that's what Jasper wants—what he's always wanted. Up until now, he's achieved it through stealing the psychic energy of others. Now, it seems, he plans to do it through money." He studied Nikki for a moment, and her expression became defiant. She knew what he was about to say, and didn't like it; he said it anyway. "Jake and I will hunt her. But you need to stay away from it."

"You can't find her without me."

Maybe they could, and maybe they couldn't. It wasn't worth jeopardizing her safety to find out.

"You'll slow us down," Jake commented into the brief silence. "You're a liability, Nik. Trying to protect you might well get us all killed."

"We'll be moving in the daylight. We'll have the advantage, remember?"

"Zombies have no problem getting around during the day." It wasn't exactly a lie. Zombies *were* mobile. It was just they were more like insects, acting on instinct rather than any rational mode of thought when Jasper was in deep sleep. Still, they certainly were more than capable of defending the bastard. However, if Michael admitted as much, he'd have no chance of convincing Nikki to stay behind. "And Jasper has proven he can move around more than just at dawn or dusk."

She lifted her chin, looking stubborn, determined, though he could hear the unsteady pounding of her pulse. "I'm going. I refuse to let fear rule my life."

Or anything, or anyone, else. He clamped down on a surge of anger and glanced at his watch. "It's past four now. We'll have to give it a few more hours before we move. That way we'll be sure to find them asleep—if we find them."

Jake frowned as he poured some soup—which was

undoubtedly cold by now—into two coffee cups. "And you? Won't you be affected?"

Nikki raised an eyebrow, looking calm when she was anything but. Even from where he stood, Michael felt the surge of her anger. It ranged through his mind like a sudden summer storm, and left an uneasy sense of guilt in its wake.

"You told Jake," she said, her voice flat. "But not me?"

"I had to explain why I couldn't—"

"*That,*" she said, cutting him off, "is nothing more than an excuse."

Perhaps it was. Perhaps he *should* have told her. But he couldn't change the past, so there was no point arguing about it. He glanced at Jake and said, "As long as we avoid the sun between ten and two, I'll be fine."

Jake handed a mug to Nikki. "I'll be back here at eight, then. That way, we'll have two hours to hunt. Nice soup, by the way."

Michael walked him to the door. Jake turned the handle, and hesitated. "Don't let her come with us," he said softly.

Michael raised an eyebrow. "You know I can't stop her."

"Find a way. I don't care how. Just don't let that madman get his hands on her again."

This from the man who had basically admitted it was nigh on impossible to get Nikki to do anything she didn't want to do. But Michael nodded and closed the door behind Jake, then turned to find her watching him. Her knuckles were almost white against her soup cup. She expected a fight from him. Maybe even wanted one.

He took a different tack. "If you intend on coming with us, you'd better get some rest. Jake was right. In your current condition, you'll slow us down."

Her eyebrows rose in surprise, and he smiled grimly. "I don't intend to argue the point any more. If you want to commit suicide, who am I to stop you?"

Anger glinted in her eyes, but all she said was, "I've slept enough. I don't need any more."

"*I do,* though, and I can't if you're going to stand there glaring at me. So, please, at least get into bed and either watch the TV or read the newspaper."

Her expression was mutinous, but she did little more than place the soup down and pick up the remote. The TV came on, the noise sharp against the silence.

"Do you need anything else?" he asked. Their thoughts touched briefly, and passion caressed his mind. He tensed and quickly broke the contact.

She sighed. "No."

"Wake me if you do." He ran his fingers through his hair and turned, walking to the chair. He slept, but it wasn't restful, because his dreams were filled with the fire of her touch.

Eleven

"NIKKI, LET IT go. Break the connection." The soft words speared the madness assaulting her mind. She shuddered and fought the shadows, desperate to reach the safety of Michael's voice.

Warm hands touched her face, caressed her cheeks. The demons laughed raucously, but retreated.

"Nikki?"

She blinked, and realized she was sitting up in bed. The TV still blared, and the coffee she'd made herself sat untouched on the beside table. Jasper must have attacked her not long after she'd made it . . . Her gaze met Michael's. He sat on the edge of the bed, his dark eyes full of compassion and a certain amount of wariness. He reached for the remote and turned off the TV.

"Hold me," she whispered, pushing the blankets aside and struggling upright. "Please, just hold me."

He drew her into his arms. She leaned a cheek against the bare warmth of his chest, allowing the heat of his touch to chase the chill away. Allowed the tender caress of his thoughts to chase the last strands of darkness from her mind.

"You have to fight him, Nikki."

"How?" Her voice cracked slightly, and she bit her lip. How could she fight Jasper when she'd never been able to fight Tommy? Jasper's evil was far more intense than Tommy's ever had been.

But she'd survived Tommy, and she'd survived three nights of Jasper's insanity. She'd survive this—any way she could.

Michael held her silently, the rock to which she clung in the ever-turbulent currents of her life. Gradually, almost unwillingly, she became aware of his scent, musky yet fresh; aware of the slight tension in the arms that held her so gently. She could hear his heart pounding as erratically as her own. She lifted her head and met his gaze. His smile made *her* heart do an odd little somersault.

He gently touched her cheek, then ran his fingers over her lips. "I want you to know, Nikki, *not* making love to you is the hardest thing I've ever had to do."

Her pulse leaped beneath his touch. She kissed his fingers, and with her own traced the firm line of his jaw. "I don't want your restraint, Michael. I want you."

Just touch me. Hold me. Love me. She bit her lip and looked away from the understanding in his eyes. What she was doing wasn't fair, but she couldn't think of any other way to drive Jasper from her thoughts. Was it too much to ask for just an hour, maybe two, without Jasper's darkness staining her mind?

He sighed and closed his eyes. Fighting the needs of his body, she thought. It was a battle she didn't want him to win.

Leaning forward, she captured his lips with hers.

He groaned and tightened his arms around her, his lips suddenly harsh.

Then he pulled away. "Don't do this, Nikki." His voice was ragged, his dark eyes troubled.

"Why not?" What was wrong with wanting to kiss him, make love to him, until the darkness that was Jasper's presence in her mind was erased and there was nothing but the two of them alone? Couldn't he see she needed this, needed to keep the insanity at bay?

"Nikki, it's wrong."

She raised an eyebrow. "Why?"

He didn't answer. She trailed tiny kisses up his neck, and gently bit his earlobe. He made no move to stop her, no move to encourage her, yet she could feel the tension under her fingers and wondered what, truly, he was so afraid of. Vampires might not be able to love, but they *could* make love, and that was all she was asking of him.

She ran her hand down the warm length of his body until she touched the waistband of his jeans. Fingers trembling, she slowly undid his fly.

"Nikki . . ." He hesitated, his body tensing as she touched him. "This isn't right . . ."

She closed her eyes and briefly rested her forehead on his shoulder. He was correct. This certainly *wasn't* the right time nor the place for them to make love. But what other choice did she have? She had to stop the stain of Jasper's darkness growing stronger in her mind.

"Please, Michael. Just make love to me."

He groaned again and crushed her to him. She kissed him fiercely, savoring the taste of his lips, his mouth. He caressed her breasts, her stomach, her buttocks, his hands gentle yet his touch urgent, setting her aflame with need. She reveled in the play of muscles across his shoulders, the feel of his skin, so smooth and warm against hers.

"Lay down with me," she said softly.

And, at last, he did.

Surrendering, finally, to his desires, Michael ran a hand down the gentle curve of her side, watching the desire darken her amber eyes. Yet he could also feel the desperation in her thoughts, the urgent need to deny Jasper's control over her. Michael touched her cheek, following the outline of her jaw. Her skin was soft and smelled so good, like honey and cinnamon. She captured his finger with her mouth and sucked on it gently. Heat ran through him—a smoldering fire threatening to explode.

There was no denying the strength of his desire for her. He might have been a three-hundred-year-old vampire but, in some ways, he was still very human.

"I cannot offer you anything more than this moment, Nikki." Not the words any woman wanted to hear, by any stretch of the imagination.

Her dark amber gaze met his, and he accepted that she wanted nothing more than this moment—that all she cared about was time without Jasper's intrusion in her thoughts.

And it hurt somehow, though God knew it shouldn't have. She was simply using him in the same manner he'd used scores of other women during his life.

At least he would have the memory of loving her in the long nights of loneliness left ahead.

"Good." Though her voice was light, there was an edge that made him wonder if she'd heard his thoughts. "Because if you had stopped right now, I would've killed you."

He touched her lips and ran his finger lightly down her neck to her breast. "The only thing likely to stop me now is you."

"Then quit talking," she murmured.

Power shivered between them, a gossamer touch that slowly tugged his jeans from his body. He laughed against her lips, and pulled away slightly. Using his own kinetic abilities, he eased the shirt up and over her head and tossed it across the room.

"Now I know what romance novels mean when they say he undressed her with his mind," she teased.

Though her smile was easy, he saw fear flicker deep in her eyes. She'd remembered what he was, what he was capable of—and yet he knew she wouldn't stop. Her fear of Jasper was far greater than any fear she had of him. There was only one way Michael could convince her he'd never harm her, particularly at a moment like this, and that was to make love to her with every part of himself—body *and* mind. So he kissed her, savoring the sweetness of her lips as he drew her closer. Their minds entwined in a gentle dance of fire, sharing each sensation, each emotion.

The link between them was drawing tighter, but at that moment he didn't care. He had Nikki in his arms and it was all that mattered now. He touched her, caressed her, explored her body until he knew every inch of it intimately, until she was moaning and squirming under his touch and the heat of her desire burned through their connection, setting him aflame in ways nothing ever had before. God, it was incredible. *She* was incredible.

"I need you," he whispered. Needed to feel her lithe, wonderful body underneath him, needed to lose himself within the heat of her. Become, for just a moment, nothing more than a man loving a woman. He held her tightly, breathing in the scent of her hair as he battled the urgency pounding through his body, his heart.

"Then take me," she murmured, her hands trailing down his back, igniting fires wherever she touched.

She felt so good, so right. How in the hell was he going to walk away from this? How could he deny the harmony of their minds? How could either of them?

Nikki ran a hand through his hair. "Hush, Michael. Just love me. Let tomorrow worry about itself."

Tomorrow was something he *didn't* want to think about. Not when everything felt so perfect right now. He shifted position, gently nudged her knees apart, and slowly slid into her. She groaned—a sound he could only echo. He held himself still as her muscles clenched around him, wanting to enjoy the moment, to make it last. She groaned again and clasped his face, kissing him fiercely as she began to move underneath him. He had no choice but to move with her, slowly at first, then faster, and faster, until her moans became a gasp and she was shaking and shuddering underneath him. Only then did he give in to his own needs and finally, completely, lost himself within her.

* * *

Michael gently caressed Nikki's thigh. Lord, it felt so good, lying here beside her in the warm aftermath of their lovemaking. Her thoughts were as quiet as the gentle rhythm of her heart. As much as he wanted nothing more than to extend and enjoy this moment, he couldn't. If she was to have any hope of breaking Jasper's link to her mind, she had to confront what had happened in her past. Until she did, Jasper would continue to use the guilt she felt over her part in those events against her.

"Nikki, we need to talk," he said softly. He brushed some silken strands of hair away from her face.

Her eyes opened, and a smile twitched the corners of her mouth. Only the sudden wisp of wariness in her thoughts had him resisting the impulse to kiss her.

"I gather vampires are immune to the make-love-then-collapse syndrome that seems to affect so many men."

"No, they're not. I'm not." He would have liked nothing more than to fall to sleep with her in his arms. But Jasper was out there, and Jake would be here soon. "Nikki, we have to talk."

"What about?" A flicker of guilt ran through her thoughts, and he wondered if she was already regretting their lovemaking.

"Tommy."

It was not what she'd expected, and her thoughts were suddenly chaotic. "Why?"

"Jasper's using your guilt against you, Nikki. He's using past demons to grind down your resistance."

She tensed. "What do you mean?"

But she knew what he meant. He could see the images in her mind, skittering like scared rabbits. "It's time you faced the past, let go of the guilt."

She was silent for a long moment. Michael held her gently, listening to the beat of her heart—a rhythm filled with jagged fear.

"Tommy has nothing to do with any of this," she muttered finally. Heat crept up her cheeks and she looked away. "And you've no right to ask."

And no right to care. It was a thought that tasted bitter. He ignored it. One way or another, she had to face the guilt centered around that part of her past, or she would have very little hope of resisting Jasper's final call. In many ways, Jasper represented the darker side of human existence, and guilt was part of that darkness. It drew her into Jasper's sphere of influence, made it all that much easier for him to attack her mind.

"Jasper wouldn't use Tommy's memory if he didn't think it would help break your spirit, Nikki. It's time you told someone what happened."

Her face was as pale as the tangled sheets beneath them. "If I tell you, will you promise never to bring the subject up again?"

"Yes." It was an easy thing to promise, given he had no intention of staying around. He might have the *desire* to stay, but desire was something he rarely succumbed to.

Tonight had been a miraculous exception.

She stared at the ceiling. "I met Tommy several months after my mom's death. I was pretty messed up at the time, and on the run. My grandparents

wouldn't take me in, and I didn't like the other options." She hesitated, and shrugged. "Tommy led the
street gang I started running with."

No wonder she'd empathized with Monica. While
their family situations were completely different,
they'd both been young and confused, with no one
listening to what they wanted. An easy target for evil.
Though why she thought Tommy was in the same
league as Jasper, Michael couldn't say.

"How did you meet him?"

She licked her lips. "I was in a store his gang was
robbing. One of the kids was bashing the old guy at
the register, and I stopped him."

"Kinetically?"

She nodded. "It was the first time it happened. Up
until that moment, I'd been able to move small things
around, but little else."

"How old were you?"

"Fourteen."

And in the midst of puberty, no doubt. Most talents didn't fully manifest before then. Add the fact
that not only had she been fourteen when her mom
had died, but unwanted by anyone else in her family,
and it was no wonder she'd been pretty messed up.

And in many respects, still was.

Michael might not be able to stay here with her and
share his dreams or his heart, but he could give her
peace. *If* he could keep her talking. "What happened?"

"Tommy happened. He swung around and our
gazes met." She hesitated, then shrugged. "I know it
sounds corny, but at the time, it felt like I'd just met

my destiny. He was gifted, like me, and seemed to know I needed help."

More than likely he'd seen the potential of her abilities and had known the power that one day would be hers. And had wanted it, as Jasper did. Michael clenched his fists. Nikki glanced at him, and he forced himself to relax. "So you joined his gang?"

She nodded. "He was good to me, at least at first. He taught me how to survive the streets, taught me how to control and use my gifts."

Pain swirled around him, a gossamer veil he could almost touch. "When did it all change?" Though he could see the answer in her thoughts clearly enough, he wanted her to talk about it. Maybe then she would see that Tommy hadn't been the savior she thought him to be. The bastard had done little more than take advantage of a frightened young girl.

"When I turned fifteen." She shuddered, and he had to resist the urge to hold her close and caress all the hurt away. "Everything changed. He became possessive, never letting me out of his sight. Sometimes it felt as if he was in my mind, governing my thoughts, my actions."

If Tommy's telepathy had been as strong as she seemed to think, that was probably just what he'd been doing. Fifteen years old and barely in control of her gifts, she would have had little resistance when it came to subtle mind merging. He clenched his fists again, and slowly straightened them out. Tommy was dead, and there was nothing Michael could do about the past—other than help her through the pain of it.

"When did this extend to trying to control your gifts?"

Her gaze jerked to his. "How did you know?"

He grimaced. "It wasn't hard to guess, given your reaction to our link."

Her gaze skittered away, but her thoughts were clear enough. She still wasn't comfortable with the link, still wasn't comfortable with him. Maybe she never would be. Attraction or not, it was only the thought of stopping Jasper from invading her mind that kept her on the bed with him right now, kept her talking.

At least he had something to thank Jasper for.

"What happened?" he asked again, softly.

Fear shimmered through the link. "Tommy gave me a ring for my next birthday. He told me he loved me." She hesitated and swallowed. "What did I know of love? He was my world, all that I'd had since my mom's death. But maybe he could see the doubts, because he asked me to prove what I felt for him."

"How?" The question came out more abruptly than he'd intended, and she looked up quickly. He forced a smile, though it was the last thing he felt like doing. "What did he ask you to do?"

"Merge minds. Even though I sometimes feared him, and what he could do, I actually saw no harm in it. It was something we'd been practicing for a while." She shuddered. "Only this time it was deeper. This time it was complete."

He could see the chaotic results in her mind. Her gifts, controlled by Tommy, had been used for violence. No wonder she now feared any sort of mind link.

"What did you do?"

"What could I do?" Her question was almost a plea. For an instant she was very much a confused and frightened teenager, not a twenty-five-year-old woman. "I was sixteen years old and had no one I could turn to for help. Not that Tommy would have let me. He knew my thoughts, and he could make me do things . . ." She paused, and a tear ran down her cheek.

The first crack in the wall, Michael thought, resisting the urge to wipe the tear away. It wasn't over yet. She had to face the destruction she'd unwillingly caused.

"What sort of things?"

She wouldn't look at him. He placed a finger under her chin and gently tilted her face upward. "What did you do, Nikki?" he said, closing his heart to the pain in her eyes.

"Tommy pulled a bank robbery, and it went wrong." She jerked away from Michael's touch and dashed the tears from her eyes. "I'd refused to take part in it, and for some reason Tommy hadn't been able to make me. Instead, I waited a block away with a getaway car. The police had received a tip and were waiting at the bank."

Which didn't explain the pain he could almost taste. "What happened, Nikki?"

"Tommy escaped, and the cops and security guards chased him. He came straight to me. He used my gifts to . . . to . . ."

She hesitated again, and more tears ran down her cheeks. He made no move, though he ached to comfort her.

She took a deep breath. "He used my kinetic abilities to destroy several police cars. He threw one of the security guards through a store window. The falling glass cut the guard's throat. Another is now in a wheelchair as a result of Tommy throwing him into a wall. I couldn't stop him, Michael. I fought so hard, but I just couldn't stop him."

That's why she'd made him vow never to make her do anything against her will. A sob escaped her control, and he drew her close. At least she was finally letting go of the pain she'd held in for so long. But he knew it wasn't over yet. "How did you escape the police, Nikki?"

She laughed—a bitter, brittle sound that made him wince. "I didn't. Tommy escaped. They told me later that I'd been lucky he hadn't grabbed me as a hostage. They never knew it was me who killed that guard . . ."

"If one man uses a gun to kill another, you blame the man who pulled the trigger, not the weapon, Nikki." And that's what she'd been, a weapon. She sniffed back her tears, but wasn't ready to let go of the past just yet. "How did Tommy die?"

"The streets caught up with him. His violence had made him a lot of enemies, and in the end, it came back to him."

Then why did she feel so guilty about his death?

She shifted in his arms, resting her cheek against his shoulder. The warmth of her skin burned into him. He fleetingly wished they could just stay here, on this bed, and forget about everything but each other.

"Because I dreamed it was going to happen," she whispered, "and I didn't tell him."

She was reading his thoughts as clearly as he was reading hers, he realized suddenly. And link or not, she shouldn't be able to. But he couldn't think about that now—there was more Nikki needed to release.

"Why not?" he asked, knowing that in the same situation, he would have wished the fiend to hell and laughed as he died.

But Nikki didn't have three hundred years of weariness behind her.

"*Oh God . . .*" Her hand clenched against his. "I told him that I hated him. I told him he could burn in hell for all I cared. Ten hours later he was dead. I felt his soul leave his body, Michael. I felt it encased in the fires of hell. I could have stopped it, but I didn't. Just as I didn't stop my mom's death. They both died because of me."

She'd seen her mom's death? Why hadn't she warned her? Surely not out of hate. She had loved her; that much was clear. "Tommy's soul was cursed long before you came along, Nikki. You did nothing more than trust the wrong man."

"But he was good to me. He cared for me."

Michael was pretty sure the only person Tommy had cared about was himself. But he knew Nikki wasn't ready yet to face that. "He only wanted to make you trust him, make you need him. Where Jasper has tried force and drugs to subvert your will, Tommy used your emotions."

"I did love him."

Yet even as she whispered the words, there was doubt in her thoughts. It told him that, for the first time in years, she was looking past her fear and truly seeing the man Tommy had been.

"He didn't die because of that love, Nikki." He

hesitated, then added, "He was a vicious thug who got what he deserved."

"Maybe. But there's still my mom."

Three hours ago she wouldn't have confided this much. And yet he sensed it wasn't so much trust as the need to finally purge her demons. Perhaps she saw the necessity as much as he did. "Want to tell me about it?"

"No." She took a deep, somewhat shuddery breath. "She was going away without me, taking off on a vacation with her new boyfriend and leaving me in the care of a nanny. I was so furious with her. So when I had the dream, I didn't tell her."

"You were a kid, Nikki. All kids do horrible things at one time or another."

"Not all kids watch their mom die. Not all kids feel the caress of their mother's soul as she passes away."

Which was surely punishment enough for her childish rush of spitefulness. "Would your mom have believed you even if you'd told her about the dream? Would it have stopped her from going?"

"Mom was gifted herself, remember. I think she would have listened."

"Fate has a way of getting her own way, no matter what you do, or who you try to save. I've lived long enough to be certain of that, if nothing else."

"That isn't an excuse for not trying." But even as she said it, there was an odd mix of uncertainty and acceptance in her eyes.

He smiled and brushed that stray strand of hair off her face again. For now, that mix was enough. At least she'd seen beyond her guilt and released some of her pent-up pain.

The deaths in her past would no longer be a weapon Jasper could use. It might not be much, but it was a start.

She gently touched the silver cross resting on his chest. "Where did you find it?"

"In the tunnel." He placed his hand over hers, pressing her fingers to the flesh above his heart. "Do you want it back?"

She hesitated, then shook his head. "No. Keep it . . . if you want."

He did want. It was a small piece of her he could take with him when he left. He glanced at the clock. Seven A.M. Time enough, perhaps, to create a final memory to last a lifetime.

He met her gaze. There was understanding in her eyes, acceptance in her thoughts. Just one more time, he vowed, and he reached for her.

Twelve

THE LIGHT SEEPING past the closed curtains washed across Nikki's face, painting her pale skin gold. Michael smiled. She looked so much younger in sleep, almost childlike.

Yet the image was a lie. Nikki was an old spirit in a young body. Her mom's death and her brief time with Tommy had forced her to grow up far too early. She'd lived through the nightmare and somehow survived. Maybe now that she'd finally confronted her memories and guilt, she'd be able to do more than that. Maybe now she'd live—and love—without fear.

He eased his arm out from under her head and watched her snuggle into the blankets. Lord, he didn't want to leave her. Not now, and not in the future. But he had no choice about either. He ran a hand through his hair and looked away. This morning had been a mistake. He should never have touched her a second time, should never have let their minds entwine so strongly. For now he could no longer deny he was human, with human wants and needs.

He'd played with fire and lost his heart.

Yet if he *hadn't* taken that risk, she would not now be sleeping, but rather preparing to join them on the hunt. Because he'd done the one thing he'd promised he wouldn't—he'd slipped into her mind when she was at her most vulnerable and ordered her to sleep.

She would hate him for it.

He rose from the bed and moved across to his clothes. He might not be able to erase Jasper's stain from her mind, but he could keep her safe. *That* had to be his first priority, now more than ever. He couldn't risk the fiend capturing her again. Anger washed through him at the thought, and he savored its taste. It would help him hunt this morning.

He glanced at the time, and saw it was just before eight. Jake would be here any minute—and right on cue, the sound of his soft steps echoed in the hall. Michael finished buttoning his shirt, then moved back to the bed. Bending, he gently kissed Nikki's cheek. She didn't stir, and her thoughts were full of warmth and contentment. For the moment, at least, she was free from Jasper's taint.

But how long would it remain that way?

Damn it, he *had* to find Jasper and kill him. And the quickest way to do *that* was to unhinge the monster's plans—not just for Nikki, but for Monica, too. Destroy the teenager, and Michael destroyed the plans Jasper had for her—which would piss Jasper off. And while an angry Jasper was undoubtedly more dangerous, he was also more careless. His anger was the reason Michael had been able to kill Jasper's brother all those years ago.

Besides, the teenager would know where her master was, and one way or another, Michael intended to get that information out of her before she died.

* * *

After several hours of aimless driving, he finally had to acknowledge their quest was futile. Nikki was right; they needed her help. Lyndhurst was a maze; Monica could be anywhere.

Michael rubbed his chin wearily, and winced as the sun caressed his arm. He shifted uncomfortably in the passenger seat, glancing at the clock on the dash. It was just past ten.

"Let's call it a day," he said into the silence.

Jake gave him a quick look. "The sun getting too much?"

"Yes."

"Oh."

Jake's fear washed through the silence. Michael crossed his arms and controlled the urge to touch the other man's thoughts. For the first time since he'd turned, Michael wanted someone to accept him without any sort of force. He smiled slightly. Nikki was a bad influence.

After a moment, Jake cleared his throat and gave him another quick look. "Where to, then?"

He glanced at the clock again, felt the beat of the sun through the windshield. It would take them too long to get back to the hotel. He gestured to a small bar just ahead. "Feel like a drink?"

"Anywhere, anytime."

Jake's grin was slightly forced, but at least he was making the effort. And it would be good to sit back and wait out the day's heat with an icy beer. If he couldn't be with Nikki, it wasn't a bad alternative—a normal pastime in his abnormal life.

Jake stopped close to the entrance, and Michael climbed out. The sunshine raced heat across his unprotected flesh. It was a warning he dare not ignore.

He ran up the steps and ducked inside. The interior of the bar was dark and cool and smelled of sweat and stale smoke. It didn't matter. All he needed was someplace to wait out the worst of the day. He ordered two drinks from the disinterested barman and moved across the room to a table hidden in deep shadow.

Jake sat opposite him and took a sip of his beer. He smacked his lips in appreciation, and gave Michael a shrewd look. "So," he said, "just what do you plan to do about Nikki?"

He knew Jake wasn't referring to the fact that they'd left without her. The man saw too much. "What is this?" he asked lightly. "A fatherly inquisition?"

Jake shrugged. "I've known her a long time and, in many ways, I *have* been a father to her. I don't want to see her hurt."

"Neither do I." Michael drank his beer, then added, "When did you two meet?"

Jake smiled. "When she was sixteen. She saved my life."

Michael raised an eyebrow in surprise. "How?"

"I was tracking a runaway for his parents and got cornered by his gang. Nikki came out of nowhere and faced them all down."

It was easy to imagine the skinny little ball of fierceness she must have been. He smiled slightly. Nothing much had changed. "So, she was a hellcat even then."

"But a vulnerable one," Jake said sharply. "Her toughness is just a shell."

"I know."

Just like he knew she had issues with trust—something he certainly *hadn't* helped by forcing her to sleep this morning. He'd be lucky if she didn't throw his ass out the goddamn window and fry him in sunshine.

He took another drink and met Jake's gaze squarely. "I'm here to do a job, nothing more. Nikki knows that."

"Women are strange folk, buddy. What they know and what they understand are often two very different things."

True. But that wasn't the case with Nikki. She didn't want *anyone* close. She might concede to physical attraction, but would definitely allow nothing more. "I don't think that'll be a problem here."

"Until the last few days, I would've agreed with you. But you've cracked her shell, no matter what either of you might say—I have eyes, I can see what you're both denying."

"I'm not denying I'm attracted to her," Michael protested. "I'm simply saying that I've been honest with her, and that *she* understands the situation." Honest where it counted. Up to a point anyway. "Believe me, I have no desire to hurt her."

Jake nodded. "I just needed to know she's in safe hands. Let's enjoy our drinks, my friend."

Michael picked up his beer and stayed silent.

* * *

Nikki blinked the sleep from her eyes, and flipped the sheets away from her face. Bright sunshine caressed her skin, filling her with warmth. She felt contented and lazy and, for the first time in ages, happy. Like a big, fat cat rolling in the sun.

And this is one fat cat who's not had enough, she thought with a grin, and reached across the bed. Only Michael wasn't there.

The hotel room was silent, empty. She clenched her fists against the sheets in sudden anger. Damn it, Michael'd left without her. But how? No matter how energetic their lovemaking had been, she certainly hadn't been tired enough to sleep—not after all the damn rest she'd been getting over the last few days. Then she remembered a gentle whisper in her mind as her orgasm hit, telling her to sleep, and fury swept her.

"Damn you to *hell,* Michael," she muttered, and flung the blankets aside, climbing out of bed. If he and Jake thought they had her beaten, they were wrong. She'd go after Monica alone.

The thought sent a chill down her spine, but she ignored it and quickly dressed. Jake and Michael had forgotten one major point: She was still the only person who could accurately zone in on Monica's whereabouts.

Or was she? Nikki frowned, walked across to the percolator and switched it on. Last night, when their minds had merged so completely, she'd felt the enormous power behind Michael's gifts. He'd never actually *said* he couldn't find Monica.

Did that mean the second time between them had

been little more than a convenient way to enter her mind and make her sleep?

She didn't want to believe that. She really didn't. He might have used their lovemaking to make her sleep, but surely to God their minds had entwined too closely for any emotional subterfuge to survive? And yet, with the strength of Michael's gifts, how could she ever be sure? Tommy had been able to make her believe he cared, and he'd only possessed a tenth of Michael's abilities.

She crossed her arms and stared at the smoke-stained wall. Why did it matter so much anyway? One night, that was all she'd asked for, all she'd wanted. One night free from Jasper's taint. And Michael had surely given her that.

So why did she suddenly feel so cheated?

Because, she thought bitterly, he'd not only betrayed her trust, he'd betrayed the emotions they'd so briefly shared. Emotions that had *seemed* real, even if it was now obvious that they weren't . . . at least on his part.

And she couldn't forgive him for that.

The percolator began to do its stuff. She waited until the mug was full, but as she picked it up, she spotted a newspaper sitting on the nearby chair. Jake must have dumped it there earlier. The headline leaped out at her. *John Trevgard Murdered!*

She took a gulp of coffee, almost scalding her throat in the process. How in the *hell* had Monica gotten to her father? They'd warned the cops about her . . . Nikki grimaced. Like *that* would matter when it came to Trevgard getting his own way. He'd never believed ill of his daughter when she was alive, why would that change now that she was dead?

She picked up the paper and quickly scanned the article. Trevgard's body was found just after eight P.M.; witnesses reported a male running from the mansion around seven-thirty. The brief description fit Jasper, and the timing was certainly right—he hadn't appeared outside the hotel window until four A.M.—but why would he allow himself to be seen like that? Unless, of course, he did it to give Monica an alibi. It would be hard to get his hands on her millions if Monica was convicted of killing her father. And it was certainly warning enough that Jasper's plans marched on, however much he appeared to be playing with her and Michael. They had to stop him—but first, they had to stop Monica. If nothing else, it would put a dent in Jasper's plans, and that could only be a good thing. She put the cup down and shoved a hand into her pockets, dragging out the locket she'd swiped from the mansion. Obviously, Jasper hadn't bothered searching her clothes when he'd stripped her.

She wrapped her fingers around the locket, and the sheer depth of malice emanating from it chased horror through her mind. Monica's evil had grown. Images began to push forward, but Nikki held them at bay and sat down.

And did nothing, because fear suddenly assailed her. The last time she'd tried this, Jasper had been waiting for her. Michael was nowhere near to rescue her this time if Jasper attempted to do it again. Hell, given the connection Jasper had forged with her through torment, maybe he didn't *have* to snare her.

Maybe all he had to do was whisper for her to stop, and she would.

She closed her eyes and pictured the images of the two servants Monica had murdered. Conjured up the darkness, the madness, in the teenager's eyes when she'd attacked Nikki and Jake. She *had* to be stopped, and this was the only way to do it.

She took a deep breath, clenched her fingers tightly around the locket, then opened her mind to hell.

Darkness flooded her senses. Through it, she heard the faint strains of music . . . *an organ.* Frowning, she tried to broaden the view. She needed an exact location, not merely the sounds and images of Monica's den.

A man dressed in black . . . the cross. Two old cypress trees dusted with snow . . . The pictures gradually formed into an area she recognized. Monica hid in the bowels of an old church up in the hills.

Nikki smiled at the absurdity of it. Yet what better hideaway *could* Monica find? No one expected a vampire to hide in such a place. Not even Michael . . .

What place?

She jumped. The question sounded so clear he might as well have been standing right next to her. She put her hand on her chest, and took a deep breath to calm the rapid pounding of her heart.

Nikki, what place? Where is Monica?

In a church. An honest answer, but not one that would help him. There were at least twenty churches scattered in and around Lyndhurst. It would take him forever to find the right one.

Where is the church, Nikki?

Annoyance seared her. She smiled grimly. Good.

Maybe next time he'd think twice about breaking promises and leaving her behind. But there wasn't going to be a next time, was there?

Nikki?

The hint of sadness behind his question made her wonder if he'd heard her thoughts. Given the connection between them, he probably could.

All I know is it's in the northwest, toward the mountains.

Thank you. He sounded surprised, as if he hadn't expected an honest answer. *We'll find her, Nikki.*

Maybe they would. And maybe she would. The bracelet would lead her straight to the teenager's lair.

Stay in the hotel, Nikki. Stay safe.

Yeah, right. She rose and called for a cab. Her car was still parked in front of the agency, and, hopefully, her old set of knives remained hidden under the dash. Even if a knife wasn't an effective weapon against a vampire, she still felt safer with them strapped to her wrist.

She glanced at the time. Two o'clock. She collected her jacket and went outside to wait for the cab.

Thanks to traffic, it took her nearly an hour to get to the old church. She stopped her car and climbed out. This was the place. She took off her sunglasses and leaned against the car to study the church. A priest puttered around in the front garden, tending to a few winter flowering plants. Two old cypress pines dominated the grounds on the right side of the old building, but the back and left side were bare and open.

She squinted slightly and looked at the sky. It was

barely three, but the sun's strength was beginning to wane. Michael had said any exposure to the sun was dangerous to the newly turned, but she wanted to be sure that Monica died. The later it was, the less likely that became.

It wouldn't wait until Michael arrived. She didn't question the certainty that he was coming. As he'd warned, the ties between them had been strengthened by their lovemaking, and he was using that connection to find her—and Monica.

Maybe she *should* wait for him . . . but something drove her on. Something told her she couldn't afford to.

She locked the car door then crossed the road. The priest moved back into the old building.

How could she rid the church of its unknown guest without raising the priest's suspicions? She frowned and turned down an old stone path that led through the trees. There had to be a second entrance at the back of the church. Maybe she could get in there.

Luck was with her for a change. She climbed over a small fence and approached the second door. It was locked. She looked around to ensure no one was watching, then quickly zapped the door with kinetic energy.

It creaked open. The hallway beyond was dark, still. The murmur of several voices came from a room to her right, and someone moved around in another room farther down the hall. Below them all was a sense of evil, sleeping.

Thirteen

SWALLOWING HEAVILY, NIKKI stepped inside. She reached into her pocket and dug out Monica's locket. It pulsed lightly against her palm, a muted beat that would lead her straight to the teenager.

She moved forward quietly. There were no windows in the small corridor, and the gloom closed in. She resisted the urge to turn on her flashlight, knowing the proximity of the voices meant there was a chance they'd see it.

A cobweb trailed against her face, and she jumped sideways but managed, with effort, not to scream. Heart pounding unevenly, she stopped and listened. The soft murmuring in the other room continued unabated.

Sighing silently, she walked on. The corridor ended at a set of stairs. She hesitated, stomach suddenly churning. She'd climbed a similar set of stairs to escape Jasper's clutches. Was he here, as well?

She couldn't feel his presence, only Monica's, but the fear that she was walking blindly into another trap was a cold weight in the pit of her stomach.

She turned on the flashlight and shone it into the gloom. The dust-caked steps showed no trace of footsteps, yet she could feel Monica's presence in the darkness below.

Could vampires fly? Bile rose in her throat. She closed her eyes, swallowing heavily. It was ridiculous to think vampires could fly. They didn't have to, when they could move faster than the eye could see.

What if Monica was awake and waiting for her? The rhythmic beat in the locket spoke of slumber, but how could Nikki be sure a vampire's heartbeat was in any way the same as a human's? Because now that she thought about it, she really hadn't heard the steady beat of Michael's heart when she'd been resting in his arms. And she should have.

Sweat beaded her forehead. Biting her lip, she walked slowly down the staircase. Dust stirred—a cloud that stung her eyes and nostrils. She wrinkled her nose, fighting a sneeze. The door at the bottom of the stairs was closed. She touched the doorknob, and hesitated again. What if Jasper *was* here? What would she do?

Probably die of heart failure. If she was lucky.

The locket told her nothing. Nor did she really expect it to—it was Monica's, not Jasper's. Mouth dry, she turned the knob and opened the door. The air that rolled out was thick with age and a musty dampness that spoke of leaking pipes. She swept the light across the layers of darkness. It illuminated the slimy floor but little else.

A hand came down on her shoulder, and her heart almost stopped.

She screamed and spun, only to find the priest she'd seen earlier.

She swallowed and gave him a somewhat shaky smile. "Father, you gave me a fright."

"It was not my intention, I assure you." His voice was gentle, as if he feared he was talking to someone not quite sane. "I merely wanted to know what you were doing down here."

Should she lie? She eyed him for a moment, and decided against it. Something in his green eyes told her he'd seen enough of life to know the truth from a lie.

"I'm a private investigator." She pulled her wallet out of her jacket and shone the flashlight on her license. "I got a tip that an escaped criminal was hiding in your cellar."

The priest frowned. "I don't see how. The doors are kept locked, and I've seen no one about."

No one but herself, she surmised from his look. "The side door was open, Father. If I got in, someone else could have?"

"Possibly."

But not likely, his expression seemed to suggest. She glanced over her shoulder. Something stirred in the darkness—or was it only her imagination?

"Is this criminal dangerous?" he added.

Damn it, why wouldn't he just leave? If Monica stirred, Nikki doubted his robes would offer him much protection. "Yes, she's dangerous."

"In that case, perhaps it would be better if we called the police."

Nikki hesitated, and glanced back to the dark cellar. At least the priest would be out of the way if he went to call the cops. And maybe it *would* be better if they were the ones to drag Monica into the sunlight and death. As long as they arrived well before sunset, there shouldn't be any sort of danger.

And with Monica out of the way, the only nightmare left would be Jasper—and the zombies. Although his death would at least take care of them.

Foreboding pulsed across her skin. "How far away is the local station?"

"Not far. It would take maybe ten minutes for them to get here."

"Call them. Tell them Monica Trevgard is in the basement. I'll stay here to insure she doesn't escape."

His gaze widened at the mention of Monica's name, then he nodded and moved back up the stairs.

Nikki watched his retreat. Did he know Monica? Maybe Nikki should warn him what might happen . . . But, priest or not, he wouldn't believe her. Hell, it had taken Jake long enough to accept the fact that she was a vampire, and *he* trusted her.

The minutes ticked by, and the silence grew heavier. She glanced at her watch. Perhaps the priest had decided to call the loony bin first, just to ensure she wasn't an escaped nutcase.

She cast her senses into the back of the basement, checking that Monica was still there. The wash of evil was answer enough.

A few minutes later she heard the sirens. Yet she couldn't escape the notion that something was wrong, that *she* was doing something she shouldn't. But they had to get rid of Monica, for everyone's safety.

Didn't they?

Footsteps pounded down the hall. She rubbed her arms, wishing they'd hurry up and get to her.

MacEwan and three other men clomped down the

steps. MacEwan stopped beside her, and the others several feet behind him. "This better not be one of your tricks."

His breath washed over her, and she screwed up her nose. Too bad garlic didn't affect vampires. "How the hell did you get here so fast? This isn't your precinct."

"Happened to be in the area, and heard the call over the radio. Monica is *my* case—you sure it's her down here?"

"Yes. And she's all yours."

She offered him her flashlight, but he shook his head and produced one of his own. "Jenkins, make sure she stays put. You other two, follow me."

The three men stepped into the basement. The darkness closed around them; only the bobbing light gave away their position. Nikki clenched her fists, half expecting Monica to wake and try to escape. But no sound broke the silence except for the occasional footstep.

Minutes later, Jenkins' two-way buzzed.

"Call the paramedics in, Jenkins." MacEwan's voice sounded annoyed, even over the two-way. "And get them to bring down a stretcher. The girl isn't looking so good."

"What should I do with Miss James?"

"Tell her to stay put, or her ass is mine."

The young officer glanced at her. Nikki smiled sourly. "Message received. My ass isn't moving."

He grinned slightly then headed up the stairs. Nikki shifted her weight from one foot to the other, waiting uneasily in the darkness. She wanted to go down there and see Monica for herself, but knew MacEwan had meant what he said.

Though with Jasper still on the loose, maybe jail was the safest place to be.

Jenkins returned a few minutes later, but Nikki felt no safer with him. She glanced at her watch. If MacEwan didn't move Monica soon, he might well find himself trying to control a very angry, and very awake, vampire.

Footsteps sounded down the hall. Two paramedics pounded past them and disappeared into the darkness. More minutes ticked by.

Finally, MacEwan reappeared. Just behind him, the two paramedics carried Monica on the stretcher, with the two other police officers following them.

She let the five men pass, and followed them up the stairs. The teenager looked more dead than alive. She was limp, boneless, and her skin was pallid and unhealthy-looking. Nikki frowned. Something didn't feel right . . .

She crossed her arms. However Monica might look, she was still a monster. Like the fiend she'd taken as a lover, Monica enjoyed the terror she inflicted on her victims. It had been all too obvious in her eyes when she'd attacked both Nikki and Jake.

Now evil's mistress was about to meet her deserving end.

MacEwan glanced over his shoulder. "I don't want you disappearing. I'd like a word with you first."

She nodded. She had no intention of leaving anyway. Not until she was certain of Monica's fate. She followed the men down the hall, stopping as the first paramedic stepped outside. Beams of sunlight touched

Monica's still form, washing her skin with warmth. For an instant she looked like the Monica of old—a carefree, innocent teenager. Nikki bit her lip and half reached out to stop them. Then she dropped her hand to her side and watched the two paramedics carry her fully into daylight.

Monica screamed—a high, tortured sound that ricocheted through Nikki's mind, filling her with echoes of pain and confusion. *Oh Christ . . .* somehow, she was connected to Monica, and feeling what the teenager was experiencing. She took a step forward, though whether it was to stop the paramedics or to warn them what was about to happen, she couldn't really say. But at that moment, the fire that assaulted Monica's body leaped through Nikki's brain, and she doubled over, gasping in pain, eyes watering as she struggled to see the teenager.

Monica kicked and twisted against the straps holding her captive. She screamed and cursed her father as her exposed skin turned red and began to blister. The paramedics swore and struggled to keep hold of the stretcher as the teenager's convulsing became more violent. There was a tearing sound, and suddenly she was free and on the ground. Her eyes flew open, revealing a sea of red where there should have been white. Tendrils of smoke began to rise from her flesh. She hissed—a low, inhuman sound—and began to crawl toward the doorway, the safety inside the church.

In Monica's unnatural gaze, Nikki saw past the layers of agony to the child deep within—a lost and lonely child, desperate for hope and love. *Me,* Nikki thought, *if it hadn't been for Jake and MacEwan.*

She stepped forward, though again she wasn't entirely sure whether she intended to help Monica or end her suffering, but the fire in her brain intensified. Gasping, Nikki dropped to her knees. There was nothing she could do—nothing but watch Monica die. Tears ran down her cheeks when she met the teenager's gaze. Deep in the blue depths of the girl's eyes, Nikki saw the sudden flash of understanding—and hate.

"Christ Almighty! Somebody do something." MacEwan's voice rose harshly above the noise surrounding the old church. "Throw a blanket over her!"

The priest ran to obey. But they were far too late. Monica burst fully into flames. Nikki closed her eyes, not wanting to see any more. The pain in her head exploded, and she bit back the urge to scream, as Monica screamed.

She'd been wrong about one thing. No matter what Monica had done, she hadn't deserved a death as horrid as this.

The screams finally faded into silence, and the fire, the pain, eased for Nikki. The priest returned with a blanket and an officer threw it over what was left of Monica's body. And still, the fire burned unabated, the flames so fierce they took the blanket with them. Dark smoke climbed skyward.

Soon there was nothing left but ashes. Fury ran through Nikki's mind—so deep and endless that her soul quivered in utter fear. Jasper did *not* like his plans being thwarted.

Well, good, she thought resolutely, even as she knew he'd make her pay.

She took a deep breath and wiped the tears from her cheeks. There was nothing she could do about Jasper at the moment, and nothing she could do for Monica, other than mourn a life so wasted.

"I've heard of things like this happening." MacEwan's voice was harsh, full of the pain he would never show. "Never thought I'd see it, though."

She rose and walked over to where he stood. The priest began to murmur over the burned soil and a few scraps of blanket—all that remained of Monica's pyre.

"How in hell am I going to explain this downtown?"

She glanced at him, wondering if he expected an answer. His face showed no sign of emotion, yet she knew the appearance was a lie. MacEwan—the tough, no-nonsense cop—hated losing a kid, no matter how bad that kid had gone. Despite all his years on the streets, he still believed they could be saved, given half a chance.

"You can't." She shoved her hands into her pockets to ward off the chill of the freshening wind. "No one would believe you if you tried."

He lit a cigarette and sucked on it almost greedily. "You knew this would happen, didn't you?" he said, after a moment.

She didn't reply, not trusting him for an instant. Fair cop or not, he was just as likely to march her downtown and interrogate her all night if she admitted too much. Yet her silence was answer enough.

"So," he continued, exhaling a long plume of smoke, "what was she?"

She gave him another uncertain look. How much had he guessed? "What do you mean?"

He gave an exasperated snort. "No games, or I might be inclined to get nasty. Normal people do not explode into flames when the sun touches them. Certainly it's not a problem Monica Trevgard has suffered before."

And wouldn't again, Nikki thought with a shiver. She watched a wisp of blanket turn in the breeze. The intensity of the fire had left the soil under Monica's body a charred mess. She doubted if anything would ever grow there again.

"She was a vampire." It was time MacEwan knew the truth, whether or not he chose to believe it.

He made no comment. She'd always found him hard to read and now had no idea if he believed her or not.

"And this madman we still have on the loose?"

"Monica's lover. Another vampire."

"I see."

Did he? There was little emotion on his face, but his eyes were thoughtful.

"And do you intend going after this madman?"

She nodded, half expecting him to warn her off the case. As usual, though, MacEwan did the unexpected.

"Well, keep me informed of all developments." He dropped his half-finished cigarette on the ground, crushing it under his boot heel as he gave her a wintry smile. "I am not as blind as you might think. I've seen things . . ." He hesitated and shrugged. "Let's just say I'm not unwilling to believe there are some things on this earth that defy explanation. Just be careful. I can do without the extra paperwork."

He gave her a brief nod and walked away. She turned her gaze to the priest, watched him sprinkle holy water over the soil.

The back of her neck tingled in warning, and she turned. Jake walked across the road and entered the church through the main gate. Michael wasn't with him, but he was near. His anger washed over her, almost smothering in its intensity.

"I heard over the police radio that they'd found Monica." Jake stopped and regarded the priest's actions with interest. "This all that's left?"

Nikki nodded. "She went up like a torch."

"One down, one to go." There was little remorse in his voice. He took her elbow and pulled her away from the church. "But just what the hell did you think you were doing? You could have gotten yourself killed!"

She wrenched her arm out of his grip and glared at him. "What the hell did you think *you* were doing, leaving without me this morning?"

He shrugged. "We did what we thought best to keep you safe."

"I thought we were a team, Jake."

"We are, Nik. But sometimes you scare me. It's almost as if . . . as if you have no sense of your own well-being. You just keep pushing yourself." He looked at her grimly. "Sometimes I think you have a death wish."

She snorted softly. And yet there'd been times in the past when she certainly hadn't cared whether she lived or died. Maybe that was why she had been such an easy target for Tommy. "Even if I did, what business is it of yours?"

"Damn it, do I have to spell it out? You're like a damned daughter to me. I don't want to see you hurt!"

She was an idiot, no doubt about it. She touched his still bandaged arm gently. "I'm sorry."

He sighed and shook his head. "You've been on your own too long, kiddo. It's about time you let someone in."

He was talking about Michael, she guessed, not himself. "Father figure or not, does the phrase 'mind your own business' mean anything to you?"

"It's one I have great trouble with." He held a hand out. "Give me your keys. I want you to go talk to Michael. Now, Nikki," he added when she hesitated.

She swore softly but knew better than to argue when he used *that* tone of voice. She dug the keys out of her pocket. "If I didn't know better, I'd swear you've been drinking."

"One or two. I'm safe to drive."

"My car's parked across the road. I'll see you back at the office."

He nodded. "Trust him, Nik. Let him in."

She scowled and turned away. She had no intention of letting anyone in, especially Michael. It was too damn dangerous. *He* was too damn dangerous.

Jake's Mercedes was parked in the shadows of an old elm. The darkly tinted windows prevented any view inside, and yet she could feel Michael's anger as if it were her own.

She opened the driver's-side door and climbed in. Michael watched her silently, eyes hidden behind dark glasses. He made no comment as she started the engine and slowly drove off.

Though she kept her eyes on the road, she couldn't help being aware of every little move he made. Now that she was here, she feared talking to him. But just what did she fear? Him? Or herself?

"Why?" he asked softly, after several minutes.

"That's a question I should be asking you. But I guess it would be useless, because I already know the answer. Promises mean nothing to you—not when they get in the way of something you want."

"What I wanted was to keep you *safe*!"

She ignored the undercurrent of anger and frustration in his voice, and kept her own voice level. "You're not my keeper, Michael. If I want to risk my life, then I *will*. Monica had to be hunted down and destroyed—you said that yourself."

"Yes, but not before she'd led us to Jasper."

"Jasper would have killed her before he allowed that to happen, and you know it."

"Jasper would have been in undead sleep when you found Monica," he retorted. "I could have snatched the information from her mind and dealt with Jasper before he even realized what was happening."

"And just how long have you been chasing the man? Do you really think it would have been that easy?" She snorted softly. "Besides, Jasper woke when Monica burned. I felt the tide of his fury."

"That still doesn't excuse the risk you took—"

"I guess my sin is as great as yours, isn't it?"

He made a sound suspiciously like a deep-throated growl. "No other observations, while you're at it? No other accusations?" His voice was almost mocking, hinting at the anger she couldn't see but could sense.

"There was when I woke alone, but I've had time to think since then."

"I just bet you have."

She shot him a quick look, unsure how to take his remark. His face was as remote as ever.

"So what did you come up with?" He shifted slightly in his seat, facing her.

She didn't trust his tone. It was too polite. Too controlled. "One question."

"And that is?"

A quick glance at his face told her little, yet she caught a wisp of uncertainty in his thoughts. She unclenched her fingers against the wheel and bit her lip in indecision. She didn't want to voice her doubts, didn't want to hear his answer. And the demons whispering madness in her mind could never force her to do this. But she had to know.

"What did our lovemaking mean to you?"

His gaze, though hidden by dark glasses, burned into her soul. "What do you think it meant?"

She couldn't look at him. "That it was a little more than a means to insure I slept."

A tide of anger seemed to leap into the car and swirl around her. She kept her eyes on the road, hands tense against the steering wheel. She didn't want to face the fury she could feel building.

"If that had been my sole reason, I could have achieved it when we made love the first time." His gaze burned into her. "Think about what we shared, Nikki. Look inside your own heart."

No. Never again would she trust what she felt in

matters like this. People died when she did. As the light ahead changed, she slowed the car and risked another quick look. His face remained impassive, giving no indication he'd heard her thoughts. But even if he had, she still needed to know.

"You are a fool, Nikki. A fool who will not listen to her own intuition."

"Intuition has nothing to do with this." Because intuition was telling her to trust him, telling her to grab on tight and never let go, no matter how he fought. But it had told her the same about Tommy, and it had never been more wrong.

"I have to ask, Michael. Surely you can understand that?"

"The only thing I can understand is the fact that I am a fool twice over."

The sudden hint of weariness in his voice frightened her. She glanced at him quickly. What had he meant by that?

"I will not deny that I used your vulnerability during our lovemaking to make you sleep." He took off the sunglasses and rubbed his eyes. "As for what it meant—I warned you before, Nikki, it can never be anything more than just a moment we share."

His words cut through her. While she knew he couldn't stay, she'd hoped it might have been something more than just a physical release to him. Because to her, their lovemaking had been, at least, something of a revelation. She'd never realized that two bodies could become one so completely. That two minds could share a dance so poetic, so full of care and desire.

She blinked, then shifted the car into gear as the light turned green, and the traffic flowed on.

"Remember, I was not the initiator, nor am I made of stone," he continued softly. "And there's one more question you should ask. Just who was using whom last night?"

Heat crept into her cheeks and she bit her lip. There was no denying the fact that he was right. She *had* used him, used his warmth, the caress of his thoughts, to keep Jasper's nightmares at bay.

But while she regretted her reasons, she didn't regret making love to him. Those memories she would treasure in the years ahead.

"I'm sorry," she said. "I was wrong to do that. But so were you in leaving me."

He made no comment, and she drove the final few miles to the office in silence. She parked in front of the building and glanced at her watch as she climbed out of the car. It was after five. She frowned. Why wasn't her car here? Jake had left the same time as she had, and she'd been going decidedly slowly . . .

Her psychic senses sprang to life, and pain ran like fire across her body.

Only it wasn't her pain. It was Jake's.

Jasper's dark laughter whispered through her brain—a teasing gloat, edged with warning.

If she wanted Jake to live, she would have to take his place.

Fourteen

NIKKI GRIPPED THE edge of the car door and closed her eyes. She couldn't go back to Jasper . . . yet she couldn't let Jake die in her place.

"Nikki, listen to me." Michael's voice seemed to come from a great distance. "He won't kill Jake just yet. He'll make sure we have enough time to attempt a rescue. Jasper likes his little games. Break the contact, Nikki. Break it now."

She bit her lip and concentrated on pushing Jasper from her mind. His poison slid away, but the effort left her trembling.

Michael turned her around and pulled her toward him. She leaned her cheek against the warmth of his chest and wished she could stay in the safe circle of his arms forever. Why couldn't the rest of the world just go to hell and leave her alone? Better yet, why wasn't there a way to simply turn back the clock to the time before Monica and Jasper had walked into her life? Though that would mean not meeting Michael. Perhaps some good had come out of this whole mess, no matter how brief.

After a moment, she sighed and pulled away. "If

Jasper's actually mobile in the daylight, he's stronger than you thought."

"Yes." Michael finally removed his dark glasses and glanced at the sun. "Although it's nearly five, and the winter sun is weak. But more than likely it was the zombies who grabbed Jake. Jasper would not risk sunlight when there was no need."

"Just how much do you know about Jasper?"

He shrugged. "As I've said before, he and I are old foes. I make it my business to know my enemy."

"Do you make it your business to keep your allies in the dark?"

"I've never been comfortable giving more information than is needed."

She clenched her fists and tried to ignore the desire to yell in frustration. "Well, right now I need to know everything I can about Jasper."

He nodded, though his dark gaze was suddenly distant. "As I said earlier, he's a twin. He and his brother survived the San Francisco fires of 1906, but the rest of their family did not. We're not sure when they both changed, but we do know it occurred shortly after the fires, when they were fifteen." He hesitated, his face grim. "Even so, Jasper was responsible for the murder of at least five people before his rebirth."

She shifted from one foot to the other and tried to ignore the need to move. Finding Jake would take all the caution and cunning she could muster—and every scrap of information about Jasper and his need for revenge. "You mentioned the royal 'we' again."

Michael sighed, though it was a sound filled with annoyance. "I am a member of an organization known as the Damask Circle."

"Are you all vampires?"

"No. But neither are we all what you'd term *human*."

Human. The bitter emphasis he'd placed on that word spoke volumes. He'd heard her thoughts, all right. She bit her lip and glanced away from the accusation of his gaze. "And this circle of yours goes around killing people like Jasper?"

"Yes. So people like you can rest easier at night."

People who fear what cannot easily be explained. People who cannot trust what their hearts know to be true. She closed her heart to his thoughts. This wasn't the time to argue about her refusal to trust. "Is that why you killed Jasper's brother?"

Again Michael hesitated, and pain rose through his soul. She wanted to reach out and tell him she understood. Instead, she clenched her fingers and waited for him to continue.

"Yes. I was sent after them both, but I only managed to bring down his brother. And in return, Jasper killed Patrick and another that was dear to me."

Revenge. Everything was based on revenge, and it could end up killing them all. "How often have you and Jasper met in the past?" She paused and frowned. "If you're three hundred years old and Jasper is over a hundred, wouldn't your brother have been well and truly dead before Jasper and his brother were even born?"

The pain in Michael's soul became sharper. "Patrick was a vampire."

And Michael had turned him. Nikki wondered why. "How often have you and Jasper met in the past?"

"Three times."

And each time Jasper had somehow slipped from Michael's noose. But it wouldn't happen again, she thought. Deep in the dark depths of his eyes she could see the promise of death. One way or another, Michael was determined to finish it here in Lyndhurst.

Foreboding pounded through her. Shivering, she turned away and locked the car door. Dark laughter ran through her mind, taunting her. She closed her eyes briefly and took a deep breath.

"Let's go inside," she said, avoiding Michael's gaze and walking around to the front of the car. "I should be able to find something to trace Jake with."

She climbed the steps and unlocked the door. The office was as cold as the ice forming in the pit of her stomach. Dark laughter again scurried past the edges of her mind.

"Nikki." Michael swung her around to face him. "Jasper's only taunting you, trying to make you fear every step."

"He's doing a damn good job of it," she muttered, wishing Michael would wrap his arms around her and hold her until the stain of evil left her mind. But it was no use wishing for things that could not be. He couldn't stay. She didn't want him to stay.

So why did the thought of him leaving hurt so badly?

He placed a finger under her chin, raising it until her gaze met his. "He can't control you, Nikki. He can only undermine your confidence."

It was a lie. He knew, as she did, that Jasper only had to call, and she'd go running. "Why is he bother-

ing? Why doesn't he just kill me if he wants to own
my gifts so badly?"

Michael's smile was edged with anger, his eyes lay-
ered with a darkness that chilled her soul.

"Because he taunts me through you." He raised a
hand, pushing a wisp of hair away from her eyes. His
touch trailed heat against the ice of her skin. "I came
here to protect you—he undoubtedly knows this now
through his connection with you. He wants me to
suffer the knowledge of your capitulation, and death,
before he achieves either."

She shivered, fighting the need to fall into his arms,
to beg him to hold her, protect her. "Why? Isn't that
a rather dangerous game to play?"

"It's one we've played before, and unfortunately,
one he's won." His voice was distant, distracted, as
he ran a finger lightly down her cheek and neck.

She licked her lips. It was hard to concentrate with
him touching her so gently. Lord, all she wanted to do
was fall into bed with this man . . . but she couldn't.
The time and the place were all wrong. Damn it, *they*
were wrong. A man who couldn't love and a woman
afraid to love—what hope would there ever be for
them?

Michael's hand stilled near her breast. She glanced
up quickly, but he avoided her gaze and stepped away.
It didn't matter. She knew his thoughts. She knew he
wouldn't touch her like that again.

"I'm sorry," he said softly.

She nodded. It was as much her fault as his. She
should have pulled away the minute he'd touched her.

She walked across to Jake's desk. There had to be

something here that held enough of Jake's vibes to enable her to track him.

She found it within a few minutes—an old fob watch lost among the junk in his bottom drawer.

"It has his imprint?" Michael asked, sitting on the edge of the desk.

She nodded and tried to ignore the sensations running through her fingers. "How do you want to go about this?"

"That would depend on how much you're willing to trust me."

She gave him a sharp look. He was sitting on the edge of the desk, swinging one leg slightly. So very casual in appearance, but she could feel his tension. She could see it around the edges of his dark eyes.

"What do you mean?"

"Jasper knows you will attempt to find Jake, so he will have set some sort of trap again."

She nodded. That much she'd guessed. But she had to find Jake, and this was her best option. Probably the only option, if they wanted to find him alive.

"You have a plan to stop him?"

"Yes. But it would involve joining my mind to yours." He hesitated and shrugged lightly. "Completely."

She stared at him. Merge minds? Know each other's thoughts and desires?

"We already know each other's thoughts, Nikki."

"But I can't—"

"You can." He studied her, face grim. "And all too often you have. It's something neither of us can really control, something that gets stronger every time we . . ." He hesitated. "The point is, do you trust me enough to allow our minds to merge?"

"I trusted your promise not to make me do something against my will, and look where that got me."

Anger flitted around her, sharp and bitter. "I will do nothing to alter your will in any way, Nikki. But you are more than welcome to attempt to find Jake on your own if you prefer."

She bit her lip. Jasper would be waiting for her, of that she had no doubt. And with the connection he'd forged between them, there was no guarantee whatsoever she'd have the strength or the will to stop him from snaring her completely.

"How deep a merging would it be?" Even saying the words made her stomach turn. Did she really want Michael to know all her wants, all her secrets and fears?

"It would have to be complete enough to allow me some kind of control if I need it. But I promise not to open any doors you wish kept closed. And you must promise the same."

She wondered if promising something like that even mattered. Michael's abilities far outstripped her own. There was no way on earth she'd be able to control him. "But how will this merging screw up the kind of trap Jasper had waiting last time?"

"I intend to direct your abilities along a slightly different path."

She licked her lips. For all intents and purposes, he'd have control of her. Her willingness to go along with this would allow Michael to succeed where Jasper had so far failed . . . and would give him the access Tommy had wanted but couldn't fully control.

"Damn it, Nikki, I'm *not* Jasper. Or Tommy."

He rose and moved around the desk, stopping only a foot away from her. She couldn't help the instinct to retreat, and only stopped when her back hit the wall. The wood paneling felt cool against her palms when compared to the fire of his gaze.

"I don't *want* control of your mind—or your body—or anything else, for that matter. When will you get that through your head? I just want you to trust me."

Never, she thought, as she stared at him. He'd betrayed her once—what was there to stop him from doing it again? And yet, if she wanted to rescue Jake and keep safe, she had no choice. Deep in his eyes she saw a flicker of anger, but deeper still was longing. She knew in that instant he wanted something more than he'd ever admit or allow.

She flexed her fingers, fought for calm. "Tell me what you intend to do."

He sighed and turned to the window, staring out through the lace curtains. "Instead of merely tracking Jake's whereabouts, I intend to join his mind. That will prevent Jasper from detecting us, and it will give us a better idea of what's going on."

So Michael would have control of two minds. She remembered how easily he had made the waiter do as he asked, and shivered. But that had only been surface control. This would be so much deeper. "Won't it be dangerous?"

"Anything that deals with this kind of mental intrusion can be dangerous."

"For us or for Jake?"

"For everyone."

She swallowed to ease the sudden dryness in her throat. "Will we be able to feel what he feels?"

"Yes. But I will protect you from it as much as I can."

"I don't know—"—*if I can cope with Jake's fear on top of my own.*

"You must," Michael said gently. "If you want him to survive."

She took a deep breath then nodded. Jake was the closest thing she had to family. She didn't want to lose him. "What do I do?"

"Sit in his chair and close your eyes."

She did. Michael held her hand. Heat burned through her flesh, warming the ice formed by her apprehension.

"Now relax."

She listened to the rhythmic flow of his breathing and tried to match it. Gradually, she felt the tension begin to leave her limbs.

"Relax, relax." Michael's voice was a whisper that soothed her soul. "Allow our thoughts to touch, to become one."

Heat danced through her, warmth that burst like an explosion through every fiber of her being. It was a caress, a lover's kiss, and nothing like the invasion she'd imagined. The fire that burned when they touched was nothing when compared to the inferno they raised as their minds became one.

Concentrate, Nikki.

The cool breeze of his thoughts whispered through her. His mind ran like a wave before hers, separate yet united with her own. She could see his thoughts before he spoke them. See his emotions—a blaze of color that almost left her blind. Could see the areas he wished kept hidden, vast tracts of forbidding darkness.

Find Jake, Nikki.

She reached for the watch. The metal was cold against her skin, but her hands twitched, burned by the images rushing from the fob. Her senses leaped away, following the trail that led to Jake. Shapes began to form. She felt a tremor of fear, only to have Michael chase it away.

Concentrate on Jake, Nikki. See him. Feel him. Become one with him . . .

. . . Pain throbbed through his temples. Jake cursed and ran a hand through his hair, only to stop when he felt the sticky dampness matting it.

What the hell? He struggled into a sitting position and tried to remember what had happened. Cold stone nudged his butt, and a breeze pulled at his wet clothes. Where on earth was he? The air was heavy with age and the scent of decay. Somewhere ahead in the darkness he could hear the steady drip of water.

It had to be a cave of some kind. But how in hell had he gotten here—wherever here was?

"Hell is an apt enough description of this place, my friend."

The words came out of nowhere, reverberating around the walls. Jake tensed, studying the darkness.

"Who are you? What do you want?"

"Questions." The stranger's voice dripped cold sarcasm. "Always questions from my captives."

Jake swallowed. Now he knew who had him. Knew why.

"Nikki won't be fool enough to fall into your trap a second time."

"We shall see." The darkness moved, forming shape. Became a man with the eyes of a demon.

It was easy to understand Nikki's fear, Jake thought, studying the muscular form warily. He wasn't psychic, but he could feel the power that oozed from the man. And those eyes . . . they were almost hypnotic.

Don't look, he thought with a frown.

"Interesting," Jasper murmured. "You have a certain . . . strength I did not expect."

Jake made no comment and studied the darkness beyond Jasper. There had to be some clue as to his whereabouts, some way to warn Nikki not to come after him.

"You will find no escape."

His gaze darted back to Jasper. He noted the insanity entrenched in the blue depths of his eyes. Knew he was a man who enjoyed toying with his victims. *No, not a man. A vampire.*

Jake cleared his throat. "Where are we?"

"Underground. Deep underground." As Jasper spoke, a tremor ran through the ground—a vibration that shook the air and rushed wind through the darkness.

Were they in a tunnel? Did some sort of vehicle passing through cause the vibration? Maybe a train?

"Not even close," Jasper mused. "I could, of course, tell you, but I doubt it would do you any good."

"Nikki won't look for me," Jake replied, trying to sound casual, though tension knotted his gut and constricted his throat. "She won't run the risk of falling into your trap a second time."

"You lie, little man. I know how much she values your friendship."

Jake closed his eyes. "They will stop you," he whispered. "No matter what it takes."

"I like a man with confidence." Jasper smiled. "But what if the cost is your own life?"

Jake shrugged. He would die no matter what happened. He could see it in the monster's eyes. But he wasn't about to give Jasper the pleasure of his fear.

"I can read your mind, little man. I know what you feel."

"Then you know I loathe you more than I fear you."

The chill in the mad blue depths sent ice splintering down his spine, and for an instant he regretted his rash words.

"Bravery must run in your profession," Jasper said. "As much as I'd love to stay and chat, I must go tend to my traps. But first, a drink is called for, I think."

The fiend lunged at him. Jake scrambled backward, but talonlike fingers caught his arm, tearing into skin. Jake swore and kicked out. Jasper only laughed. Fear slammed through Jake's entire being, and no amount of fighting could stop the inevitable.

"Struggle, little man. Struggle as hard as you can. I like my meal accompanied by fear."

Teeth tore into his neck. Jake screamed as the warm gush of horror plunged him into darkness . . .

* * *

Nikki's scream echoed through Michael's soul. He tore her from Jake's mind and lurched forward, catching her as she fell sideways out of the chair.

"Easy, Nikki. We're safe. You're safe," he whispered and held her gently, one hand caressing the silky length of her hair.

She shuddered and wrapped her arms around him, holding on as if she'd never let him go.

Which was about as far from the truth as you could get. "I'm sorry, Nikki. I should have pulled us out earlier."

"Yes," she agreed softly.

Linked as they were, he could see the visions running riot in her mind, feel her shudder as she remembered Jasper's teeth tearing into her flesh . . .

"Jake's memory. Not yours." *It will not happen to you, Nikki. I won't allow it.*

"My memories, because we were there."

"Hush. It's over."

She sighed into his chest, her breath warm against his skin. "For us. Not for Jake."

True. He pulled away from her, though it was the last thing in the world he wanted to do, and held her at arm's length. "If we want to save him, we'll have to move quickly."

She sniffed then turned and sifted quickly through the papers of Jake's desk. "There's a map of the area . . . Here it is."

"Right." He stood, giving her no time to dwell, no time to fear. "Where are all the tunnels situated?"

She frowned, studying the map. "If it was a rail tunnel, there are three." She pointed them out with a trembling hand.

He ignored the sudden desire to comfort her again. They had no time, nor was it right for him to keep touching her like he cared. "What about old caves? Mine shafts?"

"This section of the mountains is literally littered with old mines. I know a lot of them were filled to stop people falling down them, but there are about a dozen that still remain. Jake could be in any one of them."

But Jasper couldn't. The shaft would have to be deep and long to provide the protection he needed. "The tunnel was wet. We heard drips, remember?"

She nodded, chewing her lip thoughtfully. "There are two old mines near the new dam they're building here." She pointed to an area on the western edge of the map. "I'm pretty sure one of them goes into the mountain rather than down."

He saw her glance at the watch in her hand, saw her fingers twitch against it.

"Is he there, Nikki?"

"I think so," she whispered. "But I've been wrong before."

And it had resulted in death. Too much of her young life had been affected by death, and there wasn't a damn thing he could do about it. But he'd do everything it took to stop Jake dying on her as well.

"We'll need some supplies," he said.

"Out back."

She stood, but rather than brush past him, she took the long way around the desk and walked across to the storeroom. He shook his head and followed her. She'd trusted him with her soul, but still wouldn't trust him with her heart. He wondered if she ever would.

But what in hell would he do if she did?

He leaned against the doorway and watched her collect some chocolate and a few cans of soda and throw them in a backpack. She pulled on a heavy coat and turned to face him. Fear dominated her thoughts and brimmed in her eyes.

"Ready?" he said softly.

Ready to dance with the devil himself? Never. Her thought ran through his mind like a frightened gazelle. Her gaze was grim when it met his.

"For Jake," she said softly, "yes. Let's go."

Fifteen

NIKKI LEANED AGAINST the trunk of a scrawny old pine, her breath coming in ragged gasps that tore at her throat. She'd thought she was reasonably fit, but climbing this mountain had quickly put that notion to rest. She eyed the darkness ahead and wondered how much more they had to climb. And how in hell she was going to make it. The muscles in her legs were on fire. She couldn't possibly walk another step.

"Have a drink." Michael took a soda from the backpack he carried and handed it to her.

"Thanks," she replied, and popped the top.

He nodded, his gaze sweeping the still night.

"Anything?" she asked, after a long drink of the lukewarm cola.

"Nothing. You?"

Her gaze skimmed the darkness and ice crawled across her skin. There wasn't anything she could pin down, just instinct, warning her. "He's here, somewhere."

Michael nodded. "He'd hang around to watch the fun."

She looked at him in irritation. "Attempted murder cannot be classed as fun."

"To a man like Jasper, it can." His gaze, when it met hers, was assessing. "Ready?"

No. She quickly drank the remains of the cola and handed him the can to enclose in the backpack. As she followed him up the slope, she couldn't help noticing the ease of his gait. He walked like he hadn't a care in the world. Yet tension and worry washed down their link. She still couldn't fully read his thoughts, but then, she didn't really want to. Not if it meant knowing how small their chances of pulling off this rescue were.

She wrapped her fingers around the fob watch in her pocket. Its warmth comforted her, as did the slow but steady beat that told her Jake was still alive.

The entrance soon loomed before them—a cavernous hole framed by timber that looked older than Lyndhurst. Older than Michael.

"The timber's not *that* old," he said, half smiling as he handed her the flashlight. "Here, hold this."

She shone the beam at the entrance. The light penetrated only a few feet into the darkness before being swallowed. But it was enough to see the footprints. Michael squatted on his heels and ran his fingers around the outline of the prints.

"Zombies," he said, indicating a scuffed section on one print. "See? Their step is heavy, and they drag their feet."

"We knew he'd have traps waiting." So why hadn't her psychic senses kicked in and warned her?

"They won't." Michael stood and brushed the dirt off his hands. "Jasper's using the psychic net again—I can feel it pulsing. It's shielding this entire area, and probably interfering with your abilities."

"But I can still feel Jake's heartbeat through the watch."

"Only because Jasper wants you to find him."

She shivered. "Then the rest of my abilities will be useless?"

"Probably. But you can't find out without trying, and the net will catch you if you do."

Her stomach twisted. While she'd often wished to be normal, to be free of the gifts that had somehow always set her apart, she knew deep down that she relied on them too much to ever let them go. And her brief time with Jasper had proven just how useless she was without them.

Michael wrapped his fingers around hers. "You're not alone, Nikki."

She closed her eyes, fighting the warmth that sprang through her body. It wasn't right to want someone as much as she wanted Michael. Wasn't right to need his touch, the comfort of his arms, to chase the demons away.

"I'll always be alone," she said, and stepped away from him. It couldn't be any other way. Not when her love was a curse. Michael might be a vampire, but that didn't make him invincible. Monica had proven that vampires could die as quickly as any human. "Let's go."

He made no comment and stepped into the cave. She followed him into the darkness, her shaking hands making the flashlight's beam dance erratically.

The steady drip of water was all she could hear above the sound of her footsteps. Michael made no noise, as silent as a ghost. The chill in the air crept past the layers of her clothing and touched her skin with icy fingers.

She shivered and inched closer to Michael's broad back. Her psychic senses might be useless at this point, but she could still feel Jasper's evil all around. Even the air they breathed seemed tainted by it.

She swept the flashlight's beam across walls slick with slime. Rivulets of water ran down the slope past their feet, but to where? She remembered how damp Jake's clothes had been and guessed, somewhere along the line, they'd hit water. Hopefully it wouldn't be too deep.

Michael stopped abruptly, and she plowed into his back. "Give a girl some warning next time," she muttered, rubbing her nose as she stepped next to him.

The path led into a wide, still lake. She groaned. It didn't seem to resurface anywhere near, if at all.

"How well do you swim?" Michael knelt and dipped his fingers in the water.

"Like a rock." She shone the flashlight onto the water. There was no telling how deep it was. It was too dark to see the bottom.

Michael sniffed the water on his fingers, then carefully tasted it. "Putrid," he muttered, and spat. "Whatever you do, don't swallow it."

"I don't even want to go in it, let alone drink it." She backed away from the edge. The more she stared at the water, the more certain she became that it was a trap. Every sense she had was urging her to flee . . .

Yet if she did, Jake would die.

Michael touched her hand, and this time she didn't pull away.

"Keep close and hang on to my hand, no matter what happens."

His concern ran down the link—a fire that warmed her soul. She squeezed his hand lightly. "I intend to, believe me. Whether I'm *allowed* to is another matter entirely."

He brushed his fingertips along her cheek. "Just hold on to me. As a vampire, I can't drown, because I don't really need air to survive, but you're vulnerable."

As if she needed reminding. He tugged her forward. Black waves rippled across the lake's surface as they walked, side by side, into the dark waters. The water crept up her leg and past her hips, and every step forward became more difficult. She kept her arm raised well above the lake's surface, allowing the flashlight's beam to wash across the darkness. But she kept an eye on the water—just in case something jumped out and tried to grab the light.

The link suddenly flared to life and Michael touched her thoughts. Warmth wrapped around her, a cocoon of comfort and strength. *A girl could get used to this,* she thought, and alarm stabbed through her heart. Because she *was* getting used to it, and it would only make his leaving all that much harder to bear.

They plowed on through the icy water, but each step felt as if they were forcing their way through molasses.

Michael squeezed her hand gently. "Halfway there. Don't worry, we'll make it."

"You mean there is an end to this lake?" If there was, the flashlight couldn't pick it out.

"Yes. And the path's beginning to slope upward again."

They'd been following a path? She stepped on something slimy and slipped sideways, yelping in fright. The flashlight dipped under the water and darkness closed in, thick and heavy . . .

Michael yanked her upright, almost pulling her arm out of its socket.

"Great," she muttered, hoping she didn't sound as scared as she felt. "Now I'm completely wet."

Amusement and concern ran down the link. "Are you okay?"

She gave the flashlight a shake. Droplets of water sprayed across her face. The bright beam flickered then stayed on. "Now I am."

"Good. Don't slip again. You'll give me heart failure."

She glanced up sharply. The seriousness behind his light remark shook her. It sounded like he cared—really cared. He'd told her vampires didn't have feelings, that they couldn't love. Was that a lie? Every once in a while he said or did something that made her think it was.

"Ready to move?"

She touched the fob watch. Its beat was shallow. "Let's go," she said.

Shivering, she shone the light across the water. Tiny waves continued to roll away from them, fanning out across the darkness. In the distance, water dripped steadily, but the lake seemed to swallow all other noise.

Still, someone was out there, watching them. She

licked her lips. It was getting harder and harder to ignore the urge to run. "Michael—"

"I know." His voice was terse. "Just keep moving. There's nothing we can do here anyway."

The water level began to drop, inching down from their chests to their hips. But it still had the consistency of glue, making every step a challenge.

Then something pushed at her wet jeans. Biting her lip, she battled the desire to run. The soupy water made any sort of haste impossible anyway. She'd only fall . . . and that was probably what Jasper had in mind.

But she wished she knew what was touching her ankle.

Again it trailed past, more solidly this time.

"He's playing games." Though Michael's voice was calm, anger burned along the link.

"So you don't think we'll be attacked?"

"Not here. Not yet."

She wished she could share his certainty. But the dark water receded farther, and walking became easier. She swept the flashlight's beam across the darkness ahead, noting the tunnel was beginning to close in around them. The roof was only inches above Michael's head.

"I hope we don't have to crawl," she muttered. The thought of getting down on her hands and knees made her stomach churn.

"I can't imagine Jasper doing it, so I doubt we will."

"You really do know him well, don't you?"

"It pays to. As I've said, he's eluded our circle for years."

"And was your circle after him before or after he killed your brother?"

"Before."

But it became personal when Jasper killed Patrick. "Does the circle attempt to kill every vampire who has a thirst for human blood?"

He shrugged—a movement she caught in the edge of the light. "Not all. There are some who can restrain the urge to kill when they feed." Some, but not many, she deduced from his tone. "Those we leave in peace."

She wondered how he'd managed it, how long it had taken him to curb the lust all too evident in Jasper.

"Jasper is a killer," Michael continued grimly. "He always was. Even before the change, he feasted on the suffering of his victims."

And now he feasted on Jake. Her stomach turned. She swallowed and forced a little lightness into her voice. "And his sort gives the vampire world a bad rep, huh?"

He squeezed her hand. "Something like that."

She swept the light across the shadows ahead of them. There was nothing to be seen, yet she had a sense of something going on in the darkness beyond the reach of the flashlight.

Michael stopped abruptly. "Movement."

"How far?"

"Where the tunnel rounds a corner. Something moved in the shadows."

She shivered. It had to be the zombies. It wouldn't be Jasper, not this soon. He'd toy with them a little longer.

Power washed through the link as Michael used his abilities to study the threat ahead. Why didn't Jasper's net affect him?

"It's not aimed at me. There are two zombies up ahead."

"What do we do?"

"*We* do nothing. I'll take care of them." He brushed a kiss across the top of her head, then faded into the darkness.

"Michael?" she hissed as his hand left hers. "Michael!"

No answer. Wonderful. What if the zombies were just a diversion to separate them?

Movement whisked around her legs. Biting back a yelp of fright, she shone the light down at her feet. The water stirred, and something slick and brown and sinuous rose briefly to the oily surface before slithering back underneath.

Her mouth went dry. Snakes. There were snakes in the water with her . . .

Sweat broke out across her brow as the dark waters began to churn, the snakes bumping against her legs. Were they real, or some form of illusion?

They sure *felt* real. One entwined around her legs, and she kicked out. A sleek brown head rose from the water, hissing. She screamed and swiped at it with the flashlight. It sank back down and joined the circling pack. She leaped over them and ran forward, heading for the zombies and Michael.

The beam of the flashlight jumped erratically, creating crazy shadows on the slick walls. The darkness beyond the light seemed oppressive, a monster waiting to pounce. She splashed on, cursing Michael for leaving her.

The snakes followed. Real or not, they were coming for her. She gripped the flashlight tightly and tried to run faster.

Michael! Frantically, she reached for the connection between them. There was no answer, just a sense of absence. Could he hear her when he was little more than a shadow?

It was just one more thing she didn't know. Heart pounding faster than her feet, she listened to the sounds of pursuit above the noise of her own panicked flight. She was tempted to use her psychic abilities, but Jasper would snare her the minute she tried.

Damn it, she wasn't *completely* helpless without her abilities. She had her knives. She could use them to defend herself. Why play Jasper's games any more than she had to? She stopped and swung around, but the water was still, silent. The snakes, if they'd even been real, were gone.

Almost with you, Nikki.

She closed her eyes and took a deep breath, trying to calm her churning stomach. It had been nothing more than a game. Once she'd stood her ground, Jasper had backed away. He might want her abilities, but maybe he also feared them.

The thought did little to ease the sick tension in her stomach. She turned and shone the light across the waters ahead again. Ripples of movement stirred the surface, but she couldn't see Michael. Only when he was near her did he shake himself free of the shadows.

He brushed his knuckles lightly across her cheek. "Are you all right?"

She wished he'd just take her in his arms and hold her until the chill and the fear left her. But they had no time. Jake was dying. They had to get to him quickly.

"Yeah, sure." She ran a hand through her damp hair. What would he think if he realized she'd been running from nonexistent snakes? "This place is just starting to get to me. What about the zombies?"

"They've disappeared."

She raised an eyebrow. "How can zombies just disappear?"

He shrugged. "I don't know. As soon as I neared them, I lost all scent."

She studied the darkness uneasily. If Jasper could fool Michael's keen senses, they might be in big trouble.

"Come on." He ran his hand down her arm and clasped her fingers gently. "There's nothing we can do but move forward."

The warmth of his touch made her feel more secure as they walked on. But after a few minutes, they stopped again.

"Fork in the tunnel. Which way, Nikki?"

She closed her fingers around the watch fob. It pulsed lightly, its rhythm slower, more erratic than before. They had so little time left.

"Left." She swung in that direction, but Michael jerked her back hard, again almost dislocating her shoulder in the process. She swore softly. "What's wrong?"

"The zombies are back."

She shone the light into the tunnel but could see no movement. "We can't just stand here, Michael. We have to get to Jake."

He hesitated, then shrugged. "All right, let's go."

The walls began to close in, threatening to smother them. Ghostly tendrils of slime brushed against her clothes and felt like long green fingers of the dead.

Twenty feet on, they came out of the ankle-deep water and into a cavern. She blinked and stopped, astonished. The flashlight filled the cavern with dancing shadows—dark demons that teased her imagination. Something about the air conveyed a feeling of vast emptiness.

At that moment, she saw Jake huddled against an outcrop of rock. With a small cry, she ran over. Squatting beside him, she frantically felt for a pulse. It was there—but slow, erratic, weak.

"He's dying," Michael said softly, stopping just behind her.

She swallowed the lump in her throat and blinked back sudden tears. "No. I won't let him die."

"Jasper has fed on him. There's barely enough blood left to pump his heart . . ."

Michael's voice faded, and she glanced up quickly. He was listening to the silence, his face as still as his thoughts, giving nothing away. Evil swirled around them, and her heart lurched in sudden fear. She reached out and touched Jake's pallid cheek. His skin was colder than her fingers.

"Jake? Please, wake up."

No response, nor had she really expected any. They needed to get him to a hospital if they had any hope of saving him.

Michael said softly, "We can't stay here—"

"I won't leave him!"

"Nikki—"

"I don't want to hear it, Michael." She clenched her fists and glared at him. She wasn't about to leave Jake here to die, as she'd left everyone else in her life she'd cared about.

"I was only going to say we have to get going. Move aside so I can pick him up."

She did as he bid and watched him haul Jake's unconscious figure upright. Something quivered in the air between her and Michael. She spun, but too late to see what it was. She bit her lip and clenched her fists again. Jasper was playing games, again. Damn it, she had to ignore him, had to . . .

An explosion ripped across the silence. The ground bucked and she screamed, staggering sideways as the darkness was suddenly filled with fire and death.

Michael grabbed her arm and held her upright. An ominous rumble ran through the darkness. Jasper wasn't finished with them yet.

"Go," Michael shouted, and thrust her forward.

She ran, dodging falling dirt and stone, the flashlight's beam barely picking out the ground a foot away. Dust filled the darkness—a thick cloud that tore at her throat, making it difficult to breathe. She had no idea where she was going. She just ran, staggering from side to side in tandem with the earth's contortions.

Michael was at her back, his breathing labored. She knew they would all die if they didn't get out of this tunnel soon, and the thought sent fresh energy surging through her.

"Swing left!" he ordered, voice harsh.

Her foot slithered on the slick footing and she threw out an arm for balance, struggling to stay upright. Hopefully, Michael had better balance than she. The falling debris changed everything. It was difficult enough to breathe, let alone remember which tunnel was where.

Another explosion ripped across the darkness and rocks rained down from the ceiling. She threw up her arms, trying to protect her head. Debris hit her, bruising her hands and shoulders. She stumbled, falling, and jarred her knee. Michael's arm went around her waist. With a grunt, he lifted her up and kept running.

After several minutes, he released her and pushed forward once more. "Move, move!"

His fear was tangible, filling the darkness. Not fear for him, but for her. The knowledge lent her feet wings.

"Turn right!"

She swung, dodging rubble, her breathing sharp and labored under the thickening cloud of dust.

"Watch it—"

Michael's shout echoed as her instincts cut in. She twisted sideways, barely avoiding the foul grasp of a zombie. She slipped and cursed, but somehow managed to twist around and shine the light into the creature's eyes. It leaped at her anyway. She dodged and flicked her knife into her palm.

Michael grabbed her arm and pulled her back.

"Let me," he said, and thrust Jake at her.

Jake's weight hit her and she grunted, staggering backward into a wall. Rock dug sharply into her hip and pain ran down her legs. She cursed but wrapped an arm around Jake's chest, holding him upright.

Another rumble ran through the darkness. She glanced upward, wondering uneasily if Jasper's plans included bringing the entire mine down on top of them. A chill ran through her. Jasper was close, so very close. She sensed his evil, felt his gloating . . .

Come to me, he whispered. *Come to me now.*

She closed her eyes and fought the urge to obey. But Jake slipped from her grasp, she turned around and started walking.

See? Jasper whispered. *You are mine. You always were.*

No, she thought, and somehow found the strength to stop. *No!*

Jasper laughed, the sound clawing at her nerves. Footsteps echoed behind her. Nikki swung around, her fingers clenched around the knife. A figure loomed out of the darkness. Michael, not Jasper. Relief shot through her, shocking in its intensity.

He glanced at Jake, at her, his expression suddenly concerned. "What's wrong?"

"Thought I heard something." She half shrugged. "Whatever it was, it's gone."

"Go," he said, and picked up Jake.

"What about the zombie?"

"No longer a threat."

Given there were at least four more out there, that wasn't much comfort. The water began to climb up her body once again, inching toward her chest. She remembered the snakes she'd encountered and faltered. Then, just as another explosion ripped across the darkness, a hand grabbed her ankle and pulled her down under the water. Jasper's chuckle surged around her, as thick and dangerous as the water suddenly was.

"Nikki!"

Michael's cry was cut off as she was pulled deeper under the foul water. Dirt and stone fell around her, striking her arms, her body, but doing nothing to hinder Jasper's grip on her. Kinetic energy surged through her body and she flung it downward. Jasper's grip was ripped from her ankle, and the surge of bubbles that suddenly danced around her suggested he'd been flung away with some force. His fury swept her mind, accompanied by the demand that she stay, but her chest burned and her head ached, and if she didn't get some air soon she'd die. She thrust upward, kicking as hard as she could for the surface. Rocks continued to fall, churning the water and confusing her senses. The need to open her mouth, to suck in air, grew desperate.

A rock smashed into her shoulder and she thrashed sideways. Another hit her head and red fire spread through her brain. She gasped in agony, and the waters rushed in as darkness engulfed her.

Come to me, pretty one. Come willingly, and fear not death.

The voice was soft, as alluring as the darkness that surrounded her. Yet it filled her with fear and confusion. She had no idea where she was, no idea what was happening to her. She couldn't feel her body, couldn't feel anything. She just floated in blackness, waiting.

For what?

Another voice—softer, more desperate—invaded the darkness. *Nikki, Nikki! Hear me!*

There was an edge—a desperation—in that frantic call that pulled at her. Something within her wanted to reach out, to grasp the hand that she knew would be waiting somewhere out there in the blackness.

No, the dark voice said. *Heed not the betrayer.*

Betrayer? *Tommy.* He had to mean Tommy. But he was dead, killed long ago as a result of his own recklessness.

Not Tommy. Michael. He lies to you, pretty one. He has always lied to you.

Perhaps, she thought. But there'd been truths, both in his words and his actions, as well.

Enough, the darkness whispered. *Come to me. Now!*

The command swirled around her, tugging at her confusion, her will. She half turned. In the distance, blue light flared. Twin beacons of power, bright and alluring.

Damn it, Nikki! Listen to me! Don't answer Jasper's call. Don't take the path of death.

Path? But even as the word formed in her mind, golden light filled the stillness around her, freeing her from fear, filling her with peace and an intense need to be one with the light.

NO!

Gentle music washed across her senses, flooding her cold body with warmth and releasing her from the dark whispers and the weight of pain holding her captive. Suddenly free, her spirit drifted toward the long golden tunnel.

Stay with me!

Something in that urgent plea made her hesitate, and the call of the golden light became muted. Yet she didn't have the strength to go back, didn't have the courage to face the fear and the pain. The honey-eyed light pulsed, welcoming her, calling . . .

Nikki, I need you. Don't leave me.

The cry made her heart ache. She wasn't worthy of the urgency in that entreaty. She wasn't sure she was even capable of understanding it. And it was too late. Far too late. Dancing in seductive brightness, she drifted closer to the light.

Nikki, do you want to live?

Did she? The question echoed through the soft warmth surrounding her, and images of Michael ran through her mind. Oh yes, she wanted to live. But only with Michael. And that was an impossible dream.

No! If you trust me, there is a way.

No! Not as a vampire. Better death than a vampire.

Cold steel filled his thoughts. *Do you trust me?*

Trust was a flickering fire, easily put out. So few people had earned its warmth after her mom's death. Only Jake, and he, too, was dying.

Jake needs you, Nikki. I need you.

She closed her eyes against the pain in his entreaty. Michael didn't need her. He didn't need anyone. Maybe that was half her problem. He could walk away, and it wouldn't matter to him.

But Jake had to live. He couldn't die because of her.

Come to me, Nikki. Let me save you. For Jake's sake, if not for mine.

She spun in confusion, afraid to go forward and afraid to go back. The warm light pulsed, healing and calming. Here at last was the peace she had searched so long for. It would be very easy to give in to its warmth. Easy . . . But was it right? She didn't know, and that scared her more than the thought of dying.

Forgive me, Nikki. I can't let you do this.

Something grabbed her soul and yanked her away from the golden light. She wept and reached out toward it, a desperate swimmer fighting the tide, but her efforts were in vain. The light disappeared, and she was thrust through layers of darkness and gathering pain.

Then the red mist enclosed her brain and swept her away.

Sixteen

.

MICHAEL?

The harsh whisper ran through his mind. He closed his eyes and leaned back in the uncomfortable hospital chair. The last thing he felt like doing was talking to anyone right now, particularly Seline. Yet she was the one person who might understand.

Michael, what have you done?

He smiled grimly. What *had* he done? Even now, he wasn't entirely sure. He'd risked his life and cheated death, but until Nikki regained consciousness, he wouldn't know if it was worth it. There could be aftereffects, either from her ingesting so much putrid water or his own intervention. There was a very real possibility he might have destroyed the very thing he was trying to save.

He raised his Coke and took a long drink. It didn't ease the burning in his throat.

Michael?

Worry shot through Seline's mental tones. He sighed. She'd be in Lyndhurst in a flash if he didn't start answering. And the last thing he needed was a face-to-face confrontation with the old witch.

Here.

Michael, what on earth have you done? Half the circle had visions of you in jeopardy.

It was unusual enough for Seline to worry. No doubt his ice-cool reputation had been shot to hell, as well.

I think I've fallen in love, Seline.

Heavens, boy, why do you think I sent you to save her?

He snorted softly. He'd known the old witch was up to something, but he would never have imagined it was matchmaking. *You could have warned me, Seline.*

And why would I do that? Especially given your renowned determination to remain a lone wolf. Amusement ran through her mental tones. *Now stop avoiding the original question, or I'll come over in person and box your ears.*

The threat made him smile, as she no doubt intended. Seline—who barely reached his shoulders—was a thin, frail-looking woman. But she didn't look the one hundred and eighty years Michael knew her to be, and she certainly didn't act it.

We've known each other a long time, Michael. I thought trust was part of what we shared.

Trust wasn't his problem. Would she understand the sheer desperation that had made him act as he had? Would she accept his need to break a vow? Would she understand that he might lose Nikki, anyway, because of his actions?

She was dying, Seline. I shared my psyche with her.

He had made her live, against her will, by fusing her life-force to his. And in the process had linked them together forever and made her as near to immortal as any human could get without crossing over to become vampire. But it was an act that could have killed them both. He closed his eyes and took another long gulp of cola.

The sudden tension down the mental lines told him Seline understood the risk he'd taken.

Dear heavens, Michael, are you all right?

Exhausted. Weak. But alive. Obviously.

Can you cope with Jasper? Will you have the strength?

I'll cope. And Jasper would pay for every ounce of pain he'd put Nikki through.

Is she . . . all right?

Michael opened his eyes and studied Nikki's still features. She lay unmoving on the hospital bed, her skin almost translucent, as if she was still suspended between life and death. He couldn't reach her mind, couldn't open the link between them, and it worried him.

I don't know.

How did all this happen?

Jasper set a trap, using Nikki's boss as bait.

That Jake still lived was a miracle. With the injuries he'd sustained, he must have survived on sheer force of will alone until they reached the hospital. Michael only hoped the hospital could sustain that miracle— and not just for Jake and Nikki's sake, but for his own, as well. Jake was a rare discovery in this day and age—someone who looked beyond fear, beyond humanity, to see the person that lay beneath.

Do you need a hand? Gail's available.

I'll handle it.

But—

I said I'll handle it.

Concern ran down the link. *Are you sure? Gail's ready to go.*

The bastard's mine!

Her thoughts recoiled from the force of his anger, and he cursed. Lashing out at his friends would help no one, least of all Nikki.

Sorry.

I understand, Michael. Just be careful. You're no good to Nikki if you're so damn weak you can barely stand.

I know. He took another gulp of Coke. *What the hell am I going to do once all this is over?*

What do you think you should so? What do you want to do?

What he should do and what he wanted to do were two very different things.

They don't have to be, Michael. She's a very resilient young woman. She'd fit nicely into our circle.

And share his world? As much as he ached to do just that, to finally have someone to walk by his side, it wasn't right or fair to ask her to do so. Darkness had been too much a part of her life already.

You should at least give her the opportunity to refuse, Michael.

She doesn't want me in her life. She doesn't want anyone in her life.

Amusement filtered down the line. *That sounds terribly familiar. I wonder where I've heard that before?*

He grimaced. *I have to leave her. I have no real choice.*

Believe an old witch when she says the future is

clouded when it comes to the two of you. There is no clear-cut choice here, no right or wrong.

He ran a hand through his hair. *Fat lot of good that advice does me.*

Then listen to your heart, Michael. It may be buried deep, but I know it's there. Now get something to eat before you fade into shadow.

She broke the contact. He sighed and finished the rest of his Coke. Seline was right—he needed to eat. If he couldn't touch Nikki's mind now, after all they'd shared, what hope did Jasper have?

He pushed out of the chair that had been his home for the last six hours and walked across to the window. The morning light washed across his skin, but even in his weakened state, it held no threat.

But fatigue did.

He had to regain strength as quickly as he could. When he finally caught Jasper, he had to be fit enough to take him.

The bastard had to die.

Nikki woke in a room that wasn't her own. She blinked, confused, and wondered where the hell she was. And how she'd gotten there.

She bit her lip and looked around. Sterile whiteness met her gaze, but it still took her a moment to realize she was in a hospital bed. The clock on the wall opposite said it was just after nine, and the sunlight pouring in through the window to her right meant it was A.M., not P.M. There were three other beds in the room, and a chair beside each, but none of them were occupied. There was also a chair beside her bed—it was also empty. And had been for some time. Michael was several miles away, gaining nourishment from a herd of dairy cows.

She blinked. How could she possibly know that without reaching for the link? *What has he done to me?*

She clenched her fists and closed her eyes, trying to recall the last moments in the mine. She remembered the golden light and its comforting warmth, and her need to let go, to be at peace. Remembered Michael's desperate pleas. Then something had yanked her back into darkness and pain.

Michael, breaking his vow yet again.

He may have saved her life, but at what cost? Was she even human anymore?

Desperate to know, she pulled out the IV, scrambled out of bed and ran across to the window. If she *had* been turned, then what she was about to do would be deadly, but she didn't really care. She'd rather die than become a vampire.

Nothing happened.

The sunlight caressed her skin, warming but not burning her. She leaned her forehead against the windowpane and closed her eyes. So she wasn't a vampire. At least Michael had heeded her wishes in *that* regard. But how had he saved her? Why did she feel no pain, no aches, after swallowing so much foul water and being trapped under rocks and debris? How had he saved her, and at what cost to them both?

Her senses danced with the knowledge of change, yet blurred into confusion when she tried to understand how. And though she needed answers, she didn't want to reach for the link to Michael. But she sensed nothing would ever be the same—not with her life, and not with Michael.

A nurse entered the room. "Nice to see you're finally awake," she said, although her smile faded quickly when she noticed the detached IV. "But I'm not sure you're supposed to be getting out of bed just yet. And you certainly shouldn't have unhooked the IV."

"I didn't. It must have come out on its own." Nikki half shrugged. "But I'm fine."

The nurse gave her the sort of look that suggested she wasn't buying the lie. "Be that as it may, perhaps you'd better get back into bed until the doctor says otherwise."

Nikki opened her mouth to argue, but the nurse, for all her sunniness, gave her the sort of look that suggested she wasn't the type to be easily swayed.

Nikki sighed and got back into bed. The nurse checked her over, reinserting the IV, and patted her hand before saying, "Can I get you anything? There's water on the table beside you—unfortunately I can't offer you anything to eat until the doc clears it, though. I can get you some magazines to read, if you'd like."

"I'm fine." Nikki hesitated, then said, "Tell me, is Jake Morgan also a patient here?"

The nurse frowned. "I'm afraid I can't talk about other patients—"

Meaning he was? Nikki's stomach suddenly began to turn itself into knots. "He's my boss. I just need to know if he's okay."

"I'm sorry, but I can't." The nurse patted Nikki's

hand again. "The doctor will be here soon, and if he gives the all-clear, I'll remove the IV. Just use the buzzer if you need anything."

Nikki blew out a frustrated breath as the nurse bustled out, and reached for the TV remote. With nothing else to do, she flicked through the various news channels, watching the different reports about Trevgard's death. It was certainly big news on the local channels—along with reports about the eight women who had now gone missing. Interestingly, there were no reports of Monica's demise. Maybe MacEwan had managed to stifle *that* little piece of news.

It was just after three when the phone on the bedside table rang, the shrill sound making her jump. Her heart accelerated as she reached for the receiver. She knew who was calling. What she wasn't sure of was why.

"Mary," she said softly, blinking back a sudden rush of tears.

"The nurse just told me you had been awake and asking after Jake." Mary's voice sounded weary, old. "You need to come talk to him, Nikki."

She had a sudden vision of Jake, pale and dying, and felt a rush of despair. *Don't let me lose him, too. I couldn't bear it.*

"Nikki?"

She swallowed the lump in her throat. "How's . . . How is he?"

"He's going to be fine. It was touch and go for a few hours, though. He's awake, but he won't settle until he sees you. I told him you were okay, but he keeps muttering something about vampires controlling my mind."

Given the time, it was possible that Jasper was awake, but she doubted he was strong enough to control either Jake or Mary from a distance. And the amount of sunlight still about meant he *couldn't* be here physically—not unless he'd taken refuge in the hospital last night, and why would he have done that? It wasn't a safe place for someone who was unable to respond to any sort of threat through the midday hours.

But that didn't mean he wasn't planning another trap. Didn't mean he wouldn't use Jake or Mary against her.

She ignored the fear that swirled at that thought, and said, "What room is he in?"

"Five-eleven."

Which didn't really help, given she had no idea where that was or where she was, but it surely wouldn't be that hard to find. "I'll be there as soon as I get dressed."

She hung up the phone, suddenly grateful that the doctor had given the all-clear for her IV to be removed—and had, in fact, been surprised by the speed of her recovery. Which was no doubt due to Michael and whatever he'd done to her. She thrust the thought aside and climbed out of bed, padding across to the small closet. Her clothes were inside, all scrunched up in a plastic bag. The smell just about knocked her out when she opened it. There was no way in *hell* she was going to put them back on. She gathered the rear of hospital gown together with one hand to stop it flapping open, then headed out. She found Mary pacing the hall on the other side of the hospital.

The older woman didn't immediately say anything, just gathered Nikki in her arms and hugged her fiercely.

"I'm so glad you're okay," she said, after a moment.

"I'm glad *everyone* is okay," Nikki said, blinking back tears as she pulled gently away. "He *is* okay, isn't he? Really?"

"He's beaten, bloody and mauled, but he's alive, and that's all that matters."

It certainly was. Nikki hesitated, then asked, "Did he say what attacked him?"

Mary grimaced. "He seems a little fixated on vampires at the moment. The docs said it was a rogue animal of some sort."

"Well, that's more likely than a vampire," she agreed. Mary obviously didn't know or believe the truth, and Nikki wasn't about to enlighten her without talking to Jake first. "Are you sure it's okay—"

She stopped when Mary gripped her arm. "Go, talk to him. I'll wait out here."

Nikki stepped into the small, bright room. Jake's broad body was almost lost among the machines and tubes surrounding him. She stepped closer, smiling when he opened his eyes.

"Nikki." His voice was harsh, forced through thin, pale lips. "I was so afraid that bastard had gotten you. I just needed to see for myself . . ."

"Jasper didn't get me. And he won't." If she said it often enough, maybe she'd believe it. She placed her hand on his. "You're looking good."

It didn't matter that his color was ghostlike, that there were tubes sticking out of every bit of him, or that he had a huge bandage around his neck as well as a smaller one around the stitched cut on his forearm. He was alive. That was all that mattered, all she cared about.

"Liar." His gaze pinned her, shrewd despite the pain haunting his pale features. "How are *you*?"

She shrugged. "I'll live."

He turned his hand around and squeezed her fingers. His grip was weak, yet oddly reassuring.

"I'm not going to die on you, Nik. I'm far too stubborn to let the likes of Jasper win so easily."

Tears stung her eyes, but she blinked them back. Jake didn't need her tears; it would only make him worry. "I'm glad."

He squeezed her hand again. "I just needed you to know. I don't want . . ." He hesitated, looking uncomfortable. "Nik, not everyone in your life has to die. Don't be afraid to live because you're afraid of death. Don't let fear close your heart."

His words cut through her. She stared at him, wondering how he'd known, how he'd guessed.

"I'm no fool, Nikki. I've watched you grow from an untamed urchin to a warm but distant woman. Let someone break the ice, kid. If not Michael, then someone else. You can't go on as you are."

Why not? Why was everyone so intent on changing her life when she was happy?

But am I really?

Awareness raced like fire across her skin, and she knew without looking that Michael had stepped into the room. Still holding Jake's hand, she turned and watched him walk to the opposite side of the bed.

She wondered if it was a deliberate choice. His gaze, when it met hers, was dark, emotionless, and there was a similar stillness in the link. He was keeping his distance and it made her uneasy.

"Good to see you're alive," Michael said softly. Though his gaze had turned to Jake, she knew all his attention was on her—waiting, assessing.

She shivered and bit her lip. She didn't want the confrontation she sensed was coming. She wasn't ready for it. How could she be? Her whole life had changed in some unfathomable way, and the man standing so calmly on the opposite side of the bed had worked that change.

"As I was just explaining to Nikki, I'm too bloody stubborn to die." Jake's smile was a pale imitation of its usual self. "But, if you both don't mind, I really need to rest. I might suggest, though, that you find somewhere to sit and talk."

"God, not even a vampire's attack can stop you from being bossy," she muttered.

Jake smiled, and closed his eyes. "Hey, that's my job."

And she was *so* glad he could still do it. She leaned forward and dropped a kiss on his forehead, pulling her hand from his. He really did need to rest. And she needed to get out of this hospital. She couldn't do anything when she was stuck in here.

"Let's go," she said softly, glancing at Michael.

He nodded and stepped away from the bed.

"Get the bastard for me, Michael," Jake murmured as they left.

Michael's gaze was bleak as it met hers. "I will."

The promise of death was in his voice. Nikki gave Mary a brief hug, asked if she could borrow her coat, then headed back to her room. Once there, she exchanged the hospital gown for the coat, collected the stinking bag of clothes, and—against the advice of the nurses—checked herself out.

"He'll live," Michael commented as they waited for an elevator.

"I know." She glanced at him, studying his still features. "Thank you for not leaving him in the tunnel."

He nodded. The elevator doors opened, and several people got out. Nikki stepped inside beside Michael and pressed the lobby button. When the doors opened again, they walked in silence to the car and drove to Nikki's home.

Her nerves were stretched to the breaking point by the time she opened the front door and entered her apartment. Michael followed her inside with ease, and it took a moment to remember that she'd actually—accidentally—issued an invitation a few days ago. She couldn't stop him even if she'd wanted to. And she didn't want to—did she?

Frowning, she stripped off the coat, walked into her bedroom to throw on some clothes, then headed into the kitchen, turning on lights as she passed them. It might be only four, but the afternoon shadows seemed to be closing in thick and fast. Michael leaned on the counter and watched her make coffee. The time for confrontation had come. She feared it . . . and sensed she wasn't the only one.

Apprehension stole through her heart but she ignored it, finally turning to face him. "What did you do to me, Michael?"

He didn't answer her right away. She gripped her coffee cup tightly, watching him, waiting.

Eventually, he said, "I saved your life."

"But at what cost? Why do I feel so different?"

"You were dying, Nikki."

"And maybe *that* was my fate. But no, you had to step in and break your vow yet again."

"It was necessary—"

"*What* was necessary? Answer the question, damn it! I have the right to know."

"But do you have the courage to look beyond it?" A trace of bitterness haunted his words. "What I have done cannot be undone."

"*What* can't be undone, Michael?"

He hesitated, then said, "I gave you part of what I am."

Horror rose anew. Did that mean she *was* a vampire?

"No, it does not." He moved quickly toward her, but stopped when she took an instinctive step back. "All I've ever asked of you is trust. I wonder now if you are even capable of it."

His contempt lashed at her. She flinched but made no comment, waiting for him to continue.

"What I did was give you part of my . . . psyche, part of my strength. Part of my life-force, I suppose. It gave you life."

And linked us together forever.

She took another step back. Linked for the rest of her life, never to be separated. The one thing she was desperate to avoid.

"Not your life. *My* life."

Her heart skipped several beats. She clenched her fists against the fear pounding through her heart. "What do you mean?"

"Your life-force is linked to mine. As long as I live, you cannot die."

She groped for the edge of the bench, her knees suddenly weak. "Oh God, Michael, you're kidding . . . right?"

"No. Unless you're beheaded, or otherwise rendered brain-dead, you will not die. Even a shot through the heart will not kill you. Your body will simply heal itself, just as my body heals itself." There was no remorse in his voice, only an odd harshness that somehow spoke of pain.

She ignored it. She was immortal? As eternal as the moon and the stars . . . and Michael?

But Michael wasn't immortal. He *could* be killed. Did that mean . . .

"That if I die, you die? Yes, that's what it means."

"Damn it, I don't want my life to be dependent on a man who hunts vampires for a living! Nor do I want to spend eternity linked to a man who lives in shadow, a man who could rule my every thought and desire!"

His anger rolled across her. "I have *no* desire to control your every thought and deed, Nikki."

Energy burned at her fingertips. She clenched her fists against it. "But could you, if you tried?"

He seemed to hesitate. "I couldn't before—not without a lot of effort. Now . . . I don't know."

She closed her eyes, fighting terror. Michael wasn't Jasper. He wouldn't want to control every aspect of her life. At least not now. But what about one hundred, two hundred years from now? What would happen when he tired of her?

"Questions like that mean nothing, because *nothing* will ever come of this. You do not want me in your life, Nikki, and I . . ." He hesitated. ". . . cannot have you in mine."

Cannot, or would not? Either way, it made little difference. "Then why save me? Why not let me die?"

Again he hesitated. "Because I couldn't let Jasper win. Because I couldn't risk the possibility that he might raise you, even though your death was not directly at his hands."

Well, that certainly wasn't something she'd have wanted, either. She rubbed her arms. "How did you share your life-force, Michael? How is something like that even feasible?"

"I'm not sure about the mechanics of it myself. I only know it can be done when two people are . . . compatible."

What had he originally meant to say? She shook her head, not sure if it even really mattered. "Is this the first time you've attempted something like that?"

"Yes." And the last, if the acidity in his voice was anything to go by. "Do you think it was easy, Nikki, to tear part of what I am away so I could give you life?"

She winced at his anger. She wasn't a complete fool. Life was a miracle she surely didn't deserve. She was just trying to understand the ramifications.

"Can all vampires do this?"

He hesitated, and doubt ran through the color of his emotions.

"Very few. There are problems. I know of only one other, and he found himself in need of an . . . assistant."

"A servant," she corrected tightly.

He sighed. "There were reasons, Nikki, and his friend was very willing."

"Well, at least the friend was given a choice!"

He made a short, sharp movement with his hand, his eyes glittering with fury and some deeper, darker emotion she couldn't define.

"What *is* your problem, Nikki? Why do you refuse to trust me? Why can't you just accept the gift I gave you?"

I can't trust you because I might love you. And I don't want to die just because you die.

"I have no intention of dying anytime soon, Nikki," he said, voice bitter. "So you can wipe that fear from your mind."

"But I don't *want* eternity, Michael. I don't want to live with the fear that one day you will turn on me."

His breath hissed through clenched teeth. "If you think me such a monster, kill me. Take a knife to my throat and behead me."

She snorted. "And kill myself in the process? Unlikely. I may have wanted to die back in the mine, but I'm not particularly suicidal right now."

He swore softly—vehemently—and walked to the other side of the kitchen. It was a distancing that was as much mental as it was physical. And though this was what she had wanted, it still tore at her.

"What are we going to do, then?" he asked after a moment. Arms crossed, he leaned against the wall, his face impassive, distant. As cold as when they'd first met.

She studied him. Anger she could cope with. Frustration and bitterness she could understand. But this? "I don't know."

And while she had no idea what they were going to do, she *did* know what she wanted—and that was for someone to cherish her, love her, for the person she was rather than what she was capable of. But she also feared that sort of love, particularly now, with him, because her love had always signaled death. Vampire or not, he could die.

Better to live a lifetime alone than face the weight of one more death on her conscience.

Only now it wasn't just one lifetime she had to face, was it? And it wasn't just the fact that she could only die when he did, but rather having to face the death of Jake and Mary and anyone else she might care about in the future.

"Perhaps it is best if I simply leave," he said softly. "At least we can continue on as we were, and perhaps eventually it will be as if we never even met."

But they *had* met, and he'd linked them eternally, so pretending it had never happened was not going to be an answer. Not now. Still, what other choice was there? She couldn't risk him staying, and he didn't want to anyway.

He turned and walked to the door. But as he reached out to grab the door handle, she found herself whispering, "Don't."

He glanced back at her. "Jasper won't come near you again. I vow that, and I mean it."

She wasn't afraid of Jasper right now. She was

afraid that Michael would walk out that door and she'd never see him again.

Yet wasn't that what she wanted?

"Bye, Nikki." He turned and left. The door slammed shut behind him, rattling the display case in the living room. A crystal vase rocked and fell to the floor.

The sound of it smashing was like the sound of her heart shattering into jagged pieces.

Seventeen

THE SILENCE DROVE her crazy. Nikki prowled through the house for hours, trying to find something, anything, to do. Now that she had time to think, it was the one thing she was desperate to avoid. Michael had walked out the door, probably forever. And she couldn't help the notion that, in a lifetime filled with mistakes, she'd just made her biggest. *I want to be alone. I don't want to share my life with anyone. I don't want to share my heart . . .*

But did she really want to spend eternity alone?

The answer to that was simple. She had no real desire to spend *this* lifetime alone, let alone the next three or four.

But what other choice did she have?

She stopped in front of the window and stared out blindly. Night had finally arrived and Jasper was out there somewhere. While she could feel his darkness in her mind, he hadn't as yet called to her. The fact that she'd resisted him in the mine—and used her kinetic powers despite a net supposedly designed to stop her—suggested neither he nor his influence on her was as strong as he'd led her to believe. By the same token, she had no desire for that suspicion to be tested.

She crossed her arms. Outside, a young couple strolled hand in hand across the road. She wished she had their courage. Wished she could find it within herself to take a chance.

She turned from the window and walked across the room. Maybe she needed to work. Maybe if she buried herself in mundane office tasks, she wouldn't have to think about Michael or Jasper or the long, *long* years of loneliness ahead.

She went to the bedroom to collect her coat and keys, brushing past the bed. Memories rose to haunt her—being in Michael's arms, in his bed, his throaty laughter as she'd whisked his pants off him. The fire of their minds, touching and loving.

How could she have given it all away? How could she have thrown away her one chance of lasting love?

She froze. There, she'd finally admitted it. She loved him, no matter what he'd done. But it didn't matter a damn. She didn't want him to die, so they simply couldn't be together. Not even after Jasper was dead.

She spun away from the bed and her memories and retreated to the front door. Where she stopped. Jasper was out and active, and she needed something other than kinetic ability to protect herself with. She walked across the room and opened the closet door. Squatting, she dragged out the old cutlery set and took out two knives. They were badly tarnished, but hopefully it wouldn't matter. They were still silver— though just how pure she couldn't say. She pushed a knife down each boot, then rose and stamped her feet lightly. The knives might make walking slightly uncomfortable, but she felt better for their presence. After a quick glance around to check that everything was off, she opened the door and went outside.

The night was clear and held the promise of cold. A chill ran up her spine as she unlocked the car door. It had nothing to do with the wind's icy fingers teasing the back of her neck. Someone was watching her.

She ignored the sensation and got into the car. There was little else she could do. It wasn't Michael or Jasper, so it was more than likely one of the zombies. And she sure as hell wasn't going to confront one of them.

But if only one zombie was watching her, what were the others up to? Foreboding pulsed, a warning of trouble ahead. She grimaced and drove out of the driveway. It would be nice if the warnings were a little more specific.

The first thing she saw as she walked into the office was the flashing light on the answering machine. Throwing her keys on her desk, she grabbed a pen and paper and sat down to answer some calls.

It was nearing midnight when she stopped. She rubbed at the crick in her neck and closed her eyes in sudden weariness. *I need a drink,* she thought. *Something strong.* Only Jake didn't keep any alcohol in the office. It was probably just as well. The mood she was in, she'd most likely get drunk and end up feeling sorry for herself.

She leaned back in the chair and rested her feet on top of the desk. For some reason, she felt safe in the office. All the doors and windows were locked and barred, so if anyone tried to break in, she'd hear them. A few hours' sleep would not go amiss. She closed her eyes and drifted.

Images formed in her mind. Images that were indistinct and blurred, but full of panic. Figures lurched and spun in a gentle yet terrifying dance. Death laughed, white teeth flashing across the darkness.

She jerked upright, her feet crashing to the floor. Now she knew what the other zombies were up to. Jake was in danger.

She reached for her link with Michael, but stopped. It wasn't fair to call him every time she or Jake was in trouble. He was in Lyndhurst to find Jasper, and she shouldn't keep distracting him from that. And yet, if the zombies were attacking Jake, it would be on Jasper's orders.

Damn it, no. She had other options and it was time to start using them. She picked up the phone and quickly dialed MacEwan's number. He answered on the second ring.

"It's Nikki James. I need help," she said.

"To do what?" His voice was terse, annoyed.

She wondered if she'd woken him. "It's one of those situations that can't rationally be explained."

Silence met her reply. She waited, her knuckles white with the intensity of her grip on the receiver.

"Tell me what's going on," he said after a long moment.

She sighed in relief. At least he hadn't dismissed her outright, as many others would have. Of course, he *had* seen Monica burn. "The man responsible for the recent spate of murders is going after Jake. Only he's sending his people to do it."

"Isn't Jake still in the hospital? He should be safe enough there, what with hospital security."

"No, it's not that simple." She hesitated, then softly cleared her throat. "The people being sent are . . . Well, they're zombies."

MacEwan made no sound. Even the soft rasp of his breathing had disappeared.

She added, "You'll be looking for two of the eight women who went missing in Highgate Park."

MacEwan swore softly. Once again, she had no idea whether he believed her or not, and all she could do was wait. Jake was in danger and needed help. If MacEwan wouldn't assist her, she'd have no choice but to turn to Michael. She couldn't cope with two zombies on her own, and she wasn't going to let Jake die.

"And to think I was worried about explaining Monica Trevgard's sudden crisping. Jeez . . ."

If he had any doubts as to Nikki's sanity, she didn't hear it in his voice. Maybe he *had* seen too much on the streets to be fazed by anything life threw at him now. Or maybe he was just humoring her while he called the men in white coats with his spare line.

"So how do we deal with these people?" he asked.

"I'm told the only way to stop them is to break their necks."

"So I'm supposed to order my men to break the necks of a couple of formerly missing women?" His voice was scratchy with either disbelief or amusement. Maybe both.

"There's no other way to stop them." And time was running out for Jake. She had to move.

"Maybe." Disbelief was stronger in his voice this

time—not that he seemed to doubt *what* they were dealing with, more the *way* they had to deal with them. "We'd better meet at the hospital. Ten minutes?"

"Ten minutes," she confirmed and hung up.

She stood, then hesitated. She had the silver knives in her boots but would they work on zombies? She could probably use her kinetic ability to break their necks, but if there were more than two and they took her on en masse, she wouldn't have much hope. And although she was psychically strong, fighting too many at one time was likely to be beyond her. So what else? Salt? Michael might have laughed at the idea, but it was used as a barrier in many witches' spells—at least it was on some of the TV shows she watched. And really, what did she have to lose? At the very least, throwing it in their eyes might distract them.

She walked across the room and opened the small cupboard under the sink. Jake had a fetish for extra salt on his food, so there had to be some in there somewhere. She moved several jars around, eventually finding a large shaker. For good measure, she grabbed the pepper and shoved both in her coat pocket.

She retrieved her keys from her desk, locked the office and ran out to the car.

MacEwan was waiting for her at the hospital, leaning against the side of a car almost as battered as her own and smoking. Two officers waited near the hospital's main entrance. She knew there would be others guarding the remaining exits. When MacEwan did something, he did it properly.

She stopped her car beside his and got out. "How many men do you have?"

He exhaled a long plume of smoke, then dropped his cigarette, crushing it under his heel. "Six. Two men guarding each of the exits."

Six men, plus the two of them. Surely it was enough? "Have you been inside?"

He nodded. "Just to let the staff know what's going on."

She stared at him. "You told them about the zombies?"

He snorted. "I'm not a fool."

"And your men?"

"They've seen pictures of the missing women. I've told them to expect the unexpected." He shrugged. She knew in that moment he didn't *really* believe he'd be confronting zombies. "You ready to go in?" he continued.

She looked around, and nodded. She didn't sense anyone watching her. Maybe she'd lost the zombie. And maybe it had somehow beaten her here and joined its brethren.

Seven men might not be enough to cope with the inhuman strength and speed of two or more zombies. Just because intuition had told her there were only two here didn't actually mean that was true. There were eight women missing all told, after all, and even if Michael had killed two, that still left them with six. If two were at the hospital, there were still four more at large . . .

God, she missed Michael. She missed his strength, his ability to make her feel safe. She missed all his secrets and irritating ways. *Admit it,* she thought, *you simply miss him.* But as tempting as it was to reach for him, she couldn't. Jasper's last two traps had almost killed her. If he succeeded with the third, she didn't want to take Michael with her.

Then she stopped suddenly. She couldn't die. Michael's gift of life meant Jasper couldn't kill her—not unless he severed her head. And if he did that, he couldn't raise her, because the one sure way of killing a zombie was to break its neck.

The implications were more than a little mind-boggling.

MacEwan opened the hospital door and frowned back at her. She hurried forward. The nurse stationed at the front desk looked up, but MacEwan flashed his badge and she made no effort to stop them. Nikki led the way to the elevators.

MacEwan spoke into a handset as they got into the elevator, ordering his men to keep sharp. She watched the floor numbers roll by and hoped the men listened to him. Their lives might depend on it.

The doors opened on the fifth floor. MacEwan held her back and looked out, then made her follow him as he led the way down the hall. When they reached Jake's room, he motioned her to one side of the door, stood on the opposite side and slowly pushed it open. Nothing happened. After a few seconds, she peered around the corner of the doorway. The room was dark—and even though it was well after midnight, this was a hospital and rooms were never totally dark. Not unless someone had deliberately engineered it.

Foreboding pulsed in her brain as MacEwan reached out and turned on the lights. They didn't work, so he unhooked the flashlight from his belt and flicked it on. The room was empty. Jake was gone.

MacEwan swore and spoke quickly into the handset. Nikki quickly moved forward, hand outstretched as she neared the bed, desperate to find something . . . There! She grabbed his reading glasses. Her palm burned as images rose. Jake was alive.

"The stairs!" She pushed past MacEwan and ran from the room.

He cursed and spoke quickly into the handset as he pounded after her. He grabbed her arm as she reached the stairwell and wrenched her backward.

"Don't be a fool," he said. "You're unarmed. Let me go first."

He drew his gun and cautiously opened the door. It was useless protesting, especially if he wasn't entirely convinced they were up against zombies.

It was also a damn good reason for contacting Michael. But maybe that was what Jasper actually wanted—calling Michael here to help when the odds were on Jasper's side.

The stairwell was silent, dark. MacEwan pointed his flashlight upward—the emergency lighting was totally smashed. The zombies, obviously. She clenched her fingers around Jake's glasses. Warmth pulsed through her mind, whispering secrets.

"They're on the roof," she said, keeping her voice soft.

MacEwan gave her a curious look, but didn't refute her statement. She followed him into the stairwell, squinting up into the darkness, straining to see something, anything, that might indicate Jake was near.

The sound of a dragged footstep rasped across the silence. The handset squawked.

"We're heading to the roof," MacEwan answered.

Though he spoke softly, his voice echoed. The zombies would know they were coming, if they didn't know already. She licked her lips and followed MacEwan up the stairs. Somewhere above them, a door opened, then slammed shut. She gripped the handrail tightly. They didn't have much time left.

"Quickly," she whispered.

"I'm going as fast as I can."

Tension edged his whisper. She smiled grimly. Maybe MacEwan wasn't the cool, calm and collected type he liked to appear. They reached the door to the roof. MacEwan opened it and peered out. A cold wind blew in, whipping around her ankles. She shivered and peered over his shoulder, trying to see Jake.

MacEwan nudged her back. "I see them. Wait here."

He disappeared out the door. Nikki snorted softly. *Stay here indeed.* Slipping out, she ran in the opposite direction. The warning pulse coming from the glasses grew more urgent. The zombies were dragging Jake to the edge of the building.

She raced around a crumbling chimney, then stopped. The wind slapped against her face, as cold as ice. The zombies were heading for the roof's edge, Jake's half-unconscious figure held between them. MacEwan stood twenty feet away, gun drawn but by his side.

"Police! Stop or I'll shoot," he warned.

The zombies paid no notice, ambling on toward the edge. Again MacEwan shouted a warning, this time aiming his gun. The zombies continued to ignore him.

The gunshot reverberated through the night. One zombie halted, and dropped its hold on Jake and turned ponderously to face MacEwan. The other limped on, dragging Jake by his wounded arm. Blood was beginning to stain the bandage, meaning the cut had split open again.

Nikki broke into a run. Out of the corner of her eye she saw MacEwan take a step, saw him raise the gun.

"Stop or I'll shoot!"

The creature continued to ignore him. Another shot reverberated. The zombie staggered sideways as the bullet hit, but it kept moving. She didn't know if MacEwan had aimed to wound or kill, but it didn't really matter—unless . . .

"Try a head shot," she shouted, even as she kinetically wrenched Jake's unconscious body away from the creature, hauling him across the darkness and into her arms.

She staggered under his weight, her mind reeling with pain. She'd never attempted to move anything as heavy as a man before, and it was harder than she'd imagined it could be. Sweat broke out across her brow, only to be chilled by the cold wind. She thrust her shoulder under Jake's arm and, holding him tight, walked away as quickly as she could.

The zombie howled in frustration. Heavy steps followed.

"How the hell do you stop these things?"

MacEwan's sharp question jarred the silence.

"Other than breaking their necks? I don't know. But, like I said, you could try shooting their fucking heads off." She barely glanced at him, all her attention on the exit at the far side of the roof. A warning pulsed through her, and she paused.

The door opened, and two of MacEwan's men stepped out. They looked around, then ran toward the detective.

Behind them, the door opened again. Three more zombies stepped out. The exit was now blocked, and there was no other way off the roof.

They were trapped.

The plaza pulsed with music and light. People danced and drank, filling the night with heat and music.

Michael kept a close watch on the partygoers from his vantage point above the square. Jasper wove his way through the unsuspecting crowd, a red haze in the darkness, easy to follow. Michael sensed the other vampire's hunger, felt his need. Knew he would attempt to feed tonight. He watched him move from figure to figure, searching for easy prey, someone to lead off into the night.

Only, Michael had already made sure there were no loners in the immediate area. Jasper would have to extend his search to a less populated section of the city.

And there he would die. And Nikki would be safe.

He stirred, shifting from one foot to the other. He wouldn't—couldn't—think about her. Not when he had a murderer to catch. Maybe not even after.

But the memory of her smoky amber eyes, clouded in confusion and fear, kept running through his mind.

He sighed and leaned wearily against the wall. He

had never wanted to fall in love. Not with Nikki. Not with anyone. His life was too dangerous, and human life was too tenuous, too short. But right from the beginning, he'd had no choice. He might have told himself he was only using her as bait, but the truth was, that was simply an excuse to stay near her. She was a flame, a bright torch that had pierced the darkness surrounding him. He needed the touch of that fire. Needed *her*.

He didn't want to return to the emptiness of an eternity alone. Better death, if it came to a choice. Except now his death would also kill Nikki.

He frowned and watched Jasper move back to the center of the square. What was the fiend up to now?

The younger vampire found shape, intercepting the attentions of a pretty young woman, spinning her away from her partner in a dance both erotic and sensual.

Why the hell was Jasper dancing? Why was he risking exposure like this? Michael stood up straight. Something was going on, though he wasn't sure what.

The younger vampire turned. Their gazes locked in a battle Michael knew neither could win. Then Jasper sneered and mouthed a word.

Jake.

Michael clenched his fists. Jasper was going after Jake. Probably with the zombies again, he thought, and wished he'd killed them all when he'd had the chance. Not that he'd really *had* the chance. Besides, Jasper could easily create more. He jumped to the ground and moved forward, slipping quickly through the crowd. There was nothing he could do for Jake right now. As much as he liked the man, as much as his death might hurt Nikki, he wasn't going to let Jasper slip through his fingers now that he almost had him . . .

Jasper's sneer faded. His eyes widened as he suddenly realized his plan wasn't working. He turned and ran, pushing his way through the crowd.

Michael smiled grimly. Jasper could never escape, no matter how fast he ran. Not when the air recoiled against his evil.

He walked quickly through the crowd, following Jasper's trail. They moved out of the square and into the main street. Jasper crossed the road and moved into an alley. Michael hesitated as a car drove by, then pulled free the knife he'd retrieved earlier from his kit at the hotel.

Jasper's life-force shimmered ahead. Michael tossed the knife in his hand, glanced toward Jasper and threw it as hard as he could.

The blade arrowed through the air fast and true, striking Jasper high in the shoulder. He yelped, staggering forward for several steps, and, yanking the blade from his flesh, twisted around and threw it back violently—without any accuracy. Michael avoided the blade easily enough, and for the first time he read fear rather than gloating in the younger vampire's thoughts. He scooped up his knife and ran after the fiend.

Jasper crossed another street. He was heading for the docks, perhaps hoping to lose Michael among all the old warehouses.

The tang of salt air grew heavier on the wind. Michael listened to the waves breaking across the wharf supports—an angry sound that matched his mood. Jasper ran down a wooden walkway and into a building.

Michael studied it. The warehouse appeared deserted. There was no one about, either inside or in the nearby buildings. A trap waiting to be sprung.

He stopped near the door, and moved around to the left. Turning a corner, he saw a small structure in the shadows of the next warehouse. He walked across, keeping watch on the first building to make sure Jasper didn't make an escape attempt.

The door was padlocked, from inside. Michael wrenched it open. *How fortunate*, he thought, seeing a dozen or so cans of gasoline.

Picking up two, he moved back to the warehouse. Jasper hadn't moved. Michael could see his red haze hunkered down in one corner.

He opened one of the cans and splashed gas across the building's wooden wall. Then he stepped back, reaching into his pocket for the matches he'd picked up when he'd left his hotel this evening.

The fire wouldn't kill Jasper, but it would make him sweat. It would make him relive the horror of his childhood. It would terrify him, as he'd terrified Nikki.

Lighting a match, Michael flicked it at the wall, and stepped backward quickly as it exploded into flame.

The sensation of fear hit Michael, almost suffocating all his other senses. Only it wasn't Jasper's fear. It was Nikki's.

He immediately opened the link and reached out, demanding to know what was wrong. But her mind was closed to him, refusing to acknowledge his call.

He cursed softly. He'd feared this might happen. When he'd shared his psyche with her, he'd not only strengthened the link between them, but he'd also strengthened her ability to ignore him.

He glanced back at the fire. Hungry fingers of flame were beginning to spread along the roof. It wouldn't be long before the whole building was ablaze. Jasper hadn't yet moved. He would wait until the last possible moment. But Michael couldn't.

Nikki was in danger. He had to leave.

At least dawn wasn't far off. With a bit of luck, Jasper wouldn't have the courage to do any further hunting tonight.

And that, in turn, would weaken him—a distinct advantage for Michael. Because when he had shared his psyche with Nikki, he'd lost a lot of his own strength. If Jasper fed, he would be hard to beat. Not that it mattered. Michael had no intentions of dying— not when he would take Nikki with him.

He turned and broke into a run, heading for the hospital and Nikki.

The zombie charged. Nikki leaped away, but not quickly enough. The creature's fist clipped her jaw and sent her flying. She hit the concrete hard, her breath whooshing from her lungs. The zombie turned, its movements ponderous yet not exactly slow. A sick grin marred its once pretty features.

Nikki rolled over and scrambled to her feet as the zombie rushed her again. She reached for kinetic energy, but pain lanced through her brain and brought tears to her eyes. Hauling Jake away had cost her *big-*

time, but she didn't regret it. It just meant she'd have to do this the old-fashioned way. She dodged sideways, barely avoiding the creature's fist, and glanced toward the shadows at the chimney's base. Slowly, foot by foot, she was leading the zombie away from Jake.

A shot rang out through the silence, then a string of curses and the sound of running footsteps. From the sound of things, MacEwan and his men were trying to deal with three of the creatures. Another zombie held guard near the door.

Nikki's undead foe rushed her again. She ducked, but not fast enough. Its hand smashed into the back of her skull and sent her flying. Her knees skinned against the concrete and she shook her head, fighting tears, and the stars dancing before her eyes.

From behind her came the sound of a scraping footstep. Panic surged. She twisted away, but the zombie hit her hard, knocking her sideways, back onto the concrete. It laughed—an oddly vacant sound that chilled her soul. She blinked away tears of pain and tried to roll to one side. The zombie reached down and stopped her, putting its hands around her neck and hauling her upright. It felt like it was trying to rip her head off—and maybe it was. After all, that was one sure way to kill her.

But Jasper *couldn't* know she now shared Michael's psyche. And if he didn't, the zombies didn't, either. Unless . . . Just how deep did the link he'd created go?

The creature's grip tightened. Gritting her teeth against the pain, gasping for breath and trying not to panic, Nikki reached into her pocket.

The edge of darkness was closing in fast. She

quickly took the small container out of her pocket and, loosening its top, flung the salt into the zombie's face.

The creature roared and let go, clawing at its eyes as it staggered away. Nikki pushed herself upright. She could barely see through her own tears, and her throat felt raw, as if it were on fire. It hurt to breathe, let alone move. But she had to move, before the zombie returned.

A warning pulsed through her mind. She scrubbed the tears away and turned. Her attacker sniffed the breeze, using scent instead of vision. Then it spun and charged.

Nikki didn't move. The creature was too fast to outrun, and too strong to fight. No matter how much it hurt, she was going to have to use her psychic abilities.

She took a deep breath and prayed for a miracle.

Thrusting a tight beam of energy at the creature, she halted its charge. It screamed in fury, struggling against the invisible cords holding it immobile.

Sweat broke out across Nikki's brow and dripped into her eyes, stinging them. She didn't blink, didn't move, fearing either might cause her to lose her kinetic grip. Fire ripped through her mind—a red haze of agony she had no choice but to ignore as she battled to contain the creature.

But simple containment wasn't the answer. The zombie had to die, or else it would come back again and again. The vampire who controlled its mind wanted Jake dead. The zombie would follow the wishes of its master until it succeeded.

Or perished.

She had no choice. She flung out a cord of kinetic energy and wrapped it quickly around the creature's neck. It screamed—a sound so human, Nikki hesitated.

In that instant, the creature broke her grip and surged forward again—running straight for the shadows that protected Jake.

Nikki gasped and dropped to her knees. She couldn't do it again. She bit her lip and hugged her body tightly. But she had to. This zombie had to die, or more people would. People like Jake, who'd done nothing except be her friend.

She forced past the pain and snapped tight the noose of energy still wrapped around the creature's neck. It halted mid-stride and struggled desperately, wrenching and twisting against the invisible leash that held it captive. Pain rippled through Nikki's every fiber, every cell. She ignored it and tightened her hold, then, with a last, desperate effort, yanked the creature's head back and down, snapping its neck. The zombie fell, lifeless, to the ground.

She closed her eyes and rocked back and forth, desperately trying to catch her breath. She felt like she'd run a marathon—and it wasn't over yet. Unless MacEwan had started shooting their heads off, four zombies still remained, with a fifth unaccounted for.

Another gunshot shattered the night. Nikki licked her lips and climbed unsteadily to her feet. MacEwan appeared out of the shadows to her left, half carrying one of his men. A zombie followed, dragging one leg.

Nikki clenched her fist and threw a ball of power at the creature. It staggered under the impact and stopped, giving MacEwan the chance to escape.

Then it turned. A roar of anger bit through the night. Giving the creature no chance to charge, she sent another whip of power toward it, knocking it sideways.

She reached for more psychic energy, but agony locked her mind tight. She fell to her knees, fighting tears, fighting the red tide that threatened to engulf her. She'd done too much, pushed too hard. Now there was nothing left. Nothing but pain . . . and quite probably death.

I don't want to die.

Not that she could, unless someone decapitated her, of course. And she still had no idea whether Jasper knew that or not.

The zombie's steps drew near. She had little choice but to close her eyes and wait. She'd find out soon enough just how much the zombies—and their master—knew.

Eighteen

THE FOOTSTEPS STOPPED. An eerie silence followed.

Confused, Nikki opened her eyes and looked up. Pain shot through her head at even that smallest of movements and she blinked back tears, unable to believe what she saw.

The zombie lay on the concrete, ten feet away, its neck twisted at an odd angle. *What on earth . . . ?*

"Nikki?" The soft question flowed out of the night.

Michael. Her heart leaped, rushing heat through her body. She turned carefully, searching for him, but saw nothing but shadows.

"Are you all right?" Again his whisper cut through the night.

"Yes." Why didn't he show himself? Was it MacEwan's presence that stopped him? Fear pounded through her heart and she reached out to the link, only to be stopped by a wall of pain.

"The remaining zombies are all dead. You are safe. Take care, little one." His voice was distant.

He's leaving me. She squeezed her eyes shut, and tried to control the panic pounding at her pulse. This was for the best. It's what she wanted. But fingers of fear wrapped around her heart, squeezing it tight.

Tears trickled past her closed eyelids. Maybe she was a fool for letting him go, but what choice did she really have? She'd always been cursed when it came to love. Jake had managed to survive its touch, but she didn't love him the way she had loved her mom, and Tommy. And now Michael.

She had to believe it was better that he left. It was the only way he could survive.

Footsteps approached. She opened her eyes. MacEwan eyed the dead zombie warily, his gun at the ready. Any other day, the look on his face would've made her laugh.

"Shooting their brains out does appear to stop them, but damn, you have to be *fast*." He nudged her zombie with the toe of his boot. "Care to explain how this one and the two near the door were killed? My men and I took out two, and I'm guessing you took out one, but how the hell did the others die?"

"One of those situations that can't be explained." God, it hurt to think, hurt to move. But she had to do both. She couldn't stay here.

His gaze was disbelieving; Nikki ignored him. She didn't have the energy to even try to explain Michael's intervention.

After a moment, MacEwan shrugged and put his gun away. "Who am I to question deliverance? Need a hand up?"

She nodded. He clasped her arm and hauled her upright. Pain shot through her brain and she gasped, fighting the urge to be sick.

"You don't look so good." MacEwan studied her with a frown. "Maybe you should go downstairs and let one of the doctors take a look at you."

She gingerly shook her head. The last thing she needed was to be prodded and poked. She was fine. Mostly.

"Then at least let me get someone to drive you home—"

They both turned sharply at the sound of the exit door opening. More police officers. She sighed in relief.

"The cavalry, at last," MacEwan commented dryly.

"Too late, as usual." She rubbed her temples. Would the pain ever go away? It was a white-hot fire, eating at her brain.

MacEwan gave her a wry look and waved his men over. "Would an earlier arrival have saved us? How many men does it take to kill a zombie?"

Only one—if you're a vampire. "Isn't that a bad joke?"

He laughed—a startling sound in the now quiet night. "Probably." He turned as one of his men approached. "Jenkins, drive Miss James home, please."

The young officer nodded and MacEwan turned back to face her. "I dare say my superiors will want to talk to you later."

"You know where to find me." She glanced across at Jake, still safe in the shadows of the chimney. "Will you get a doctor up here for Jake, as quickly as possible?"

MacEwan nodded and spoke into his handset. Nikki waved away Jenkins' offered arm and walked slowly toward the stairs. Every step sent lances of fire shooting through her brain. She bit her lip and fought the urge to howl like a baby. It hurt, sure, but pain, in one form or another, was something she was used to, something she'd learned how to handle. But did she want to cope with it alone for the rest of her life?

"Nikki?" MacEwan called as she neared the door. She glanced back at him. "If you find the man behind this trouble, give me a call."

So you can do what? It was only thanks to Michael any of them were alive tonight. She nodded, too tired to do anything else, just wanting to get home and sleep.

But she felt MacEwan's gaze on her back long after she'd left his presence.

Michael watched her walk away. His heart ached with her pain, yet there was nothing he could do to help her. Nikki had to get over her intimacy problems without interference from him. Until she did, there was no hope for them.

But there had never been any hope, really, not from the very beginning. He'd long ago stepped past the threshold of humanity. What made him think he could ever go back?

When she walked through the exit, he turned and moved across to Jake. The man was still heavily drugged, but otherwise appeared unhurt. He'd hate to think how Nikki would react if he died now, after all she'd been through to save him. Her emotional dependence on Jake was frightening. Michael grimaced wryly. If he was being at all honest, it also made him wildly jealous.

Which was a human emotion he could live without, he thought bitterly. That and love.

Several hospital staff came running up and he

stepped away, watching them bustle Jake onto a stretcher. As they took him back downstairs, Michael glanced at the sky. Dawn was beginning to stretch golden fingers through the night. So much had happened, yet so little time had passed. At least Nikki was now safe. Jasper wouldn't attack her with dawn so close. He would be on the run, searching for a place to wait out the day.

Michael turned and walked back to the stairs. It was time to resume his hunt.

The voice whispered through her brain, its touch evil, full of menace. Nikki twisted and turned, desperate to escape. But there was no running from the demons taunting her dreams.

Not even when she was awake.

She sat up on the sofa and studied her living room. Shadows hunched in the corners, but through the window she could see the red and gold tendrils of sunrise spreading across the stormy sky.

She glanced at her watch. She'd been asleep for little more than half an hour.

Evil whispered around her, shimmering through the air, filling her mind with its malice. Her breath caught in her throat, and sweat broke out across her brow. Jasper was coming for her.

She rose quickly. For an instant the room spun and she grabbed the arm of the sofa, holding on tight. The spinning eased, but not the knife-edged pounding in her brain.

Jasper was coming, and she was without any form of defense. Panic ran through her, closing her throat and making it difficult to breathe. *I can't do it. I can't face him alone.*

Her gaze fell on her boots. Silver gleamed briefly, firefly-bright in the half-light of morning. But the thought of facing the vampire with only a silver knife made her mouth go dry—he could easily take it from her, without any effort, without any movement. All he had to do was command her to drop it and she would.

Yet she had nothing else. She sat back down and quickly dragged her boots on, tucking the knives close to her shins. Again malice whispered through the silence. She clenched her fists against a wash of hopelessness.

You are mine, and I will prove it. Fighting it is useless.

She *couldn't* be his, thanks to what Michael had done. To kill her, Jasper had to behead her, and that meant he could neither raise her nor siphon her powers into himself. And yet the thought offered no comfort. He was a monster—she had no doubt that if he couldn't use her, he would torture her. Even if Jasper wasn't aware of the psyche-sharing, Michael's actions in rescuing her time and again had made her the perfect bait to draw him into Jasper's net.

And that's what he intended, she finally realized. All these games, all these little tests, were nothing more than a means to weaken *her* so that *she* had no psychic means to fight him.

But she was more than just her abilities, and she would not give up against Jasper. Maybe he was right, maybe it was futile to fight him, but she had to try.

His laughter slipped around her, as cold as ice. She resisted the temptation to flee. Jasper would find her, no matter where she ran, no matter where she hid. The link between them was strong, but he didn't seem to be picking up all her thoughts, and it surely wasn't stronger than the link she shared with Michael. She closed her eyes and tentatively tried to reach out to him. Pain lanced through her brain, and she gasped, blinking back tears. *In saving Jake, have I destroyed that part of myself forever?*

And if she had, did it matter? Jake was alive and, in the end, his survival meant more than the gifts that had caused so much trouble in her life.

She waited. There was nothing else she could do.

Open the door . . .

The command washed across the silence, threatening yet enticing. The urge to do as he demanded surged through her. Clenching her fists, she rose and backed away. Jasper was just beyond her apartment door. She could feel his heat, his depravity.

Hope flared. If she could feel that, then her psychic senses weren't dead. Her head might pound every time she moved, yet maybe, if she pushed hard enough, she might be able to defend herself.

Open the door.

No. *Never.* She reached down and slid one of the silver knives from her boot. Power swept around her, black wings that beat against her resistance. Where was Michael? Why wasn't he here to stop Jasper?

He will not arrive in time to help you. The trail is long and twisted.

Nikki closed her eyes and tried to ignore his mocking confidence. Jasper couldn't harm her unless she allowed him in her house. She had to keep resisting.

His amusement slithered around her. She shivered. The only thing twisted around here was Jasper's mind.

I will never be yours.

You are mine already, sweet thing. Shall I prove it to you?

She made no reply, just backed farther across the room, the knife clenched so hard in her hand that her fingers were going numb. Power washed through the apartment—a psychic beam that wrapped around her like a chain, heavy and cold.

Open the door.

"No!" she screamed. Yet her whole body trembled, muscle fighting muscle, the urge to obey battling the will to fight.

The chains drew tighter. Cold sweat ran down her back. She wouldn't give in, she wouldn't . . .

He laughed, and the sound stung her heart.

You have no choice. Open the door, pretty one.

Power whipped around her, beating at her resistance, searing her senses. She fought the urge to obey with every ounce of strength she had.

To no avail.

One foot slipped forward, then the other. She screamed in terror as she was slowly forced toward the door.

The warehouse was gutted, a blackened shell that stood out starkly against the morning twilight. Michael made his way past the fire engine and moved on, following the trail along the docks. Jasper's scent was faint. He studied the street ahead uneasily. Something didn't feel right.

The trail led past a series of well-lit factories. There was no hiding place here for Jasper, no hope that he could find an easy feed. The area was too full of people and light. So why had he come here? Why meander like this after leaving the burning warehouse, when there was so little of the night left? If Jasper had intended to feed, he would have done it quickly, then moved on to find shelter to wait out the day.

But Michael had been away an hour, and that was a long time when you could move as fast as the wind.

Michael frowned and studied the lights ahead. The trail was beginning to take him eastward, into an area of Lyndhurst he did not know. An area on the opposite side of town to Nikki.

Michael stopped cold. *Nikki.* Revenge. It all centered around revenge, she'd said. And she was right. Jasper didn't meander. Michael was a fool. God, what a fool!

He turned and ran back through the darkness, the night a blur, fear beating through his heart.

All he could do was hope he wasn't too late.

"Come in." The words were forced through gritted teeth.

Tears rolled unhindered down her cheeks as Jasper walked into the apartment, angelic and smiling.

Their gazes touched and her heart quailed. Once his eyes had been dead, showing little emotion; now they were consumed by madness. He was over the edge and out of control—and yet totally in control of *her*.

Jasper came into the living room and sat casually on the sofa. The leash loosened—but not enough to allow her to run through the door to freedom. Instead, she backed away from it, away from him. She still held the knife. She might yet have the chance to use it.

"Drop it," he said quietly.

She clenched her fingers around the hilt. The silver burned into her hand—a clean fire that fought the dark chains wrapping tightly around her.

"No. Take it from me, if you dare."

He smiled in amusement and locked his hands behind his head, leaning back to study her.

"You think I'm afraid of the toothpick you hold?"

She didn't think anything. She only knew it was important to keep him talking. Michael was out there somewhere. Even though the pain in her head had stopped her from contacting him, surely he'd realize something was wrong. He'd known when she was in trouble at the hospital. Sooner or later, he would come to her. He'd promised to keep her safe from Jasper. He'd keep that promise, no matter what.

Jasper raised a hand. Power pulsed through the silence, a fiery tendril that wrapped around her. She clenched her teeth, gathering her own energy despite the bitter ache in her head.

Jasper laughed, flicking his fingers outward. Nikki yelped as she was lifted off the ground and flung across the room. She crashed against the wall and slithered to the floor. For a moment, she lay there, struggling to breathe against the fear locking her throat. She'd never beat Jasper. Not in a million years. He was as strong as Michael when it came to psychic gifts. Perhaps even stronger.

But she had to try.

She dragged her arm close to her chest and hugged the knife tightly. The cold metal burned into her skin, fighting the darkness, giving her strength.

"That . . . that the best you can do?" she said, when she could.

He laughed. "Such courage."

Power surged again. This time, she met his thrust with her own, shoving his lance aside before rushing on, pushing him to his feet—pushing him back, toward the gathering dawn. For an instant she saw fear in his eyes and knew for sure, in that one moment, that she'd been right. Jasper *was* afraid of her powers.

But fire ran through her brain and her head felt ready to explode. She couldn't hold on . . . couldn't . . .

Her psychic energy slipped away. She gasped and hugged her body. Tears fell onto her arm as she rocked back and forth, desperate to shake the pain locking her mind. Desperate to ignore the laughter surrounding her, tightening the dark chains once again.

"Drop the knife."

She clenched it even tighter, eyes closed, huddled in on herself. Warmth spread through her hands and chest—a lone fire in the darkness surrounding her.

Jasper took a step toward her. "Release it."

Black wings of energy beat against her. Her fingers twitched in reply, and his elation grew. But still she made no move to drop the knife.

He took several more steps. Energy lashed at her.

She quivered under the blows, but refused to move, refused to answer the growing need to obey.

Another step. The heat of his body washed over her, burning the bare skin along her arms. Her muscles twitched in agony, but she ignored it, concentrating on Jasper.

Just a few more steps, she pleaded silently. *Just a few steps closer.*

As if drawn by her plea, he moved. Nikki unfolded, thrusting up in a fluid movement and ramming the silver knife into his stomach.

Jasper screamed and lashed out, smashing his fist into her face. She slid across the floor and landed in a heap near the kitchen doorway. Gasping for breath, she shook her head, trying to clear it of the pain falling in a red haze around her eyes. Or was it blood?

Jasper hissed and she glanced up quickly. The force of his gaze made her cringe. Jasper was through playing games.

She scrambled to her feet. He took the knife in two hands and drew it slowly from his abdomen. Small tendrils of silver fire licked against his fingers, and the smell of burning flesh filled the air. But he showed no sign of pain, and his eyes were blazing murder.

"You will die for this," he hissed, holding the knife up in his fist. "Come to me—*now!*"

Sharp probes of energy lashed at her, knocking her back to the floor, filling her body with fire. It burned through every fiber, every muscle—quick, deadly and powerful. *God I should crawl to him, beg his forgiveness . . .*

"No!" she screamed, raising her hands in front of

her face, breaking the lock of his gaze and the force of his will.

The chains of power curled up her body and around her neck. They snapped tight, cutting off her air, pushing her neck slowly up and back. He knew what Michael had done. Knew how to kill her. He wanted to do it slowly so that Michael would feel every inch of her pain. She gasped, struggling against panic, struggling to breathe. She threw a lance of energy at him, trying to thrust him away, but he barely rocked on his heels. His laughter whipped around her, cold and mocking. Nikki blinked back bitter tears and reached for the other knife. But the black wings lashed at her and fire consumed her mind, making it difficult to think, to breathe. *If this is what hell feels like, I definitely do not want to die.*

But maybe the choice had never been hers to begin with.

Nineteen

ENERGY SPUN THROUGH the room and the deadly force around her neck abruptly ceased. Nikki waited, sucking in great gulps of air, her body shuddering with pain, for the axe to fall again. It had to be another of Jasper's games, another way of extending the torture to both herself and Michael.

She closed her eyes, wrapped her arms around her body, not looking up, not doing anything other than waiting. She wouldn't give Jasper the satisfaction of her fear.

"Nikki, get up."

Michael's soft order seemed more a shout in the heavy silence. She glanced up quickly, elation, relief and fear tumbling through her.

He leaned against a wall near the doorway, his arms crossed and his face impassive. Yet death and fury filled his eyes.

"Go," he said softly, not looking at her. "Get out and do not come back."

She clung to the door frame and pulled her aching body upward. The room spun and she gasped softly, fighting the urge to be sick. She took a deep breath and forced herself into motion, slowly edging toward Michael and safety.

Jasper's gaze burned through her soul, but he didn't move. Power whispered around her—a touch so different to the dark flames that had beaten at her only minutes before. Michael was holding Jasper still so she could escape.

She reached him and hesitated. His dark gaze met hers. For an instant the link flared to life, and their souls met in a dance that was as fierce as it was powerful. Then regret flickered, and the link died, lost in a blaze of pain that made her eyes water.

She stared at him and he reached out, gently touching the cheek swollen from Jasper's blow. She closed her eyes, leaning briefly into his touch.

"How very touching," Jasper commented dryly into the silence. "Be assured that I will take good care of her when you die, Kelly."

She ignored the mocking laughter that danced through her mind. "Michael—"

He put a finger to her lips. "Leave us, Nikki. Don't come back, no matter what happens. Promise me."

Her eyes widened in alarm. "No."

"Promise me. If you remain anywhere near, Jasper will attempt to kill you."

And if I go, he will kill you. And that, in turn, would kill her. But did it really matter now? Did she really want to live without him, if that choice had been available?

"Michael. Don't—"

"Hush," he said softly. "Promise me, Nikki."

Dread pounded erratically through her heart. She

closed her eyes and took a deep breath. "I promise. As long as you make me a promise in return."

Wariness flickered in his eyes. "What."

"Don't die."

He smiled grimly. "I have no intention of killing myself—or you. Now go."

She stared at him a moment longer, then turned and walked out the door.

The door slammed shut behind her, a harsh sound in the silence. Michael listened to her fading footsteps and knew his heart went with her. But it didn't matter. Nothing did, except killing this bastard and keeping himself alive, so that she might also live.

"I shall savor your defeat, as I shall savor your woman in your memory," Jasper said.

Michael pushed away from the wall and shook his arms, loosening tight muscles. "You must win first."

"Oh, I shall."

Michael quirked an eyebrow. "As your brother won?"

Jasper snarled and power seared the room, washing around Michael. He watched Jasper's body twitch, and knew he wouldn't be able to hold him much longer. Jasper was close to his equal now that Michael had shared some of his strength with Nikki.

With a snap that stung his mind, the chains shattered. Jasper howled and launched himself across the room. Michael dodged and swung his fist, smashing Jasper's jaw and knocking him sideways. It was totally unnecessary, but the sound of flesh smacking against flesh appeased something in his soul.

Jasper shook his head, laughing as he turned. Energy gathered in the room like an approaching storm. Michael shifted his stance, watching Jasper warily. Madness lit the younger vampire's eyes. Michael would have to be careful. Jasper was as cunning as a cobra and, in this mood, probably ten times more deadly. No matter what else happened here today, he had to make sure Jasper died so Nikki could live her life in peace—and without fear.

Energy hit Michael, flaring around him in a red wave of heat. He flung a bolt of his own and followed right after it. He hit the younger vampire side-on, knocking him backward, closer to the window and the warm morning light.

Jasper laughed again—a high, inhuman sound. Too late, Michael felt the presence of silver. He thrust backward, but the knife pierced his side, the blade snapping in half as it entered his flesh. It would kill him if he didn't get it out quickly. But he had no time to do that now—he had to take care of Jasper first.

He staggered upright. Energy lashed at him; Michael ignored it, walking forward, watching Jasper's eyes, seeing the hint of fear grow as the younger vampire backed away. Ignoring the pain pounding though his body, dredging up every reserve he had, Michael reached out kinetically. The cords of power wrapped chains around Jasper, stopping him cold.

"How long has it been since you tasted the sun? Can you remember its warmth, Jasper? Can you remember the feel of it against your skin?"

Jasper made no comment, struggling against Michael's hold, fighting with mind and body to survive. White fire ran through Michael's mind. The blade lodged in his body was weakening him, weakening his ability to hold on. But thankfully the window was only a few feet away.

He stepped forward and wrapped his arms around Jasper, picking him up. Ignoring Jasper's struggles, ignoring the whips of energy beating through his mind, Michael thrust a cord of power at the window, smashing it. Holding Jasper tight, he dove forward, throwing them both through the shattered window and out into the light.

Nikki stopped abruptly, her body stiffening with shock. Pain washed heat through her, almost suffocating her. Michael was hurt. Maybe even dying.

"No!" She didn't want to die. But, more importantly, she didn't want *him* to die. She spun and ran to the house. She'd stood back and watched her mom die. She had watched Tommy die. She sure as hell wasn't going to repeat the same mistake with Michael—and not *just* because their life-forces were linked.

Glass shattered. She slid to a halt and glanced up. Michael and Jasper tumbled out the front window and hit the ground with bone-breaking force.

Jasper's hiss filled the air with venom, but he didn't immediately burst into flame as Monica had. Still, Nikki could feel his desperation, as clearly as she could feel Michael's determination.

He was holding on to the younger vampire, but just barely. And with every moment that passed, he was weakening.

She hesitated, needing to help but unsure what to

do. Jasper's struggles were becoming more frantic, his movements more desperate, but he might still have the power to control her. And she didn't want to end up attacking the man she was trying to save.

She bit her lip and watched the two men roll down the slight grassy incline and onto the sidewalk.

Michael's dying.

Jasper's whisper ran through her mind, full of malice. She swore and retrieved the second silver knife from her boot. The first hadn't killed him, but maybe a second would. A wash of energy hit her, sending her staggering backward.

"Stay . . . back!"

Michael's command was hoarse. Tears sprang to her eyes. Jasper was on top of him, fighting with fists and mind against Michael's grip.

Did he really expect her to simply stand here, when it wasn't only his life that depended on the outcome of this fight?

She took a step forward, but stopped. Something glinted brightly between the two men . . .

A piece of her knife, wedged deep in Michael's side. Killing him, as she'd attempted to kill Jasper.

"No!" she screamed, and smashed the barriers of pain aside. Reaching out kinetically, she ripped the blade from his body and flung it as far away as she could. She glanced at the knife in her hand and threw that away, as well. Just in case Jasper managed to break free from Michael's hold.

Both men were weakening. It was evident in their struggles, in the weakening wisps of power running around her. In a last, desperate effort, Jasper screamed, surging upward, smashing free of Michael's grip and staggering away. His desperation to escape the growing heat of the sun filled her mind . . . and then he turned and met her gaze.

He smiled suddenly. Nikki clenched her fists and backed away. Energy flowed through her—a desperate shield, a last defense.

"Mine," Jasper whispered harshly, and lunged at her.

She hit him with every ounce of kinetic power she had, but it wasn't enough to do anything more than thrust him away. She watched him rise, panting harshly. Ignoring the bright beat of pain smashing at her temples, she hit him again.

This time he slammed to a halt and the link between her and Michael flared to life. His thoughts caressed hers, and their powers combined.

Now, Michael whispered.

Together, they thrust Jasper skyward, holding his struggling body up to the bright sunshine. He screamed, his white skin flaring as he began to burn. Again energy pulsed, a thin strand of power wrapping tightly around Jasper's throat. His fear washed around them, his struggles becoming more violent as dark flames began to lick around his arms, his hands.

Nikki dredged up the last of her reserves, battling to hold her share of the psychic cage. The strand of power snapped tight, and there was a sickening crack as his neck broke. Jasper's eyes went wide with shock an instant before death took his soul.

It was over.

The last of her strength ebbed away and she dropped wearily to her knees. Everything hurt—her brain, her body and her heart—but it was worth it. Jasper was dead.

With the strength of the psychic cage gone, he flopped back to the pavement. His skin was still burning slowly, but it didn't matter. His neck was broken, and he would not rise again. The sun was only finishing what she and Michael had started.

She closed her eyes and took a deep breath. They'd won—together. She reached out to the link but it was little more than a void, as if Michael had never been a part of her.

Fear slammed into her heart. She pushed upright and staggered to Michael's side. He didn't move. She dropped to her knees and felt frantically for a pulse.

Nothing. No pulse, no sign of life.

"Damn it, Michael, don't die! Don't you *dare* die and take me with you!"

She rose and grabbed his arms, dragging him back toward her house. Every muscle was screaming by the time she reached the front steps. She hesitated, looking up in despair. Six of them. It was all that stood between her and home, and they'd never appeared such a mountain before. Michael was too heavy to carry, too much dead weight . . .

Her limbs suddenly felt weak, and an uneasy feeling washed through her. It was like nothing she'd ever experienced before, a chill caress of something not of this world.

Death, she thought, and panic surged.

Damn it, no!

She reached for what remained of her kinetic energy. Warnings beat through her mind. She'd done too much, pushed too far. If she kept on, she might lock her mind in an eternal nightmare of pain, never able to use her gifts again.

She closed her eyes and reached regardless. It didn't matter. Nothing mattered, as long as Michael survived. Not because she didn't want to die—although she couldn't deny that reason existed—but because she loved him. Because she wouldn't want to live if he was dead anyway.

Energy came. She opened the door, lifted Michael and thrust him through. The world spun drunkenly. She grabbed the banister, holding on tight. Gritting her teeth, her breath little more than wheezing gasps, she eased him to the floor. She didn't know how much time he had left. She had to hurry if she wanted to save him.

She slammed her apartment door shut behind her then staggered over to the shattered window, pulling the blinds closed. If he was to have the slightest chance of life, she had to make sure there was no sunlight to weaken him further.

She knelt by his side and picked up his hand, holding it close to her chest, close to her heart. Reaching forward, she gently brushed dark wisps of hair away from his damp forehead.

"Come back to me, Michael."

There was no response. Tears sprung to her eyes. *Michael, I need you to live. Not just because I don't want to die, but for the possibilities that remain unexplored between us.*

"Damn it, you promised me you wouldn't die!"

Still no response. A sob tore past her throat and the weakness assailing her got stronger.

Weakness . . .

He'd torn part of himself away—and undoubtedly weakened himself severely—to give her life. What if *that* was the only reason he was dying now? What if he simply *didn't* have enough strength to go on?

She bit her lip, pushed upright and ran to the kitchen. Michael might not drink human blood anymore, but she had a feeling he needed it if they were both going to survive.

She grabbed a knife from the rack, then hesitated. He wouldn't thank her for doing this. She had a feeling his control over his bloodlust had not been a battle easily won. But what other choice did she have, other than letting him die?

She walked back to his side.

"Forgive me if I'm doing the wrong thing, Michael, but I love you. I can't sit here and let you kill us both."

Leaning forward, she kissed his forehead. Taking a deep breath, she sliced her wrist, then forced open his mouth and let the blood drip down his throat. He swallowed convulsively after several seconds, and jerked spasmodically. Lunging forward, he grabbed her arm, holding her still, his grip bruising as he sucked quickly, greedily, at the wound.

He wasn't awake, wasn't even aware of what he was doing. He could drain her without knowing . . . and she knew it wouldn't matter. As long as he lived, as long as he broke the curse, she didn't care.

Through a growing haze of pain, she formed a thin lance of psychic energy. Touching his forehead lightly, she closed her eyes and thrust deep into the darkness holding his mind captive. She plunged into his consciousness, deep into the shadowed areas he'd kept well hidden when their minds had last merged.

Don't die! she screamed through the darkness of his mind.

Something burned in answer. A single heartbeat, weak and uncertain. Elation trembled through her. It was working. Breathing harshly, she dove deeper.

I need you! I love you! You can't do this, Michael. You'll kill us both!

Another beat ran through the silence, stronger this time. A dark haze ran across her vision. An odd sort of lethargy was beginning to creep through her body, sucking the strength from her limbs. She ignored it.

Live, damn you, live! she silently screamed, pouring the last of her energy, the last of her strength, into him.

Then the blackness claimed her, and she knew no more.

Twenty

MICHAEL LEANED A shoulder against the wall and watched the dawn rise through the lace-shielded windows. From behind him came a steady beeping—Nikki's heartbeat, recorded by the intensive care instruments that still surrounded her, strong at last.

Not that he needed the instruments to hear her heart. The demon within him had finally woken from its long slumber and was hungry to taste her again.

He shuddered and clenched his fists against the need beating through his soul. Three days had passed since he'd awakened and found her lying still and pale by his side, her life still hot on his lips.

He'd come so very close to killing her.

He'd never thought to warn her against offering her blood. It was the one thing he'd never expected her to try.

He scrubbed a hand through his hair. His need to taste her again was growing. He had to get out of the hospital, had to go somewhere far away from any sort of human habitation until he could bring his demon under control. Until that happened, he was a bigger risk to Nikki than Jasper had ever been.

The door to his left opened and Jake entered.

Though he still wore the thick white bandage around his neck, his movements were stronger.

"How is she?" he asked, walking to her bed.

"Alive." Like a siren song, the pounding rush of blood through Jake's veins called to the darkness in Michael. His canines lengthened in anticipation. He swallowed and looked out the window.

"I was just talking to the doctors. They said she'd lost almost eighty percent of her blood. They have no idea how she managed to stay alive."

She was lucky she'd only lost eighty percent. Lucky he'd awakened in time to stop.

"Don't suppose you'd like to explain how it happened? I mean, you don't take human blood, right?"

He didn't have to turn to see Jake's bitterness, the sudden mistrust in his face. It was all too obvious in his thoughts. "I was unconscious, probably dying. She cut her wrist and offered it to me. She gave me life." *To save her own.*

"And you almost killed her in the process!"

Michael closed his eyes. "Yes," he said softly.

"What about that bastard, Jasper? He still around?"

"No. We killed him."

"Good," Jake muttered. "At least something positive has come from this mess."

Maybe it had. Jasper was dead. Michael had his revenge. But at what cost?

He walked over to the bed and gently brushed the dark strands of hair away from her eyes. Her face was still pale, despite the strong beat of her heart. But her thoughts were finally stirring. She would awaken soon. He had to be gone before then.

He met Jake's gaze. "Take care of her for me, will you?"

Jake raised an eyebrow. "After all she's been through for you, you're not sticking around until she wakes?"

"I can't." He smiled, revealing lengthened canines. Jake took a hasty step back. "When she gave me her blood, she destroyed the hold I had on my vampire urges. I can't stay here, can't stay near her, until I get that control back."

"Good idea." Jake swallowed and ran his fingers through his hair. "But there's a lot of unfinished business between you two. I don't think fate will let you go so easily." He hesitated. "And I know for certain Nikki won't. She'll keep looking for you, no matter how long it takes."

"She can look all she likes. She'll never find me."

"Want to bet? You've seen how tenacious she can be."

Michael smiled grimly. Tenacious or not, she wouldn't find him unless he wanted to be found. After three hundred years of existence, hiding was one thing he'd become very adept at.

And yet . . . part of him hoped Jake was right.

The other man frowned. "What do you want me to tell her when she wakes?"

"Tell her . . ." Michael hesitated. *Tell her I love her. Tell her I'll come back for her if I can.* "Tell her to take care."

Jake raised an eyebrow. "That's all?"

"Yeah." It wasn't fair to offer anything more, to offer hope when there might not be any. He bent and brushed a kiss across her cheek. Breathed, for the last time, her scent.

Then, without glancing back, he turned and walked for the door.

Leaving his heart behind.

If you loved *Dancing with the Devil*,
be sure not to miss the next thrilling installment
in the Nikki and Michael series!

HEARTS IN DARKNESS
by
Keri Arthur

The third and fourth books in the Nikki and Michael
series—*Chasing the Shadows* and *Kiss the Night
Goodbye*—will follow at one-month intervals.

Here's a special preview of *Hearts in Darkness*:

THE BREEZE WHISPERED around her, its touch like a
furnace. Sweat beaded her skin, staining her T-shirt
and dripping from her ponytail.

Around her the night pulsed a bass-heavy rhythm.
The air was rank with the scent of sweat, alcohol and
chlorine.

Nikki stood in the shadows of an oak and sipped a
lukewarm soda. Below her, on the main pool deck,
bodies writhed in time to the music, unmindful of the
heat or the closeness of others.

They had to be mad. If *she* had any choice, she
would be in the pool, allowing the cool water to wash
the heat and sweat from her skin. But instead she was
stuck here in the shadows, nursing a lukewarm cola,
awaiting the next move of a wayward teenager.

It was an all-too-familiar feeling. Six months before, she'd followed another teenager and had found herself caught in the middle of a war between two vampires.

Pain rose like a ghost and she bit her lip, hard, blinking away the sting of tears.

It was her own stupidity that had driven Michael away. Her refusal to trust, to admit what she'd felt—until it was far too late—had worn him down as surely as the sea wears down a rock. Of course, allowing him to feed on her in an effort to save his life hadn't helped all that much, either. According to Jake, it had left Michael's hard-won control over his bloodlust in tatters—at least when he was around her. She wasn't entirely sure whether to believe that, though, because surely three hundred years couldn't be so easily undone.

But what hurt the most was the fact that he'd left without saying good-bye.

She'd looked for him, of course. She'd spent the first two months after she'd awakened in the hospital doing little else. But America was a big country, with lots of places to hide. And when the man she was hunting lived most of his life in the shadows, what hope did she have of finding him?

None. Not that it really mattered. She'd keep looking until she found him—though what happened then would very much depend on how he reacted.

The two-way clipped to her lapel squawked. "Nik, are you there?"

It was Jake, her boss and best friend. He sounded as bored as she felt. Nikki pressed the button. "No, I'm at home enjoying a nice, cool bath."

"Forget the bath. A cold beer would go down beautifully right now. The kid still in your area?"

She scanned the crowd. Matthew Kincaid, a red-headed, jug-eared teenager, stood out from the mob. But it wasn't so much his looks as the fact that he towered a good foot or more over his peers. Basketball material, for sure—if someone could teach him to shoot a ball. Or bounce it. But then, given he was a computer whiz with a genius-level IQ, he really didn't need to be risking life and limb—or at least limb—on the basketball court.

"Yeah. He's hovering near the tent housing the bar, trying to convince some of the adults to buy him a drink." She hesitated and took another sip of her cola. The warm liquid slithered down her throat and she shuddered, upending the rest into the dirt. "He's not acting like a kid on the verge of running away from home."

"I know. But his mom's paying us to watch him, so watch him we will. Besides, we need the money."

"When don't we?" They'd been working together for close to ten years, and she couldn't remember a time when the business hadn't been strapped for cash. Private investigators didn't make a lot of money—not in Lyndhurst anyway. And Trevgard—a former client, and the one potential windfall they'd had in the last year—had died before he could pay them. "Why is Mrs. Kincaid so convinced he's going to disappear tonight?"

"A conversation she overheard when passing his bedroom last week. Apparently, he's been chatting with this girl over the Internet and has formed quite a relationship with her. He arranged to meet her during the party."

Nikki frowned. "That doesn't explain why she thinks he's going to run away."

"The kid's unhappy at home. Hates his dad, who's an alcoholic, and argues constantly with his mom."

"He sounds like an average teenager to me."

Jake laughed softly. "Yeah, I guess. But lately the kid's been saying that he doesn't need them anymore, that he's found someone who understands him."

Nikki raised her eyebrows. "The Internet friend?"

"Maybe."

"Has Mrs. Kincaid talked to Matthew about this?"

"Yeah," Jake said, voice dry. "And the reply is one I'm not about to use over the two-way."

She grinned. "Has she tried going into his computer when he's at school?"

"He's password-protected and encrypted both his e-mail and chat logs."

"Clever kid."

"Doesn't take a genius to do that sort of stuff—which he is, remember. It's easy."

Maybe it was standard procedure for the kid and Jake, but computers had never been her strong point. "That doesn't explain why he's going to such lengths to stop his mom reading his e-mails. I would think a kid with his—let's be polite, and say 'unusual'—looks would be letting all and sundry know he's in contact with a hot girl."

"We don't know that she's hot."

"We don't know she's not," Nikki retorted. "But maybe he lied about his looks. Plenty of people do on the Net."

"Yeah, but there's no indication he's done that, either."

Maybe, but given his height, his coloring and those ears, it was more than likely that he *had*. The Internet would have given him not only anonymity, but also the ability to reinvent himself.

So why would he risk all that to meet this woman and reveal the truth? And why did Nikki have a feeling that it could all go horribly wrong?

She glanced at her watch. "It's close to eleven-thirty now. Does his mother have any idea when the meet is going to happen?"

"Midnight, apparently."

Witching hour. The time when all things dark and deadly came out to play. Things like Michael. Or Jasper.

She shuddered and rubbed her wrist. In the worst of her dreams, she could still feel Jasper's touch—in her thoughts, and on her skin. But Jasper was dead, decapitated, burned to ashes by the sun's heat. His evil could never touch her again.

Michael, on the other hand . . . Thanks to the events surrounding Jasper's capture, her life was now linked to Michael's. As long as he remained alive, so would she. But wherever he was, whatever danger he was embracing, if he died, then she would, too—out of the blue and with utterly no warning.

A chill ran through her. She hated being dependent on anyone—and especially on the man who had broken her heart. But, on the positive side, nothing short of decapitation could kill her as long as Michael lived—and her psychic senses told her she'd be in need of such protection tonight. Because she couldn't shake the certainty that evil of another kind was on the move in Lyndhurst. And if that *were* true, then Matthew Kincaid could be a target. From what she'd seen, evil liked preying on innocents.

The bass-heavy pounding faded, replaced by a gentler, more romantic song. On the pool deck, the teenagers drew close. There was probably more kissing going on than dancing.

She looked across to the bar. Matthew was staring at the crowd, his expression a mix of envy and anger. He slammed his drink onto the counter, then walked away.

"Heads up. He's on the move."

"Where?" Jake sounded relieved.

Matthew had disappeared behind the tent. Nikki moved, keeping to the shadows as she skirted the sweating mass of slow-dancing teenagers. Matthew came into sight, his arms swinging as fast as his legs as he strode along the path.

She slowed, not wanting to get too close and attract his attention. "He's heading for the back gate," she said quietly into her two-way.

"Is anyone else in sight?"

"Not unless you want to count the teenagers getting busy under the trees."

Jake snorted softly. "I'll bring my car around. Keep me posted."

"Will do."

Matthew reached the gate and stopped to unlatch it. Nikki stepped behind a tree. The kid threw the gate open, then glanced over his shoulder. His look was petulant, like a child grabbing at candy he knows he shouldn't take.

It wasn't his family making him run, she thought with a grin. It was his hormones.

He headed out, turning right. She pressed the two-way, informing Jake, then followed the teenager.

Matthew's long strides had taken him a good way down the street. She crossed to the other side then stealthily jogged over, closing the distance between them. The slow beat of the music began to fade and silence closed in, broken only by the occasional roar of a car engine or the blast of a horn.

Matthew strode on, looking neither right nor left. She swiped at the sweat trickling down her forehead and studied the street ahead. They were in the Heights—a ritzy and very expensive section of Lyndhurst nestled into the western edge of the mountains that ringed the town. Below them, lights blazed—a neon sea of brightness that outshone the stars. Matthew could have been heading toward any one of those lights, but her gaze stopped at the docks.

That's where he's going, she thought.

The two-way buzzed softly. "Nik, I'm in the car. Where are you?"

She pressed the receiver. "Ocean Road, just past Second."

"I'm parallel on West. Let me know if he changes direction or meets a car."

"Will do."

They continued on—Matthew striding out, her half running to keep up with him. Boxlike shapes began to loom around them as houses gave way to factories and warehouses. The faint wash of traffic seemed to die completely and, in the silence, her breathing seemed strained and harsh.

Ahead, Matthew stopped in the puddle of an over-head light and glanced at his watch. He looked briefly to his right, then turned left, heading into a small side street.

She pressed the two-way. "He's just turned into an alley. He's heading your way."

"Last cross street?"

She frowned, thinking back. "Sixth."

"Just passed it. I'll park and wait."

She stopped near the alley entrance and peered around the corner. Matthew was nowhere in sight.

Swearing softly, she hurried down it, keeping an eye on the fences lining either side, looking for gaps or gateways the teenager could have used. Nothing. But halfway down, on the right, she came across an-other small street. On it, Matthew was a dark shadow moving quickly away.

She sighed in relief. "He's turned off again," she told Jake. She glanced up, studying the unlit street sign. "Heading down Baker's Lane, toward the docks."

"That street comes to a dead end."

She hoped it was just a figure of speech and not a reality. "It's a rather odd place to meet an Internet friend, don't you think?"

"If it is a friend he's meeting, yes. But all sorts of perverts go trawling the chat rooms looking for in-nocents like Matthew."

She kept close to the fence on the off chance that the teenager might turn around. At least in the darker shadows lining the fence, she'd be harder to spot. "The problem is, I've got a feeling it's not your aver-age pervert we're dealing with."

Jake groaned. "That's all we need. I'm heading in—and bringing a gun."

"Be careful, Jake. I really don't like the feel of this."

"Then maybe I'll call the cops, just to be safe."

"And tell them what? That I've a got feeling?" Even Col MacEwan—a senior detective and the officer who'd helped them during the mess that was the Trevgard investigation—wasn't likely to come running over something like *that*. He might believe in her psychic abilities these days, but he'd still want something more concrete than a feeling.

Jake grunted. "Don't do anything stupid until I get there."

Meaning she could do something stupid after? She grinned, though it didn't ease the tension knotting her stomach. "You do remember that I really can't die, don't you?"

"*If* Michael is to be believed," Jake retorted. "And even if he is, that's no reason to needlessly throw yourself into danger."

"Trust me, I'm really not planning to do that anytime soon." Because while it might be hard for her to die, she *could* get injured—and badly enough that she might *wish* to die.

The street narrowed, and the warehouses on either side seemed to loom in on her. She skirted several Dumpsters and screwed up her nose. From the amount of garbage overflowing onto the street, they hadn't been emptied for at least a week. Combine that with the heat of the last few days, and the result was revolting.

Matthew stopped. She ducked behind a stinking Dumpster, holding her breath as she peered around.

He was studying the buildings to either side, but after a few seconds he turned and ran toward the fence on the left. She waited until he'd disappeared over the top, then followed.

"He's just climbed a fence. Third warehouse from the end."

"Wait for me."

"I might lose him if I do."

Jake swore. "Damn it, be careful."

"You be careful. I'm not the one most at risk here."

"But you're not immortal, either, and I'm positive Michael didn't tell you everything about his gift of life everlasting."

She smiled grimly. Michael had never told her more than what he thought she needed to know. Bare facts, and nothing more—especially when it came to anything concerning his past or what he did for a living. Or how greatly he risked both their lives . . .

"I'm heading over."

She grabbed the chain link and pulled herself over the fence. Dropping to the ground on the other side, she crouched, her gaze sweeping the darkness. It had to be some sort of produce warehouse. Packing crates were lined in neat rows, those closest containing the limp remnants of lettuce leaves.

Matthew could have gone anywhere, so she stayed where she was, listening intently. The wind moaned through the silence, raising the hairs on the back of her neck. She rubbed her arms, then reached down, withdrawing a knife from her right boot. Made of the purest silver, it was one of two she'd had specially designed after her encounters with Jasper. If an old kitchen knife with only the smallest amount of silver in it could stop him, her new knives should stop just about anything. That's what she was hoping anyway.

From the right came a soft, metallic squeal. She rose, padding quickly through the rows of crates. An old brick building loomed ahead. She stopped at the end of the row and peered out. To her left were several large entrances, all shuttered. To the right was nothing but a brick wall. The sound had come from around the corner.

She moved swiftly to the wall, then edged forward and looked around the corner. Matthew's sandals were disappearing through a window.

"Jake, Matthew has just entered the warehouse through a window on the right side of the building. I'm about to follow."

"I'm almost with you, Nik."

Almost wasn't good enough, and she couldn't afford to wait. The sensation of danger had risen tenfold and was threatening to stifle her.

She made her way to the window. It was a foot or so above her reach, but there were several packing crates stacked close enough to use as a ladder. She climbed them carefully and peered through the window.

There was no sound, no light. Just a darkness thick enough to carve. Yet the warehouse was far from empty. Somewhere in there, evil waited.

Fear rose, squeezing her throat tight. Nikki closed her eyes and took a deep breath. If she didn't go into the warehouse after Matthew, Jake would. And though he was armed, they both knew from experience that guns weren't much of a threat to a vampire.

Though why she thought it was a vampire who

waited, Nikki couldn't say. Evil came in many forms—some of them human, and some of them not. Maybe it was just Jasper's memory teasing her fears to life.

She'd let those fears get the better of her once, and had lost Michael because of it. Even before she'd shared her blood with him, her refusal to admit to her own feelings—a refusal that stemmed from a past of losing everyone she'd ever loved—had all but forced him away. That sort of fear would never get the better of her again.

She pulled herself through the window and hunkered down, listening for any hint of sound. Beyond the harsh note of her breathing, the silence was absolute—as impenetrable as the darkness. If Matthew was moving around in this, he had to have the eyes of a cat.

Keeping one hand against the outer wall for guidance and the other in front of her, she slowly moved forward. After five steps, she hit another wall and followed it deeper into the warehouse.

A sound broke the silence, something heavy clattering across the concrete. A soft curse followed.

"Lizzie? Are you here?" Matthew's voice held a combination of petulance, bravado and fear. "Why don't you stop playing games and come out?"

"You lied to me, Matthew."

Though the words were soft, there was something in them that spoke of death. Ice crawled across Nikki's skin.

"Only about my age." The whine in Matthew's voice was more evident this time. "And only by a few years."

"Years matter, especially to someone like me."

The husky voice was drawing closer to Matthew. And so was the sense of death. A chill chased its way across Nikki's overheated skin. She closed her eyes briefly, restraining the urge to scream for help. If she did, Matthew could die.

"So what if I lied about my age? It doesn't change who I am or what I feel."

He was close, maybe a few steps away. Nikki edged to her left, the knife grasped tightly in one hand and the other outstretched. She'd probably scare the life out of him if she touched him, but at least it was a touch he'd survive. She doubted he'd be so lucky if his husky-voiced girlfriend got to him first.

"It changes everything. Your age means people will worry about you. It means people will follow you and attempt to protect you."

Nikki froze. The woman knew she was here. Knew she was following Matthew.

Air stirred sluggishly, whispering past her cheek. Someone was moving, someone she couldn't see or hear. Someone other than the woman Matthew had come here to meet.

Sweat trickled down the side of her face. She ignored it, not daring to move, her breath lodged somewhere in her throat.

The sense of impending doom was so thick her skin crawled with it. Kinetic energy crackled across her fingertips. She clenched her hand, searching the cover of night, looking for the source of the movement.

The air stirred again, and with it came the sound of a soft step behind her.

Nikki spun, and hell broke loose.